HALDERWOLD

February 21, 2007

To Marilyn

From Carolyn

HALDERWOLD

A Novel

Carolyn Maine

iUniverse, Inc.
New York Lincoln Shanghai

Halderwold
A Novel

Copyright © 2007 by Carolyn L. Maine

iUniverse books may be ordered through booksellers or by contacting:

iUniverse
2021 Pine Lake Road, Suite 100
Lincoln, NE 68512
www.iuniverse.com
1-800-Authors (1-800-288-4677)

This is a work of fiction. All of the characters, names, incidents, organizations, and dialogue in this novel are either the products of the author's imagination or are used fictitiously.

ISBN-13: 978-0-595-40785-9 (pbk)
ISBN-13: 978-0-595-85149-2 (ebk)
ISBN-10: 0-595-40785-4 (pbk)
ISBN-10: 0-595-85149-5 (ebk)

Printed in the United States of America

To my friend, Franki Wilkinson, for her enthusiasm and support.

CHAPTER 1

Today would be a busy one for Paige Nelson. Just as she was leaving for morning class at the school where she was training to be a clown, the phone rang and the high school office administrator asked her to come in today as substitute teacher for a two o'clock algebra class, and she had a birthday party scheduled for five.

Driving to school, Paige repeated out loud to herself what was lately becoming almost a mantra. "I can do it all if I just stay organized." Organization was the key, plus a little luck.

And luck seemed with her as she pulled into the last parking space in the lot across the street from "The Allister Cormick School of Comedy," known among the locals of the Town of Gifford, New York, as "Cormey's Clowns." She was about one minute late by the hall clock over the door to the classroom.

And Allister was in one of his moods—just what she didn't need. Paige had barely found a chair when he stomped over and hovered in front of her, hands bulged into fists jammed into the pockets of his baggy checkered pants. "Miss Nelson, have you by any chance, in your extra time, found your hat?" he asked in a tone that sounded like a demand.

"My ... wha?" Paige stuttered. "I ... I didn't lose anything."

Titters from the whole class filled the room, more nervous than hardhearted. When Allister got like this, each student knew he or she might easily be his next victim. Of course, it being after all a clown school, laughter was common and usually a favor to the person in the forefront of attention, so it was pretty much a group habit. But that was different from being laughed at because you'd suddenly become the group fool without even trying. And these scholars of all subtleties of humor knew it well. It was never fun to be the butt of one of Allister's peculiar methods of making a point. And the point here was clearly her tardiness.

The instructor was in such bad humor today, his usual outfit, a two-foot flowered tie and long curled-toed shoes were completely out of sync with his sour, down-turned mouth and imperious glare. Paige knew that most of the students were doubled over, ready to laugh at anything, partly to quell the nervous giggles that rose involuntarily when they looked at him, and partly to make themselves as small and inconspicious as possible to avoid drawing his attention to themselves.

Allister paced back and forth across the front of the room in the meandering manner he had developed as his stage entrance: looking as if he had lost his way and just wandered in from some back alley. Sometimes he even carried a mangy cat on his shoulder, which he would then pretend to discover and get rid of. He was a highly-talented comic, respected by all the students of his school, but no one enjoyed coming under his direct scrutiny, especially if it engendered his particularly cutting brand of sarcasm.

Paige wilted with relief when he meandered away from her. She had just taken in a deep breath that would have become a sigh of relief, had his next comment not come before she could let it out. Looking up at the ceiling, he bellowed, "Now, here is a classic case of lack of commitment to one's chosen profession!"

Paige flinched as if he had let her have it in the face with his lapel waterflower (a tactic he was not above using for emphasis every now and then) as he twirled around and pointed his whole arm directly at her. "Miss Nelson, do you or do you not remember my long-winded lecture of last week on the importance of a would-be clown finding his—or her ... *own hat*?"

"Oh, yes. I remember," she replied quickly. "And I've been looking. I just forgot what you meant there for a minute. I mean, I'd just come in from outside—hat and coat, you know. Outdoors."

"Don't babble!" he commanded, coming back to stand over her again, his gaze piercing and dour. "I've been *looking*," he repeated in a mocking, wimpy voice.

That was enough. Paige sat up straight and looked directly at him. "Yes, I have been looking, Mr. Cormick."

His head waggled from side to side. "And where have you looked? Under your bed?"

A couple of low giggles escaped the other students, though it was obvious from the many hands over mouths that they were making every effort to hold them in.

"Just about everywhere," Page said in the steadiest voice she could muster, determined to face him down. "In store windows, my friends' closets, people on the street, television. But I haven't seen anything that really suggests what I want to express about my own approach to humor."

One of Allister's ridiculous shoes was tapping on the floor. "Your approach to humor. And what *is* your approach to humor, Miss Nelson?"

Page finally lowered her eyes. "I … can't really put it into words …"

"Then I don't see much hope of your putting it on your *head!*" he shot back sarcastically, whirling away from her.

At that some of the others burst out laughing in spite of their attempts at control. Paige's face flamed. She bit her lower lip, ready to run out of the classroom if he said another word to her.

But he had turned away, already launching into a tirade about hats in general. "A clown's hat is his performing partner, his best friend, his straight man, his main prop. Or *hers* if you will, ladies." He bowed ridiculously low to a group of female students sitting together. The women sat expressionless, hoping to avoid his personal comments, as he continued, "It must state what manner of clown he is, his particular brand of humor … his very philosophy of life!"

He stopped and opened his arms in a great sweeping motion. "A clown does not really have an *identity* until he has … FOUND HIS HAT!" He tossed his broken-down derby into the air with such vehemence that he missed catching it when it came down. A strange silence filled the classroom as all the hands that were not clamped over mouths now tightened over stomachs.

When class finally ended, Paige couldn't get out fast enough. In the parking lot, a fellow student, Sue Gates, ran to catch up with her. "The old man was in rare form today, huh?" Sue cried.

Paige was unlocking her car. "It had better be rare. I, for one, don't think I could take that kind of harassment as a steady diet."

"Oh, he was just letting off steam." Sue's voice became consoling. "You don't want to let that get to you. It's just one of his ways of testing us."

Paige opened the door, threw her bag into the car and stood there frowning. "Testing us?"

"Yeah. A clown has to get used to being laughed at you know. Being the center of attention even if it turns negative—like when you're off your mark and not funny. You can't quit. We have to get so professional it doesn't bother us the least little bit."

"Sue, that's different!" Paige cried. "Being laughed at when you're trying to entertain, and being belittled in front of your peers—well, those are just two completely different things."

"I know, but they have something to do with each other," Sue insisted. "You remember his lecture on detachment? How you have to learn to sort of psychically stand aside and watch yourself when you're performing so that nothing that happens will destroy your control?"

"I think so." Paige got into her car and shut the door, then rolled down the window since Sue was still talking.

"Well, you have to get to that place where nothing bothers you when you're doing your act," Sue continued. "Being laughed at—not being laughed at. Wouldn't not being laughed at when you're performing be worse than what Allister was doing in there today? We know he's just teaching no matter how bizarre it gets."

Paige looked up at Sue. "I hadn't thought much about it. I'm always laughed at when I perform." Then she added. "But that's probably because my audience is mostly under four feet tall."

"Much too easy." Sue shook her head. "Girl, you want to be a professional? Just think about it."

Paige had already started her car. "I will when I get time, Sue. Right now I've got to run. I have two more jobs today. See you next class."

Sue was right, Paige thought as she drove to Pomona High School. I have to learn to be less sensitive or I'll never be a successful clown. I must try to be more like Aunt Holly. Holly, her father's sister, wasn't a professional clown but she seemed to run on non-stop comedy. That was just who she was, and Paige's parents took it for granted that Paige had inherited Holly's 'gene' for comic performance.

Page wasn't so sure it came naturally. In fact, if she didn't soon get rid of her leftover teenage shyness, she wasn't sure she'd even make a good teacher, let alone a clown. Or even a person who could enjoy her own life without going into psychic devastation every time something embarrassing happened. Yes, she had to work on her self assurance. It was ridiculous for a college graduate and a teacher to go around dying inside over little things like an adolescent.

In fact, most of the ninth grade girls seemed to handle themselves with more confidence than she sometimes felt. Of course, there was no telling what those girls were really going through inside when they were acting so grown-up and sophisticated. By that age she'd learned to mask her sensitivity too, mostly thanks to having gotten into clowning.

Mrs. Thorne, her seventh grade teacher had cast her as a clown in a school play, carefully explaining that she'd chosen her because her bouncy red curls would look perfect falling out from under the funny, old-fashioned ladies' hat and not because there was anything silly about her as a person.

Paige had accepted the role and quickly discovered a new dimension of herself. When she was in costume, all her fears of appearing ridiculous or stupid vanished like magic, all the misgivings she had come to consider just part of being awake fled from her mind. Gone were the nagging doubts that her clothes might not be fashionable, that her hair was too frizzy or her slight figure immature compared with other girls her age.

And she could get all the attention she needed without having to speak in front of people—she had hated speaking in front of people, as herself. To cook up a goofy voice and walk funny and say nonsensical things, that was completely different. That was fun. If she clumsily tripped over something, all she had to do was exaggerate it by either falling flat on the floor or hopping around on one foot, holding the other and making faces, and laughter and applause would rise from any other kids who happened to see her. They knew she was just clowning around.

"Well, you've certainly taken to this part," Mrs. Thorne had told her, smiling. "I'm glad I picked you. You've turned out to be a natural."

Paige had just nodded and grinned the grin she loved to flash, with one tooth blackened. She couldn't tell Mrs. Thorne that some days she never wanted to take that clown suit off and be just Paige again. Paige with all her little fears and worries.

Coming back to the present, she stopped at a fast food restaurant for a chicken sandwich to go. She'd have a few minutes in the teachers' lounge before class, and they always had coffee on.

"My hat, my hat, my hat." Paige realized she was muttering out loud as she got her coffee and settled down on one of the vinyl sofas in the teachers' lounge. Good thing no one else was around. It was quarter to two. The other teachers ate lunch as soon as classes ended at noon, and most were back in their classrooms by now.

Paige didn't need much preparation time as a substitute for ninth grade algebra. All she had to do was find a piece of chalk and borrow a textbook. No real preparation was even possible since many times she didn't even know ahead of time that she'd be teaching that day. She would just ask the students where they were in the book and carry on from there. She had taken calculus in college so high school algebra was one of the things that didn't scare her in the least.

The sandwich finished in her usual hurried manner, too close to what could be called 'gobbling,' she wandered over to toss the container into the trash. The teachers had lockers, but sometimes they left their coats and hats in a corner closet near the trash can. The closet door stood partly open, and it had become a habit to check out any hats she came across. Without even thinking, she pushed the door wider and glanced up at the shelf above the hangers. There were a few pairs of gloves, probably forgotten from last winter, a couple of folded scarves, and a cap. She reached up and took it down. It was a soft wool cap, the kind men wore in old pictures when they rode around in topless cars, or the favorite headgear of kings and dukes playing golf. It was a brown tweed and the stiff brim was held to the front by a large snap. She turned it over in her hands, snapping and unsnapping the brim a couple of times.

There was a mirror on the inside of the closet door. Paige perched the cap on her bright curls that were extra-frowzy today from her quick shower, forgetting the conditioner. She tried cocking it at several different angles to see if she could get a comic effect. With the hat down over one ear and the brim sideways, she twisted her neck to look at herself from either side. She giggled, seeing in the mirror a nineteen-thirties newsboy who couldn't afford a haircut. Would something like this work? She turned the brim around and made a face at herself in the mirror. Someone behind her cleared his throat.

"Miss, if you're through with your performance, I wouldn't mind having my hat back."

Paige's hastily-eaten lunch lurched inside her stomach as she spun around to stare wordlessly into the mocking face of a tall man with well-cut sandy hair that fell thickly onto his broad forehead. She knew who he was—Tremain Tate, a senior English and film teacher, but they had never spoken. He was handsome, or so she had thought previously. For the moment, the mocking laughter in those blue eyes and the wide grin that revealed even, white teeth were not one bit attractive. They seemed to cast humiliation over her like a clown's pail of wood chips. She wanted to back into that coat closet, close the door, and never come out.

Stupidly, she stood there, the hat on her head tilted at a zany angle, until he began to laugh and, reaching for the hat, said, "Well if you're not going to give it up willingly, I believe I'll just reclaim my property."

He turned the hat in his hands as if it needed reshaping. When she still didn't speak, he looked at her again and said, "I don't think it was all that flattering on you anyway. It looks much better on me." He brushed back his hair and fitted the hat onto his head with an exaggerated dapper air.

"I … was just …" What could she say? What could she possibly say? *I'm a clown, you see, and I'm looking for my hat?*

She never went around telling the sensible people she met that she was a clown. They usually didn't believe her anyway, at first. The few times she had mentioned it to new acquaintances, it was something like, '*Nooo. A nice, pretty girl like you?*' Of course it was never meant as an insult, but yet it was, sort of. To her, it implied that she must not have enough brains or talent to match up to her looks and education, she didn't know any better than to make a fool of herself. Now she chose to simply turn away from that smirking face, grab her purse, and walk hurriedly out the door.

"Now don't go away mad, Miss." That deep, taunting voice followed her out of the lounge and several steps down the corridor. "You're welcome to borrow my clothes anytime, if you ask nicely."

Thankful there were no classrooms within hearing distance of the lounge or anyone passing in the hall just then, burning with embarrassment and fury, Paige somehow reached the classroom where she was to teach algebra. There was no excuse for such insolence over a *hat!* The man was rude, uncivil and completely over the line—and not even very funny, though he seemed to think he was. Why, the next time she laid eyes on that stupid hat, she'd set a match to it, whether he was wearing it or not. Even better if he were.

"Hi, Miss Nelson." The cheerful face of Cheryl Aimes, ninth-grade algebra star, beamed at her. "Are we going to get into polynomials today?"

Paige stopped for half a second to gather her wits. Of course, she was the teacher now. Not a clown, nor a bashful, angry twelve-year-old. The teacher. In a suddenly controlled voice, she answered, "Oh, I don't think we're quite ready for that today, Cheryl."

The girl bent her head sideways, pursing the little pink mouth in her plump face. "I get so *impatient*," she sighed. "My father's been showing me polynomials for a month now and I'm *dying* to get to work on them in class."

Paige gave a small, good-natured "Hah," which surprised her as much as the grip she had gained so quickly over her voice. Maybe there was something to the '*mastering*' that Allister swore he would teach every last one of his students if it killed him (and them).

"Well, young lady," she told her student. "We just have to bear in mind that the others don't have scientists for fathers. We have to go at the best pace for the whole class. In fact, I'd get in trouble with the school board if I didn't. Polynomials aren't in the ninth grade curriculum, you know. And probably won't be any time soon."

Cheryl pouted and tossed her head around, apparently meant to be a nod, and followed her teacher into the classroom.

The class went better than Paige had expected. Maybe that rush of anger had sparked up her brain energy or something, she was thinking as she left an hour later.

But the effect was only temporary. No sooner was she on the road than the big letdown set in, and she felt so tired she wanted nothing more than to go home and crawl right into bed for the night. But there was still the birthday party. Enough time for a shower and maybe an energy drink before the makeup, and she'd be off to entertain a room full of five-year-olds. Much as she loved keeping busy, days as packed as this one could be demanding to the point of exhaustion.

To say nothing of the stress. She could handle the work load just fine—she'd done that plenty of times, she thought, getting mad all over again. First, it was her turn for humiliation from Allister and then that … *jerk* at the school, and his damned hat! Of course, that scenario was actually a continuation of the hat thing Allister had started. "I should mark this day on the calendar as *Hat Day*," she snorted out loud, giving the steering wheel a brutal twist onto her street. "Hats and Humiliation Day! Oooh. Men!"

But her hat problems for the day were not over. No sooner had she reached her second floor apartment, shed her work clothes and turned on the shower, than she remembered tossing away the shower cap that had ripped the last time she'd used it in one of her frenzied, fast showers. She had meant to drop into the pharmacy and get another one today, but it had completely blown out of her mind, even when she passed the store.

Well, there was no time for hair drying. She turned off the shower faucet and gave herself a fast sponging off. Ten minutes later she caught the front of her hair back in a wide headband, and sat down at her mirrored table to begin putting on her clown makeup.

Tonight she would be what was called in the business a 'comedy whiteface.' Pre-schoolers loved a clown halfway between a decoration—a giant-sized doll—and a buffoon. Removing the cover from the small tub of white grease-paint, she dipped in her fingers and carefully covered her face. She had tried this with a brush, even a sponge, but fingers did the most efficient job. After washing the paint from her hands, and drying them thoroughly, she picked up a cotton sock full of white talcum powder, a device of her own manufacture, and shook it until the powder worked its way through the fabric to cling to the outside of the sock.

The kids would probably get as much of a kick out of watching her get ready as watching her antics, she thought, as she patted the sock gently all over her face until the paint no longer appeared greasy. She waited a couple of minutes before feeling her skin with her fingertips. You couldn't always tell if all the grease was gone from the white paint by just looking in the mirror.

Switching to black greasepaint, applied with a sable brush, she outlined an exaggeratedly large lower lip, extending it to line up with the outsides of her large blue eyes, the proper place to end a clown mouth. She made no upper lip at all. Next, she drew a small heart near the top of each cheek, and filled the lower lip and the hearts with red greasepaint.

Satisfied, she started on the eye makeup, for which she used an ordinary black liquid eyeliner. She disliked putting the greasepaint so near her eyes. Highly curved black eyebrows drawn far above her own reddish brown ones and several uneven inch-long eyelashes were added. Surveying her work in the mirror, she nodded at her reflection. It looked right; and better, it was helping her get into a clown mood.

Now for the outfit, and she didn't have much time left. She dressed in a pair of shorts and a tee shirt, over which she pulled a loose, one-piece suit, red with big yellow polka-dots. Five-year-olds loved this one. She pulled off the headband. There was no reason to tuck her hair up under the curly red wig that she put on like a cap. The natural curls that bobbed around her shoulders and streamed down her back looked nothing like the yarn of the wig, of course; but they seemed to blend with it, and she hated tucking her hair up anyway. It got so hot under that wig, and then the hair was all flat and weird after she let it down. There was no denying it would be nice to find just the right comical hat, then she could dispense with the wig. She put it out of her mind. Hats brought back the unsavory events of her day.

Her long white shoes matched the ruffles that encircled her neck and ran down the front of her suit on either side of the big purple buttons. Last of all, came the round, red nose.

"Ready to rumble," she told her reflection in the mirror. She was no longer Paige. She was Poppy. Poppy the Clown, her celebrated persona, beloved alter ego, embarrassed by no accidents, hurt by no barbed remarks, stopped by nothing.

In the kitchen, she realized she'd forgotten to make and down her blender drink before the makeup job. "What was I *thinking?*" she asked herself as she removed her nose to drink the yogurt and fruit after she'd whipped it up. That done, she touched up her broad lower lip, put her nose back on, and was finally off.

The party was a jubilant success. By the time Paige got there, she was well into her clown personality, staggering, walking with knee-dips and tilting her head at a different angle for every giggling little admirer in the room. After a few 'magic' tricks, she did one of her most popular skits: walking, losing, chasing, and retrieving an invisible dog. It was great, for her and the children. She liked teaching, but she *loved* clowning, making little kids happy.

A girl named Hanna with her arm in a cast told Paige all about being in the hospital. "I was only there one night," she said with a sad little pout, "an' I missed my mommy so much. But some of the kids have to stay there a long, long time."

"That's very hard," Paige told the little girl, trying to be sympathetic without losing her comic facade. "But I'm sure their mommies visit them often."

"One girl," Hanna continued, her eyes growing large and her voice rising. "One girl named Mollie only sees her mommy one time every month 'cause she lives way out west."

"That's really too bad," Paige said. "I'll tell you what. Why don't we go visit Mollie? You and I. Is your mommy here? I'll ask her if we can."

"That would be *great!*" The little girl was excited. "I'm sure Mommy will say 'Yes.' She feels sorry for Mollie too, and all the other kids in the hospital. But she's not here yet. She's coming to get me at seven."

"Then we'll ask her at seven." Paige smiled a smile that, of course, looked like a crazy grin, and it made Hanna laugh again, and forget her sadness.

The next day, after clown class, Paige went to the gym. Alister had been pretty tame today, sitting to watch each student fall down. Falling is a major art in clowning, he had told them over and over, and clowns have to work hard at it. Falling that looks comical but doesn't hurt is nowhere near as easy as it appears. Paige had discovered that at the tender age of twelve. You can't just stagger and hop and let your body fall any old way without ending up with some nasty bruises, or worse. And as you get older and less flexible (Paige was feeling a difference already at the ripe old age of twenty-four), you have to work even harder at staying in shape.

After her regular workout on the machines, Paige claimed the only available mat. Not one of the large ones she liked, but it would have to do. She began by doing regular somersaults, then trying different postures from which she could launch into a somersault.

Kids seemed to get a big kick out of the skit where she pretended to be perplexed over an invisible mosquito that kept her slapping at, but never getting, then turning around several times to look for it until she was almost whirling. From her whirl, she would fall backward, landing on her hands to do a backward somersault. She had been working on continuing from there into a cartwheel, and had brought it off a couple of times at the gym, but she wasn't ready to try it without a mat, or, God forbid, demonstrate it for Allister. Five-year-olds would find it hilarious no matter how it turned out, but that wouldn't do for a professional. The stunt had to be perfected.

Paige went through the mosquito slapping and looking around just for practice. None of the regular body builders or overweight toilers at the gym paid much attention to her routines; they were used to Cormey's Clowns working out among them. But she was having trouble ending up at the right spot on the small mat. After she got through the preliminary whirls and rose from her backward somersault, she twisted sideways to do the cartwheel and the foot holding her weight slipped off the edge of the mat, bringing her down heavily on her back.

Before opening her eyes, Paige heard someone giggle. Not very nice, she thought foggily. Laughing at a person taking a tumble like that. Maybe they thought it was meant to be funny? The giggling continued. When she finally got her eyes open, they closed again of their own accord, the light was so dazzling.

"Why is it so … *bright?*" she asked out loud, trying again to open her eyes.

"Because it is a lovely day," a chipper voice answered. "The sun is shining."

Paige's bewildered squint finally focused on a young girl bending over her—Cheryl Aimes. What on earth was she doing here in the gym during school hours? And what was that brilliant electric blue behind her? It didn't make any sense, but after trying to see through her squinched-up eyes for several moments, Paige said, "Oh. It's the sky."

"What do you usually find up there?" the girl asked, followed by another spasm of giggles.

"Where am I?" Paige was becoming alarmed. "How did I get outdoors?" She attempted to sit up, but it just didn't happen. From her supine position, she continued her questions. "What's going on? What are you doing here, Cheryl? And who brought me out here?"

The girl became serious. "That I was going to ask *you*," she said, kneeling over Paige to look at her more closely. "Ahhh," she gasped, looking into her eyes, which were open now that the shadow of her own head shaded them. "You are *Larian!*"

"I'm … *what?*" Paige demanded, making a greater effort to sit up. Finally, she made it, with the girl helping her, and now holding onto her wrists and looking at her with what seemed to be admiration, or even awe.

"What kind of a cock-eyed dream is this?" Paige was becoming downright concerned, now that she could look around. "Or if it's not a dream, where on earth are we, Cheryl?"

An amused snort overcame the girl's awestricken manner. "I am *Cherry*," she said. "Not … Cheryl. Whoever heard of such a name?"

"Never mind, I'm sorry … *Cherry*," Paige said. She hadn't known Cheryl had a nickname. And she was acting awfully silly. Probably too much advanced algebra. In spite of the brightness, she could see that the gym was nowhere in sight. Neither were any of the other buildings on the street. Neither was the street. She gave 'Cherry' a pleading look. "Please. Just tell me where we are and how we got here."

"We are in Halderwold, of course," said Cherry coolly. "But how did you come here from Laria?"

"I … don't know." In her sitting position, Paige was able to hold a hand over her eyes to shield them from the glaring sunlight and take a better look around her. A quick three hundred and sixty degree sweep showed her to be in the middle of a field of grass and bushes. Here and there flowers of various shades tossed in the breeze. Looking straight ahead, the field seemed to go on forever, on her right, at some distance, lay a dark green forest, backed by a very distant ridge of purple-grey mountains that nearly wrapped them around, she noticed, as she turned to see that behind her, nearer than the mountains, the land slanted down to a silvery-aqua gleam of water. To her left, along a bend in the river, she was looking down on a not too distant town—but not like any town she had ever seen in North America. All the buildings appeared to be made of bluish stone, mostly sprawling and low, except for a rise on the distant side of the town with a very large building at the top of a hill. Narrow greyish streets entered the town haphazardly, and the river flowed, glistening, through it.

If this was some weird hallucination caused by her fall, she might be seriously injured. That was—her real body. The one she was experiencing right now felt perfectly okay except for a slight dizziness, but it couldn't be her real one since that one belonged to a completely different world. With Cherry's help, she got onto her feet and felt reasonably stable, but also incredibly *physical*

"How can I be dreaming?" she asked out loud, pounding a thigh with her fist.

"You cannot be." Cherry was grinning up into her face. "Because I am not dreaming and we are here together."

The girl seemed much shorter now, and very young, hardly a teenager. And definitely not Cheryl. She was wearing some kind of pink Swiss Alp type of dress with long sleeves and a gathered apron, and she was obviously Paige's only hope.

"Cherry," Paige said. "I need your help. I'm very frightened. You see, this isn't where I'm supposed to be, and I can't remember how I got here."

"Oh, that can be frightening," Cherry replied, no longer smiling. "But do not worry, lady. My grandmother can treat you. She is a mender."

"A mentor?" Paige asked, puzzled.

"A *mender*," the girl repeated. "She helps people get better when they are unwell."

"Oh, a *healer*," Paige said.

"I guess so," Cherry replied. "But Grandmother says wounds heal themselves, after she mends the people."

Oh, God, Paige thought, realizing how medieval this whole scene appeared. *What kind of methods might this woman use? Leaches? Spells?* "What kind of mender?" she ventured.

"What *kind?*" Cherry wrinkled her cute, round face. "A mender mends people who have something ailing them. What other kind could there be?"

"I mean what kind of medicine or … er, methods of treatment does she use?" Paige wondered whether to run for the hills or the water.

"Oh." Cherry's creases of perplexity smoothed out. "Mostly herbs. With quietness."

"Just herbs?" Paige let our her breath with relief. "You mean tea and oils and leaves—things like that? Stuff rubbed on your skin?"

The girl nodded. "Yes, and bulb paste and soup and wine …" She broke off and ran a few yards over to a patch of shrubs, from which she retrieved a basket and came running back slightly out of breath. "I almost forgot. I was picking blueberries for grandmother's wine."

Blueberry wine. That didn't sound half bad. Paige remembered taking a stiff swig of blueberry brandy once on a skiing trip that had done no harm. In fact, it had brightened up the cold world considerably.

CHAPTER 2

Well, what the heck. It was only a dream anyway, or at worst a concussion. If it was a concussion, there were plenty of nice people at the gym, some of whom knew first aid. They had surely gotten her real body on a stretcher by now, maybe even in an ambulance heading for emergency. They'd take care of her. She herself had all she could manage with this cockamamie situation. And just in case it didn't end real soon, she would have to cope. She couldn't just stand here in the middle of a field indefinitely.

"Would your grandmother mind my coming to visit her?" she asked.

"*Mind?*" Cherry's brown eyes sparkled. "She will be honored, of course."

"Because …?"

"Because you are Larian, naturally," Cherry said, nodding her head vigorously. "As I am honored to be the one to find you in your discomfiture."

This girl's words were as long as her skirt. Maybe she was some kind of verbal equivalent of Cheryl, the math whiz kid.

"Let me ask you another stupid question." Paige pressed her fingers against her temples. "Please excuse me if I speak inappropriately. My memory is really out of sync today. My brain is just … not working very well. How exactly do you know I'm a Larian, and why does that make me anything special?"

Cherry giggled heartily, but, Paige noted to her relief, she was not offended. Before she met any of the adults in this strange society, she needed some clue to how she should act, and what kind of attitude they might take toward her. What exactly would it mean to be 'honored?'

"Lady, you are in desperate need of help," Cherry said. "I know you are Larian because of your eyes. And you are important because there are so few of you in Halderwold. Just a score or so left now, besides my father."

Paige was relieved. At least she wouldn't be expected to wield unusual powers or anything. "Your father is Larian? Doesn't that make you Larian too?"

Cherry sighed, as if from an end of patience. "Are your lovely blue eyeballs not working either? What color are my eyes?" She opened her eyes widely and stared into Paige's.

"They're brown," Paige answered meekly. "And very pretty."

"Huh!" Cherry snorted as if she didn't believe her, then her cheerfulness returned. "You really think so?"

"Absolutely. But couldn't we please talk about *me* right now? Just until I get the help I need?" Paige crossed her arms and thought hard. "Now, how important will I be here and why?"

"You will be an honored guest as I have told you," Cherry said slowly, as if explaining to a child. "By everyone who meets you. Even the king."

"The *king!*" Paige's heart made an alarming jump. *Oh God, a king. But of course, what would a medieval dream be without a king?* But didn't kings in these kinds of fantasies rule with an iron hand? Didn't they ... she wouldn't let herself think of it right now. "I can't imagine why your king would want to meet *me*," she said.

"Of course he will," Cherry insisted.

"Well, do you think he'll ... *like* me?"

"I am sure he will," Cherry assured her. "So long as you do not laugh. I have been told that Larians still laugh."

"Laugh! Why in the world would I laugh?" Shaking her head vigorously, she added, "I swear I will *not* laugh at your king. Now can I ask one more dumb question?"

Cherry nodded and she went on, "What *is* a Larian?"

With that, Cherry had to set her blueberries on the ground to keep them from flying out of the basket with her giggling. "I must get you to grandmother at once," she said when she could get her breath. "Lara, Lara," she began to sing, holding up her arms and turning in circles, reminding Paige very much of a dark-haired Julie Andrews twirling in her apron in the flowery meadow among the mountains. Cherry came to a stop in front of Paige and pointed to the ground. "Lara."

"Lara, what?" Paige said stupidly.

Cherry got down on her knees and pulled a clump of grass up by the roots. Holding it up, she repeated, "Lara."

Paige looked carefully at the grass root, wondering what she was supposed to be seeing. Then she noticed that the mud clinging to it was of a definite bluish grey cast. In fact the grass itself had a bluish tinge. She looked around. No wonder the sky appeared so dazzlingly sapphire. It was bluer than the grass and bushes—and they ranged anywhere from a deep teal to a greyish violet. She hadn't noticed the range of shades at first. It had taken her eyes a while to adjust to the light. "You mean the color? The bluish shade?"

Cherry tossed the grass and got to her feet.

"Is the earth here blue?" Paige asked her.

"Earth?" Cherry looked puzzled, then shrugged and pointed downward. "You mean Lara?"

Paige stamped her foot. "That is Lara? This, what we are standing on. Is that Lara?"

"All is Lara," Cherry said. "Everything. The whole planet. But especially your land, Laria."

"Where is my land?" Paige asked. "And why is the ground there any more Lara than this land here?"

Cherry was showing impatience again. Turning toward the unending meadows with a sweeping gesture, she said. "Your land is over there, and you were the first. That is where the people generated. That is why your eyes reflect the color of Lara."

"How far is it?" Paige asked.

"The land of Laria is far. Far beyond the swamp, which is far beyond the grasslands. Larians do not come here anymore. They cannot pass through the flatlanders' swamp." She turned and held out her arms in a sweeping gesture. "And those mountains you can see are impossible to traverse. It is said they contain deep lakes bounded on all sides by steep cliffs. I hope you will remember how you came here. It will be important news, even for the wise ones."

Paige decided to stifle her curiosity about the 'wise ones' for now. They would no doubt have some connection to the king, and she wasn't ready for it. First she would deal with Cherry's grandmother. She now had an idea who she was supposed to be, and a reasonable assurance that she would not be harmed—so long as she didn't laugh at the king, which seemed just about the most remote possibility imaginable. She was ready to get going. Somewhere. She pointed toward the town. "You live in that city?"

Cherry nodded her head and picked up her basket. "There is nowhere else to live. No one would *choose* to live in the swamp."

Paige tried for a more casual turn in the conversation. "What do you call those little blue flowers in clusters everywhere? They're so sweet."

"These?" The girl stooped to pluck a couple of the delicate, pale blue blossoms. "They are bluets. You like them, lady?'

"Very much."

"Then you shall have a bouquet." She set down her basket and gathered a handful of the flowers. "You shall have these by your bed this night."

A bed. So she was pretty sure of a place to sleep. "That's very sweet of you Cherry. I appreciate it. Can we go meet your grandmother now?"

Cherry stood for a moment as if thinking, then burst out in a howling laugh.

"What's so funny this time?" It was a good thing she *was* a clown and used to this, Paige thought. Only she saw no present reason for it.

"We must do something about the way you are dressed." Cherry deposited the flowers into her basket and untied her ample apron, which she placed around Paige's waist, going behind her to tie it.

"This is awfully generous of you, Cherry," Paige told her. "But I don't really think an apron goes with the clothes I'm wearing.

"I am trying to cover you as best I can," Cherry explained. "We don't want everyone we meet to see you this way. It will embarrass them to be amused by a Larian—someone for whom they should be showing respect. They may even be tempted to laugh."

"But what's so wrong with my clothes?" Paige didn't like the apron over her gym clothes. What could be more ridiculous? Heaven only knew she was accustomed to dressing funny, but this was supposed to *keep* people from laughing? She was wearing a pair of orange sweat pants and a long sweater that was knitted in a pattern of yellow, green and maroon. Not the most tasteful outfit to be sure. The sweater had been one of Aunt Holly's wacko gifts, but it was pure cotton and comfortable, and she wore it mostly for jogging and exercising. "Let me guess. The women here don't wear pants?"

"We wear pants." Cherry pulled up her skirt to reveal a pair of lovely lavender bloomers.

"But never without a skirt over them?"

"No. But it is not the pants. It is the colors."

"Well, nothing matches, I know. But I was only working out in the gym, for goodness sake," Paige sputtered.

Cherry looked as if she hadn't understood a word Paige had said. "Do not worry. Grandmother and I will dress you. But first I must get you home." She picked up her basket again. "What is your name, lady?"

"Oh, sorry," Paige said. "I forgot to introduce myself. I'm Paige."

Cherry brought forth a guttural laugh that nearly brought her to her knees. "I think not."

"Why not?" Paige demanded. This was getting *too* silly. *Everything* couldn't be funny.

"You are not a boy and you are not a page. Anyone can see that."

Paige was beginning to feel drained. "Then how about … Poppy?"

"Poppy." Cherry repeated approvingly, nodding her head up and down. "A very nice name."

"Great. Let's get going—just one more question. Why do you laugh at everything?"

"Why, because I am nearly thirteen," the girl answered matter-of-factly, with a touch of incredulity at the question.

"Oh," was all Poppy said. *Well, she* is *practically a child. And children love to laugh or I wouldn't have a career in comedy*. But something still didn't make sense and she was afraid she was going to find out what it was—probably sooner than she was ready.

They set off toward town, Poppy following her guide through the long grass along a narrow path that only Cherry could see. It all looked like a sea of fluttering, blue-green waves so pristine that no one had ever walked through it before, but each time Cherry took a new tack, sure enough, a path emerged behind the swaying pink skirt for Poppy to follow. As they approached the edge of the field, a neatly mowed, level stretch appeared through which a rather winding road led to the outskirts of the town.

Though not paved, the road was hard and dry, easy to walk on except for a few pebbles, and tending more toward grey than the bluish buildings of the town. Now that there was room for them to walk side by side, Cherry shifted her basket from one arm to the other and took Poppy's arm. "It is still too early for most of the workers to be coming home," she said in a voice seemingly meant to be comforting. "We will be able to reach my grandmother's house without meeting many people."

"Yeah, sure," Poppy replied. "We wouldn't want to embarrass the whole town with my outlandish garb."

Cherry laughed as if she believed Poppy was trying to amuse rather than express sarcasm. Steering her companion onto a wider road that became whitish and wound among the first houses, then down to a lower level nearing the river, she explained, "Our house is down on the flat. We do not have to walk up through the city."

"Fine with me." Poppy was watching the first person to come toward them. A man in loose grey clothing with a large hat of a peculiar shape. It seemed to have a triangular crown, and a brim curled upward and inward, like that of someone rushing to report that the British troops were coming, or a high church official of the Middle Ages. Of course these people obviously *were* in the Middle Ages, what with Cherry's talk of pages and kings. She hoped it was a gentler version of that period than her own world had produced.

"Growing weary?" Cherry had heard her sigh. "We will be home soon."

"I'm okay," Poppy said. "Just feeling a little befuddled."

Cherry began to smile at the word *befuddled*, but to Poppy's surprise, seemed to gulp back the giggle that she expected to follow. Instead, the girl straightened her shoulders, lifted her head very high and called out a sober greeting to the approaching traveler. "Fair weather, Armand!"

"So may it remain," the man answered, nodding courteously. Getting nearer, he glanced at Poppy and, after another polite nod, turned his face away quickly, but not before she saw his face muscles tighten to avoid smiling.

"Well, we got past one of your townsmen without cracking him up," she remarked.

Cherry was making a sound inside her throat—a stifled laugh.

"What do you say when it's raining?" Poppy asked.

"What?" Cherry rolled her eyes upward and held out the flats of her hands. "Well, look at it rain." She shot Poppy a suspicious glance. "But it is not raining."

"As a greeting?"

"Oh. We say, 'Water is needed.'"

"And the other person says?"

After another of those *how stupid can you get* looks, Cherry replied politely, "May the land never turn to swamp."

The few minutes it took Poppy to mull that one over brought them onto streets with houses on either side. Considerable bustle seemed to be coming from inside the houses, through high windows, but few people to be seen. After they had walked a few more steps, half a dozen children ran out from a side alley, yelling some kind of chant—a game no doubt, took one look at Poppy, and went weak in uncontrollable mirth.

Poppy's clown persona kicked in, and her weariness seemed to melt away. She had never had such a ready audience as these kids. How could she resist just a moment of performing for them? Ignoring Cherry's alarmed expression, she pulled up her apron, jumped into the air, kicked her heels together, came down and attempted to turn a cartwheel, lost her balance and fell on her butt. The children roared with delight.

Cherry grabbed Poppy's arm in a surprisingly strong grasp. "Get up!" she whispered frantically. "Get up *now*, lady! Please!"

"Sure." Poppy scrambled to her feet and felt a wave of faintness. "I guess I'm still a little woozy." She put a hand to her head and leaned on Cherry with the other.

"No time for that!" Cherry yanked on her arm with seeming desperation. "Please try to hurry. We must get to grandmother's."

Poppy followed with no further comment, concentrating on the street directly ahead, though she was peripherally aware of several women in long skirts appearing in doorways as they passed.

Cherry rushed her past the women with no greeting. "At *last!*" Poppy heard the girl breathe as they entered the vestibule of a large house. An archway brought them into a sort of anteroom, then they passed through the open door of a room which had furniture, including a table and several chairs. The floor was the same hard, bluish grey as the streets, though softened somewhat by several large scatter rugs, and the high windows had no glass or shutters. Cherry settled her charge quickly in a chair, a sort of rattan with deep, soft cushions, then disappeared through an inner doorway.

The room was cool, much cooler than the street, and Poppy was able to regain a measure of her stability in the few moments she was left alone, though she was still trembling from the furor outside, and the unthinkable craziness of the day. Her chair was comfortable, and a delicious smell of food cooking wafting from the interior of the house calmed her a little more. She realized her wooziness might be partly from hunger; she had eaten nothing except a slice of toast before leaving for the gym this morning. Then she wondered if hunger could affect her dreaming self. Although she had no sense of how long she had been unconscious, she now had an unmistakable sense of dinner time.

Cherry appeared with an older woman dressed in a long grey dress. "This is my grandmother," she said, sounding much calmer than when she had rushed Poppy into the house.

"I am Kandra." The woman approached Poppy, then bowed slightly with her palms held out as if something lay upon them, but there was nothing there. "Welcome to our dwelling."

"Thank you very much." Poppy tried to get up but found it such an effort, she sank back into the cushions. "I am Pai ... Poppy, and I'm sorry to just pop in like this, but I was out in the field and ... I don't even know how I got there."

Kandra raised a hand and made a motion toward her guest indicating that she should remain seated. "Cherry has told me," she said gently. "Do not distress yourself, lady. You must rest and take nourishment. We will speak later, after my son-in-law, Lorimar, comes home."

Son-in-law? Cherry's father? Poppy longed to ask a hundred questions, but was afraid it might be bad manners in so strange a culture. Better to wait and see how much they tell her. "It's very kind of you to take me in like this. I don't know what I would have done if I hadn't met Cherry."

Kandra smiled, and it made her look much younger. The grey hair and dress did nothing to flatter her. With a closer look, Poppy could discern no deep wrinkles, just a middle-aged softness to her face, which was rather sweet when she smiled. Good heavens, if she were to put on some bright make-up and take a package of red dye and an egg-beater to her hair, she'd be a dead ringer for Aunt Holly! Poppy gasped a little which brought a look of concern from her hostess, so she just settled back and tried to smile.

"Cherry will bring you fluid," Kandra said. "I must return to my duties."

She left, and Cherry came immediately with a cup of charming periwinkle pottery. Poppy sniffed at the "fluid" inside, but it seemed to have no scent. She took a sip. It was delicious. Something like the tea Aunt Holly made from the various flowering herbs she grew in the sprawling backyard of her upper New York State home.

Poppy leaned back and continued sipping the warm liquid, and thought about Aunt Holly. Actually, she hadn't seen her in weeks. She'd have to be sure and call her as soon as she got back … woke up, whatever. She must be getting too comfortable, forgetting the unbelievable pickle she was in. But she would certainly not allow herself to imagine never getting home again, of her parents and Aunt Holly never knowing … No, she would absolutely not even think of such things. So far on this strange adventure, nothing bad had happened to her, and she felt safe here with Cherry and Kandra. Though, except for the traveler on the road in the triangular hat—who had acted quite civil and polite—she had met none of the men of this place as yet. She hoped Cherry's father, and the others, would turn out to be, if not as protective as the women, at least as genial as the bizarrely-hatted man.

In spite of her unfathomable problems, the drink was bringing an amazing calm, yet a feeling of new energy also, which Poppy decided to save until it should be needed. "What's the name of this drink—this *fluid*, Cherry?" She asked. "I really like it."

Cherry had been disappearing into the inner room and coming back regularly to check on Poppy. "Vigorwart," she answered. "Everyone loves it. It will make you strong again."

"Yes. It's working already," Poppy told her, draining the last of the cup. "Is there anything I can do to help? I mean, I smell cooking and I'm guessing you and your grandmother are making a meal."

Cherry smiled and took the cup. "Malina and I are all the help grandmother needs to prepare supper. It will be a simple meal of soup and poufla." She took the cup back into the other room.

Poppy tried to relax. Poufla? Oh, well. It smelled good, and after that tea—whatever they called it, she felt more than ready to try their food. She lapsed into a light sleep, and again had no idea how much time had passed when voices awakened her. Others were in the room now, and a man's voice pierced her senses. She opened her eyes and saw, at first groggily and then clearly as she sat up with a jolt, the man who was bending over her, looking closely at her. Tremain Tate!

CHAPTER 3

She must be at the high school, but why on earth had they brought her here instead of the hospital? And what business did *he* have hovering over her? "*You're* here?" She practically yelped at the man.

"Yes," he replied calmly, drawing back and surveying her as if she were some specimen from another planet. "Because I live here."

He *lived* at the school? Shaking her head, Poppy realized she was still in the strange house in the strange place, and the man she had yelled at was not Tremain, although he could be his twin brother.

"Oh, I.... didn't mean to be rude," she stammered. "I've had a very rough day and I just fell asleep, and ..."

The man smiled slightly, exuding none of the reassuring warmth shown by the women. "So I have heard." Then he made the same palms-out bow that Kandra had offered, and continued, "Cherry has apprised me of your meeting. Most peculiar, lady. You have no recollection of traveling here from Laria?"

"Laria. Oh, yes." Poppy had almost forgotten about being a Larian. "I mean, no. I'm sorry. I have no idea how I got here. I don't remember anything except waking up in the field, hearing Cherry laughing."

He nodded, casting an askance look in Cherry's direction as the girl came back into the room carrying a stack of plates, then brought his attention back to his guest. "Yes, I am afraid she laughs at every opportunity. Please excuse her. Of course it will soon cease. I hope you can bear with it a few more days."

"Oh, it's no problem. She's a regular ray of sunshine." Poppy hoped he didn't mean he was going to throw her out after a few days, even if she had nowhere to go.

"By the way, I'm Poppy." She got to her feet with a little effort, strengthened by the tea and the nap, and held out her hand, then withdrew it when he looked as if he had no idea what to do with it. Well apparently shaking hands was out of style here. She held her hands out, palms up, and bowed, as he and Kandra had done.

"My name is Lorimar," he said, bowing again.

She felt a giddy relief that he wore no hat. She had been picturing Cherry's father coming home wearing something like the topper that man on the road had been sporting, and herself having to struggle against laughing. Or was it only the king she mustn't laugh at?

Then, an even giddier thought occurred to her. If she ever did meet the king, she hoped he was not a hat person either. Since she wasn't supposed to laugh in his presence, she wanted nothing about *him* to amuse her. Of course he would be wearing a crown, wouldn't he? And why should she ever meet the king anyway? She was nobody. Then she remembered. Here in this other-worldly place, she was one of those esteemed Larians, whoever they were. She was babbling mentally, she realized. The smell of food increased and she looked up thankfully to see the two women carrying steaming dishes to the table.

Lorimar pulled Poppy's chair over to the table as the others settled themselves. Tea was served first, a bluish (what else?) herb tea that tasted like blueberries. A nice familiar taste. Everyone sipped quietly, then Lorimar put his cup down and began ladling what looked like stew onto deeply indented plates—almost bowls—that had been placed by his elbow.

To Poppy's surprise, the stew or soup was light brown, as stew should be (she was expecting another bluish dish), although she could not identify the herbs or the vegetables except for some type of beans. It seemed to contain no meat. By the time she had finished it, something like turmeric had impressed itself upon her taste recollection. Or not. It didn't matter. It tasted fine and she had been famished.

The poufla was good too. It turned out to be an airy bread that raised into crunchy bubbles, a lot more filling than it looked. Then there was another "fluid" as these people termed it. Almost a milk shake, fruity and creamy. The smaller spoons with the long handles were obviously provided for digging the dregs out of the deep cup in which it was served. Poppy congratulated herself for doing quite well with this unfamiliar cuisine. She hadn't noticed a single raised eyebrow all through dinner, but perhaps these people were just too polite, or had some gesture other than raised eyebrows, something she wouldn't notice like tapping a foot, when faced with poor table manners.

No one had spoken much during the meal, and satisfying her hunger, Poppy looked Lorimar over more carefully while he was attending to his dessert. Now he looked a little older than Tremain, maybe by five years or so; or maybe he'd had a harder life. His charcoal grey knitted clothing, a long night-gown-like dress with a round neckline ringing his muscular throat, with a darker grey cape tossed behind his shoulders in a way that would have surely fallen off but for the silver clasp that held it together in the front, certainly gave him no more of a youthful appearance than Kandra's grey dress gave her.

Poppy strained to make out the carving on Lorimar's silver clasp, but twilight had fallen, and the room was not brightly lit. One large candle-type lamp sat on a shelf near the table. She took in the greying sandy hair (which Tremain kept nattily cut), brushed back from his face and falling over his shoulders, and the face that was rather stern, in striking contrast with Tremain's perpetual smirk. Or weary. The eyes, when he looked directly at her, were deep blue, the soul of gravity, but as aloof in their gravity as Tremain's had been in their mockery. Lorimar's eyes did not mock her, but they were not friendly either. They seemed to hold something akin to suspicion, or even worry. Poppy couldn't seem to get a comfortable take on his attitude. But then, how could she expect to read someone else's mind, especially someone who probably didn't exist? And why wouldn't he be suspicious of her, a strangely-dressed woman appearing out of nowhere?

Being fed, she suddenly felt very tired again. She hoped they intended to keep her. No one had exactly invited her to stay the night. She had nothing to give her confidence except Cherry's promise of flowers by her bed.

Her fears were relieved when Kandra said, "You have spent a weary day, Lady Poppy Larian. Cherry will lead you to your place of rest."

"Thank you. *Thank* you," Poppy said. As much as she appreciated the hospitality of the older members of the family, she looked forward to being alone again with Cherry.

"First a relief breach," Cherry told her after they left the room.

A … which? Poppy followed her down a flight of stone stairs, then along a winding corridor to a large room that turned out to be a lavatory. The toilet was made of stone, as was everything else in the room, with a surprisingly comfortable knitted ring to sit on. Poppy could hear the sound of water rushing far below but the room was so dimly lighted by one small lamp on the wall, and the one Cherry carried, she could see nothing down inside but darkness.

There was a small wash basin, like a drinking fountain, for hand-washing. Poppy hoped that was not the only mode of bathing, but she decided not to ask right now. Something that important would surely be shown to her soon enough. The family members had all seemed neat and clean. And Cherry sometimes got so impatient with her questions.

The house seemed much larger now than it had appeared from the street as they climbed back up the stairs, then up two more long stone staircases and down a corridor to what Poppy soon realized was Cherry's own room, dimly lit by some kind of old-fashioned lamp that was quite pretty, sitting on a high chest of drawers.

"I hope I won't be intruding terribly," Poppy said, noticing the jar of bluets that sat on a small table between two narrow beds.

Cherry pushed her playfully onto the softest mattress she had ever experienced, and she wasn't the least bit difficult to upend.

"I get lonely," the girl said. "Your company is welcome." Then she came close and said in a near whisper, "We can laugh together in here, no? And even jest."

"Sure, why not?" Poppy replied, already wiggling into a nest of comfort. "But not tonight. I'm not in a very humorous mood." Then she opened her eyes wide and sat up. "But you really have to tell me what I did that was so wrong out there on the street—just before we got here."

Cherry gave no answer, her smile gone.

"It was something serious, wasn't it?" Poppy pursued. "You have to explain these things to me so I won't goof up again."

Cherry giggled softly. "What is *goof up*?"

"Just making a mistake. You know. I don't want to offend anyone here. You have to teach me to be nice."

Cherry was gazing at her in disbelief. "You do not know the danger in what you did?"

"No. I do not, Cherry. Honestly."

Cherry sat down on the bed beside Poppy's, and was silent for a long moment before saying gently, "We will speak of it tomorrow. You are weary now."

"That I am," Poppy agreed, flopping down again. "But first thing in the morning. Before we go out anywhere. Okay?"

"Okay," Cherry echoed in a tone that indicated she had never heard the word before, but understood what its meaning must be. She crossed the room and opened a drawer, pulling out a length of white fabric that turned out to be a very comfortable nightgown. Poppy forced her body up again to struggle out of her maligned clothing and into it. It was sleeveless, and knit of a material very much like cotton. The sheets and pillow also felt knitted, and they were so soft. Her last effort was to crawl under the covers. Her last utterance was "Ummm."

On first opening her eyes, Poppy found the morning light so strong she had to scrunch them together again and open them more gradually. In the process, she began to recall the incredible dream she had experienced. Now, her strangely bright surroundings brought an almost overwhelming wash of distress.

She looked around a room much larger than her impression of last night in the dim lamplight, at pale walls covered in some kind of light yellow stucco. *Not blue, thank goodness.* Several large, high, arching windows were letting in all that incredible brightness. There seemed a lot of space between the two narrow beds and the tables and cabinets arranged around the walls. No wall hangings decorated the spaces between the tall furniture and the arched windows, but the floor was laid with a nice honey brown rug that blended very well with the yellowish walls and seemed to ameliorate the harsh brightness into a buttery tone. The other bed was empty and the plain grey coverlet neatly made up.

Her own bed matched the other, she noticed, then became aware of a third bed on the other side of hers, made up in the same color. A regular dormitory, she thought, wondering if someone she hadn't yet met belonged in the third bed. But she must not ask about it, she reminded herself, thinking how her questions were sometimes met with hesitation, even astonishment. Maybe Cherry had married sisters who visited, or had even died. She would be careful not to exhibit inappropriate curiosity, to wait for information to be offered to her.

The trouble was, they seemed more interested in getting information out of her, and she had none to give. At least they seemed to understand amnesia—lucky for her, until she could come up with something better. Another thing, she schooled herself silently under the covers, her slitted eyes gradually growing accustomed to the light: I'd better watch what I tell them. Dropping in from another world might not be the right information to provide until I find out whether they believe in witches and things like that. This Larian thing may have saved me from heaven knows what, and I'll probably be smart to go along with that as long as possible.

By time she heard footsteps, her behavior planning had focused her on the day she must get up and face and dulled the anguish of her disappointment at not waking up in her own bed. Still squinting, she was able to greet the fully dressed Cherry with almost as much cheer as the girl brought into the room with her.

"We will breach our fast outside," Cherry announced, carrying a large tray past the beds and out through an arching doorway that Poppy, from her supine position, had taken for one of the windows.

Getting out of bed, Poppy found the air warm and the nightgown enough, especially since there was no sign of a robe for her to put on. She followed Cherry out onto a balcony that looked as if it spanned the whole side of the house, which was indeed a large one. While Cherry busily arranged the items from the tray on a table, she approached the outside wall of the balcony that came up to her waist and, shading her eyes with a hand, gasped as she took in her surroundings.

The house sat on the bank of the shining aquamarine river that slid away in either direction as far as her sight could follow, from the mountains on one side away between the meadows on the other. Along the banks grew vegetation ranging in shade from ice blue evergreens to deep teal river grasses, and scattered throughout the blues and greens were flowering shrubs and gardens of all colors, though dominated by the bluish hues.

Most of the other houses, all bluestone, were lower than the one she was looking out from. Many appeared to be one-story bungalows with walled rooftops charmingly but sparsely furnished; about one-third of them were two-storied with balconies ringing the outside of the second floor, some with what appeared to be lived-on roofs as well. Only here and there was a three or four-storied building, all directly on the river bank with terraced flower gardens leading down to the water. Strangely, she saw only one or two small piers, a few very small boats and no large ones, and that left the whole river as pure and uninterrupted as liquid crystal.

Farther off in the direction from which she had come, the fields waved in gentle ripples as they had yesterday when she was among them, and still farther, the forests off to the side appeared to gradually darken until the mountains turned back toward bluish mauve and the sky screamed its uncompromising, intense blue. An occasional fluffy cloud was edged with a shade of lavender or pink. She wondered if there were robins here in this colorful land. There certainly ought to be, the color of their eggs would fit in so nicely.

Poppy had always been partial to orange and gold tones, and these she did find scattered here and there in hazes of bushes throughout the fields and along the river banks. The blue-grey roads held many people: men, women and children apparently going about their morning business, whatever that was. With relief, she noticed that they wore a variety of colors, especially the children. In fact, from her perch, they looked like large flowers moving along. The whole panorama was breathtakingly exotic, and Poppy had squinted at it much longer than comfort allowed. Finally she had to hold her hands over her searing eyes to let the cool darkness ease the ache.

"What a beautiful landscape!" she exclaimed, turning back to where Cherry was sitting, waiting for her company at the table. "It must get painted all the time."

"*Painted?*" Cherry replied in a little shriek. "How could anyone paint the lara?"

Poppy paused. For a moment she had almost forgotten that there was nothing here she could take for granted. "You don't mean to tell me no one ever paints this?" She waved her arm in a sweeping gesture toward the scene spread out beneath the balcony wall.

"It would take a great deal of paint to cover it all," Cherry answered, but her grin revealed that she did comprehend Poppy's meaning. "You mean a likeness?"

"Yes. A likeness. Of course. You didn't think I meant we should start throwing buckets of paint at the river from here, did you?" Thank God for her sense of humor, and for that of her young companion as well. Already the pain of waking up here was diminishing.

"We are not allowed to create likenesses," Cherry said simply, picking up a cup. "Please, lady. Take some fluid and food."

Poppy obeyed, taking a seat at the small table and tasting the steaming "fluid" Cherry had poured for her out of a large, covered pitcher that looked very heavy. The fluid tasted deliciously like coffee, sort of an herb-laden espresso, very heartening. She had thought after last night it was going to be one herb tea after another ad nauseam. Tea was okay, but she really loved her coffee in the morning. As for food, she found by using her imagination, she could be eating crunchy pancakes with blueberry syrup. Actually, it *was* blueberry syrup.

While they were eating, Cherry jumped up suddenly as if she had forgotten something important, and fetched a blue shawl from the bedroom which, without a word, she deftly wrapped around Poppy's shoulders.

"Thanks, dear, but I really wasn't cold." Poppy said.

"The arms," Cherry told her. "Bare arms outside the house. I should have thought of it before you stood over by the wall."

"Oh, I guess I shouldn't be out here in just my nighty, huh?"

Cherry shrugged. "You are covered. It is allowed except for the bare arms."

The nightgown was almost exactly the same fashion as the dress Kandra had worn last night except for the tie around the waist, and the sleeves. Poppy made a mental note: the arms must be covered at all times when in public. "Does the arm thing apply inside the house if there is a man present?" she asked.

Cherry shook her head, chewing. "Just outside."

Poppy suddenly remembered the question that had occurred to her when she was looking down at the river. "I was wondering why there are so few boats, and no big ones. That river looks so inviting."

Cherry looked at her as if she had taken leave of the little sense she had. "The boats we have are sufficient for fishing. Why build bigger ones?"

"Well, doesn't anyone travel on the river?"

The girl shook her head at her hopeless questioner. "The River Halder passes through Halderwold peacefully, but further down, there are many steep rapids, and upriver the mountains. No one can travel from here by the river. And we know of nowhere to travel, except Laria, which is on the River Lar and could not be approached from the Halder even if there were no rapids."

Poppy nodded, finished her breakfast, or 'breach of fast,' as it was called here, then leaned back with her cup and looked seriously at Cherry. "Now. Tell me what was so awful about making those kids laugh yesterday."

Cherry looked almost as frightened as she had last night, rushing her guest into the house. "It is all right to make children laugh," she explained. "But it is *never* done in public. Do you not have rules of conduct in Laria?"

"I think I've just forgotten a lot of the things I knew, along with how I got here," Poppy replied." The amnesia excuse had better have a lot of mileage. It was all she had. "I think you'd better refresh my memory, even in the small matters," she added. "There's nothing I'd hate more than to embarrass you or your family."

"It would be much worse than *embarrassment*," Cherry's dark eyes grew large and solemn.

Poppy got a sinking feeling that she didn't even want to know how much worse it could get, and she wondered if it was going to be possible for her to negotiate the customs of this land without getting herself and this family into big trouble of some kind.

She spoke quickly. "I'll *never* do it again, Cherry. I promise. Just try to tell me what I mustn't do before I do it. What about making grown-ups laugh?"

The girl stared at her in absolute astonishment. "Poppy, you must not jest about such things." She jumped up and ran to look over the wall, down onto the street, then came back to her chair. "Not even when we are alone. You never know who might hear you."

"Don't tell me," Poppy said in a near whisper. "I think I've got it figured out. You never—absolutely *never* try to make an adult laugh. Right?"

"Never," Cherry confirmed in a low voice.

"Not even the slightest little joke—jest?"

Cherry's dark waves slid around on her shoulders with the vigorous shake of her head. "Never. You could be the cause of their losing control."

Poppy drained her cup in a long, thoughtful draft. God, what a place for a clown to land, even in her wildest dreams—and this was definitely the wildest. "But why is everyone here so uptight—so down on humor, Cherry?"

"It is not allowed. Against the law," came the simple reply.

"Against the law." Poppy sat there trying to take it in. "Wait a minute. All you did yesterday was laugh. Everything I said—you laughed."

"We were alone out there." Cherry smiled as if remembering a wonderful picnic.

"But what if someone *had* heard us?"

Cherry looked thoughtful. "You are right, Lady Poppy. Even though we were far from the others, it was very thoughtless of me. Please forgive me. I might have caused you the utmost grief." The girl bowed her head as her hands dropped like lifeless things into her lap. Then she sighed deeply. "But it becomes more difficult each day as my passage draws near."

"What passage?" Poppy felt panic rise up within her. "Please don't tell me you're going away!"

"No. Where would I go? It is my rite of passage that I speak of."

"And what rite is that, Cherry? What are they going to do to you? Remember, I know nothing about your ways. And of course I forgive you. Now look at me and explain everything that's going on with you. I really need to understand. I don't see how I could survive here without you."

"Of course." Cherry drew herself up and continued. "The end of this week—the morrow—I will be thirteen."

"Congratulations," Poppy said, then after receiving a strange look from her friend, resolved to shut up until she finished.

"Most of the girls in our group have already reached thirteen. There are just three of us yet to attain the age. I will be next, then Kellith and Deema, all within the next three days. We will take our part in the passage rites to be held mid week next."

"And what's going to happen to you then?" Poppy found it impossible to keep quiet.

"Oh, wonderful things," Cherry said, without the enthusiasm that should have accompanied such words. "Our parents, and many other adults, are even now having new clothes made for us, preparing delicious foods and arranging for decoration of the Wise House where the festivities will take place. The musicians—the *king's* own musicians—and the paraders are all practicing for the passing-though. There will be great celebration. We have a large group this time. Many of us were born near the same time. There must have been many storms the prior year."

Poppy gulped back a snort. "Cherry, was that a … jest?"

"No." Cherry replied matter-of-factly. "In times of storm the people must stay inside sometimes for days, instead of going about their business. Many children are born as a result."

"Yeah, I understand that," Poppy said. "Now let me ask you some questions, just to make sure I get this straight—what you've already told me. I'm assuming this rite of passage is a ceremony that declares you girls to be adults when it's finished, right?"

Cherry nodded.

"And it's a big, wonderful celebration—a huge party. How long does it last?"

"Three days."

"What is this 'Wise House'?"

"The large house on the pinnacle outside the city," Cherry told her. "I'll show it to you. Or maybe father will."

"Why not you?" Poppy was uncomfortable about going out with another adult before she knew all the rules.

"Well, he could take you inside," Cherry answered. "I can only take you up the road to look at it from the edge of town."

"Who can go inside?"

"Only those who are authorized, and the children who are still in learning. But I am past that," Cherry said with a proud little smile, her first smile of the past ten minutes.

"You mean you're all through school?" Poppy exclaimed. "At twelve years old?"

"I completed my wisdom learning last year," Cherry told her. "Now I learn from grandmother."

"You mean ... housework?" Poppy asked cautiously, not to sound demeaning.

Cherry nodded. "Preparing food, creating materials and making clothing and household items such as bedding and rugs, preparing for storms. Grandmother Kandra has much to teach me. Unlike many others, I am also learning of the mending herbs and roots."

"I see." Poppy felt she had said enough about the girl's 'education.' "Tell me more about your passage."

Cherry rose and began gathering dishes onto the tray. "We must go to grandmother now. Your questions will all be answered as time permits."

"Let me help." Poppy reached for the pitcher. "Those look heavy."

Cherry put them all on the tray and laughed lightly, to Poppy's relief. This wonderful celebration the poor girl had been talking about had taken away more of her spirit with every word.

"I carried them in full of food and fluid," Cherry said. "I can carry them away empty." Going through the bedroom, she called back, "I will be back soon to bring you a dress. Do *not* put your own clothing back on."

"I get it." Poppy followed her as far as the bed, which she began making up. "I won't put those dreadful things on again."

After resorting to the chamber pot under her bed that Cherry had made her aware of last night, Poppy found a comb of sorts on one of the dressers and pulled it through her badly snarled hair. Her curls had been tamed as best she could manage by the time Cherry brought her a brown dress so shapeless and of such rough material she hated to part with her soft nightgown.

Noticing her look of distaste for the garment, Cherry said, "It is only for the kitchen. We will be with grandmother and the other women for most of the day, helping with passage preparations."

The bundle she left on the bed also included a pair of bloomers and an undershirt. They felt okay to the touch, though they still weren't as soft as the nighty. Poppy picked up the sports bra she had worn to the gym, wondering if she should put it on. She would feel strange without it, but Kandra had obviously not been wearing any such garment last night. Of course Poppy knew she looked quite different without a bra from women of Kandra's age. But if that was the style here ...

Cherry put an abrupt end to her pondering by pulling the bra wordlessly from her hands and stuffing it unceremoniously into a drawer in the dresser nearest Poppy's bed.

"Who are the others who will be here?" Poppy asked as the two began their climb down the stairway.

"The women who will help with the work," was the reply. "And my friends, Kellith and Deema."

After the two long flights of stone stairs, they reached the ground floor, then down another stairway to the underground level they had visited last night before going to bed. Poppy had expected to find the kitchen on the ground floor, but found herself in a huge room that wasn't exactly a basement or cellar, where there was much going on by the light of a few very high windows, many flaming lamps mounted on the walls, and a large fireplace.

On a long sideboard, women were creating mountains of dough; from an oven near them, others were taking out large trays of delicious-smelling pastries. And others, in different areas of the room, were making what appeared to be relishes and wines. Sauces were simmering in huge pots hanging in the gigantic fireplace.

Poppy was drawn to a couple of clattering devices in one corner that turned out to be knitting machines. The women working the pedals and guiding the thread were really concentrating. They gave only the slightest recognition to a spectator hovering near them. Poppy was amazed to see women running these rather sophisticated machines only a few yards from others making cheese in wooden tubs. Fascinated, she drew closer to the machines. One was turning out ordinary, knitted fabric, but the other produced smooth material, almost satiny. She couldn't resist interrupting the busy woman. "How can this fabric be so smooth? It looks as if it were woven, but I can see it's being knitted."

They both stared at her for a moment, then their intent expressions softened. "Laral works on the weft," the woman turning out the smooth fabric replied with what Poppy thought was a faintly superior smile.

The other woman shrugged and continued with her peddling and careful guiding of the yarn.

"The weft? That's the name of her machine?" Poppy asked.

They each shot her a look of pity before the first woman continued. "I work on the warp. The wales come out much smoother."

"Oh," Poppy said. Both women had turned back to their tasks, so she pursued her instruction no further. Apparently they needed to concentrate and didn't have time for an ignorant pest.

The cheese makers smiled at her, so she drifted over toward their area and nodded and smiled back at them.

Nearby, Cherry had joined two other girls in shelling and washing beans. Poppy wandered by just as one was wiping water from her face that another had splashed on her. Cherry introduced them and the girls nodded shyly, held out their hands in polite greeting and turned back to their tasks. They'd probably never met a stranger before, Poppy realized.

Wondering what she could do, Poppy looked around to see Kandra hurrying over to her, red-faced and flustered. "It is not always so confusing in our house," she explained.

"I know," Poppy replied. "The girls' passage. Cherry told me about it. What can I do to help?"

An unskilled job was found for her. Several large pots containing different colored liquids sat on a row of stone fire pits against a back wall she hadn't even noticed. "These are the dye pots," Kandra told her. "Would you be so kind as to watch them until boiling, then put the materials beside each pot into the fluid?"

Poppy agreed eagerly, and Kandra cautioned her that, once the materials had been put into the fluid, it must be stirred and poked constantly to make sure of even coloring, and the coals underneath each pot must be tended carefully with small sticks from a certain pile added when the flame diminished. Glad to be useful, especially at a job she felt she could handle, Poppy joined the busy crew, and was soon humming as she stirred the pots and savored the feeling of earning her keep among these kind and hard-working, though humorless, people. As she stirred and fed the coals, she fantasized about letting some of the material come out unevenly dyed—introducing tye-dying to this society.

Except for an occasional smile, most of the women were too busy to notice her, but the noise level precluded conversation anyway, which suited Poppy. All the less chance of her saying something inappropriate. She noticed those working together sometimes yelling into each other's ears. Once an elderly soapmaker stopped for a moment to supervise her poking at the materials, then nodded her satisfaction and walked on.

CHAPTER 4

Poppy had really begun to sweat over her steaming vats when all work stopped for mid-day break. The women drifted in ones and twos down the corridor to the lavatory, then back to gather on an outside patio beyond a short passageway that Poppy hadn't been able to see from the inside work area. The patio was lower than ground level by the look of the shrubs peeping over the high side walls and the end opposite the house was actually open to a low view of the river. Poppy found it a pleasant relief after the heat and bustle of the inside work room.

The women brought out bread and blue cheese (that didn't seem fermented), a cool drink reminiscent of ginger ale without the fizzle, and something like blackberry tea.

The three young girls joined them, but ate little, they were so busy poking each other and giggling. By now they were so weak from their silliness, they lolled around, choking on anything they put into their mouths. Some of the women seemed alarmed at their antics and tried to talk to them, but the girls only laughed harder. They were obviously hysterical, Poppy realized, remembering her teenage years.

Kandra knew how to handle the situation. "Back inside, back inside!" She waved her arms as if she were shooing away horseflies, and the girls hobbled back through the wide doorway, taking with them only their drinks, and leaning on one another in mirthful weakness.

Poppy had noticed long ago that the girls were fooling around so much they had hardly gotten anything done. The few beans that did manage to get free of their shells and washed were often accidently dumped onto the floor where the girls, bending to pick them up, would fall on top of each other, laughing. What an audience these girls would be, Poppy thought. Would I love to pop a few jokes and tricks for them. But she knew she dared not even consider it.

She had also noticed how the women tolerated the girls' behavior so long as they were inside, pretending not to notice their antics, while at the same time smirking and exchanging glances. More than a few of them cast nostalgic, openly longing glances at the youthful exhibition of high spirits. Not until they had brought their silliness outside had any of the women reprimanded them in any way.

Sitting at lunch, the women spoke only of their various projects and chores, how many more loaves would be needed, how many more gads (yards?) of material. They were friendly to Poppy, offering her more fluid and smiling at her whenever she met their mostly brown eyes, yet none of them even attempted to engage her in conversation or pose any of the questions normally asked of a stranger. Was it because she was Larian, or was it just their way? Or had they heard of her, the stranger with amnesia? After listening to them for a while, she decided it might be a little of all three.

The women seemed content to be working together, even fond of one another, yet their topics rarely touched on anything personal. None of the banter or anecdotes, retelling of funny happenings that women usually recount to one another in casual conversation. Smiles were given generously, but no one, except the three girls, ever laughed.

Poppy was soaking wet with perspiration, but proud of the lovely colors her materials had taken on when, by late afternoon, Kandra called a halt to their day's labor. The other women appeared hot, damp and weary too, but all seemed to take it in stride; she heard no one complain. One would imagine they worked like this regularly, but Cherry had spoken as if this was a special effort to prepare for the 'passage.' Still, Poppy thought she would never be able to keep up if it were not for her regular workouts for her clowning. Even now, her back really felt the strain.

The woman who had nodded at her work earlier brought another, a muscular woman, who waved her aside and poled the pieces of material out of the vats into wooden tubs and the two of them hung them over a long railing to dry. Both of the women's hands were deeply multi-colored when they finished.

"Will that come off?" Poppy asked.

"Along the way," one woman replied casually, wiping hers on her skirt.

Soon the others left, leaving Poppy alone with Kandra and Cherry. Secretly she hoped it was now some kind of happy hour that would bring her another cup of that neat beverage they called 'vigorwart.' They closed the outside doors and put out the lamps.

"We need to bathe," Cherry said, taking Poppy by the arm.

Poppy expected a sponging in the small lavatory they had visited last night, on the same level as this workroom, but Cherry led her past the lav and turned at the end of the corridor to follow another stairway. They descended into a much cooler room with several stone benches surrounding a small sunken pool, actually an oversized bathtub. Why, it was nearly large enough to swim in! She could hardly wait to get into that refreshing water shining in the soft light of several wall lamps in the windowless, underground room.

She was looking over some large cloths spread on a bench for some kind of bathing suit when she heard a loud splash. Cherry was in the water naked, with an expression of having found paradise on her face. Poppy didn't hesitate to follow her example. Cherry's eyes were closed in bliss anyway. When she opened them, it was to reach onto the shelf along the back rim of the pool and come up with two unevenly cut pieces of homemade soap, one of which she tossed to Poppy. The soap smelled wonderful, and held little bits of flower petals.

Poppy was surprised to find the water tepid, just right for cooling off without getting chilled. "How can this water not be cold?" she asked Cherry.

"Hot stones were lowered into it a short while ago," was the gasped reply as the younger girl rose from a ducking to wet her hair. After more questioning from Poppy, she explained that, in the afternoons, the 'stoners' went from house to house along the river—the only houses that held these lower story bathing pools—bringing stones which they heated in the fireplace and held in wire racks lowered into the water for a time.

As soon as Poppy had soaped and rinsed her body by swimming four laps, which brought her to the other side of the pool, Cherry came up behind her and began washing her hair. Without a word, Poppy did the same for her after she had finished. Then Cherry got a vial of liquid that smelled of citrus from the soap wall behind the pool's edge that turned out to be a fragrant hair rinse.

When both had their hair done, Cherry grasped a rope railing and climbed up some steps cut into the side of the stone pool that Poppy hadn't even noticed, and wrapped herself in one of the soft towels. Poppy did the same.

"I don't think I've ever felt more refreshed in my life!" she exclaimed. "This is just like going to a spa."

"A … spa?" Cherry's look was quizzical.

"A place to relax," Poppy grasped for the right words. "A place where other people take care of you for a little while."

"Oh, I shall take care of you," Cherry cried, raising her thick, dark eyebrows. "Do Larians not take care of one another as we do here in Halderwold?"

"Sure they … we do," Poppy stammered. "But a spa is something special. You spend more time there than if you were just bathing at home."

"Oh." Cherry was satisfied. She studied Poppy's dripping red curls. "Most Larians have brown or yellow hair," she remarked.

"Poppy shrugged. "I guess I'm an oddball." Then seeing Cherry's eyebrows curve again, she added, "That's an odd person. Someone who does or has things that are uncommon to others."

Cherry smiled and nodded her head slowly. "My father seems to do everything the way it is done here," she said thoughtfully. "But of course he was a child when they came from Laria."

"How did they get here?" Poppy asked, toweling her hair vigorously.

"It was different in the old days," Cherry said. "People used to travel. Now for many years no one has been able to pass through the swamp." She looked down at her bare feet and repeated. "No one ever gets through anymore."

"Do you know anyone who has tried?" Poppy asked cautiously. Maybe she would fit in better in Laria, if she could get there. That is, if she didn't wake up soon.

"Not well," was the girl's thoughtful answer. "I know of people who left, but have never returned. Of course the convicts cannot return. And no one from Laria ever comes here any more. No one except you." She looked her friend straight in the eyes as if there were still something Poppy wasn't telling her.

"I wish I could tell you more than I already have," Poppy said quickly, getting the silent message.

"You cannot tell what you do not know," Cherry said mildly, as if afraid she'd made Poppy feel inadequate. She wrapped her hair in a towel and twisted it on top of her head. "I will go get some clothes."

Poppy waited, wrapped in her towel, drying her hair. After about twenty minutes, she began to wonder if she had been forgotten. She'd have to stay here until someone thought of her. Who knew how improper it might be to show up in the general living quarters wearing only a towel, even one large enough to wrap yourself completely up in.

Soon Cherry returned with an armful of fabric. She wore a light green gown that made her olive skin glow. Her damp hair was piled up in shining coils. "You look sensational!" Poppy burst out.

"I am practicing." Cherry smiled. "I will soon be dressing as a grownup woman."

"And you'll knock everyone's socks off." Poppy told her, then noticing the bewildered look that crossed the girl's face, she added, "Just an expression. It means you will impress everyone with your beauty."

Cherry lost her new dignity and giggled, then she held the clothes out to Poppy. "Kandra sends you her favorite Larian blue gown."

"Oh, I wouldn't want to wear her favorite dress!" Poppy cried, but seeing Cherry's disappointment, realized that was the wrong tack. Maybe it was an insult or something. "I mean, it's too good. I'd love to wear it, but what if I spill something on it …"

"Put it on." Cherry spoke as if to an exasperating child. She helped her get the shoulders right and tie the sash. It was a deep—almost royal blue, but not quite. It seemed to have a tinge of green, but yet wasn't quite teal. These people sure had a variety of blue shades.

"It's beautiful," Poppy said, looking down at herself. "I'd like to do my hair up something like yours. Could you help me?"

Cherry was happy to. After toweling the flaming curls nearly dry with a fresh towel, she braided and coiled and pinned, then looped a braid around the front of the coils like a crown. Poppy looked around for a mirror, but there were none. In fact, she had not as yet seen one in the house. She felt her hairdo with her hands. "It feels great."

"You look sensational," cherry told her. "You will knock socks off. What are socks, Lady Poppy?"

Laughing, Poppy pulled on the sandals Cherry had brought her. "In some places, when it's cold, people make knitted covers that can be pulled over the feet to keep them warm." She made motions to demonstrate how that would be done.

"Father has never told me of socks," Cherry said, thoughtful again.

"Oh … they're not that common," Popped said quickly. "Even in Laria. It's usually too warm for anything like that." She jumped to her feet. "Shouldn't we be helping Kandra with supper?"

"Malina is making supper," Cherry said. "Kandra is resting."

Poppy was puzzled. "I've seen Kandra working constantly, and doing all kinds of things—and she still has someone come in to make supper?" After it was out of her mouth, she could have bitten her tongue. Who was she to question how things were done in this house?

"Kandra lives in the house of a wise one," Cherry took on an air of bemused impatience. "She knows how to make all things, and she is making foodstuffs for my passage, as are the other women. They, who do not have to work hard, do this to honor us. Grandmother is not *required* to do her own domestic work, though she does much." Then she added with a grin, "And she has many dresses. Even others in Larian blue. So do not distress yourself over this one, lady."

Poppy was afraid to say it. "This is the house of a wise one?"

Cherry nodded. "My father."

"Lorimar is a wise one?" Poppy repeated.

"The head of the wise ones. The *nashu*. The greatest of them all."

Poppy stood very still. The tired man who had eaten quietly with them last night was the head of the wise ones. Whatever they were, they sure sounded important. Suddenly, she was overcome with intimidation. What if she should speak or act inappropriately in his presence? (As if she hadn't already done that with her shock on first seeing his resemblance to Tremain and asking him what he was doing here). She resolved to stick like glue to Cherry for culture instructions.

"What is the matter?" Cherry had started toward the door. Now she paused, looking back at her guest. "Come. I am hungry."

Poppy was experiencing an attack of self-consciousness. "I ... do you think I could just have some food in the bedroom? The way we had break-fast—breach of fast?"

"No. Of course not," Cherry said firmly. "That would not be acceptable for the evening meal. The house of Lorimar would not deny conviviality to a guest." Then, with a forgiving smile, she held out her hand. "You desire to learn how to behave among us? Come to supper, lady."

Poppy obeyed, her uneasiness growing with every step to the room where they had taken their meal last evening. Lorimar rose from a chair near the wall as they entered. "Good evening, Lady Poppy," he said politely.

"G ... good evening ... sir ... Lorimar." What on earth should she call him, she wondered. Now that she knew how important he was.

But his grave forehead creased for a moment in amusement. "Sir Lorimar? I'm afraid I lack the status to be greeted by so eminent a title."

"I'm sorry." Poppy looked at Cherry for help and found her laughing noise-lessly, her lips puckered. An ability Poppy had already noticed the girl had honed to an art.

"He is but *'Lorimar'* here at home. Of course, he is *'father'* to me," the girl said, casting a glance at Lorimar for his corroboration.

Poppy stood helplessly as Lorimar nodded to his daughter, and smiled graciously at his guest. "Please." He gestured toward the table.

What a wonderful smile he had! All the grave lines had rearranged themselves instantly into youthful crinkles, but with none of the caustic mockery of Tremain's smile. Poppy took the same seat she had occupied last evening. At least that must be okay, since everyone else took the same places as well.

There was no vigorwort for her tonight, just the same tea everyone else was sipping. The 'fluid' she had enjoyed so much yesterday was probably medicine. Something given only to the highly agitated or strangers appearing half-insane. For one madcap moment, the idea of putting on a crazy act just to get more of it hovered in her mind. *For heaven's sake, it's getting to me already,* she thought, shivering slightly. *Trying to be serious all the time. I wasn't born for it. I'm a clown for Pete's sake. How long will I be stuck in this weird place? How long can I behave?* Aunt Holly would feel so sorry for her right now if she knew.

"Pulse, lady?" Lorimar was holding out a bowl of something that looked like ambrosia, and the women were looking at her with concern.

Poppy jumped. "I'm *sorry!*" It sounded too loud in her own ears. "I guess I was daydreaming." She hurriedly accepted some of the fruit. It looked delicious. Other dishes were offered and she took some of each. They all tasted fine. Every dish reminded her of some familiar food, but didn't quite taste like it. Bright yellow noodles with blue almost tomato sauce. Nothing unpalatable had been offered to her yet—she was thankful for that. It might be rude to refuse, even if she hated it.

A surprisingly ordinary conversation grew around her, mainly about the coming festivities of Cherry's rite of passage. They discussed the progress of the women's projects, how constantly the orchestras had been practicing, and hoped for fine weather come mid-week. Poppy concentrated carefully on picking up every hint of information that might help her understand just what would be going on, and why. There was only so much she could ask Cherry outright before that look of exasperation crossed the plump face, the look that made Poppy feel like an imbecile. Of course, with the stress the poor girl was under, she couldn't be blamed for losing patience now and then.

But how long could she feign amnesia? She had already slipped up and spoken of socks; what would she give away next that would lead the girl to realize that she did harbor memories? And memories that didn't sound very Larian.

Another thing bothered her. It was plain how hard Cherry was working to act enthusiastic about her coming of age, and how abjectly she was failing. What would become of her after next week? What if she couldn't manage to stifle her natural good humor? Would they just keep her in all the time, doing housework? Liking the girl as much as she did, it was too depressing to even wonder about.

As bedtime grew near, three girls arrived to spend the night with Cherry. Kellith and Deema, who'd had so much fun all day in the kitchen, brought a smaller girl with hazel eyes; she was Sil, Deema's younger sister. In such a large house, Poppy expected to be given another bedroom, but Cherry motioned her to accompany the chattering group as they headed toward the stairs. She followed, wondering how the three narrow beds would accommodate five bodies, until they entered the bedroom. Two low cots with soft rug-like bedrolls had been placed between the beds.

Wall to wall females, Poppy thought, moaning silently. Should make for a giddy night, and just when she really needed her rest. Not only was she exhausted from her day of toil, but she'd had a tendency since childhood to lose control over her sense of humor when sleep deprived. Her first memories of playing the stooge were late in the evening when she'd been allowed to stay up past her bedtime. She would goof around until she became hysterical unless her mother noticed the signs and sent her straight to bed.

Or sometimes it worked the other way. Fatigue could also cause weakness in the optimism department, and she couldn't afford that either. She needed all her strength of mind to stay upbeat in this mind-blowing situation that she should have, by all rhyme or reason, awakened from by now. But hadn't.

The girls got busy dragging some tall screens in front of the windows. Poppy had noticed those big screens standing against the wall this morning, and had thought they looked like some kind of room dividers. She wondered why they had not been used last night when only Cherry and she had slept here. Perhaps the number of occupants might cause sounds that could be heard from the street and entice peeping toms to climb up to the windows? She decided not to ask.

With more than a little commotion, they all got into the nighties they had brought with them, or pulled from the drawers of the large chests in the room. The lamps were put out, and they all went to bed.

For about five seconds, all was quiet, then the noise began a little above a whisper, increasing steadily decibel by decibel to a low roar. Being in the bed nearest the door tonight, Poppy slid out of bed and softly slipped out of the room. Surely among all the rooms in this big house, she could find a sofa or something where she could get a night's sleep. Not wanting to venture into any of the rooms on this floor in case they were already occupied by members of the household—she still had no perfectly clear idea of how many people actually lived here, servants or whatever—she felt her way by the dim light of one wall lamp down a staircase to the second floor.

For a long moment, she stood wondering which way to go until she noticed a faint light coming from a nearby doorway. Moving carefully through the semi-darkness, she entered a room with bluish moonlight streaming through the windows. As her eyes adjusted to the pale light, she could make out what appeared to be some kind of sofa against the further wall. Approaching carefully, she found it empty and comfortable to sit on, with a knitted throw folded and lying conveniently across the back. All she needed was a pillow. Now she could vaguely make out a nearby chair, which she approached and began tugging on the seat cushion. It was loose and came off to make a fairly good pillow. Settled down and nearly asleep in no time, Poppy's eyes suddenly flew open at the sound of an inner door opening softly and footsteps crossing the carpeted floor just inches from her where she lay.

It was funny, she thought later, how her brain could be thinking: *Don't move a muscle—they won't know you're here,* while at the same time her body suddenly bolted upright. The footsteps stopped abruptly and a voice demanded, "Who is there?" It was Lorimar's voice.

"It's me, Poppy," she said breathlessly. "Is that you, sir?"

Without another word, he went back into the adjoining room and came out carrying a lamp. "Still *sir,* is it?"

She could see his smile in the yellow lamplight. "Please never call me that in the presence of the king. He might think I have been tutoring you."

The king again. "Do you really think I'll get to meet the king?" she asked, hoping for a negative reply.

But it did not come. "Undoubtedly. No Larian can show up in Halderwold without stirring the curiosity of the court."

"I ... don't think I want to be a curiosity," Poppy said weakly. "I don't know enough about your customs and ... manners. I'm afraid I would do something to shame your family ..."

"No such thing." Lorimar spoke in an almost parentally soothing tone as he put the lamp down on a small table that suddenly became visible and sat in the chair nearby, sinking quite low, since it was missing the pilfered cushion. "The court will be most eager to meet you. Your being here has already caused considerable stir. Several people asked me about you today."

"What did you tell them?" She wanted to lie down and hide under the covers, but she remained sitting. After all, she was holding a conversation with an important man.

"That you are my honored guest and they will all get an opportunity to meet you at the passage feasts."

Poppy shivered but not, she realized, because she was sitting there in her nightie and bare arms. Was that a scandalous way to appear before him, alone in a nearly darkened room? If it was, he wasn't letting on. Cherry had assured her that bare arms were okay inside the house. In fact, sitting a few feet from her without his cape, in a gown not much different in style from her nightgown, he seemed more relaxed than she had yet seen him.

Memories of her arrival and Cherry's panic at her fooling around with the neighborhood children still haunted her. Without meaning to, she heaved an audible sigh. It was way too easy to goof up here, and Cherry had only hinted at the consequences, but the hint had held a dire note.

Her host seemed to read her fears. "You are now under our tutelage and care, Lady Poppy. Cherry has taught you much already about our social situations, but let me add before I forget: the title 'sir' is generally reserved for male blood relatives of the king or queen, and I do not possess that distinction."

"I'm really paying attention," Poppy said. "But I don't think I've even begun to get it. Everyone here is so … serious. And I'm afraid to ask all the questions that pop into my mind. I don't want to appear rude or prying."

You will be taught all you need to know," he assured her softly. "Trust us."

The gentle strength of his tone made her feel that she could manage. "I'll do my best," she replied.

"By the way," he said, smiling again; almost roguishly, she thought, to her surprise. "In case you are unaware, you have bedded down in the anteroom of my study. And I was working late—that is the reason I happened to come through here."

"Oh, I'm *sorry*," she began, but he cut her off with a sound close to a suppressed chuckle. "Do not tell me. You found it too quiet in the room with the girls."

She burst out laughing, at which his face fell immediately into a somber expression. "I bid you goodnight, lady." He rose to his feet with his customary dignity, despite a moment's struggle to get out of the cushionless chair. "And I apologize for our thoughtlessness in sending you to bed with the young ones. Would you like me to leave you the lamp?"

"No. I'm fine," Poppy told him. "The moonlight is lovely. That's what drew me into this room in the first place. It's so *blue*."

He paused on his way to the door and looked back at her. "And what color would you have it?" She was glad he didn't wait for her reply before adding, "Shall I take you to view the city tomorrow evening, lady?"

"Oh, I'd *love* that!"

He nodded and was gone, with the lamp.

CHAPTER 5

She hadn't been outside the house since she'd been here, except for the balcony and the patio by the river. Hadn't even thought of going out. She'd assumed that Cherry and Kandra would purposefully keep her inside for fear of her making one *faux pas* after another, getting herself, and maybe these good people as well, into who knows what kind of hot water. But she would be safe with Lorimar; she felt almost sure of it. After all, he was the *nashu*, the head honcho of all the wise ones. Soon she was asleep, and soon (it seemed to her) awake again. And still in Halderwold.

That first moment, looking around after waking, was the worst; that moment when she felt refreshed and good and everything started to come real, only to reveal her still stuck in this sickeningly ludicrous dream. And again she had the sensation—almost pain—of adjusting to the bright daylight. But the second moment was really the most labor-intensive. This moment, when she had to gather her resolve all over again to turn her thoughts away from her real life and concentrate her energy and mental verve on the screwball life that had to be dealt with in the here and now.

She could do it, she told herself, as she had yesterday. First, she would count her blessings: she was, at least the guest of a very nice family who seemed deeply concerned with shielding her from harm. On a deep breath she affirmed that she would trust them, as Lorimar had requested last night. What else could she do? Freak out? Heaven knew where that might land her. But thoughts like this must be abandoned. She had to get up and live the life she was given, no matter how strange and unwieldy. Sitting up and swinging her legs over the side of her sofa bed, she looked around at surroundings she had not been able to see last night.

The room in which she had slept, the *anteroom* as he had called it, looked like a blend of two paintings: one of an ancient Roman sitting room and the other of maybe Sixteenth Century England. Beautiful fabric coverings and cushions were everywhere, but no tapestries or decorations. As in Cherry's room, only the lamps broke up the monotony of the plain walls. Nice wooden tables, chairs and another sofa even longer than the one she had slept on, a huge stone fireplace with some bluish-grey wood laid ready for a fire. The windows were fewer than those in Cherry's room, but the patches of sky showing through them were as brilliantly blue as yesterday's.

Lorimar's study, huh? It was just beyond those heavy doors that now stood partly open. What did he study, and what new and possibly useful information lay on the other side of that door? What might she learn about this household, this world, by peeking inside? Unable to resist, she got up and crossed a plain navy blue rug to the large doorway, then pushing open a heavy wooden door, stepped gingerly into the next room, expecting to see a desk of some kind, but there was none.

Instead, it was more like a school library, except that the row of many windows along the side of a very long room which must reach the full width of the house were equipped with what appeared to be telescopes. *Telescopes?* This was more of a surprise than the knitting machines. Being careful not to be visible from the outside, she approached one and seated herself on the stool before it. Peeping through, she could see nothing but dazzling blue that made her squint to the point of closing her watering eyes against it. Of course you can't see anything in the daytime, she laughed at herself. No wonder Lorimar was in here at night. She turned to examine the other side of the room.

"Books," she muttered. Shelves and shelves of books covered the inside wall. She had seen no trace of written or printed material in this house and had wondered if they even had such a thing. She hurried over to pull one of the cloth-bound volumes out of it's place and open it, hoping for some clue to *Halderwold.* It was all hand-printed in the neatest, most beautiful lettering. And she couldn't read a word of it. Not even a letter. It was nothing like any language she had ever seen. She would find no clues to this world here.

Much as she didn't want to think it, the thought had begun to impress itself on her that this world might actually be real. She couldn't have gotten to another planet—but maybe she'd passed into … another dimension? She'd heard of such things, of course, but mostly in science fiction movies. Too weird. She replaced the book with a shudder, took another and opened it to find the same script. Carefully, she put the second book back and, looking around to see nothing else except a couple of small, round tables with more of the backless stools like those that stood by the telescopes, and another huge fireplace at the far end of the room.

Back in her ante-room, Poppy folded the coverlet and put the cushion back in the chair. What to do now? Yesterday Cherry had brought breakfast up to her, but today she didn't even know where she was. Would it be forward of her to go down and look for Kandra and the family kitchen that she supposed was on the same floor as the room where they had taken their meals? First she would go upstairs and see if the girls were still in the bedroom. They were.

"Where have you *been*?" Cherry greeted her. "We are having such a *wonderful* time!"

They didn't need to find out where she had actually slept. "I was … just looking for a bathroom." It wasn't a lie. She really did need one, and she couldn't bring herself to dig under one of these beds for a chamber pot and put it into use with five people in the room.

"You wish to bathe *now?*" Cherry looked perplexed. "We should wait until after the day's work."

"No, I mean just a … *toilet?*" Poppy ventured. "A lavatory? Water closet?"

The four of them were looking at her quizzically, then Deema burst out laughing, and of course it took the others about half a second to join her.

"Water? In the closet?" The little girl, Sil, giggled.

"Never mind," Poppy said. "I'm sure I can find the one in the basement."

"Oh, you need a *relief site!*" Cherry shrieked, as the others fell back onto the beds laughing. She recovered quickly and, with a frown, motioned to the other girls to get up. "I am so sorry, lady. I should have shown you last night."

Sent off by a chorus of stifled giggles, Cherry led her from the bedroom to the end of the hall, where they entered a small wash room. Poppy was expecting something like the lavatory in the basement that she had visited the day before, but this was a dry lav. A wash stand held basins and pitchers of water, and on the other side of the room, three or four grey ceramic pots with covers were the accommodations. Poppy hesitated, wondering if she would be lucky enough to uncover an unused one. With a knowing smile, Cherry pointed to the one at the end and left the room. The hand-washing basins had no fountains like the one in the basement. The one she approached was just a bowl into which she poured some of the water from the pitcher beside it, but there was that lovely flowery soap in a dish beside it. It seemed that running water was only available in the very bottom level of the house. Maybe it came straight from the river.

Cherry accompanied her back to the now quiet bedroom (the girls were gone), where she put on a plain greyish lavender dress Cherry pulled from a drawer, obviously another working dress. How she longed for something yellow to wear for a change. Well, at least she hadn't been fired from her job in the big kitchen; she'd be able to keep busy.

The girls breached their fast downstairs today and Poppy finally got to see the family kitchen on the ground floor. It was nice. A large room—not as large as the kitchen down on the basement level—with a big stone fireplace sporting a built-in oven in the top. Lots of shelves full of supplies covered two whole walls, and two roomy counters with tops of stone, polished to a luster that shone in the light of the sun streaming down through the high windows, nearly filled the middle of the room. None of the windows she had seen in the house were at the level where you could look out. Or where anyone could look in.

On tall stools before one of the counters, they ate some kind of bread toasted in the fireplace, spread with honest-to-goodness butter (they must have cows here) and what tasted like grape jam although it had a greenish hue. But of course there were green gapes, even on earth. Poppy reached eagerly for the piping hot almost coffee that she was fast learning to love. And she finally met Malina. A beautiful young woman who looked enough like Cherry to be her sister. She made their toast and bowed whenever she offered something to Poppy.

"Is it okay if I tell her not to bow?" Poppy whispered to Cherry.

"You may tell her," Cherry said with her mouth full of toast. "But she is probably enjoying waiting on a Larian."

Poppy was nearly finished, so she settled for smiling her thanks at Malina. It was too complicated to figure out.

After the meal, they all reported for duty in the already bustling downstairs kitchen. The four girls were given easy tasks again, husking blue corn, and grinding it in a hand-cranked grain mill. And like yesterday, they horsed around much more than they worked, and their behavior was again tolerated with benevolent glances by the busy women.

Poppy was proud to be given a semi-skilled position today. Kandra showed her how to shape pastry dough into what would have been turnovers had they been square to begin with, ending up triangles, but of course they weren't. A lump of dough was broken out of a large piece, beaten flat and round inside a circular form with a round wooden disk on the end of a little stick, then one of the various fruit fillings had to be spooned in a little pile onto the middle of the dough before it was gathered around the filling like a little bag, and pinched firmly to make it stay together at the top. Poppy had always enjoyed baking, though, living alone, she did little of it. She learned fast, and Kandra gave her several satisfied nods in passing, a couple even delivered with a rare smile. It was good to keep busy.

As her breakfast wore off, Poppy began snitching tastes of the fillings for the tarts, or whatever they were. Most were pleasant although, except for the blueberries, she didn't exactly recognize the berries and fruits, but there was one that was very close to the taste of chocolate. Maybe it was made of the almost coffee beans mixed with something else. She tasted it a second time. This filling was thinner than the others and had to be sealed into the dough quickly to keep it from running. She broke off a small piece of dough and mixed it with the filling, then tasted it. Dang. It sure enough tasted a lot like chocolate—soft, but …

Surreptitiously, Poppy placed several pieces of the almost chocolate dough on a baking sheet by themselves and, when no one was watching, slipped them into the oven, taking them out when she put the next tray of tarts in. The brown dough cooled into something she was able to break into small pieces that tasted amazingly like chocolate chips.

None of the busy women seemed to be keeping an eye on her anymore, so she confiscated a large piece of the pastry dough and cut out cookie-size rounds with the mouth of a small jar. Then she pushed several of the chocolate chips into each one, dropped her invention on a baking sheet and slid it into the oven. Her secret endeavors brought no attention, or maybe the women had decided she was harmless and unworthy of their supervision today.

After the bread and cheese lunch, Poppy brought out a plate of her cookies and offered them first to Kandra. Her hostess looked surprised, but picked up one of the cookies, probably out of politeness, and nibbled at it. Her nod gave the go ahead to the others, who each tried one, nodding their heads at each other and smiling at Poppy as they ate.

The girls went crazy over the new treat, reaching for more until Kandra slapped at their hands and gave Cherry a warning look. "We will save the rest of them for supper," she told her firmly.

Poppy breathed an exultant sigh. She had done something *right*. She had given these people something new and good, something of her own making. She was no longer just a klutzy freak from nowhere. Well, maybe she was—but she wasn't *only* that. She was getting respect for something she had accomplished, not because she was supposed to be from Laria.

At the end of the second workday, Cherry's three friends all stayed to bathe with her and Poppy, but it was faster this time. Not leisurely and spa-like as it had been the day before. None of them washed their hair. The girls' talk, taking on a more sober tone, was of the one day remaining before the big festivities. Already, they had begun referring to their lives up until now as "my child-hood," and this afternoon they even seemed to be tiring of their perpetual gig-gling. Maybe they were just exhausted. There was no way any of them could have gotten enough sleep last night. Or maybe their impending forced grown-up status was depressing them. Even though Cherry turned thirteen today and tomorrow was the big day for Kellith, and the next for Deema, there was no talk of birthday parties. Apparently the forthcoming festivities covered it all.

Poppy put on a lovely mauve garment that Cherry brought her, and let her hair down from the fancy hair-do that had lasted all night and all day in the kitchen. She looked on the counter built along the wall of the bathing room for a hairbrush and found a reasonable facsimile. It had bristles at the end, but the handle was smoothly rounded wood and she was able to give her hair a good, stiff brushing in lieu of a shampoo. It came out partly in crinkles from the braids Cherry had woven among the coils; the rest of it going back into its nat-ural curl. Wondering if it looked funny, Poppy found a small piece of material to use as a scarf to tie back the front. Even working without mirrors, she thought the mix of waves and curls probably didn't look bad.

She was right. The girls made their admiration clear, stroking back their own shining dark tresses as if they were not worth dressing. Poppy wanted to make them feel better. Young girls should feel good about themselves, espe-cially when they were actually quite beautiful anyway, and now losing their youthful status so suddenly and so early. "When I was a kid I hated being a red-head," she said without thinking. "I used to imagine being Snow White, with white skin and black hair."

Immediately, she had their full attention. The questions came tumbling over one another: "Who is Snow White? What is snow?"

After one quick glance at Poppy, Cherry handled the situation. Busily rety-ing Poppy's scarf a little further back on her head, she told the others brusquely, "They are just stories. Just Larian folk-tales like my father's mother used to tell me." Satisfied with the scarf, she gave Deema, who was nearest, a shove. "We will be late for supper."

Although Cherry said nothing about Poppy's admitted childhood memo-ries, Poppy knew from the girl's look that she had done it again. It was hard to resist spontaneity with these friendly and buoyant young companions, especially when her education and work had been oriented around children and teenagers, and she felt so comfortable with them.

Even the family's enthusiasm over her cookies at supper failed to ease the mounting anxiety. Whatever would she say if someone were to come right out and tell her they knew she was not a Larian after all? And what would they then do with her?

Soon after the meal was finished, Lorimar declared it time for her tour of the city. Even though she wanted desperately to get out of the house and see the city, particularly under the guidance of a wise one and a gentleman, she had worked herself into a state of apprehension. She would be very careful, she promised herself. She would try to let Lorimar do most—no, all of the talking.

Her host was dressed in a dark green toga (as Poppy had begun thinking of his garment; she didn't like to call it a dress or gown, only it was longer than a toga, well below the knees) topped by the grey cape with the beautiful silver clasp. The engraving on the clasp must signify his rank, she thought, as he held out his arm to her. "I can't wait to tour your city," Poppy said as she slipped her arm through his.

His seriously handsome face relaxed and his deep blue eyes lost their preoccupied look long enough to almost twinkle. His smile, rare as Kandra's, was wonderful and would have been worth waiting for, if only it didn't remind her of *Tremain Tate*. Then she realized that to see Tremain again would mean she was back home. She wouldn't loath him nearly so much when she saw him again. No, in fact, she'd be happy to see him; he was part of her world.

But no time for mental wandering. With a smart step, Lorimar was leading her out onto the street that she had seen briefly two days ago. They headed up a long, gradual hill in a different direction from the one by which she had come into town with Cherry. Soon, she was able to turn and look down on the river and the houses along its banks, including the three-story one she had been staying in. "This hill is steeper than it looks," she remarked. "We're higher than the house already."

"We must reach the pinnacle before the sun sets," Lorimar told her, picking up their pace. "We do not want to miss it."

It was a good thing she kept in shape. After working on her feet in the large kitchen for two days straight, Poppy had to push herself to keep up with him. "What's on the pinnacle?" she managed to gasp.

"The Wise House."

"You're taking me to the … *wise house*? Now?"

"Of course," he replied coolly. "From there we will be able to see the whole city. And the sunset."

Poppy saved her breath for the rest of the climb. There were many more people around than on the afternoon she had come into town. That day, except for the women in doorways and the laughing children who had nearly gotten her into heaven-knew-what kind of a stew, they had met only the man in the tricorn hat. Now several adult couples, most of whom looked very young, strolled about, some hand in hand, some with the women clinging to the men's arms as she clung to Lorimar's, tighter as the climb became steeper.

There were men on horseback, sporting astounding hats of various shapes, bigger than Texas ten-gallons, followed on foot by boys looking for all the world like medieval pages. So they really did have pages here; that was why Cherry had laughed so hard when she'd introduced herself as Paige. Each of the men, even those on horseback, bowed to them respectfully, even solemnly, probably either because of Lorimar's position, or Poppy's Larian appearance; maybe both. Her guide was offering no explanations. *He wouldn't last a day as a tour guide in New York.*

The pages removed their small, pointed, Robin Hood hats and looked curiously but politely into Poppy's face before bowing. The women nodded and smiled cordially but shyly, obviously trying to get a closer look at her. No one said a word as Lorimar returned their bows; and Poppy, soon catching on, nodded to everyone. *Maybe they only greet one another verbally in full daylight?*

By the time the terrain evened out, the city behind them looked like a tranquil picture with the only movement the small figures walking or riding, and the little ripples on the now golden river. But there wasn't much time for looking backward. Finally, they paused before a long, grassy lawn that surrounded the bluestone Wise House which, except for it's enormous size, looked nothing like a medieval manor. Up close, its rounded top and encircling balconies seemed really ancient—or almost modern, like some kind of museum or planetarium.

Lorimar set their pace at a more leisurely stroll along a narrow path over the vast lawn. The sunset was spreading gloriously, like no sunset Poppy had ever seen. Long fingers of light, gold-white, gold-pink and deep peach stretched across the horizon. Higher, the white and gold ran into bluish tints creating unimaginable varieties of aquamarine laced with many shades of pink. Even higher, the pure blue of the daytime sky had given way to the deepest of lavender.

After pausing on the lawn, Lorimar scanned the sky and said, "We will have time to go through the house all the way to the top."

Poppy followed him, more spellbound with every step. He showed her classrooms with rows of little wooden benches and long tables, shelves of strange-looking books, maps on the walls depicting no lands she have ever known of, and posters written in a large, neat brush stroke type of print, stranger to her than Chinese or Arabic. The same kind of high windows with no glass lighted the rooms, but no picture, not even a child's drawing, graced any of the pale grey walls of the classrooms.

But there were jugs of flowers on the shelves and the teachers' tables, and huge, undecorated vases of lovely tall fronds and rushes sat here or there around the edges of the floor. There were banners too, on long poles fixed against the walls, their design mostly made of stripes, triangles and circles. Even without pictures, the atmosphere didn't seem in any way oppressive. In fact it was almost gay. She could imagine young voices talking all at once as they rushed in to take their places at the tables, or the eager bustle of dismissal.

He took her through a fantastic gymnasium with a shining hardwood floor. The use of most of the equipment, swings and benches—no machinery—could be guessed at in spite of the odd shapes; but it was the several large pads along one side of the floor that made Poppy, in spite of her fatigue, long to break away from Lorimar's side and turn a few cartwheels. Her shoulders straightened and stretched of their own accord, reminding her that it had been days since her last real exercise session, other than the 'women's work' that used only a few major muscles over and over, making an aching body even more in need all-around exercise.

Not only the physical plea from her muscles, but the recollection that bouncing on a pad similar to these had brought her here, whetted Poppy's appetite to try a couple of her clown routines in the hope that the same activity might somehow transport her back home. But in spite of her impulse to cut loose, she managed to walk through the gym in her long lavender gown, on the arm of her guide, as ladylike as she knew how.

They mounted a winding set of stone stairs to a floor where, her guide explained, young people learned trades. What a variety of things these people did: woodworking, metal work, rope-making, wire-making, glass-making, paper making, fabrics, dyes, hand-operated knitting and grinding machines, and some other machines she didn't recognize. Pipe-fitting, masonry, brickwork, architecture, carpentry were all taught here. She wondered that there were no printing presses, nor looms.

"All the material I've seen here is knitted," she remarked. "Don't the people weave?"

Lorimar paused before replying. "Looms are not … a major part of our culture."

It didn't make sense, but the serious tone of his answer caused her to drop the subject and pose her next question: "Do the girls come here too?"

He shot her an enigmatic look. "Why would you ask that, lady?"

"Just female curiosity," she replied.

"What would a girl need to learn that she could not be instructed in at home." he said. It was obviously not a question.

So the girls' lives here were as restrictive as Cherry had represented to her. Poppy made no further comment on the subject.

After touring several more departments and sub-departments of trades than she ever imagined could all be located in the same building, the pair moved on. The third floor seemed to be another school, and Poppy soon learned that those few chosen to be wise ones took their graduate level training between these walls. Except for the adult-sized furniture, it didn't look that different from the first floor to her, since she couldn't read any of the book titles or recognize the maps. The main difference was the odd-looking charts that Lorimar referred to as "star maps." She longed to ask about these maps, to find out if she could actually be in another star system from earth, but out of caution, she subdued her eager thoughts.

The next floor turned out to be a much larger version of Lorimar's study at home, only circular. The center was a huge, round library with tables and stools, and bookshelves at floor level with sliding doors. The area was separated from an outside walkway along which enormous telescopes jutted through huge windows. Low windows, the first she had seen. Stone benches sat before the telescopes. As they walked, Poppy realized the telescoped terrace went all the way around the building.

"This is amazing!" she cried.

Another peculiar glance from her companion, who said only, "Let us hurry to the top or we may miss the last light." With that he grasped her hand and hurried her up a final flight of steps to the roof.

They emerged into an world of unbelievable color. Never in her life had she realized there could be so many shades of pastels. The horizon, where the sun had set, was now in violet flames with variegations dipping into many shades of blue, pink and gold; a little higher up the cloud formations turned back to blue, then became amethyst, first light, then deepening in hues. In the opposite direction, the sky had turned a deep indigo flaunting an enormous pale blue moon, at least three times the size of earth's moon. From the deepening blue of the sky, a panoply of constellations were emerging so unfamiliar and so close that Poppy stepped backward as she gasped, nearly losing her balance.

"Careful." Lorimar's steadying arm slid around her, his warm hand on her back.

"I'm okay," she told him, almost breathless. Together they leaned against a waist-high stone wall, surveying the vast heavens.

"I myself never tire of it," he said in a voice close to her ear.

"I can believe *that*," Poppy replied, struggling against the spell she was slipping under, not only her awe of the overwhelming sunset but the warmth of his arm now encircling her shoulders.

"I hope so," he replied. "I certainly have no reason to lie."

Discomfort at what she perceived as a undertone suggesting that she *did*, brought her reply. "It was just a figure of speech." Upon which he made no comment.

What to do now? Well, he was a man—keep him talking about himself. That always worked. "How were you chosen to be a wise one?" she asked. "Was it when you were a boy? Did you have to study and pass examinations?"

But his look told her she had asked the wrong question. "I am Larian," he replied simply. "Any Larian who ever came here has been designated a wise one. Not because we are better people than those of Halderwold, but because our tendency to a degree of perceptive qualities is valued here."

"Oh." Every nerve in her body began to jangle. "Not the women, surely?"

"Of course the women. My mother was a wise one. An extremely talented intuitive."

Oh God. She just *had* to wake up soon. This situation could get way out of hand. It sounded as if they expected her to be *psychic* or something. What if ... what if they got the idea of making *her* a wise one, and found out what an imposter she was?

His arm had fallen away and she leaned against the cool stone to let the breeze temper the slow burn that was creeping over her. After closing her eyes for a moment, opening them did nothing to calm her. Lorimar had taken a step back and stood looking at her intently, and not just her face. "You blend so beautifully with the evening," he said. "The same colors."

Relieved that his attention had shifted to her physical appearance rather than her mental discomfort, she glanced down to notice the breeze molding the finely knitted mauve gown to her body. The silky bloomers and thin shift she now wore were so comfortable she sometimes felt she had on no underwear at all. She had already ceased to feel uncomfortable without a bra—had almost forgotten about it; but now, under the scrutiny of his gaze, the flush was fast becoming a flame licking up the sides of her neck and face.

What *could* she talk about to this man? She looked down at the sprawling city. "I can't see the edges of the city," she said. "It must be much vaster than it appeared from the field when I first saw it. And you know I still can't help wondering ... when Cherry and I came into town, we only met one man. There are many people on the street tonight. Where do they all work during the day?"

"Some work in the craft shops and granaries," he answered. "And in the houses and stables and pastures. Blacksmith sites and vendor shops. Some go to the mines out toward the mountains, and some are guardsmen in the palace and the places of detention. Among the women in particular, some follow the crafts of growing herbs and healing. But most go to the fields and orchards beyond the city. Not the wild meadows out toward the swampland where you met Cherry. The children sometimes gather wild herbs and berries there, but the sown fields and orchards are in the other direction. Though our cultivatable land is not vast, we make good use of it. We grow many kinds of grains and fruits."

"Yes, I've realized that from the wonderful variety of ingredients we women have been baking with," she babbled, glad to stretch out the casual subject matter, and speak of something she knew about. Also, she wanted him to know she had been making herself useful. "And the teas and fruits. Ummm."

"The wines are made outside the city also," he told her. "We have large vineyards. You will see it all in time."

"So you're totally self-supporting," Poppy said. "That's great."

"How else would we obtain our supplies?" he asked.

"You don't trade at all? I mean with other, ah ... city-states?"

He looked at her a long moment. "City-states," he repeated. "What an interesting concept. Yes, I suppose that is what we are. But how else could we be set up? We must live in shelters and use the fields to support us. And a governing body to keep order."

Another wrong turn. Damn. Remember—talk about *him*. Her eyes lighted on the silver clasp on the front of his cape. "I like that beautiful clasp you wear. The design is so fascinating. You can hardly tell where the circles end and the swirls begin. What does it mean?"

Again his reply was to observe her in silence.

"So." She tried to gather her wits, suddenly feeling an overwhelming hope-lessness. "You've been a wise one just about all your life, then. At least a poten-tial wise one. Cherry said you came here as a small child."

"Not that small," he replied. "I was ten years old. I remember things from long before that."

"Oh, me too." she blurted out. "I can remember when I was *three!*"

Her hand came up over her mouth as he motioned her to a stone bench. "Sit, lady." It was more a command than an invitation.

CHAPTER 6

Poppy sat, and Lorimar sat beside her, at enough distance to turn and face her. "So you have memories." He said it as if he were not surprised.

Poppy nodded, looking down at her hands.

"Not of Laria," he said.

She shook her head. "No, not of Laria." After a moment of silence, she glanced up at him. "Am I … in trouble?"

"Of course not," he replied evenly. "I have told you that you are under my care. Besides, I have known all along that you were a stranger. Even without the 'socks' and 'Snow White'—yes, Cherry told me—but everything about you, your hair color of course, the clothing you wore, even the way you handle table utensils. Not Larian."

She waited. At least she didn't have to fear being immediately thrown out of his house.

"Besides," he continued. You speak with nothing close to a Larian accent. Even though my mother and I were the last to come here, and I have probably grown up speaking as the Halderwoldians do, she never lost her way of speaking." He paused a moment with a hint of a smile. "And we *never* had … what do you call them? Chocolate chip cookies? in Laria. As a boy, I would have remembered those."

A small giggle escaped her, mostly from nervous relief but partly because of the funny way he pronounced cookies. It was more like 'kookies.' Then, even though he had not reacted to it, she got hold of herself. *Mustn't giggle. Be serious.*

"And as for the design on my clasp," he continued. "It signifies the central force of the universe—the power and mercy of the Unbounded One. It hangs over every Larian child's bed from birth. A Larian could forget his own name before this symbol, the Uniplax."

Foiled again by the uniplax. When will I learn to listen to my mother, the dentist? Poppy was growing dangerously giddy and she knew it. "I'm getting cold," she said. "And rather tired. Kandra and her ladies are not ones for letting a person sit idle."

Lorimar rose from the bench, practically whipping off his cloak. As she stood up, he wrapped her in it. "Going back will be much easier," he assured her gently. "We will get a cart."

Almost wordlessly they retraced their way down the several stairways and halls, and out across the lawn. The dewy grass brushed her sandaled feet with damp that chilled her bare toes. *Why in the world* haven't *they ever thought of making socks, with all their knitting.*

As they reached the city and started down a street, Lorimar hailed a page who was strolling alone and sent him for a cart. As they waited, Lorimar turned to her and said in a low voice, "Until the passage celebration is over, you must be a Larian, then we will decide upon a course."

Poppy could only nod. Soon a small cart arrived, pulled by a beautiful white horse. The rear seat had just enough room for two. Lorimar handed Poppy up the one step gallantly and she sat, surprised by the comfortable padding of the seat. Up front, the driver's place was hardly larger than a bicycle seat. *Can the word 'bicycle,'* she warned herself. *I haven't seen any around here, so don't even think it or next thing you'll be saying it.*

Poppy was truly exhausted when Lorimar thanked her graciously for her company and left her in the dining/sitting room just inside the vestibule, from where she heard him mounting the stone stairs up, she supposed, to his study—or bedroom, wherever that was.

She felt a little hungry after all that climbing and wandering beyond the dining area, found the door to the family kitchen, wondering if it would be improper for her to go in and look for a snack. Even if it were, the family seemed to take her constant breaches of decorum pretty much in stride. They must understand by now that she *wanted* to do things right. And besides, hadn't she worked her fanny off all day helping with the baking? Convinced she could get away with it, she pushed the inner door open only to find Kandra approaching from the other side.

"Oh, I'm sorry," Poppy gasped. "I was a little hungry. Thought I might find a leftover cookie."

After a little intake of breath that showed Kandra as startled as Poppy, the older woman reached up to smooth her silvery hair and smiled. "In truth, I was coming out to wait for you, my dear."

Poppy felt a little flush of comfort over the 'my dear.' It almost made her feel part of the family. She just couldn't get comfortable with that 'lady' business. "We just got home," she said. Then feeling ridiculously like a teenager coming in late, added, "Lorimar and I. He took me to view the city from the Wise House."

Kandra nodded. "I know. I am happy you enjoyed a respite from your indoor detainment." She smiled again, which surprised Poppy and brought a painful twinge of homesickness. She reminded her so much of Aunt Holly when she looked pleasant, Poppy almost wished she would remain austere.

"You are hungry," the older woman continued.

"If it's not a problem."

Kandra's outbreath came close to a laugh. "With all the food we have been preparing? How could hunger be a problem?" A motherly arm slid around her shoulders and Poppy was guided into the kitchen and over to a comfortable armchair beside the huge fireplace rather than the stools where she and the girls had breakfasted. "You rest, child," Kandra said kindly. "Let me bring you a little pastry and wine."

"But you worked all day too." Poppy objected. "You're always working when I get up in the morning."

"Hush." Her hostess was already bustling around the shelves. "I've been sitting all evening, sewing clothes for Cherry." She brought two of the filled pastries that Poppy had put together and baked.

After the first bite, Poppy had to resist gobbling. "These are so delicious. The lopsided shapes I made some of them into won't even be noticed."

Kandra shook her head slowly. She had taken a chair across from her guest. "No one will mind. We all enjoy the wide array of foods at the passage celebration."

Poppy sipped the wine. It was cool but at the same time bright and mellow. "This wine is fantastic!" she said. "Will we be having more of this at the celebration?"

Kandra's smile was faint now. "All you desire. And other fluids as delicious. It is a time for making and enjoying all that we are capable of assembling."

"And doesn't it begin right away?"

"Tomorrow night." Kandra looked at her directly. "And I wish to ask a favor of you in regard to the festivities."

Poppy was ready to be asked to stay out of sight, and would much prefer it, so long as they saved her a generous selection of goodies. But she answered with forced enthusiasm, "I'll be happy to do anything I'm able to, Kandra. You've taken me into your home and treated me like royalty."

A slightly sardonic expression attended Kandra's smile, reminding Poppy once again that she *was* practically royalty here. Of course Lorimar and Cherry, and probably Kandra too by now, knew she wasn't really a Larian. Would that make a difference in her future treatment? Well, she would have to worry about that when the time came. Right now Kandra was continuing, "Your ... talent." She seemed to be choosing her words as if from a vocabulary rarely used. "As a ... I mean to say ... in humor. Comedy. Could you arrange a ... *performance* for the children tomorrow evening?"

Poppy sat her wine down on a nearby table so as not to spill it. "You want me to *clown* for the children? I thought that was the worst thing I could do here! The night I came ..."

Kandra's hand waved as if sweeping the episode into a dark corner. "This is completely different. Tomorrow night is the last night of childhood for the boys and girls making passage. It will be a night of merrymaking like no other. Oftentimes, they have to create their own entertainment since there is not always an adult who can come to their aid. This time we have you. You could make it so enjoyable—so wonderful for them, and some of the younger children too. If you would, lady."

Ouch, there was that 'lady' again. "Of course, I'd love to, Kandra," Poppy replied. "It's just ... the last thing I expected you to ask. I'll give them the best show I can possibly come up with." She peered at her hostess over the rim of the wine glass she had retrieved from the table. "So long as you're sure I won't get into trouble."

With another dismissive wave and a passable Aunt Holly smile, Kandra assured her she would be in no danger. "It has been the custom for many years to make the young people as happy as possible on the evening before passage."

Poppy squelched a half-conceived wisecrack about an underage bachelor party. "I'll do it, and gladly, Kandra. But I probably won't sleep a wink tonight wondering just what I will do. I have no clown costume or any of the props I use for my tricks. What time will we be starting the entertainment tomorrow night?"

"Immediately after supper for the children." Kandra looked around as if to remind herself of the million things still to be done. "As soon as the girls bathe—well, they will bathe early since we will not require them to work tomorrow. Nor will you." The look of fondness Poppy received blended with the wine to give her the best feeling she had experienced since arriving here.

Good thing I could answer 'yes' to her request for an act. Looks as if I'm an insider for now. But the swift sensation of belonging soon brought on a stab of cheerless nostalgia for the people in her real life. Suddenly it occurred to her how lucky she was not to be in love. How awful it would be to be stuck in this *parallel dimension,* or whatever the heck it was, if she had left someone back home that she longed for even more than her family and friends.

"But we must find you garments," Kandra was saying. "Aside from your ... entertainment costume, you will need two gowns. One for the Day of Passage, and one for the evening at court ..."

"*Court!*" Poppy almost choked. Gone was the comfort—the feeling of fitting in. "Surely you don't mean '*court*' as in where the *king* will be ... as opposed to ... No, I was hoping I wouldn't be dragged into the other kind of court on charges of inappropriate clowning of something, either. I mean, you've just promised me I'll be in no trouble ..." She was babbling again.

"No trouble," Kandra assured her quickly. "But certainly you will attend the festivities at the king and queen's court tomorrow eve. They all wait to meet you. Did Lorimar not tell you?"

"No!" Poppy was on the verge of panic. "What will I be doing there?"

"Just feasting," Kandra explained with as much exasperation as patience. "And dancing. Nothing difficult will be required of you. Just be respectful and sober and ... but surely I should not speak to you as if you were a child. Please excuse me."

"No. Not at all, Kandra," Poppy replied with restrained desperation. "I need every word of advice you can give me. So, I'll actually be meeting the king?"

"Of course. And the queen also. But it is no monumental event for a Larian to meet with Halderwold royalty," Kandra told her calmly. "However, you are not like any Larian I remember, though Lorimar and his mother were the last to come through the flatlands, and that was long ago ..." Her voice trailed off as her eyes took on a distant cast.

"Why have no Larians come here since then, Kandra?" Poppy ventured. She could be patient no longer, waiting for information on a 'need to know' basis; and felt an acute desire to speed up the process. What if they were so busy they forgot to warn her of something crucial to her behavior at this upcoming celebration? "Why can't they get through the swamp—the flatlands?"

Kandra showed a look of surprise. "Why, cannot they get through? Surely you know ..." She stopped. "Oh, I forget your affliction ..." Apparently Cherry and Lorimar had not shared their suspicions of her origins with Kandra, a native of Halderwold.

"I still don't remember coming here," Poppy said. "I'm sorry. Please forgive my impediment and instruct me in any way I might need to show proper respect for your royals." *Good grief, I'm beginning to sound just like one of them.*

Kandra rose and rested her hand on Poppy's shoulder. "Do not worry. Lorimar will be with you at court. He will see that you are properly guided. Now, we must find garments for you. Come." She picked up a lamp.

Poppy nearly groaned to get up from her chair, but Kandra being considerably older and probably twice as tired, she followed obediently.

In the far reaches of the upstairs, further along the third floor corridor than Poppy had dared wander by herself, her hostess drew a large key ring from her pocket and let them through the first locked door Poppy had seen in this house into a large room filled with baskets, trunks and closets of fabrics, gowns, mantles, scarves and simple but exquisitely cut and burnished jewelry in cabinets that Kandra unlocked with another key on her ring. After much rummaging, a silky gown of orchid—more pink than blue, with trailing sleeves edged with vermillion to match the V neckline and hem, was chosen.

Then, sorting carefully through a chest of pendants, Kandra at last chose a chain of bluish silver from which hung an oval-shaped stone of dark red. Not as dark as garnet, yet not as orange as carnelian, but yet not ruby, Poppy thought as she tilted it one way and then another in the lamplight, astonished at the sparkle of the stone, the shine of its metal setting. So simple and yet so stunning. "Surely, this is too fine for me to wear," she began. "Too expensive ..."

"Do not speak so. Such is customarily selected for a guest, though it has been long since we have had one, except for Cherry's friends." Kandra looped the chain over Poppy's head, then held the gown up against her. "The pendant hangs perfectly within the neckline," she said with satisfaction. "But you must put it on to be sure it fits."

Poppy slipped out of her dress and into the pink gown. It did feel right and the skirt flowed beautifully when she turned.

Kandra fastened the necklace around her neck and it fell exactly inside the V neck. Standing back, she smiled. "Now for the other costume. Something for the evening. At court," she added with a slightly teasing lilt.

Their efforts again took some time, but finally Poppy stood in a satiny scoop neckline gown of a hue she thought of as midnight blue. Silvery trim edged a simple, delicate design—just interlacing 'x's and a flash of silver here and there as she turned suggested that silver threads, nearly invisible, had been knitted into the fabric. And how they created that shiny finish on knits was still a mystery to her. She hadn't really understood all that stuff about warps and whatnots.

"This is exquisite!" she breathed, turning slowly, letting the light dance gracefully over the material as she looked down on it. There were, as usual, no mirrors in the room.

"It suits you, Poppy," Kandra told her with a smile of satisfaction. "You honor our house to wear it."

Then she chose a strand of large beads, blue and silver, alternately strung, to be worn with the blue dress. No image appeared on the beads, which were more disc-shaped than round, and their luster was breathtaking. "And this goes well too." Kandra held up a piece of silvery netting that Poppy realized was a snood.

"I … never cared much for hair nets," Poppy began to object. *I worked in a hospital cafeteria when I was sixteen …* No, she hadn't said it aloud. She let out her breath and began to examine the almost ethereal weblike beauty of the net as Kandra brought it closer, turning it to catch the light. "It is not worn over all the hair," Kandra explained. "It looks best if you work the front of the hair high, then gather the falling back tresses into the net. The women will help you dress the hair. Of course, if you don't like it, no matter. You will look lovely anyway."

"What women?" Poppy fingered the snood. It was like silver silk.

"Two or three women will come to help us dress," Kandra explained. "You will not be expected to manage everything by yourself."

"Oh. Well, I guess that would be a big help," Poppy said. "And I'll be happy to try the … hair net." She smiled apologetically, not wanting to seem ungrateful.

Kandra nodded. "Now," she said with an air of finality. "Some clothing for … what do you call it? *Clowning?*"

Poppy nodded, wondering what could possibly be found among these beautiful clothes and fabrics that would even remotely serve for a clown outfit. But Kandra was already dragging some large baskets from a dark corner on the other side of the room.

Poppy moved to help her but the gown wasn't easy to get out of and, by the time she had shucked it, Kandra was pulling some brightly colored garments from the bottom of a basket—much brighter than any Poppy had seen on anyone in this house.

"This will be suitable." Kandra seemed to be speaking to herself, hardly aware that Poppy had approached her, as she gave the material several vigorous shakes. "It has been folded for so long …" She looked up at her guest. "Yes, this will do wonderfully. Try it."

To Poppy, the shapeless material seemed to take on form as it was handed to her. She held it up and observed it in wonderment. Could it be? It was. A clown suit—of sorts; more like a jester's outfit really, with each arm and leg made of a different material of wildly clashing hues. "You mean … it'll be all right if I wear this? Oh, I should be able to make the kids laugh in *this!*"

"It will be appropriate." Kandra nodded and smiled. "It will be wonderful for the children, but only for tomorrow night. After that, it goes back into the bottom of this basket until the next passage eve—if there is then found one worthy to wear it."

Poppy's hands moved all over the suit, finding the openings, the fastenings, fingering the many tassels, thinking just how she would wear it. It seemed quite large but that was fine. Too big was always comical. Her mind raced, and her heart did too. How she had missed silliness, even in these few days.

"What can I wear on my head?" She spoke more to herself than to her companion. Then she stifled a rueful giggle. *I can go to another world and I still have that damn hat problem!* Then she remembered the hats she'd seen on the streets. "Do you have any really big men's hats?"

Without a word, Kandra went to a large closet and began dragging a huge basket down from a shelf. Poppy rushed to help her and the dust flew as they let it drop to the floor. Kandra lifted the lid. There were hats—crazy, zany hats. Poppy went wild trying on one after another, attempting to judge their effect without the benefit of a mirror. This house didn't even have a dark window pane to give back a reflection. "Oh, I wish I could see myself!" she cried.

Kandra seemed to find her statement hilarious. For the first time in Poppy's presence, she jiggled with silent mirth, swaying as she squatted by the hat basket. Then she immediately corrected herself, glanced around in that nervous manner of hers, and said soberly, "My dear, how could you possibly do that?"

"Like this." Poppy went back to the table and picked up the large pendant, holding it up before her face. "If I just had something like this, only bigger."

Kandra shrugged and got to her feet. "That is the largest pendant in our stores. If there were a larger one, I would already have offered it to you."

"Oh, I don't mean for … adornment," Poppy explained. "To look into. See?" She held the pendant in front of the older woman's face. "Can you see your own face in it? Something a few times larger, but just as shiny, would give you a complete picture ..."

Kandra thrust the pendant away from her. "*Uniplax forbid!*" she gasped, glancing around as if she feared they were not alone. "We must *never* look at our images! It is as forbidden as creating images on our fabrics or walls!"

"Then how can I wear those beads?" Poppy almost wailed. "What if people see their images in them?"

Kandra fanned herself with a hat brim. "No one will stand before you and actually look into them. But if they should catch a glimpse of their own image, they will simply pretend they have not seen it. There is no danger there."

"But what if a little kid sees herself in my jewelry?" Poppy pursued. "And yells it out, like in *The Emperor's New Clothes?*"

"The *what?*" Kandra cried, fanning at an accelerated pace.

"Sorry," Poppy said. "An old ... just something I made up. I'm getting silly, just thinking about coming up with a clown act."

"If you do not care for the beads," Kandra said more calmly. "There is no requirement that you wear them. I was simply offering you the finest gems in our family collection."

"I love them!" Poppy cried. "I'm just nervous about doing something wrong! Especially on such an important occasion as the ... passage."

The older woman looked confused.

"I'll take this one." Poppy turned her attention back to a triangular hat she had picked from the basket, much like the one that first man on the road had worn, but even larger, as well as she could remember. "This hat will be perfect. Now what can I wear on my feet? Would you have any colorful slippers or anything like that?"

"I will find some. But I have something in mind," she mumbled, going back to the jewelry drawers. "Ah."

The "Ah" was breathed as she pulled a strand of sparkling blue stones from a fabric-lined drawer. The stones were as large as marbles, cut in facets too small to cast a reflection, clear water-blue and dazzling. The strand was long and would surely reach below the neckline of the dark blue dress. Poppy reached out to stroke them with a finger. "What amazing aquamarines! They're *beautiful*, Kandra. I'll be thrilled to wear them."

Kandra's face broke into her rare Aunt Holly smile. "They are not aquamarines," she said. "They are blue diamonds."

Poppy drew in a breath. "Oh, I ... can't wear something like that! They must be *priceless!*"

Kandra looked disappointed and a little annoyed. "Then, I will find you something else," she said with more than a hint of a sigh.

"No, I didn't mean *that*." Poppy laid her hand on the older woman's arm. "You don't understand. I've never even *seen* jewelry like this before. Not even in a store. Of course I'll wear them, Kandra. I just don't feel ... worthy."

"But you are the *Lady Poppy*." Kandra's look of puzzlement reminded her again of her high status here. Would she ever get used to it? The clown suit kept her clinging to a comforting scrap of her old life. To think of dressing up like a clown had made her feel a little like her old self, far from the equivalent of royalty.

"You had no jewels in Laria?" Kandra was looking incredulous.

"Not like these."

"They were my grandmother's," Kandra said, with a distant, unseeing gaze. "She used to tell me about the old days, before the decree."

"The decree? What decree, Kandra?"

Kandra actually jumped. "I didn't realize I was speaking aloud." She glanced again around the semi-darkened room. "I fear I have grown weary with all the preparations of the last few days."

"Of course you have, and I apologize for making it more tiresome by giving you so much trouble about these beautiful things you've been choosing for me," Poppy apologized. "They're all just ... *smashing*." That wasn't even a word she ever used. Who was she becoming now? Wasn't it enough that she had a new persona to work on in this place?

The old days." Kandra had slipped into her reverie again. "The days before the rite of passage of children."

"You mean this whole tradition is only a couple of generations old?" Poppy burst out in surprise.

"Five," Kandra answered, counting on her fingers. "Six counting Cherry. It was in the time of my great grandparents. My great grandmother told the stories to my grandmother, who told them to me."

"I'd love to hear them, Kanda," Poppy said softly, not to startle her again. "Are these stories secret?"

"No." Kandra shook her head slowly. "But though they are not spoken of openly, you are the first person I have met who has not heard them." She sat, or rather sank down on a cushioned stool.

Poppy had been getting back into her dress, and now she followed Kandra's example by taking a seat on the nearest basket.

"My great grandfather, Norlow, was an … artist. Not what we have now—the artisans who shape the utensils, the dishes, jewelry, but one who actually made likenesses of people on paper." She glanced warily around again. "I know there could be no one listening—we are three stories up, and it is late, but …"

Poppy held her breath and looked as interested as she could for fear Kandra might decide not to continue.

But after another sigh, the older woman went on: "My great grandfather was a young man, not only an artist but a … what did they call them? One who wrote about events that were going on and made many copies to disperse to all who wished to read about them."

"A journalist?"

"Perhaps," Kandra said thoughtfully. "I cannot remember the word, but it was like writing a journal, I suppose. His own ideas about the things that were happening. And he drew likenesses to … illustrate—yes, that is the word—to illustrate the people of which he wrote." She made a sound close to a suppressed chuckle under her breath. "They said his illustrations depicted his subjects so well, many were eager for each new … I forget the word—*issue*. Yes, for each new issue of the journal, or whatever it was, to be distributed."

"So he published a newspaper," Poppy said. "Stories of things that were happening and drawings of the people who were making them happen."

"Strange words," Kandra said, glancing at her uncomfortably. "But they have a distant ring of truth. We have not spoken openly of these things in so many years." She glanced up at the ceiling as if recalling far-off tales. "Norlow was not the only one doing such, but it was said that he was the most brilliant. His *drawings* roused much controversy, being not only excellent likenesses, but …" She paused again, grappling for words that had not been spoken since she was a girl. "Sometimes they mocked those whom they represented. Exaggerated their most uncomely features."

"Caricatures!" Poppy filled in. "Satire. Lampooning."

"You have many more words for these things than we have here. And I seem to have lost the ones we had, since we have not made a practice of speaking them." Kandra shot another nervous glance at the high, dark windows.

"Please tell me all about it," Poppy pleaded, dragging her basket closer to Kandra's stool. "Speak low—I can hear."

Kandra's memories brought that low, private chuckle again. "It seems that the king at that time—King Tullus—was not the handsomest man in the kingdom. In fact, it is said he appeared as … what *you* might call a *clown*. He had a large, bulbous nose, cross eyes and hair that could not be persuaded to lie down on his misshapen head. His jesters, to keep from … *lampooning?* him, made themselves more and more grotesque until the very sight of them frightened the little children they were meant to entertain."

"What a *shame!*" Poppy murmured.

"My dear grandmother was one of those children. It had been the custom for the king to send his own jesters, as a civic contribution, to festive occasions at the school, but this had to be discontinued when the children began to cry as soon as they appeared. Grandmother said she was much relieved when, as a child of four, they were told that only their own teachers would dress up as jesters to entertain them."

"So I'm guessing Norlow got into big trouble for drawing the king even funnier than he actually looked," Poppy said.

"Exactly," Kandra replied. "It was … 'big trouble' as you say, but it was not something that came about overnight. There were divisions among the wise ones, plots and rumors of plots that may or may not have even been afoot. Finally Norlow was imprisoned, then exiled, along with many of the other … journalists. Laws were passed forbidding all depictions of likenesses of any kind. Huge fires destroyed all the portraits of ancestors—I do not even know what Norlow looked like, though my grandmother assured me he was a very handsome man. But then, she was his daughter."

"And *all* likenesses were forbidden then?" Poppy asked. "Even pictures of the landscape and flowers and birds and …"

"All likenesses." Kandra made a sweeping gesture with both hands. "King Tullus's wrath knew no bounds. Clothes, even wall hangings and bed coverings were burned. Everything that bore a likeness. Only a few things that had patterns or symbols …" She drew a triangle in the air with her finger. "Signs or meaningless shapes were left alone, but people nearly stopped weaving or knitting even those into the fabrics. Better to be safe. If further laws were passed, it would only mean more goods must be destroyed."

"And sacred … or, I mean signs like the *Uniplax?*" Poppy ventured.

"Yes, the Uniplax has been a symbol of the blessing of the Unbounded One from time immemorial, perhaps since our first contact with Laria which is now lost from our tomes of record, though some of the tales survive. It is said that many books were illustrated, and so had to be burned. But of course the symbol itself is of shapes which were allowed, so we have it still."

Poppy nodded, and the older woman went on. "So embroidery, which my grandmother learned from her mother as a child, and did expertly, became a forbidden pastime. And my great grandmother made tapestries." Her eyes roamed the distant corners of the room with a nostalgic moistness. "Grandmother told me how beautiful they were. One especially, which she had loved. It was huge, a cover almost for a whole wall. It had a pattern of trees and children playing with a colt and two lambs. Grandmother had loved those little lambs. She used to stand before it wishing herself inside—a part of that world ..." She stopped abruptly as Poppy gave a start.

"She shouldn't have ever wished for something like that," Poppy muttered. "It might have come true."

Kandra's quizzical look brought a near apology for the offhand remark. "Just something *my* grandmother used to tell me." Poppy felt her face flush. "What happened to those beautiful tapestries, Kandra? Is there any chance you still have one hidden away somewhere in these closets?"

"Mercy, no! They were all burned in the public fires." Kandra sighed deeply and wearily. "The people who had created these beautiful artifacts were required to throw them into the flames with their own hands, along with their looms. Grandmother told me how she wept with her mother as they cast those lambs into the fire."

"What a downer," Poppy muttered. "Is that why the people here don't weave, Kandra?"

"Yes, indeed. Weaving is not absolutely forbidden. We make rugs and such, and a few plain wall hangings, but the art of depiction has been forgotten. Without the images, weaving is a lowly task. And we have grown accustomed to the comfort of our knitted fabrics."

"I can agree with that." Poppy wanted more of the story. "That king—what was his name? Tullus? He must've been an awful person."

"Quite the contrary," Kandra replied with unexpected brightness. "Tullus was a good king. One can hardly blame him for loathing to have his appearance mocked, especially since he was a person of high estate, and his face was certainly no fault of his own in the first place."

"But he imprisoned and exiled people for *using their talents*," Poppy insisted. "Surely you can't call that a positive way to rule?"

"Well, they were using their talents negatively—to use your terms," Kandra said. "Of course the decree went rather to extremes, taking in *all* the art in the land, but Tullus was completely out of patience. As I said, it took some time—several years, in fact—before the laws were actually passed, and even more before they were diligently enforced. Then immediately afterwards, you see, he instituted the passage of thirteen-year-olds into adulthood in order to spare small ones the severe penalties for breaches of the law; and he began these festivities for children up to the age of passage. All the celebration you will see, and participate in, tomorrow and the next day."

"I'm certainly eager to see it all." Poppy tried to go along with Kandra's positive approach. "I guess I arrived in Halderwold just in time."

Kandra seemed purposely to avoid commenting on her guest's arrival. She made a busyness of folding fabrics. "It grows late. And you will need an uninterrupted sleep tonight. You will sleep in my room."

"Thank you." Poppy wondered again why, with all the space in this house, she wasn't given a room of her own; but perhaps that was considered rude here. The sincere hospitality practiced in this family must include taking a guest into your own sleeping quarters. Anyway, it would be nice to sleep away from the girls. It seemed they even giggled in their sleep, and she was now beyond tired. She hoped Kandra didn't snore.

CHAPTER 7

Kandra did not snore. But Poppy, even though snug in a narrow bed similar to those in Cherry's room, experienced a night of disturbed sleep. The strange stories she had heard wove themselves into dreams of wild, uncontrollable laughter punishable by being thrown into a dungeon full of mad clowns. Once she half-awoke to see Aunt Holly looking down on her from a slender beam of blue moonlight. Kandra must have been checking on her, she thought later. Perhaps she had been talking, or worse, laughing, in her sleep.

But it was a stunning memory of Aunt Holly; she had seen her so clearly, peering at her with a concerned expression. Toward morning she fell into a sounder sleep, and was surprised to find out how late it was when she finally got up and went to find Kandra and Cherry in the kitchen. "You should have woke me," she told them as they offered her coffee and pancakes (they called them flatloaves). "There's always so much to do and I want to do my share."

"Most of the preparations are complete," Kandra told her without much spirit; not like someone looking forward to a jubilee. "And several women will be over later to begin transporting the foodstuffs to the festival court."

"Where is that?" Poppy asked with her mouth full. "In the Wise House?"

"Some will go to the Wise House," was the reply. "The rest to the palace." Mention of the palace still made Poppy's stomach contract; she asked no further questions but Cherry piped in anyway, "The festival in the Wise House will be held tomorrow, after we get back."

Cherry's friends were no longer with her. The girl sat devouring her cuticles, and hadn't so much as smiled since Poppy had joined them. "All I have to do is get my outfit together and bathe early enough that my hair will dry," she said.

"Well, I do need some time to get my act, and my outfit, together for tonight," Poppy said, eagerly draining the last of her coffee. She reached for the pitcher to pour herself another cup. "You kids deserve the best show I can come up with and I'm really looking forward to adding to your festivities."

Cherry's face brightened almost to its former cheeriness. "Grandmother told me. And I am so glad you are to be our jester! Whenever we have anyone at all, they usually choose some old man who has not himself laughed in years and thinks we are all little children who will be amused by seeing someone making faces and falling down."

Poppy smiled. "Well, I do those things sometimes too, but I'm really going to try to give you ... *grown up* young people something better than those old standbys. You know, I could really use some help finding stuff to use for make-up."

"What is make-up, Poppy?" Cherry asked.

Poppy had thought nothing of the women going about their domestic chores plainly dressed and combed, or of the young girls tinted only with their natural glow; but come to think of it, she had seen no trace of anything like make-up on any of the women out walking last night either. "I need to paint my face," she explained. "To look funny."

Cherry's mouth formed a silent "O," and she went immediately to rummage among the cupboard shelves. After a few minutes, she returned to deposit several small pots of ground spices on the counter before Poppy, who checked each one with interest.

"These should do fine," she said with satisfaction, finding several that colored her fingers when she rubbed the powder between them. But I need something ..." She looked around, then went to the hearth where she picked up a cold piece of charcoal and traced a line across the back of her hand. "And I can draw with this."

Kandra, who was filling baskets with jars of jellies, turned abruptly with an expression of alarm. "*Draw?*"

"Just lines on my face," Poppy held up her hand to show the charcoal streak. "So I can look comical, that's all."

Kandra stood still, folding her arms almost as if to protect herself. "Only the face?"

"Yes, just eyebrows and things like that," Poppy explained. "Lines and circles. I wasn't thinking of drawing any pictures ... likenesses, Kandra." Poppy felt a sudden attack of downheartedness. These people were going to be no help at all in getting her into a goofy mood. All the make-up in the world would not a clown make if the mood were unattainable. No, it was not going to be the easiest thing to pull off, especially with Cherry suddenly taking on the demeanor of a forty-year-old, and Kandra reverting to paranoia after getting her into this.

"Of course." Kandra turned back to her work. "Excuse me, lady."

"No, Kandra. Excuse *me*," Poppy said, wondering if she had spoken sharply. "I didn't mean to alarm you. I'm sorry if I did."

"I will help you with these, grandmother." Cherry ran a reassuring hand along Poppy's arm as she moved toward Kandra with a new air of maturity. "I have my garments nearly all laid out anyway."

"Wear a sturdy cloak over your finery tonight," Kandra told her. "Here, you can mount the stool and get down the higher jars for me."

Then she looked at Poppy. "I try not to worry," she said in voice close to a whisper. "But I ... all the tales my grandmother told me have been coming back all night, ever since I recounted some of them to you. I ... I had some dreams ..."

"I understand," Poppy said in a sincerely conciliatory tone. "Are you *sure* it's all right for me to do this entertaining tonight?" Heck, last night Kandra had been all gung ho on this, assuring her that all was well. But Poppy understood what she meant about the effects of dreams.

"It is allowed," the older woman said. "And expected. Only the children will be with you. You ... we are all perfectly safe so long as you entertain only at the children's gathering." She deposited the two jars in her hands into a basket, then added. "You will find a cloak on your bed. Wear it over your jester garments tonight until you enter the room with the children, even though you will be inside the house."

Poppy started toward the stairway, then turned back. "Kandra, last night ... I had some strange dreams too. And I just want to know—did you lean over me during the night? I mean did you check on me or something—in the moonlight?"

Kandra stood still for a moment, as if trying to recall, then shook her head slowly. "I do not remember leaning over you, or getting out of bed. I slept through the night—except for the dreams."

"Okay, I guess I just dreamed it then," Poppy said with forced lightness and headed toward the stairs again. *But it was so real, Aunt Holly looking down on me.*

In Cherry's room, Poppy fairly sweated all afternoon, preparing her act. These poor kids hardly ever had any entertainment other than just being silly among themselves. She had to give them the best clown act she could possibly come up with. Her outfit was fine, but the slippers Kandra had given her weren't funny at all. And sandals, the only other footwear they seemed to have here, would need bright socks in them. A clown just had to have wacky shoes. She chuckled a little remembering Alister's foot-long brown and whites with the curled-up toes. Well, she could use strips of fabric to tie big bows on her sandals, but ... She stopped in the middle of walking the floor. Why, the jogging shoes she had come in, of course. She found them jammed into one of the closets. The jester suit could spare a couple of the large tassels; added to the toes of the shoes, they would do the trick. The shoes themselves must look peculiar enough to these people, which was beyond a doubt why Cherry had diplomatically hidden them away and left her a pair of sandals.

She took her costume, completely assembled now, to Kandra's room where she was less likely to be interrupted by Cherry or her friends. Sitting cross-legged on the bed she had slept in, screwing her eyes up tightly, she mentally commanded all her knowledge of professional clowning to pass before them. But right now, even after being a clown for years, her knowledge seemed amateur and totally uninspiring.

The loud snort she heard was her own, exhaled at the realization of how much she was wishing she had Allister here to help her. Casting her eyes up to a sunbeam on the ceiling, she promised silently: *If I ever see that crazy-assed character again, I'll never get mad at anything he says or does.*

The clown school course covered a whole year and she had been a student there for just a few weeks; it had started in August, before the high school year. Well, she would just have to fall back on what she'd learned so far. And her prior years of winging it, making up her own persona and comedy routines. One way or another, she had to come up with a show in the next few hours.

To begin with, she mentally lectured herself, for this audience she would have to keep words to a minimum since many of her expressions would mean nothing to these children, and could bring unanswerable questions from them—or who knew, maybe even the danger of sounding offensive or politically incendiary. Many of these kids were twelve and thirteen and, if Cherry could be taken as standard issue, pretty savvy in spite of a propensity for silliness. And, though she knew it was absolutely necessary to her psychological stance to put Kandra's fearful attitude aside, this was without doubt the most challenging job she had ever landed.

So, even though verbal comedy had been her specialty, now she must forget about jokes or silly stories and songs, or interviewing a child from the audience. That had always been a great way to get laughs. Not only could you ply them with humorous questions designed to get giggles, but some of the answers kids came up with were pure gold—so offbeat you couldn't have made them up. But that wouldn't be a good idea here.

She was pretty good with magic, too, but she'd better not chance using her made-up magic words—they might mean something here. And what if—the thought occurred to her again—in this sort of medieval culture, they believed in witchcraft? So far, she had heard nothing about it one way or the other; but sooner or later they were bound to find out she wasn't Larian, and then who—or what—would they decide she was? So many questions to be considered, yet must be left undealt with for now in order to concentrate on what she *was* going to do. Anyway, since there could be no tricks or guessing things she shouldn't know, magic too was out.

What did that leave? The show would have to rely almost completely on physical action. Mime? She hated mime, probably because she stunk at it. Once she had ended up blushing right through her whiteface on realizing the laughter was because she'd been walking back and forth through a garage door she had already pulled back down. In mime, it took serious training to remember where and how you'd left all the invisible things. (Somehow the audience never had any trouble keeping the picture straight.) And mime didn't come until Allister's second semester; she hadn't even touched on it yet, and didn't care if she never did. Besides, would these kids comprehend the objects and symbolic actions she was expressing in body language? She couldn't pull out a wallet or a notebook or a pocket calculator or cell phone. Or fly a balloon or a kite, or run from a dog or slip on a banana peel. She had seen none of those things here. These kids might have no concept of the ordinary things that came to her mind. She sat on the bed squeezing her head between her hands.

Okay. There could be no audience participation, magic or mime. No songs or music. No help from other clowns, animals or puppets. No props like balloon art, explosions, squirting devices, unicycles (she could actually ride one), stilt walking (which she had never tried yet anyway), rubber chickens or invisible dog harnesses. No puns, verbal or visual (like a box labeled "baby rattler" that turned out to be a baby's rattle), trick cabinets or chairs designed to fall apart when sat on.

Poppy slumped back onto the bed and let out a groan. How had she gotten herself into this? She had wanted to contribute to this culture, these too-soon-grown-up children, to be useful. The way her costume had come together so well had encouraged her, made her temporarily unmindful of all the other elements that had to be faced. So what in heaven's name was left? Juggling and balancing. And she was still pretty lousy at both.

She lay there, thinking. A clown after all, wasn't *supposed* to be good at things, unless she was a whiteface paired with an auguste. Then the whiteface played the 'straight man,' and the auguste the bumbler. Poppy's usual makeup and costume had evolved from a childish, pieced-together affair through the classic 'neat whiteface' to the more personalized character who was no one but *Poppy*—until she had landed here. And who was Poppy, anyway? She asked herself ruefully. Who had Poppy ever been? *No one but a poor clown who can't even find her hat!*

She sat up and picked up the huge tricorn hat and held it at arm's length. How was this going to work? Juggling, she wasn't going to be able to see around the brim, and as far as balancing, tilting her head back to hold something on her forehead certainly didn't seem too promising. She'd have to take it off altogether to do that. Heck, maybe it wasn't even funny-looking here. She'd seen more ridiculous headgear on the road—but none on women. She was counting on that.

Props. Props, she needed first; then she'd work out a routine. By now she was pacing the room. What could she juggle? She hadn't seen a ball since she'd been here. She could probably make some out of dough or something, but what if balls didn't happen to be common either here or in Laria? Kandra's plates were earthenware and would probably break easily, and that might not be very funny from Kandra's point of view. She stopped in the middle of a stride. Beans! Yes, they had beans here and she had seen large jars of them in the kitchen.

By the time she got to the kitchen, her brain was buzzing with ideas. Soon she had lovely bean bags, four of them, made from scraps torn from a knitted towel. Kandra had also given her two small plates that she said could be broken if it came to it, and permission to appropriate a two-foot metal tube from a defunct telescope that Cherry had been using to roast nuts over the fire. Taking a last look around, she asked for and was given a small jug that could also be broken, the rest of the towel, and a broom handle.

By late afternoon, Poppy was ready. *As ready as I'll ever be.* Carrying one of the bathing sheets from the bedroom, and a cloak, since she wouldn't be dressing until she got back upstairs, she went downstairs to the bath. The girls had already bathed and dressed for the evening; she had heard their shrill voices in the hallway an hour and a half ago as they returned to Cherry's room to dress.

Having the pool all to herself, once in the nearly warm water, Poppy felt the tension seeping out of her body. She would get through the clown show; she'd even get through the evening at court, she reassured herself. Anyway, that was later. Maybe it was a good thing she had to concentrate so hard on the kids' entertainment—it didn't leave much brain-space to worry about the adult party. One thing at a time. Right now, just relax and feel ready for the evening and whatever it might bring. She was among friends who had promised to guide her. That was all that mattered.

Today's soap was exquisite, smelling of some heavily perfumed flower like gardenia, and slightly oily, like cocoa butter. Maybe it was some special blend made for the festival. She lathered herself, rinsed, then did it again—it felt so lavish. Her hair had to be washed, but she had drifted into near suspended animation, half-floating in the warm water, when someone entered the bathing room. Poppy's eyes opened and her nerves lurched, losing all relaxation, when her eyes lifted to see Lorimar, wrapped in a bathing sheet, approaching the pool.

Bending her knees to keep only her head above water, she waited for him to discover her, apologize, and leave. No, she should be the one to speak first. Even though no schedules had been mentioned, she obviously shouldn't be here at this time. He must have assumed she had already bathed with the girls, and he would now have the pool to himself. Before he reached the edge of the pool, she called out, "Sorry about my timing. I'll be out in a few minutes."

He simply nodded cordially, but rather than withdrawing from the room to give her a chance to get out of the water as she expected, he showed no sign of turning away. "There is no reason for haste, lady," he replied casually, coming up to the side of the pool.

"No, really. There's no problem," she said, getting nervous, grabbing the floating cake of soap and beginning to swipe at the wet ends of her hair "I just need to wash my hair—I'll make it quick, then I'll be out ..."

But she stopped soaping, and breathing, when he suddenly dropped the bathing sheet and lowered himself into a sitting position on the edge of the pool. It was only after he slid into the water, and not in any particular hurry, that she realized she had been staring right at him all the time.

Poppy quickly turned her back on her companion, and not knowing what to do next, she began soaping and digging furiously at her scalp with her fingernails. Then, to her further astonishment, his voice, close behind her, said, "You are being too rough, lady. Let me." And he actually took the soap from her hand and began washing her hair.

There was absolutely nothing to do but let him. Not seeming to even notice that she couldn't manage a response, he lathered her hair, gave her back the soap, then rinsed her hair, picking water up several times in his cupped hands and letting it run down over her head. Then he combed it all back with his fingers so that it hung into the water behind her. She was still half-squatting with her back to him.

"There. It is done," he said, as if he expected her to turn around, which she did, slowly, not knowing what else to do. Did he expect her to wash *his* hair? No, he was now busy on his own shoulder-length locks. Should she offer? She couldn't. And she still couldn't believe he had so casually appeared naked in front of her and joined her in her bath.

Poppy wanted desperately to get out of the pool, but didn't know how. She certainly wasn't going to just climb up those steps before his very eyes. She hunkered down in the water, waiting, beginning to feel shriveled. Holding up her fingers, she saw they were becoming as wrinkled as dried apricots. What would he do after he had finished bathing? Would he stay, expecting her to chat, or would he just leave? Would he … her brain hurt. The tension she had hoped would dissolve in the water was nothing compared to this dilemma. How much better off she would have been going without bathing altogether.

But she didn't have to wait long. As soon as his hair was washed and rinsed, Lorimar flung it back with a couple of swipes, quickly soaped his face and body, ducked underwater to rinse, then turned and mounted the steps. As nonchalantly as if no young woman from another world watched, as astonished by the movements of the firm muscles of his buttocks as she was at her own inability to shift her eyes away from the youthful body that so belied his mature and serious face. Again wrapped in the bathing sheet, he was gone without a backward glance.

And Poppy was able to let her breath out. After climbing out of the water, she sat on the stone bench, her bathing towel wrapped tightly around her. It must be just the custom here; something like the whole family bathing together in Japan—but after being told not to wear *sleeveless gowns!* What kind of an upside-down, cockamamie world was this? The people she had met all seemed sensible and demure to the extreme, until this.

She sat longer than she had time for, wishing she could straighten out the tangled ideas rampaging through her head as easily as she could comb the tangles from her hair. Finally she shrugged and reminded herself that, after all, she was living in a dream, so anything could happen. Only … if only it all didn't seem so darned *real.*

Just as she was gathering her things, Cherry arrived, dressed in a gorgeous red satin dress that came just below her knees. Underneath it were leggings of the same material that almost covered her sandal straps. Her hair was plaited back off her face. "Your garments for tonight are in grandmother's room," she told Poppy as she draped the cloak around her, over the bathing sheet she was already wearing. "And you are invited to eat supper with us—the *passers*, and the younger children, before your jesting."

"I'd love to," Poppy said. *Great! I won't have to face him at the supper table!* "Will all the children be allowed to come to my show?" She felt a twinge of worry that some of the children might not be able to handle a heavy dose of humor. She'd had kids get hysterical on her before, and that was in the world of daily television cartoons.

"None younger than six," Cherry answered. "They are allowed to join us for supper and the jesting, so they will not be afraid when their turn comes for passage. They must go home when we passers leave."

"Leave?" Poppy asked as she followed the younger girl up the stairs, pulling her cloak tighter around her.

Of course. We must leave the city tonight," Cherry explained. "So we can come back for the *passing through* in the morning."

"What will you actually be passing through?" Poppy was beginning to hate asking questions—afraid of the answers. Cherry was obviously under stress, but Poppy was beginning to worry that the young people were about to be away from the city for a while, and she still shrank from the thought of living here even a day without Cherry as a companion. Kandra was kind, but she wasn't the least bit young-at-heart like Aunt Holly.

She tried not to think what living in the same house with Lorimar would be like after his little performance in the bathing pool. Would he next show up unannounced in the bedroom? (She wouldn't sleep in his ante-room again, that was for sure). If he did, would she get herself expelled from the house if she were to throw him out?

"In the morning," Cherry was telling her. "We will come from the forest between here and the mountains and pass through the city to the Wise House for the afternoon festivities, then the evening celebration."

"And where will you spend tonight?" Poppy wanted to know. "Surely not out in the woods?"

Cherry nodded. "Indeed. It will be the first time I have ever been in the forest, but we will all be together and our keepers will make a fire and carry torches."

Poppy gasped. "Is it safe? Are there any wild animals? What about those … flatlanders from the swamp? Do they ever come around here?"

Cherry's usually dancing brown eyes underwent a somber darkening. "We are no longer children; and so far as we know, no one lives in the swamp. We must pass through the dark night and the festive day before we sleep."

"You're not even going to *sleep* tonight—at *all?*" Poppy was getting mad, but she knew she might as well get over it. No one here was going to change their traditions because of her opinions. She remembered the tizzy her all-night high school graduation party had thrown her mother into. But she had been *eighteen.* "Why on earth don't they wait until you kids are at least sixteen before they put you through all this?" she sputtered.

"What *is* that *earth* you speak of, lady?" was all Cherry said, not looking too interested in receiving an answer.

"It's just an … old-fashioned expression," Poppy said. "We talked about it before, remember? Out in the field. It means the planet we're standing on."

"Oh, yes. Lara," Cherry said absently.

"Yes, Lara."

Cherry drew in a quick breath, as if she suddenly remembered the practical things that must be done. "May I help you dress, lady? We need to get to the storm room soon."

"The storm room?" Poppy stopped in their progression up the second staircase. "There's a storm coming? With you kids going out into no-man's-land for the night?"

"There is no storm." Cherry took her friend's arm in her new, motherly way. "The storm room is a room without windows in the center of the house. It is where we go when the storms do come." Her voice fell an octave even though there was no one else on the stairway. "It is also the *'laughing'* room. That is what children call it. Many adults do also, when they are with the children. It is the room for private family life." With a sly smile and a squeeze to Poppy's arm, she added, "Tonight it is the other but we must call it the *storm room* in case we should be overheard by the *wrong ears.*"

Poppy said no more until they reached Kandra's room, lest she should be overheard by the *wrong ears* even though she had seen no other person on the last two floors.

The two beautiful gowns were carefully spread out on one of the beds and the jewelry she and Kandra had picked out to go with them placed on one of the dressers. The snood was there too, the silver net, softly shining in the lamplight. But it was the clown outfit that had to be dealt with right now.

Cherry forgot her new maturity and chuckled with delight as she arranged the items of clothing for Poppy, who was looking into the shiny bottom of a metal box from the top of one of Kandra's chests of drawers to apply her clown makeup.

Helping her into the costume, the girl was completely losing her self-control by the time they got to the tasseled jogging shoes. "I had forgotten all about those *boats* you were wearing on your feet when you came here."

Funny thing, Poppy thought, that she hadn't worn socks to the gym that day. She'd needed the traction of bare feet on the mat to practice her moves, and didn't want to bother with pulling them off and on. She wondered what Cherry would have said about them.

Cherry pulled herself together enough to help her friend braid and fasten her damp hair and put on the yarn wig Poppy had hastily created, but it was the final addition—the hat, that destroyed the girl. "Why are you wearing a tricorn hat?" she fairly shrieked.

"Just to look silly," Poppy told her, trying to cock it at a rakish angle without shutting out her view, but the hat was so large, even over the wig it fell forward and hid her face, so she pushed it back onto the top of her head.

"Do you know the meaning of it?" Cherry asked.

"The meaning?" Poppy said. "The hat has a meaning? What does it mean?"

"It means you are a happily married man!" Holding her stomach, Cherry fell helpless across Kandra's bed.

"Well, good then," Poppy replied, throwing on the cape. "It'll be funny. I'm all ready. Let's go." She pulled her friend up by the wrists, and felt much better, seeing her giggling uncontrollably again.

Poppy was eager to see the storm room. After several days in this house, this was the first she had even heard of it. It was below ground level, down the three stairways again. As Cherry led the way, Poppy figured it was in the middle of the house, between the large kitchen, which was in the back of the house by the river, and the lavatory.

CHAPTER 8

The room turned out to be a mini home with everything a family could possibly need to survive for several days. On one side was a fireplace, warmly glowing with a large screen in front. The walls around the room were covered with shelves stacked with provisions. Jars and pots and packages of all sizes. Why, it was a regular bomb shelter! Almost like those magazine pictures from the fifties.

At the center of the room stood a large table covered with what Poppy considered a "buffet dinner" obviously for children, heavy on sweets and finger foods, like a birthday party without the cake. And the children were digging in, enjoying it to the full. The remaining walls were taken up by built-in beds with shelves and cupboards above and underneath, like on a boat. Even without any windows, the room glowed with many wall-mounted lamps. It was cozy. Poppy was glad to be having supper with the kids.

Only she couldn't even think of eating. Her quick perusal of the room was snatched to a chorus of giggles from the moment she entered. The children—there had to be a couple of hundred—who weren't circling the table, were parked on benches and the floor in random order, their hands full of food that seemed to be forgotten. All the faces that lifted toward her shone with an eager excitement she rarely saw in her usual humor-inured audiences. Suddenly, she felt confident. These kids would laugh—no doubt about it. She would do okay.

Thanks to Cherry's mood upstairs, and her reception by these children, she was well into her clown personality now, and really looking forward to entertaining these humor-starved children. She would do better than okay; she would do her very best. They deserved no less.

Standing as near the center of the room as possible, sharing her space with the large table, Poppy began a soft shoe step dance with hands on hips, dipping her head in the huge hat and humming along with a goofy rhythm in her mind. Just that got them going. She turned and pushed some plates out of the way. She placed her bag of props, made of a towel tied at the corners, on the table so they could all see it.

With no music or jokes to start with, she reached into the bag immediately, took out her beanbags and began to juggle them low, keeping them within her view below the hat brim. She began with two, then added another. Three was the most she could handle. A complete hush filled the room as inhaled breaths were held and all eyes followed the beanbags. She tossed them higher until they started landing on her hat. When all three were balanced on her hat, she pretended to be peeking up into the air, waiting for them to come down.

One large exhale became laughter that rose from every side as she finally doffed her hat, allowing all the beanbags to tumble off the back of it, and scanned the upper air for a better view. She pretended to have no idea that the bags had fallen on the floor in spite of the children's calls to look behind her, and continued looking up in the air, bending her knees and taking comic postures, for a couple of minutes. Then she turned to her bag of props and, poking around inside it, came out with the fourth beanbag. She juggled that alone, then yawned hugely to show boredom (a yawn had to be universal, or multi-universal, whatever). Then looked in her bag again.

She brought out the jug which she tossed into the air with the beanbag, then she pulled out one of the plates and juggled the three objects, to sounds of heavy appreciation from the audience. Then the plate fell and broke. The crash and her exaggerated gestures of distress brought the house down. Even a few older boys standing in the back, who had begun with arms folded in unflappable maturity, burst out laughing. This was good. She was doing all right.

After a few turnabouts, and pulling out a few strands of the yarn wig in exaggerated distress, she reached into the bag for the other plate. As she went through all the motions of vacillating between fear of juggling this one lest it should also get broken and the urge to juggle regardless of the consequences, Poppy suddenly realized she was doing mime, and pretty good mime if she did think so herself.

Well, best to continue with what was working, particularly since mime was unlikely to bring forth any lingual misunderstandings. Poppy pretended to discover the beanbags again and picked them up, secretly ripping one so the beans came pouring out onto the floor. She acted befuddled over the mishap, pressing her hands to the sides of her face as she circled the mess. Then she reached into her bag of tricks for the telescope tube and began to gather up beans, dropping them into one end of the tube only to have them fall out the other end, which she pretended not to notice. Peeping several times into the tube, then looking back at the beans on the floor, she repeated the pickup a couple of times with different postures and facial expressions each time, slipping on the beans and falling down once. Several of the smaller children were by now squirming on the floor in uncontrollable laughter.

Finally, she placed the tube over the mouth of the jug and proceeded to put beans down it, but many of them spilled out the other end because the tube was larger than the mouth of the jug. The clown sat down to think, scratching her head, causing a serious loss of yarn hair which she then held up in front of her horrified face. That brought on much twisting around, feeling her hair to see if there was some still there.

She got up and found the towel remnant and made several clumsy attempts at tying it around her head, usually getting it over her eyes or down around her neck, where she made the mistake of pulling it too tight and wandered around with bulging eyes and tongue hanging out before collapsing on a large floor pillow.

Even the older kids were in stitches now, and two or three of the younger ones had already been rushed, retching, by the older girls to the relief site in an anteroom.

Finally, several women entered the room to bundle the sixty twelve and thirteen-year-olds in capes and caps to go off to the forest for the night. From her position on the big floor pillow, Poppy watched their sandaled feet pass her and wondered again why, with their knitting machines and all, these people hadn't come up with socks. The dewy grass got chilly at night, she remembered from her excursion with Lorimar, but the only thing between their bare feet and the dew was the leggings that came down loosely over their feet, not sealing the space between the legging foot and the sandal sole.

The departure of the older children, the passers, seemed to produce a second wind in the younger ones. They swarmed around Poppy as she lay exhausted on her pillow. "Do more funny things!" they begged. "Be a confounded one!" "Be a horse!"

"Go eat some more of those delicious pastries," Poppy moaned. "I need a rest."

But that was part of their hysteria, she realized. Besides the infrequent excitement of being entertained, the children had stuffed themselves with sweets. Now they were no longer interested in the delicacies. They pulled and tugged on her until she capitulated and got to her feet to give a feeble version of break dancing. Soon the exhausted children were rolling on the floor in mirthful weakness.

Poppy was relieved when more women came and began lifting the younger ones, none too gently, to their feet. Some shook their charges a little, and a few cuffs resounded here and there on those who resisted or let themselves go completely limp in passive resistance.

"It is over, Corve!" a mother scolded her son, practically dragging him away by a firm hand hooked under his arm. "It is all over. Now come along politely."

Poppy stretched out on the pillow again, thinking she'd stay there until she really felt like getting up. But her rest last only a few seconds. Kandra was soon leaning over her, looking surprisingly stunning in a green silky gown with emeralds sparkling in the thick plaits arranged around her head. Poppy sat up involuntarily in spite of her fatigue. "Kandra! You look *fabulous!*"

Kandra smiled. "That is something good, I hope."

"It means lovely. Better than lovely."

"Now that must be an overstatement," the older woman replied modestly. "But thank you, Lady Poppy. Now come."

Poppy obeyed, following her hostess out of the storm room she had already learned to love—it had such a feeling of coziness and safety. Soon they were in Kandra's room with all the things selected for Poppy's festival attire. Poppy was hurried out of her clown costume and directed to a basin of water on a table in the corner to scrub her face clean.

Two other women, whom she recognized from the kitchen detail, had come to help. The younger one, whose name was Sherat, examined her face and dabbed again with a wet cloth at several spots before declaring her a lady again; while the other, Cleod, stood ready with a soft, knitted shift which she pulled down over Poppy's head and tugged into place around her hips.

Directed to a stool where they could arrange her hair, their fatigued object of attention was thankful for the rest. Deftly and speedily, they took out her braids and gave her a front pompadour rippling with her own natural waves and a few escaped tiny curls ringing her forehead, and gathered the long, unruly back tresses into the delicate, web-like silver snood, which they called a 'catcher.'

While Poppy's hair was being arranged, Kandra handed her a cup saying, "You need to recover from your efforts with the children."

Poppy's first sip of the liquid brought a smile to her face. It was vigorwort. She sipped it slowly and happily, feeling it's brightening power before she finished the scant half a cup she had been given. "I haven't forgotten how good this is, Kandra," she said, hoping for as refill as she held up the cup. "You gave it to me the first night I came here. Remember?"

"And much did you need it, child," Kandra replied. "But it is given only in extreme need. Then she added in a tone that revealed her comprehension of Poppy's hint, "Not an entertainment drink." There would be no more.

Just as I thought. A pickup for hopeless cases. Poppy sat quietly after the empty cup had been taken from her, eyes closed to enjoy its effects to the fullest.

Her hair finished, a blend of rippling flame and flickering silver which she glimpsed by snatching a metal box from the table and stealing a look in it's smooth bottom before it was firmly taken from her hand and placed on a high chest, they dressed her in the silver-trimmed blue satin gown and fastened all the peculiar little hooks that seemed to Poppy to be found in the most unlikely places, like under the arms. After they were hooked, she realized how well the dress fit, unlike the knitted toga-type gowns she had been given to wear on ordinary days. If you could call any day here ordinary. They fastened the blue diamond necklace around her neck and put blue satin sandals on her feet.

"How *lovely!* How *Larian!*" the women exclaimed, until Poppy realized these words were synonyms here. Something like *"Parisian"* in her world.

Again she felt the unfairness of all this honor heaped on her for being Larian when she was no such thing, but since she had no other feasible explanation to give them, she decided once more to try and enjoy the undeserved celebrity while it lasted. Sooner or later, they'd have to find out she knew nothing about Laria and then ... Well, no time to think about it now.

"Do I look all right?" she asked brightly, burying her dark thoughts.

"Fabulous." Kandra stroked her cheek while the other women looked on, smiling with pride in their handiwork.

"Thanks, Kandra," Poppy said. "Thanks, all of you. But my face feels a little stiff after scouring off my jester makeup. Could I have something to rub on it to soften it up a little?"

Cleod was already on her way to Kandra's washing table to bring a jar containing a pink substance which she began to rub gently into Poppy's face and neck. "That feels nice, and smells great," Poppy told her.

"Cameria cream," Kandra said. "With pringo essence. That is enough, ladies. We must go."

"Where are we going right now, exactly?" Poppy was afraid to ask. She would gladly have sat there being pampered for another hour. She was both dreading and thrilling at the answer she knew was coming.

"To the court, of course." Kandra was already moving toward the door. "The cart is waiting."

The four women rode closely packed into two seats in the carriage, up the hill past the Wise House and on through a section of the city that Poppy had not seen. Finally she realized they were actually out of town, riding briskly up a gradual hill along a smooth road lined with gigantic trees hung with enormous leaves interspersed with pods nearly a foot long.

"The small lumps you used for your kookies," Kandra told her, pointing upward, "were made from the beans that grow inside those pods."

"No kidding," Poppy said, glad of anything to take her mind off where she and the others were heading, and how many breaches of courtly manners she might be capable of committing in one evening. "Cocoa beans."

Sherat and Cleod began to gulp back snickers. "They are kester beans," Kandra said.

"Kester chip kookies. Quite a tongue-twister," Poppy babbled.

The other women were now covering their mouths with the ends of material dripping from their long sleeves.

Breach number one: making grown women giggle. Poppy sighed, but her sigh became a gasp as the cart emerged from the tree-lined road into the sunset flushed meadows surrounding the palace, which, unlike the medieval castle she was expecting, was a spreading palatial structure with many rounded domes. The whole complex glittered in the light of a sunset on one side (much the same as she had enjoyed high in the wise house with Lorimer) and the stupendously large blue moon on the other. Fuller now than it had been the other night, and just rising, a ring of purple around its edges, spreading its sheen far out over the slopes and inclines of the vast grassy carpet of the palace lawns.

The women all sat silent, though Poppy imagined the others had beheld this scene many times. Still, hadn't she often marveled at moonlit scenes at home regardless of how many times she'd enjoyed them before?

Poppy's discomfort in approaching the palace became an almost unbearable combination of anxiety and awe. By the time the two drawing horses had trotted around a long circular boulevard to be halted before a huge pair of dark wooden doors, a side entrance it seemed, in spite of their size, the moon was higher and bluer, and the sun had sunk below the glowing pink-gold horizon.

The women were helped by no less than four doormen in brown livery, one for each, who appeared suddenly beside them and wordlessly handed them down the two slender steps onto the ground. Following the silent example of the other women, Poppy stifled a 'thank you' as each man offered an arm to one of the ladies and proceeded toward the large doors, which now stood open as a result of the efforts of two doormen.

Once inside, there was nothing but halls for some time, long and cool, and lined with plain or simple geometric patterned wall tiles, interrupted occasionally by colorful but plain or simply edged hangings—the first tapestries she had seen. It was all terribly elegant, perhaps even more elegant because of the vastness and simplicity. Of course what else but elegance had she expected of the king's residence?

Voices began to be heard only steps before they reached another pair of oversized, heavy doors which were swung open by the doormen's practiced manipulation of complicated cross-beams. Instantly the voices blared, joined by music pealing from at least twenty musicians on a platform in a far corner of the hall, which was larger than a high-school auditorium. Poppy's was the only audible intake of breath as the ladies entered the hall on the arms of their tight-lipped escorts.

Many lamps mounted on the dark walls shed nearly as much luminosity as electric lighting, and there was much to see. Feeling as if she had arrived at a grand costume ball, Poppy's eyes could hardly begin to take in the elan of the dresses worn by even the oldest and plainest of the women. The men were certainly splendid too, in their long toga-like outfits and cloaks of bright hues. Many of them wore gleaming, even bejeweled, clasps and broaches that held the gracefully tossed-back cloaks from sliding off.

The resplendence of the ladies, of course, immediately abolished her initial self-consciousness at the finery in which she had been decked out. Nearly everyone was chatting animatedly, circulating or standing in small clusters. Even the very old people sitting on richly upholstered benches that circled the walls were nodding and talking. The music was strange but spirited and beautiful, and elaborately arranged tables of food formed rings within the rings of the old peoples' benches. But two things were missing. In all the great crowd of people, no laughter was heard. And where was Lorimar?

No sooner had she begun looking around for him, than he appeared at her side, nodding to the doorman who immediately relinquished Poppy's arm and silently disappeared.

Lorimar greeted her with a rather formal smile, just pleasant enough to take away his usual slightly worried expression, and gallantly offered his arm. "There are many here who wait to meet you, lady," he said. Then, in reply to her tense hand on his arm and quick, anxious glance at him, he added, "All who will find you as dazzling as I do, I am sure."

Still stinging with embarrassment from their bathing pool encounter, Poppy managed a tight smile, looking around for Kandra, who had somehow disappeared. She had to depend completely on Lorimar—good thing she didn't have time right now to dwell on his earlier behavior. "The … *king?*" she whispered, then, realizing he couldn't hear her, she repeated it in a louder voice.

Leaning toward her, Lorimar nodded. "He will be among them … and the queen as well."

"What do I call them?" Poppy grasped his arm tightly, close to panic. "Your Majesty? Your Highness?"

Raising his eyebrows as if slightly confounded, he spoke into her ear, covering her trembling hand with his. "They are Vran and Avive."

"Just … their *names?*" Poppy's question was lost in the commotion of being led through the crowd to a dais near the orchestra, where several people sat on elaborate chairs, chatting much the same as the rest of those filling the hall. Lorimar stopped at the bottom of the steps leading up to the dias and bowed. "I bring Lady Poppy," he announced proudly. "The Larian."

Smiles broke out among the dozen or so notables on the dais. One youngish man rose immediately and came down the steps. "Welcome, Lady Poppy," he said, offering his arm. "May I ask you to sit with us?"

Realizing that he intended to lead her up onto the dais where two of those people must be the king and queen, Poppy said stupidly, "I … sure." Then added, "I'm Pai … Poppy." *Well, of course she had already been introduced.*

The same cordial smile all the constituents of the dais were exhibiting did no favor to the young man's plain features, which crinkled almost comically around his slightly bulbous nose. But he was cute in a way (*he'd make a wonderful comic*), and his large, brown eyes sparkled with good humor. Poppy nearly tripped over the first step when he said, "I am Vran."

And she had not even taken the arm Vran offered. But Lorimar quickly picked her hand from his own arm and placed it casually and unceremoniously on the king's. Somehow her feet managed the few steps. A young woman with dark hair and clear grey eyes—almost blue—rose and looked at her closely but not unkindly. "I am Avive."

Poppy nodded and smiled, not thinking it proper to introduce herself again, and no one ever shook hands here (at least now she remembered not to extend hers). She murmured, "I'm really honored to meet you … both of you." She glanced at the king who smiled this time obviously from candid amusement, probably at being himself an afterthought. Poppy nodded at the rest of the people and managed, "I'm happy to meet … all of you."

They all nodded and flashed wide smiles. Names were given, none of which Poppy remembered. She felt so dizzy she stepped away from the edge of the dais, wavering a little as she did, then felt Lorimar's hand around her back.

Vran's arm had fallen away as his attention turned to a man in a deep blue garment who had approached the dais and stood at the bottom of the steps, looking up at them. Lorimar moved away from Poppy abruptly and hurried down to speak to him; then he returned, nearly running up the steps, his face somber. "A storm," was all he said, looking at the king.

"The *children!*" Poppy gasped. "Will they be safe in the woods?"

"They are with adults," was Lorimar's hasty reply, but his voice lacked conviction. He was plainly alarmed, and Poppy was scared.

"Is it rain?" she asked, realizing she hadn't even been told what kind of storms they had here, her mind had been so occupied with the clown show when the storm room had been introduced.

"Probably, but that is not dangerous," Lorimar told her. "It is the wind that wracks destruction."

"Des … *destruction?*" Poppy repeated. "But don't you have these storms often?"

Lorimar gave her a quick look she did not relish. "Our houses are stone for good reason," he replied with more than a tinge of impatience. "For the same reason the windows are high and without lenses."

Obviously, he was referring to window glass. "The storm rooms," she said. "Are they the *only* safe places?"

He nodded. "In most homes. But you will be perfectly safe here. Come." He grasped her hand and nearly dragged her down the steps. Glancing back, she realized the others on the dais had already fled.

"Me?" She resisted his tug. "Don't you mean *us*?"

"I must go!" he said, letting go of her hand and trying to pull free of the hold she had taken on his sleeve with the other.

"But it's too *dangerous*," Poppy began to wail, partly from concern for his safety, and partly from fear of being left alone among all these bustling strangers. "Where are you going?" she cried. "The children are with adults already.

You can blow away like anyone else, you know! You're not *Mary Poppins!* And I'm certainly not staying here alone!"

A quizzical expression flashed in his eyes for one second—probably because of her reference to Mary Poppins, but his attention immediately riveted on the present dilemma. "You will not be alone. Now *come!*"

He removed her hand forcefully from his sleeve and took it firmly in his. Before she knew it, they were out of the large room, hurrying down a corridor so fast she had to take skipping steps, holding up her skirt with her free hand. Down a long, winding stone stairway, and another two or three corridors they fled, their way dimly lit by an occasional wall lamp—just torches really, flickering in the breeze they created as they passed. Then another set of stairs even more winding than the last.

Poppy was so confused she knew she would never be able to find her way out of here by herself. They must be dozens of yards below ground level by now. If Lorimar thought he was going to dump her in this place and leave her, he was wasting his energy. With panicky strength, she dragged him to a halt. "Are you weary?" he asked. "I will support you. We must continue."

She wiggled away from the arm he attempted to slide around her back, and, drawing in a deep breath, turned to face him. "I just want to you know that I am *not*—repeat *not*—going to stay down here without you!" Her voice echoed off the stone walls. "This place is a *freaking dungeon* and we are going to turn around right now and go back the way we came, wind or no wind. Maybe the storm has passed by now anyway. How would we know, stuck down here a mile underground?"

His face took on an almost stony expression and she felt her arm gripped so tightly she nearly cried out. Noticing her wince, he lessened his hold and, in an obviously controlled voice, said, "This storm will last the night, if not longer, and I will not take you back up into it. You are my guest and you *must* allow me to take you to safety!"

Poppy yanked her arm out of his grasp and raised her fists in the air between them. Bringing them down on his chest, she cried, "I don't have to … don't *must* do *anything!* You are my protector. You've said so yourself. I'm part of your family. You can't just leave me down here in this horrible place! I'll follow you right back up as soon as you turn around!" Her hands went to her mouth as she burst into tears.

Lorimar spoke more gently, but still rapidly. "Come just a short distance further," he urged. "And you may decide for yourself where you will spend the night."

That sounded more reasonable. Controlling her desperation, she gulped back a sob and took his hand, allowing him to lead her down several more corridors and two more stairways, picking up speed again until they stopped before a huge wooden door, the kind that, in a movie, she thought, would have a heavy metal knocker. But there was nothing on the door at all. Not even a latch. Lorimar knocked and, after a few seconds the door opened inward.

They were greeted by the pleasant face of an old man in a simple robe, perhaps a monk's habit. "Please come in, Wise Lorimar," the man said affably, then added, "Lady," as he opened door wide, then offered the hand greeting before moving aside.

The two stepped into a surprisingly cheerful room lined with polished wood of a light hue that shone in the soft glow from the fireplace and wall lamp, plus a lamp on the table which shed its glow on an open book. The monk, or whatever he was, bowed slightly to them both. "Lorimar, a pleasure," he said. "And ..."

"This is Lady Poppy," Lorimar introduced her.

"From Laria, of course," the other man finished for him. "I am Hesh," he said, directing his words to Poppy. "The watcher."

What in the world does he watch down here? She was so stunned by the coziness of the room after their trip through the dank corridors and ghastly stairways, she could hardly find her voice to greet him. "So nice to meet you, Mr. Hesh," she managed in a croaky voice, then sniffed loudly from her recent tantrum.

"There is a storm," Lorimar told the old man, who nodded, as if no further explanation were required.

"You will be perfectly safe here for the night," Lorimar was telling Poppy. "I will come back for you tomorrow, as soon as it is possible."

He was so eager to be off, she tried to let him go without further comment, but her consternation forced her to look around the medium-sized room that was obviously occupied by this elderly man and ask, "For the night? Where ..."

"Oh, there is room." Hesh spoke up reassuringly, and moved to open an inner door that revealed another comfortably appointed room as far as she could discern by the light entering from the one they were in. "Come and see," he offered with a gesture of his hand.

"Hesh is a man known to me from my childhood," Lorimar said with what sounded like forced patience. "A man who holds a highly trusted office. But, as I promised, you may stay here or come back with me, as you choose."

Poppy went to peer beyond the door the brown-robed man had opened for her and now stood holding the lamp fetched from the table. He followed her into the other room, where a bed, made up plump and inviting sat in the middle of the room, beside a table and a fireplace in which the makings of a fire were already laid.

"I will light the fire in your room immediately," he told her, setting the lamp down on the table.

"Oh, but I couldn't take your room," Poppy began, but stopped when Hesh shook his head and turned to leave the room, motioning her to follow. He crossed the main room and opened a door on the opposite side. "This is my room."

Poppy caught a glimpse of a glow on the far side of that room that had to be a fire. "You will not disturb me in the least," the kindly old man continued. "Indeed, I shall be very glad of your company, even if only for a few hours. Not every day does one in my position have the honor of a visit from a Larian Lady."

Poppy stepped back into the main room and shot a quick, anxious glance at Lorimar, now standing by the door as if ready to bound through it, and appearing to have more serious matters on his mind than possible slip-ups of her Larian masquerade. Still, he seemed to understand her worry. "I have every confidence in Hesh as a suitable companion for you, lady," he said, shifting his feet to show that he could not afford to wait longer.

Poppy took a deep breath. "I'll stay here," she said. "But don't forget to come back for me tomorrow."

"Tomorrow," he said and, with a quick nod to Hesh, was gone.

CHAPTER 9

Seeing the heavy door close, Poppy experienced a moment when she had to restrain herself from running after him, to face the storm with him; but she knew she would be—had already been—more burden than help. It was just so scary to let him out of her sight. Ever since landing in this alien place, she had never been apart from all the members of her adopted family at the same time. She trusted Lorimar's judgment of her new host and felt okay with him personally, but thinking how far underground they must be … well, as usual, she would have to force herself to concentrate on the cheerful components of the situation. Count her blessings one more time. At least, she hadn't been caught out there alone in the storm. Obediently, she sunk into the chair offered to her.

The effects of the underground dank and chill soon became a memory as she felt the warmth of the fire on her skin. Then her host selected a brand from the fire and carried it into the cool bedroom. "Your room will soon be as warm as this one," he told her when he returned.

The cup of tea he gave her was warm in her hand, the old man's calm and kindly presence reassuring as he took the chair opposite her. "How long have you been here, lady?" he asked.

"Never at the palace before tonight. We came to the passage festivities."

He nodded thoughtfully, as if he had almost forgotten the yearly celebration, even though he lived, for all the vertical distance, practically in the palace itself.

"Don't you ever go up to ground level?" Too late, she hoped the question was not inappropriate. Maybe he wasn't allowed up there for some reason; maybe the poor old guy was under some kind of house arrest.

Hesh appeared to sense her insecurity, and responded with a kindly smile. "I have nearly lost the inclination to go above, living so comfortably. Never a storm to worry about, and I have excellent company down here."

He couldn't possibly mean her—she had just arrived. "Are you a member of an ... order?" she asked tentatively. "A meditative or ... religious group?"

At that the old man laughed heartily, his pale blue eyes sparkling. "I would certainly wish for time to meditate," he replied. "And serving the Unbounded One would probably suit my temperament. But as a watcher, I have little time to myself."

"May I ask what it is you watch down here?" Poppy asked, heartened by his friendliness.

But he only chuckled at her inquiry; then, assuming a serious bearing, he said, "Tomorrow you shall see for yourself. Surely your protector will not return to take you away from me before we can tour my dominion. Tonight, I see that you are in need of rest."

In fact, the vigorwort had long since worn off, and Hesh's friendly aura of safety and the comfort of her softly cushioned chair, along with the lavender tea or whatever it was, had brought a realization of deep fatigue, but also deep relaxation.

Poppy looked at her companion, slowly shaking her head. "I've had a day like no other. I was allowed to entertain the children before the older ones went to the forest. I was so nervous all day ... but it came off wonderfully. They're the greatest audience I've ever had. But it was exhausting. And then I had to get scrubbed down and change into these gorgeous clothes that Kandra lent me, and come here to meet the king and queen for the first time!" *To say nothing of the shock of the day—Lorimar in the bath!*

"And now this *storm*," she continued. "I'm so worried about the children—all of them, even though Cherry and a couple of her friends are the only ones I really got to know." She stopped to let out an audible breath, and glance at Hesh to check for any sign of disapproval or boredom.

"The people here are accustomed to the storms," he told her gently. "That makes them no less dangerous, of course, but of all the men in the Kingdom, Lorimar is beyond a doubt the most capable. You are fortunate to be his guest."

"You're telling *me*," she agreed. "That's why I was scared to death to let him go."

"But you will be perfectly secure here," he assured her.

"I believe that," she sighed. "You are very kind to take me in this way."

"It is an honor, as I have said, lady," he replied. "But tell me. Why were you selected to entertain the children? As my memory serves, one of the instructors from the school is generally chosen. And are you not but lately come to Halderwold?"

"How do you know that?" she asked.

He smiled. "I receive frequent tidings from above. I am not cut off from the populace; simply required to live here because of my office."

"So you've heard of me?" Poppy was intrigued. "What do they say? How do they speak of me?"

"Nothing ill, I assure you," he answered. "The wonderment of all is how you made the journey. Surely you know that it has been a generation since we have been graced with a visitor from Laria?"

Poppy took a thoughtful sip of her tea before she said, "Well, I can't enlighten you any better than what you've already heard. I woke up in the middle of a field and Cherry—Lorimar's daughter—found me and took me home with her. How I got here is as big a mystery to me as it is to everyone else."

His look gave the impression that he was too mystified to reply.

"For some reason, I can't remember how I came here," she continued. "Or very much else," she added as a precaution against further questions.

Her host nodded in polite silence.

"And as for my being chosen to entertain the children, my abilities, if not my memory, have remained with me. I am a clown. A ... jester?"

"Truly," he responded as if astonished. "A *lady*?"

"Yep. And Kandra asked me to do the entertaining. And of course I was honored to be chosen."

After a thoughtful moment, Hesh changed the subject. "I believe you will be most interested in meeting my charges. That is probably one reason Lorimar sought me out as your temporary caretaker, as well as his concern for you."

"Your charges?" Poppy yawned. "Who are they?"

"Tomorrow," her host said. "You are weary, lady. Allow me to say good-night."

A delicious aroma reached her senses before she opened her eyes to see a young woman tending an iron griddle on a rack over the fire. Her movements caught the girl's attention, and a lovely but thin face turned toward her with a shy smile. "Greetings, lady," the girl said. "I am Nona."

Poppy had a fleeting half-expectancy of the girl's greeting continuing with, 'and I'll be your waitress this morning.' But Nona just stood there, holding a long-handled implement, waiting for Poppy's acknowledgment.

"Good … greetings." Poppy sat up. "Whatever you're cooking sure smells good. And … I'm Poppy."

Nona put the spatula, or whatever it was, down on the large, flat stone in front of the fire and took a step toward the bed, holding her hands out in the customary greeting. Poppy did the same, realizing that she had become so comfortable with this gesture, it almost felt natural.

"This is a very pleasant surprise." she said. "Do you work for Hesh?"

The girl resumed tending the food. "I have been chosen to attend you." She flipped a couple of griddle cakes and turned back to Poppy with a little bow. "A very great honor, lady. Particularly for one such as myself."

"And who is one such as yourself?" Poppy asked. "What is it you normally do down here?"

The girl's face showed astonishment and confusion. "But surely you know why I am here!" Then, lowering her eyes, "I mean no disrespect, lady, but very few come here except to be detained. I would ask the question of you—how come you to be here?"

"I was brought here to take shelter from a storm," Poppy told her. "And I'll be leaving today." She was sitting on the edge of the bed, staring at the small face she now realized was incredibly pale within the lush, dark hair, in spite of the two pink spots on the cheeks brought on by leaning over the fire (or perhaps meeting a *Larian*). A face that appeared somehow familiar.

"What is this place?" she asked, recalling Hesh's reference to his *charges*. "A girl's school? A … detention center?"

"It is a prison." Nona replied. "You did not know?"

"No. I came late last night. I was at a passage celebration up in the palace when a storm came up, and Lorimar brought me down here. I was tired and Hesh told me to go right to bed."

Nona smiled wanly. "Hesh is a kind man. Without his kindness, I may not have remained in the privileged class these past four years." Remembering the food, she turned quickly back to the fireplace. She carefully lifted the cakes onto a plate which she then placed on the table beside Poppy's bed and poured coffee from a pitcher.

Poppy took her meal still sitting on the bed, trying mentally to arrange her many questions in the most delicate approach. She thanked the girl and invited her to share the 'breach of fast.' *Remember the proper terms.* Blushing even deeper, the girl accepted as if she were doing something daring, and seated herself on the fireplace stone with a cup of coffee, even though a chair had been placed near the table.

After making sure Nona had her share of griddle cakes and syrup (the first fork-full disappeared into her mouth with a movement of undisguised eagerness), Poppy asked gently, "Why, exactly, are you being detained here, Nona?"

The girl paused in her chewing to cast another look of incredulity at her temporary mistress. "Why, for undue jocularity, of course, lady."

"Undue … *jocularity?* And how old were you when you came here?"

"Thirteen. It was soon after my passage. "I failed to manage my adult status with sufficient grace." Her head bowed briefly, but came up again quickly. "Lady, may I … ask something of you before we continue? I mean no …"

"No disrespect, of course not," Poppy replied at once. "Don't worry about it. Ask me anything, but I'll have to warn you I haven't been in Halderwold long and I may not have many answers."

"My first concern is for my mother and my sisters," Nona said. "I simply wondered if you have seen them. You made mention of Lorimar and since Deema was his daughter's friend as a child, I thought perhaps …"

"Yes, I met Deema," Poppy interrupted in her eagerness to bring the poor girl some small comfort. "And Sil too. They spent a couple of nights with Cherry at Lormar's house, and they are both fine. I didn't meet your mother, but I heard of nothing wrong with her. Deema and Cherry are doing their passage now …" She stopped. Maybe that wasn't such welcome news considering why Nona was here.

But the girl's face was suddenly wreathed in smiles. "My sisters are both well? And happy? Sil was poorly as a small child." She paused for a moment, looking up at the ceiling. "And it is Deema's passage today. I thought it was time."

"They are well and happy," Poppy replied. "Too happy." Oh, m*aybe the wrong wording again.* "I mean … not dangerously happy or anything. They were all having a lot of fun inside the house, getting ready for the festival, you know."

The dark hair fell forward as she nodded. "I know. And I feel certain that my example has not been wasted upon my sisters. They will conduct themselves with propriety and enjoy a contented life until I am with them again."

"I'm absolutely sure they will," Poppy told her in the most reassuring tone she could muster, not being at all convinced herself. "Deema and Cherry are very well prepared for their passage. Completely ready for their new life."

The expression on Nona's face brought Poppy a sigh a relief. *I haven't said the wrong thing. Not yet, anyway.*

"Time to get into our day." The voice of Hesh came through the bedroom door, which stood open, though the speaker could not be seen.

"Be up and about right away," Poppy answered, turning around and stretching her neck . "Where is he?"

Nona's face broke into a slight grin. "He will not enter your sleeping room, lady!"

Poppy experienced a now familiar confusion with the rules in this place. Lorimar had chatted with her when she was in bed, though it was the anteroom of his study, and then *bathed naked* with her for heaven's sake! Was it because he had declared her a member of his family? Now Hesh would not even step into the room where she was having breakfast with another person. Go figure. She stood up in the long nightgown she had found spread on the bed last night and looked around for her clothes. The ball gown would make an unsuitable fashion statement to girls in prison, but that was all she had with her. "I wonder where my dress is," she muttered.

"That beautiful dress has been laid away." Nona jumped up to cross the room and open a drawer in a large chest. "Hesh has instructed me to help you dress in clothing appropriate for your visit with us." She pulled out a brown knitted dress and brought it over to Poppy. "I hope this will be acceptable to you."

"It'll be just fine. But I wonder if there's any underwear in that chest."

With another little smirk, Nona replied, "Of course. Everything you need. I will bring them and dress you." She turned around with an apologetic look as if she had forgotten something. "Oh, the relief site is beyond that door, lady."

Poppy crossed the room and pushed open the usual heavy, wooden door to enter a room so chill she was suddenly reminded how far underground she was. It was small, with no bathing facility. When she emerged, Nona was ladling steaming water from a pot on the fire, to which she then added cool water from a pitcher. Testing it with her hand, she looked up. "I will now bathe you, lady."

"Oh, I can do that myself. Thanks, anyway." Poppy shucked the loose nightgown comfortably after bathing every day with Cherry and the other girls. But without a word Nona carried the basin of water to the table which she had cleared while Poppy was in the relief site, and on which Poppy now saw a chunk of soap and bathing cloths. Not to seem unappreciative, Poppy allowed the girl to do most of her brief washing and toweling. She then reached for the shift, but Nona managed to get it and the dress onto her before she could successfully manipulate the garments for herself.

Once on, the dress fell in simple lines with no decoration. Relieved to be in relatively simple garb again, Poppy sat on the bed to put on the sandals that had appeared, and a welcome feeling of familiarity enveloped her, especially after the clothing of last evening: the jester outfit, then the fancy ballroom gown. *Wow, I'm beginning to feel really comfortable in these long knitted dresses with no tight underwear or stockings.*

Nona combed her hair, using some of the pins from last evening's elaborate style to secure the curls at the back of her head. The girl seemed to be drawing out the whole procedure, taking as long as possible for every movement. When she finally declared the hair done and moved to make the bed, Poppy decided to let her do it all, and stop interfering. Heaven only knew what her usual day's occupation was going to be. Maybe this whole experience was a treat for her, a way to forestall her regular day.

When there were no more chores to be done, Nona said, "Now I am to take you to the working room, where I must remain for the day. However, Hesh has given me leave to come back and prepare the evening meal."

"Well, that would be great, Nona, but I don't expect to be here that long," Poppy replied. "But maybe some other time …" It was hard to know the proper words to use with an incarcerated girl.

"I think you will be here, lady," Nona said. "Or, Hesh would have instructed me otherwise."

"Why?" Poppy felt panic rising again. "Has Hesh got news about the storm? Is it worse than expected?"

Nona shook her head slowly. "That kind of information is not given to us here. I am simply relying on his instructions." Then she engaged Poppy's eyes with a look of desperation in her own, and spoke in a low voice. "If possible, lady, might I ask, before you go, if you could somehow let me know if the storm is passed and if no great damage has been done. And also, whether the rest of my family—my mother and my brothers are well. I know I have no right to ask, but I have six more years to think of my family …"

"*Six more years?*" Poppy could have kicked herself for the way it came out, but they gave these kids *ten years* for 'undue jocularity?' The girl simple nodded.

"Well, you can count on me, dear." Poppy patted her on the shoulder. "I'll find some way to let you know—after I find out myself. I don't know a thing right now about anyone in your family except your sisters, but I'll ask."

A sigh was Nona's reply, before she turned wordlessly to lead Poppy out of the apartment, now abandoned by Hesh, push the wooden door closed, and proceed down several semi-dark corridors to a hugely heavy door flanked by two men standing erect and silent with their arms crossed. As the women approached, one of the men lifted the iron stay from across the door, and both moved aside quickly, bowing to Poppy. *Guards.* Poppy felt a shiver go through her, but Nona led the way through the door without a glance at the men, down another corridor and emerging at last into a large, fairly well lighted room filled with rows of workbenches.

The inmates, all young men and women between thirteen and perhaps their mid-thirties, sat silently working. All faces turned toward the two women as they entered.

Hesh appeared immediately as if from nowhere. "Good morning, lady," he said pleasantly with a little nod, not quite a bow. "I trust Nona has made your rising genial."

"Oh, absolutely effortless," Poppy replied. "She hardly let me do anything for myself."

"Good girl." The old man touched Nona's arm lightly. She bowed to him and walked away, taking an empty stool before a workbench near the center of the room. Poppy watched her, delaying turning back to Hesh, not knowing exactly what to say, now that she knew who his 'charges' were.

But he left no silence between them. "Well, lady, very few of the residents from above are allowed to visit us," he said in a tone that seemed way too light for the situation. "You are the first in many months."

She didn't know whether he was just trying to be polite, or upbeat, or whether she was supposed to consider discovering this terrible place a privilege. She mustered a weak smile instead of a reply.

Apparently none was required. He continued in the same affable tone, offering his arm as if inviting her to dance, "Come, you will want to see the work these people do. Some of them are quite gifted."

She walked with him among the rows of workers, intent on their tasks. Some were doing leatherwork, some metalwork, and some seemed to be grinding lenses. She stopped only when Hesh did, admiring the fine work. "May I speak to them?" she finally whispered to Hesh. Any breach of custom here might have consequences for these poor kids.

"Of course," he replied.

"This is beautiful," she told a girl who was working diamond shaped patterns into a metal plate that looked like pewter. The girl smiled shyly, catching her eye for only a moment before casting hers back down on her work. Then, pausing to look more closely at a metal object that appeared to be a buckle, Poppy said to a young man, "That looks difficult to fit together."

The boy lifted his head, looking up at her with the saddest brown eyes she had ever seen. "It is very difficult, lady," he said in a voice that matched his expression. "But it helps me forget ..."

More than a little unnerved, she moved with Hesh toward the area where she had seen Nona take her place, eager to see what they were making. It was metal jewelry, every piece exquisitely detailed in, of course, geometric patterns. Nona glanced up with a slight smile and moved her hands aside to display a gleaming scalloped silver clasp, engraved with what appeared to be a curved-edged star.

"Why, that's *lovely!*" Poppy gasped, reaching toward it involuntarily. "May I ...?"

Nona glanced up at Hesh, who nodded and said, "Please, lady."

As Poppy ran a finger over the polished surface of the piece, feeling the delicate lines of engraving, Hesh added, "I believe Nona wishes to make a gift of her work to you, lady. Will you do us the honor of accepting it?"

Poppy hesitated a moment to figure out the proper response. She would not take the jewelry, she decided, proper protocol or not, if it made the girl unhappy.

"Please, lady." Nona held the clasp out to her, smiling hopefully.

"Well," Poppy said. "if you really want me to have it ..."

"Indeed I do."

"My charges are glad to have their work appreciated," Hesh assured her.

Poppy doubted the word "glad" would apply to any of these young dungeon slaves, except when they left this place. She held the piece against her chest. "I will treasure it."

Hesh offered his arm again, saying, "You must inspect the leather work. It is quite remarkable." As he led her through the rest of the metal workers' tables, some of the young people held up their work to catch her attention as she passed, but Hesh led her briskly on to another area where some of the workers were marking pieces of leather, some were cutting and punching holes, some working patterns with red-hot, wooden-handled bars of metal. Then some were working decorative pieces of metal, even colored jewel-like stones, into the leather of finished belts and sandal straps.

Again, she slid her arm away from her host to lean over a tawny head of thick hair to admire some red stones the girl was fitting into gold settings that had been secured into a belt. Careful not to admire the beauty of her work out loud, lest the girl feel obligated to give it to her, Poppy stared at the red stones. Turning to Hesh, she said, "These are glass stones, right?"

"No, indeed. They are rubies of the finest quality and cut," he replied proudly. "Did I not tell you we have some very gifted workers here? Well deserving of the finest materials to work on."

The tawny-haired worker glanced shyly up at them, her olive skin lusterless, her pale blue eyes (obviously Larian blood in her ancestry) sad and dispirited.

"Klepen is one of our finest leather-workers," Hesh explained, without introducing the girl to Poppy. "Skilled in setting stones as well."

Poppy gave the girl, who had lowered her eyes and resumed her work, a pat on the shoulder, hoping to convey some small encouragement.

"Now. The lens crafts." Hesh spoke as if he were proudly leading his guest on a delightful museum tour. Poppy took his arm once again and they approached the brightest area in the cavernous room. The long tables held many small lamps, one for each worker, as they bent over their tasks of hand-grinding and rubbing small circles of glass.

"This takes good eyesight and great patience," Hesh explained.

She groped for an agreeable reply to match his enthusiasm. Very few of these lens workers had even bothered to glance up at their visitor. *They've found something they can temporarily lose themselves in. Good.* But this whole scene was really getting her down. She thought of Lorimar and his telescopes and wondered if he ever thought of the lenses being ground by these confined young people as he studied the spreading heavens. "It certainly looks like a job that needs close concentration," she said finally.

Poppy was growing anxious at the thought of Lorimar coming for her. "Lorimar would wait, wouldn't he?" she said to Hesh. "If he comes back while I'm in here?"

The old man patted the hand on his arm. "No cause for worry, lady. Lorimar is a man of his word." As if sensing her apprehensiveness, he turned back toward the way they had come. "We will return now to my chambers."

Back in Hesh's comfortable main room, the dank workshop seemed a nightmare. Poppy sank into the chair beside the fireplace where she had landed exhausted last night, hoping it was. Hesh brought her tea and a plate of blue cakes and pieces of cheese a strange shade of pink. The odd food colors caused her not a second's hesitation any more. Everything she had been given in this place had been delicious. She hoped the inmates were, at least, given the same kind of food.

Hesh settled himself in a chair opposite her. "Now, lady," he began. "How can I answer your questions?"

"Questions?" she hedged, taken by surprise. "Last night I wondered what you do down here. I don't have to ask any more."

His smile was the same as if they were sitting in a sidewalk cafe. "But you will."

She took in a deep breath. "Well, I guess my only real question is *why*. Why do the inhabitants of this place … of Halderwold live like this? I mean, the law against humor was made several generations ago. Kandra explained that to me. Why keep it on the books now? I met the king and queen and they seemed very nice. Can't they be reasoned with? Can't anything be done?" She stopped abruptly as a serious expression spread over his wrinkled face. *Oh boy, I bet I've crossed the line—and this isn't Lorimar's house where I'm so well tolerated.*

But her fears were allayed by his mild reply. "That is not a question we do not ask ourselves, lady. But tradition—which is very important here—dictates that laws put in place by a king, especially those included in the oath of office, are a sacred trust to be held in the highest and most venerated esteem."

"But the young people …" she began.

But he was still speaking. "Vran is a good king, but he is bound by oath to uphold all laws already passed by his predecessors, unless …"

"Unless what?" Poppy leaned forward eagerly.

"Unless he himself should breach one."

"Then what would happen?"

"Then he would be duty-bound to banish himself from the land, along with his wife and children, and allow the next relative in line for the throne to become ruler."

"And he won't do that—even for all these miserable young people?"

"The next relative of Vran," the old man continued. "After his two children—the next in line for the throne is his cousin, Pule." He paused and pursed his lips before adding, "A born scoundrel." He looked at her with an open, earnest expression. "Believe me, lady, rule of Halderwold by Pule could be a fate far worse than the laws we labor under at this time."

"But what if the people still wanted Vran? What if they still chose him to rule over them?"

Hesh rubbed his forehead. "An occasion such as that, or even an idea such as the people *choosing* their sovereign, has never occurred in Halderwold to my knowledge, though I have heard of such an event coming to pass in Laria. But only in the most extreme situations."

Poppy sat silent, staring into the fire. *Damn. Double damn. So there's no way out of this craziness. These people have no concept at all of choosing their leader. There's not a thing I can do. If only I could just go home.* Listlessly, she took another piece of cheese, but then couldn't imagine swallowing it. She put it back on the plate. After a few minutes, Hesh excused himself to go about his duties, and Poppy napped in her chair, waiting for Lorimar.

Supper time arrived, and Lorimar hadn't come. Nona arrived, happy to prepare a meal for her new friend and her jailer. "I'm going to give the silver pin to Deema," Poppy whispered to her, even though Hesh had not come back and they were alone in the room.

Nona grasped her arm. "Oh, lady, I hoped you would. Though you are under no obligation. I truly gave it to you."

"I have no need of it," Poppy assured her, suddenly feeling her throat choke with tears. "And I know it will mean so much to your family."

The girl nodded, tears shining in her eyes as well. "It will." She picked up a poker and stoked the fire, then set about her cooking.

"Can I help?" Poppy offered.

"It is my great pleasure, lady," Nona replied. "Please rest and allow me to make you the best meal I am capable of preparing." She paused and cast a sad look at her friend. "Soon you will be gone from here, but I shall never forget you."

Sniffing, Poppy settled herself back in her chair.

CHAPTER 10

Hesh returned and, after greeting the women, went into his room. When the savory smelling meal was almost ready, he appeared, smelling pleasantly of herbal soap, his long grey hair slicked back, wet and dark. He had regained his convivial mood, poured wine for the three of them, and brought Poppy's glass to her with a bow.

"Have you heard news of the storm?" she asked, forgetting to even thank him as she took the glass.

"All is well." He settled himself in his chair before continuing. "It was a storm of serious magnitude, but Halderwold has withstood far worse."

"The children ..."

"They have been cared for. Their passage through the city has been postponed until tomorrow. There has been some damage to property, but it is being taken care of as speedily as possible."

"Lorimar ..." Poppy half rose from her chair.

"He has been busy. I have not spoken with him. Only a runner who brings me tidings. Sit down and drink your wine."

"Do you think he'll come tonight?" she pursued.

Hesh shook his head. "I think not. But are you not comfortable here, lady?"

"Of course I am." Poppy sat down and tried to relax. "I've never been so well-treated in my life, except, of course, at Lorimar's house."

"Then I can look forward to an evening of pleasant company, for which I will consider myself well-treated."

Slightly ashamed, she said, "I meant to cast no aspersions on your hospitality, sir." *Good heavens, I sound more like them all the time.*

An amused smile wreathed his shining, clean face. "I understand."

Nona had set the small round table with two places and invited them to come and eat.

"You will join us, child," Hesh told her, bringing a stool from a corner to add to the two wooden chairs that sat by the table.

Nona bowed to him and fetched another bowl, then took her place on the stool, but rose immediately to fetch a knife to cut the loaf of bread, before settling herself again.

"You haven't touched your wine," Hesh said, pushing the third glass he had poured toward her.

"This is for me?" the girl asked in a small voice, rolling her eyes up at him.

"It won't hurt you, child," he replied. "Drink up."

Nona drank and ate quietly, rising two or three times to bring more stew and some cut fruit.

Poppy could feel the girl relax as she sipped the wine. It was quite strong and did Poppy herself a world of good. *Nona has probably never had wine before. I must insist on helping her with the cleanup.*

"Will Nona be allowed to stay for the night?" Poppy asked Hesh.

He nodded. "Yes, she is here to attend you, lady."

She saw the flush come over the girl's face. *One more night and she'll be back in the dungeon. Poor girl.* She wanted to know what kind of accommodations the prisoners had for sleeping, but decided she'd rather not know even if it were appropriate to ask, which she doubted.

After supper, and the washing of dishes, Nona quietly went into the bedroom. Poppy and Hesh spoke further about the royal family, the laws and the storms, but Poppy learned no great deal more than he had already told her. It became clear that Hesh liked to talk, and, inspired by his good wine, repeated himself until he noticed Poppy nodding in her chair and sent her to bed.

In her bedroom, Poppy saw that Nona had made herself a bed on the floor by the fire. Even though her bed was narrow, she invited her to share it, but the girl was determined the keep the fire smoldering all night. Well, that wouldn't hurt, and it seemed to give her pleasure to be as useful as possible. Poppy forced herself to stop fretting and go to sleep.

Much to her relief, Lorimar arrived the next morning before the two girls finished in the bedroom. Nona responded to Hesh's knock and brought the news back to Poppy, in a none too happy tone of voice. Poppy tried to dampen her own reaction, realizing from the girl's expression that good news for herself was sorrowful tidings for Nona. This might be the only break she would get from prison routine in her entire ten-year sentence.

In spite of her empathy, Poppy couldn't get dressed fast enough. She hardly allowed the time for Nona to help her with her hair. Once more in the finery she had worn to the palace ball, including the diamond necklace that she had hidden at the bottom of a box of extra candles on the mantle, she rushed out to greet Lorimar, who appeared worn and tired. Poppy felt a stab of concern for him. "You don't look as if you've slept at all!" was her greeting.

He smiled wearily. "Not adequately. But all is well now. The rest of the debris blown from the trees and misplaced items will be taken care of by the aftermath workers."

Before Poppy could speak again, Hesh said, "Lorimar, you must eat and drink a little before going back up." When Lorimar put up a hand in protest, the old man continued, "I must insist, in the name of our friendship and my hospitality. And besides, the lady has not yet breached her fast."

With a sigh that sounded part resignation and part relief, Lorimar sat down in the chair by the fire that Poppy had favored. Suppressing her eagerness to get back above ground, Poppy took a chair on the other side of the fire and settled herself in forced patience. She looked at Lorimar and said only, "The children."

"Everyone is well," he told her. "The passing-through begins later in the day. You will want to be on the street to see them go through the city."

"Yes, I will," Poppy agreed, keeping her voice flat as she sneaked a glance at Nona, though the girl's back was turned to the others. Six more years. Six long years out of her youth before she could even see the sky and the green trees, let alone take part in the festivities of her people, or be with her family. She saw Lorimar's eyes go from herself to the girl busily cutting bread at the cupboard and then down to the cup of coffee Hesh handed him, and felt confident that no more would be said of the passage festival.

Hesh had picked up the spirit of dismay. "Is the damage extensive?" he asked, and with obvious forced joviality in his voice, "I fear I sometimes forget the struggles and worries of you who keep Halderwold in good repair so I may live down here, safe and cozy."

"There are struggles, to be sure, and constant worries," Lorimar replied. "But we do our best. No more can be asked of anyone."

Poppy noticed a glance from Nona at the others as she set up the toasting grate on the fire. Hesh and Lorimar spoke of how much of the coming harvest had been saved, new telescopes, and the progress of courses in the training for boys—all impersonal topics. Poppy went over to help Nona but the girl begged to be allowed this last service to her friend, so she took her place again with the men.

Soon Nona served thickly sliced toast and blueberry jam with more coffee, blushing as she obliged the others in their insistence that she join them at the table.

When they were ready to go, Poppy thanked Hesh sincerely for his hospitality, then hugged the girl tightly as Lorimar took his leave of their host. Trudging up the long corridors and many staircases to ground level, Poppy's brain reeled with questions, but Lorimar's labored breathing told her these concerns would have to wait until he was rested and everything normal again. As normal as her life could be in a world that wasn't anything close to normal.

The bright sunlight hit her with a shock that made her pause to cover her eyes for a moment. Lorimar noticed her discomfort and instructed her to "open your eyes slowly."

She peeked through her fingers, turning her head to take in the landscape, then gradually drew her hands from her face "It's not as bad as I expected. I saw the aftermath of a hurricane once, and ..."

"A ... hurry ...?" Lorimar looked puzzled.

Poppy glanced around and lowered her voice. "A hurricane is a huge windstorm. We had them too, in ... my homeland. But there were trees uprooted and houses completely blown apart. Of course your houses are all stone with no windowpanes ... *lenses.*" She corrected herself, noticing the perplexed wrinkles creeping into his forehead again.

He nodded and his brow smoothed out. "Yes, yes. It would be more comfortable in cooler seasons to have lenses in our windows, but as you can see, it would be folly when the storms come."

She took a deep breath and looked around, her eyes wide open now. "I'm so relieved to see everything looking as good as it does."

"The main danger of a storm," he continued to explain. "Is our unreadiness, since there is no way of knowing when one will come until the clouds gather, and by then it is nearly upon us."

She managed to suppress any remark about weather forecasting, and said simply, "Well, you seem to manage it all wonderfully."

He summoned a passing cart and they were soon approaching his house. "Kandra will be ready for your return," he told her when they were seated. "And to help you prepare for this day's festivities."

A now familiar anxiety stabbed through her as she remembered the second dress Kandra had picked out for her. How she longed to spend the rest of the day sitting quietly, speaking to Lorimar about the imprisoned young people and any possibility of changing the system.

"The palace again?" She looked up at him. "Isn't there any way we can get out of it?"

His weary smile was in response to the childlike tone of her pleading. "Tonight's festivities will be at the Wise House," he replied with a sigh. "And you at least have slept. Since I have more duties this day, I must go as I am—exhausted and longing for my bed."

She sighed. "Okay, sorry. I'll be a good soldier."

"A good what?"

"A good ... guest."

He nodded, but his face told her he didn't completely believe her. Just before turning up their street, he cautioned her, "One thing. Do not speak of your stay with Hesh, nor of the workshop. You and I will discuss it when time permits."

"No problem," she replied with a shrug. If today was going to be another party and she was expected to get into a party mood, the last thing she wanted to dwell on was her 'stay with Hesh and his *workshop.*'

Kandra was waiting in the outer doorway. She came forward to embrace Poppy. "We are all well," she said.

"Where's Cherry?" Poppy asked, thinking she may have been brought home during the storm.

"She remains with the others outside the city," Lorimar replied for his mother-in-law. "She may not return home until after passing through."

"Oh, of course," Poppy said as if she had known it all the time.

Kandra's arm still lay across Poppy's shoulders. "We must dress you for the passage and the following festivities."

"But I've hardly worn this dress at all," Poppy said. "Won't it do for today as well?"

The older woman gave her one of her hopeless glances. "No, my dear. It will not do."

No further explanation was offered and Poppy climbed up to Kandra's room to undergo another beauty session with the ladies waiting for her there. Cleod was not here this time but Sherat, the younger one, had been joined by Malina. After washing up in the nearest relief site, Poppy surrendered herself to the women once again. They both smiled as if dressing Poppy was a privilege. Down came the hairdo poor Nona had created yesterday, and new braids and coils were interwoven and pinned.

Kandra noticed her red eyes and gave her a few drops of some medicinal water for them. Absent an eye dropper, most of it missed the eyeballs when she tried to splash it in, but the couple of drops that went in felt cool and soothing.

"No vigorwart tonight, Kandra?" She couldn't resist asking.

"You have no need of vigorwart today," Kandra answered in a scolding tone, but smiled a little as she said it. She always showed a hint of pride when Poppy relished her meals or concoctions. She hadn't called Poppy 'lady' since she'd come back from underground, but was acting more like a mother than hostess, and that suited Poppy just fine. She sat quietly through her hairdressing and stood obediently to be decked out in the pinkish orchid dress and the pendant with the dark red stone.

Along with Lorimar, the women joined the crowd gathering along the main street just before the first band passed, stepping rather slowly and playing a tune that reminded Poppy hauntingly of *The Green, Green Grass of Home*. But that was probably just because of her state of mind, she told herself, from trying to repress thoughts of the young people in the underworld. And yes, she was homesick too. All the time.

Then the street was filled with older teenagers, "The ones who have gone through in the last three passages," Kandra whispered in answer to Poppy's quizzical look.

Some carried pennants, while some just waved their hands and smiled. Poppy's heart went leaden to think that Nona once belonged in this group. How many more of those bending over their crafts deep beneath them at this very minute should be among these brightly-clothed youngsters marching and smiling in the sunlight?

Two more bands passed through, separated by a group of young women, many of whom appeared to be pregnant, twirling multicolored streamers. Another band, and then the bedraggled but relieved-looking youngsters, the 'People of Passage,' including Cherry, Deema and Kellith. Cherry's red dress was rumpled and water-stained and the fatigue of a night, not only sleepless but perhaps terrifying, had taken the place of her usual cheerful expression.

Poppy heaved an audible sigh of relief, warranting an empathetic glance from Lorimar.

When the last band was marching past, stepping to a lively beat, Poppy realized that each band had upped its tempo from the music of the one preceding it, and the result had gradually and subtly raised the mood of the participants and onlookers alike to a light-hearted tempo.

All but hers. Taking her cue from the crowd, including Kandra and Lorimar, she stretched her lips in a smile and raised a hand in the air, thankful that her clown act had been two nights ago, and not tonight.

Soon she was whisked into a cart with Lorimar and Kandra, heading up the hill to the Wise House for supper and the evening's festivities. At least she didn't have to make merry in the palace again, knowing what was underneath. *Stop it! Stop thinking about it.* She shook her head and rubbed her hands over her face.

"Are you well?" Kandra asked.

"I'm … all right. Fine."

Kandra touched her arm and leaned nearer. "If you are assaying for a dose of your favorite elixir," she told her. "There will be none there."

"Kandra, you know I'm not …" Turning to face her, Poppy saw the look of sly humor, and almost laughed. *Kandra, of all people, cheering up a clown!* Well, the woman's apprehension had probably diminished considerably with the big cooking and sewing project over, the clowning party a success, with no one taken into custody, and Cherry on the other side of her passage. And the mature manner the girl had taken on, even before last night, made it appear as if she'd be able to handle her new role just fine. Yes, Kandra had had reason to worry, and it was good to see her relief. *Too bad we can't just have a rollicking giggle together.*

The music reached them even before the carts pulled up over the wide lawn of the Wise House. It pealed from the rooftop where Poppy had watched the amazing sunset several nights ago. It was earlier in the evening than the night she had come here with Loirmar, but the colors were gathering in the sky and the magnificent blue moon, now beginning to wane, was already above the opposite horizon.

There were men waiting to help the women down from the carts, not as handsomely uniformed as the ones at the palace, and no more talkative. Poppy's temporary escort was heading for the first flight of stairs when Lorimar held out his arm and Poppy was handed silently over to him.

They walked steadily up the three flights of stone stairs. On the roof, all five bands were playing at once. No wonder the music had been heard so far down the road. But it was beautiful music, more orchestra-like than band music now. Poppy didn't recognize any of the instruments, but some did have keys, and some strings, and those wind instruments pealed out like no jazz band she had ever heard, even if the musicians did look ridiculous with their heads halfway up inside them. She caught herself before laughing at the sight. It was becoming easier; the whole scene was cheering her up.

Then Cherry was at her elbow. "Welcome to our passage feast, lady," she said in a dignified but happy manner, with a little bow. "You look like a queen—but I could have done your hair in a more flattering style."

"Come here, *you!*" Poppy cried, reaching for the girl—then thinking to glance at Lorimar who nodded and smiled—and taking her in her arms in a tight hug.

Cherry clung to her as if she had been rescued from a burning building. For a moment. Then she dropped her arms and backed away. "It is wonderful to be back," she said calmly.

Poppy's eyes took her in, wondering that she still wore the stained and even torn red dress. Cherry read her glance and explained. "It is honorable to damage your passage gown. It shows that we have passed through more than just the city streets."

"I want to hear all about last night as soon as we get a chance to talk," Poppy told her.

Cherry nodded rather solemnly and spoke into her ear. "Of course. But not tonight. Tonight we must behave as if it were all nothing."

"Good little soldier," Poppy muttered, for Lorimar's benefit rather than Cherry's, since she had moved on to a group of ladies who were patting her shoulders. She enjoyed teasing him by causing that look of momentary perplexity, since, most of the time, he acted so *in charge.*

Many couples were dancing. Poppy looked at Lorimar. The party of last evening had ended so abruptly she hadn't danced at all, and it didn't look too difficult—what they were doing. She was sure she could pick up the steps with no trouble, and she was desperate for something to help her act cheerful.

As if reading her mind, he leaned near to be heard. "We will dance, but first we must find our place."

She scrunched up her face and adopted a mock pleading tone. "Not the royals again?"

"I fear it must be." Amusement tinged his weary features as he offered his arm. Obedient, she accepted it and, as they made their way around the dancers, she noticed the arrangement was similar to the palace party. The elderly people and the heavily laden tables of food were closely aligned around the edge of the roof, and a dais had been put up for Vran and Avive, and their *apple polishers,* as she now thought of them. One of which she seemed expected to become. How she wished she could just spend the evening dancing and looking at the sky, and trying not to think of all she had learned in the last twenty-four hours!

But to the dais they went, with Vran again descending to meet them at the bottom of the steps. "No need to fall up the steps tonight, lady," he teased, holding out his arm. "We are old friends now."

Her face warming, Poppy took his arm, walked demurely up the steps and sat in the chair he indicated, beside Avive. Safely seated, she turned to the queen with the intention of expressing her relief that they had weathered the storm, but decided to wait until spoken to. For all she knew there might be some wacky law against mentioning storms to the queen.

But Avive was quick to begin the conversation. "We are happy to see that you were well taken care of during the storm, Lady Poppy."

"Oh, very well," Poppy answered simply, remembering that Lorimar had told her not to mention where she had spent the night. She was getting better at this. Give out no information unless asked, then think hard and long before answering.

"And you are rested and ready to dance?"

The unfamiliar voice came from behind her. She rose before looking around at a dark, smiling face, which slightly resembled the king. "Yes. I'm ready," she replied, and was soon retracing her steps down from the dais on the arm of the pleasant gentleman. Much better to be dancing. It would require less conversation and less of her ever-hovering chances of saying the wrong thing.

The man was just slightly taller than she, extremely light on his feet, and an expert dancer, yet for some reason she was slightly repulsed by him. He had a manner of … *slickness* about him. There was no conversation at all for the first few moments of their twirling and side-stepping, and she was proud of her quick study in picking it all up. She had always been quicker at picking up physical activities than social graces. One of the reasons she had taken so well to clowning.

"You are the soul of grace, lady," her partner remarked charmingly. "Or may I call you … it is *Poppy*, is it not? Poppy the Larian?"

"Oh, I'm sorry," she said. "I just felt so much like dancing … the music is so beautiful and everything. Well, I'm afraid we should have become acquainted first."

"The fault lies completely with me, Lady Poppy," he replied smoothly. "I am Pule, kinsman of Vran, and I am honored to make your acquaintance. Unfortunately, the events of the evening before last left us no time for introductions at the palace ball."

She stumbled and very nearly tramped on his foot. Sidestepping just in time, she managed to get control of herself before looking up into his face with a forced smile. "The honor is mine as well." *Great. So I've fallen directly into the hands of* Pule. *The man Hesh dubbed 'a born scoundrel.' Why the heck didn't Lorimar do something when he saw who was making off with me?*

But what could he have done? Pule was the king's cousin and belonged among his companions, obviously tolerated by Vran and his family. She gave herself to the rhythm, the motion, closed her eyes and pretended to be dancing with her high school prom date, Charlie Briggs. Charlie had been just an inch taller than she, and they had danced so dreamily ...

And this character was now holding her way too close. Was it forbidden to walk away from a royal dance partner? She decided against it. "My feet are getting tired," she told him at last. That was no lie, after walking up from the depth of the juvenile prison, she lacked her old 'could have danced all night' vigor. "And I'm hungry," she added for good measure.

"Oh forgive me." Pule finished the twirl and brought her to the edge of the dance floor. She started for the nearest table of food but he intercepted her with a firm grip on her arm. "You will eat from the table on the dais of course, lady."

"Oh. Of course. How very kind." She allowed him to lead her back to the dais. Much better to be near Lorimar, or even Vran, now that Hesh had assured her it was not exactly his doing that these brutal laws continued in the land. Once on the dais, she got a better look at Pule. Though he did resemble Vran, his slightly comic features didn't exhibit a good-natured disposition as did Vran's. Instead she read cunning, even depravity in his face. She would ask Lorimar if he agreed with Hesh's opinion. Right now, she wanted no more to do with the man.

Now the introductions cut short last night were completed. Avive was apologetic for having had so little time with her honored guest the previous evening. Her clear eyes spoke sincerity, and Poppy decided the young queen was a genuine, likable woman.

The king as well. Vran was as pleasant as he had been the previous evening, and claimed a dance as soon as Poppy was free. He danced formally, no dizzying twirls like the ones Pule had put her sailing through. "An honor, lady," he said, bowing, when the dance was finished; then offered his arm to return her to the group.

When she returned to her chair, Lorimer leaned toward her offering a plate of pastries and a glass of wine, almost whispering, "Refresh yourself, for I have yet to claim a dance with you."

Poppy had noticed that neither Lorimar nor Kandra had called her "lady" since she'd returned this morning. She looked forward to finding out whether the knowledge gained from Hesh had given her new status in their inner circle. She hoped so. It made her feel a little more secure, especially now that she understood the severe penalties imposed here for 'jocularity.'

She was surprised to find 'kester chip cookies' one of the items on her plate. After finishing some small sweet rolls, tarts and a delicacy that tasted like a salmon pie, she took another sip of wine and gave Lorimar what she hoped was a *meaningful* look. He rose immediately and led her down the steps and onto the dance floor.

The music was slower now, the dance almost a waltz. He moved smoothly, holding her gently but quite close. Poppy wondered what life in his house would be like after the excitement of both the celebration and the storm had died down. The recollection of their bathing incident still brought the blood to her face, and she felt embarrassed all over again as she came into closer contact with his lean body. Thankfully, Cherry would still be living in the house and maybe they could sneak into the 'laughing room' now and then to unwind.

But she wasn't feeling that familiar silliness welling up inside the way she used to. Not since her visit to that ... *domain of the damned*. She let her head rest against her partner's shoulder and wondered if her natural cheerfulness had been stifled for good. She would probably be safer if it were. Maybe *that* was Lorimar's reason for taking her down there. Well, they'd have time to talk about it soon.

There were several men on the dais—she hardly remembered their names—who wanted to dance with her, and she hoped to give them each a dance in spite of her aching feet, in order to avoid Pule. She was surprised when the music changed to a kind of merry-go-round tune, and Avive grasped her hand and told her it was time for the women to dance together. The ladies on the dais flocked to the dance floor, where they formed one of the many circles that were appearing. Many of the old ladies from the sofas also came forward to be part of the dance. And it was fun. Smiling their pleasure, the ladies danced around in circles, which reformed constantly as some left one circle to join another, and some of the circles came together to form larger ones and move around the outside of another one going in the opposite direction.

Poppy found herself enjoying it. It was like being a little girl again, except for the gay laughing that should be going along with it. The smiles on all the faces were the extent of their expression of pleasure. When Poppy almost felt glee rising up within her, visions of Nona and the others down below overshadowed them, and then it was no effort at all to keep her smile from bringing forth a giggle.

The younger girls came bounding into the older ladies circles, and Cherry was there suddenly, taking Poppy's hand. Even her happy young face failed to lend any real cheer to Poppy's heart. *Lorimar was smart to take me to visit Hesh. He knew that would get me safely though these dances. He's a smart man. Well, of course he is. He's the head of the wise ones. What was that word—his title again. Oh, yeah. I mustn't forget. He's the* nashu. *And I'm a little drunk. No wonder Kandra wouldn't allow me any vigorwort. She knew the wine would be more than enough.*

When she got a moment to notice, Poppy saw that the men were dancing together in circles too, and it looked rather … beautiful. They weren't holding hands like the women, but facing each other and doing some pretty complicated steps; then occasionally they would circle each other with elbows intertwined. Their movements were graceful and masculine, almost like Russian dancing. Unlike the women, their faces were serious and concentrated, as if they were setting an example for the younger boys who had just gone through their passage, saying, *See, you can enjoy life and socialize without laughing.'* At the end of the dance, they all gave a loud stomp and a hoop. The women turned toward them and clapped, then led the way back to their seats.

Poppy was thirsty again, and she noticed that everyone else seemed to be too. Another round of wine glasses passed among them. Suddenly she felt completely worn out, wearied to the very soul, and glad when Lorimar approached and asked if she were ready to go home.

"More than ready," she replied. "Not that I haven't been having a good time, but the last few days have been busy ones, haven't they?"

"Indeed they have," he said. "But tomorrow you may rest."

"Sounds good to me." Poppy looked around, wondering what proper leave-taking entailed. Last night she hadn't had to worry about it. But Lorimar was of course taking care of that. He bowed to Vran and again to Avive with a hand on his chest. They rose and did the same to him and, turning to Poppy, gave her the same salutation. She repeated their motions and took Lorimar's arm to walk down the steps.

Kandra and Cherry were waiting for them, Cherry obviously beyond exhaustion. Poppy looked forward to hearing about her night in the stormy forest—but not tonight. As if in answer to her hopes, they rode home in comfortable silence, punctuated now and then by yawns and sighs.

CHAPTER 11

Once home, Poppy went to bed once more with Cherry, just the two of them in the girl's room, and fell almost immediately into a sound and consoling sleep. Toward morning, though, she drifted toward consciousness to sense Aunt Holly looking down on her again. She came awake with a jolt. She was *dead!* That was it! This world was some kind of way station or afterlife dimension. Maybe she'd broken her neck in that fall at the gym, and she would never go back to her real life.

But wait. Aunt Holly had a *worried* expression on her face—both times she had glimpsed her. If she were looking down at her niece in her coffin, it would be grief on her face, not concern. Poppy sat up and rubbed her face hard with both hands. This was no time to lose it, not when things were finally calming down. She resolved once more to concentrate on making the most of the life she was given.

The passage, and the storm, were over. Maybe life here would take on some semblance of routine now, and Poppy thought with relief that she would soon find out just what role she would be expected to play in the daily life of this family. Lorimar had indicated to her up at the Wise House that she was a natural candidate for a wise one; and though she'd much prefer to live here in some simple style that would attract less attention, if that were to be her role, it would be good to get on with her training.

She lay thinking about it. In a respected capacity, she might be able to exert some influence in favor of those kids down there in Hesh's charge. Maybe get their sentences reviewed, shortened or revoked or something—even a pardon for some of them. She wasn't all that familiar with legal terms, but it would be worth working for if these people had any concept of … leniency. Was that the word? Good heavens, if she'd ever dreamed of landing in a situation like this, law school would have been a much better choice than *clown school*. But life was funny that way. If this really was life. She shook the thought from her head. Of course she was alive. Didn't she have the same body she'd always had? And didn't it get tired and hungry and thirsty, and need … a relief site? Like it did right now.

Pale pink light was beginning to leak through the high windows as she slid out of bed and, trying not to waken Cherry, made her way into the dark hall-way and felt along the wall for the little room. That over, Poppy didn't feel like going back to bed, still she seemed to have no choice, so she slipped into the comfort of the warm covers and tried to take advantage of the quiet to come up with some kind of game plan for her immediate future. She was still think-ing that Lorimar had taken her to Hesh for some purpose other than safety from the storm, wanting her to find out first-hand about the prisoners. Surely Hesh would not have given her a tour and filled her in on so much of the situ-ation if he had not known that Lorimar meant him to. Most of these people had hunkered down in their storm rooms, the kids had toughed it out in the woods, so there had obviously been no real need for her to be that far under-ground for safety. Yes, he must have had a 'method in his madness,' forcing her practically screaming along all those creepy corridors and down a dozen stair-ways straight out of a grade B horror flick. He sure understood a picture being worth a thousand words. How ironic in this society where pictures were for-bidden.

She sighed, a little more settled in her mind about her role and her future here. She no longer feared the king and queen—but that *Pule*. He really was a sleazy one. It was written all over him; in his eyes, his voice. After seeing beyond his initial smoothness, he had absolutely oozed sleaze. She felt certain she would have been repulsed by the man even if Hesh had not given her his pedigree. In fact a little shiver went through her at the memory of his touching her even to dance. She would avoid *him* from now on, at all costs.

But that plan fell apart as soon as breach of fast was over. Lorimar had left before she and Cherry came downstairs.

"Father has a great deal to do with the rearrangement after the storm," Cherry explained at the table.

"I can well imagine that," Poppy replied. "It must be quite a cleanup with all those uprooted trees I saw along the roads."

"*Cleanup.*" The girl nodded with a smile, a mere ghost of her former grin. "A good name for the aftermath work. We call it '*righting.*'"

"We have taken much care to develop trees that grow low and deeply rooted," Kandra put in. "The work has been going on for at least three generations now."

"Just three generations?" Poppy was puzzled. "Why didn't they think of it before that? I mean, with all the highly developed gardening skills you have here, I'd have thought someone would have started cultivating the trees a long time ago."

Both women considered her question with puzzled expressions, then Kandra answered, "The storms were not so severe in my grandmother's time. There have always been windstorms, yes, as far back as the records show. But they have become much more frightening, even within my own memory. The one we had yesternight was equable compared to others we have experienced, and thankful I am for the children's sake." She cast a loving glance at Cherry and ran her hand down the girl's forearm.

"I am too," Poppy was quick to add, looking at Cherry. "Don't think I wasn't worried half to death about you."

"I believe you, Poppy. And you too, of course, Grandmother," the girl said respectfully, including both women in a sweeping glance accompanied by her new, retrained smile.

The first truly relaxed conversation they had enjoyed together was interrupted by a shadow that cast itself from the doorway of the anteroom across the dining room where they were drinking their coffee. Kandra rose at once to greet the visitor, who turned out to be a page—of none other than Duke Pule, who, the lad told them bowing, requested the honor of taking "Lady Poppy" for a ride. And, Poppy heard with a sinking heart, he was actually outside at this very minute, waiting in his best cart for her.

"R … right now?" she stammered, looking from Kandra to the page and back again. With a worried expression, Kandra nodded her head at the page who then left and, turning back to the others, she instructed Cherry to "fetch my best cloak for Lady Poppy."

Then, the page gone, she said, nearly trembling to Poppy, "You must go. But say little—nothing if possible, in answer to the duke's questions. Try to simply agree with anything he says. Tonight Lorimar will instruct you further."

"I already know something about our friend, the duke," Poppy told her through clenched teeth. "But if I must go, I … I'll be careful." Seeing the worried look on the older woman's face, she lay a hand on her arm. "Trust me,

Kandra. I believe I've learned a lot in a short time." Then she added with a sigh, "Just when things were calming down around here."

Kandra nodded, the fear in her eyes diminishing only slightly. "With the duke waiting, you have no time for a more courtly dress, but my cloak will cover you elegantly."

Apparently, the 'lady' title Kandra had used a minute ago was for the benefit of the page. The cloak Cherry brought was deep-blue velvet with a large and beautiful silver clasp engraved with something like intersecting triangles, the lines filled in with dark blue paint. Poppy pushed her straggling curls back and pulled the hood up over her head. It would be a little too warm for the day, maybe, but it would shield her facial expressions to some degree from her repulsive escort. Bravely, after a brief but tight clasp of Cherry's hand, she went out to follow the waiting page over to the elaborate cart.

Pule himself descended the two steps from his high cart to hand her up. Dressed in green satin embroidered with gold diamond shapes, he offered a clammy hand which she took, suppressing a shudder of distaste. Immediately they were side by side on the luxurious cushions, the page seated up front by the driver of two beautiful black horses, which were soon urged into a canter. Poppy tried to at least enjoy the scenery, marred only slightly by the ravages of the storm. Sitting quietly, she determined to allow the duke to lead the conversation, and to contribute as little as possible—as she had been warned. *This ride could be so nice if only Lorimar, or even Hesh, were beside me.*

But it soon became evident that the satin clothing had not been donned for a casual outing. "We will enjoy a midday meal in the palace garden," he announced.

"Oh, dear," Poppy exclaimed, hoping he might take her back home. "I'm afraid I'm not dressed for such an occasion."

His smile—a perverted-looking smirk—conjured up visions of cinema mental patients. "I am completely aware that I took you by surprise, lady. We will be quite alone at our repast. An intimate meal for the two of us. Your simple attire does nothing to diminish your natural beauty. I am more than satisfied with your appearance."

Just being in his presence, hearing his voice, made Poppy want to scrape the slime off her skin. "Well … I'm glad you don't mind. But I just had … just breached my fast. I … I'm not in the least hungry."

He uttered a snort so demented Poppy had to restrain herself from leaping from the cart. *Isn't he afraid I'll report him for laughing? If you could even call that a laugh.*

He sat back and stared at her. Now he reminded her of someone who should be playing the Sheriff of Nottingham in a Robin Hood movie. The little, pointed black beard, the thin mustache, the piercing crow's eyes fixed on her every move. She turned her head, trying to withdraw inside the shelter of her hood. He reached behind her and pulled it from her head with a jerk, which brought her face around abruptly, her mouth open to protest, but she caught herself. Even if he were to grab her, she told herself, she had to keep cool.

"Well, maybe I could eat a little," she told him.

"You will not be required to eat, my dear, if you are not hungry. It is your company that I desire."

That 'my dear' really rankled her. *The nerve of this jackel!* After all, wasn't she, as far as he knew, a Larian, a potential wise one? Didn't she rate a certain degree of respect? And just hearing him mouth the word 'desire' gave her the heebie-jeebies. The trick was how to cope with him for the better part of a whole day, or however long this miserable outing might last. Up until now, when she was in a tight spot, humor usually came to her rescue; but that was out of the question here.

I'll just play the ingenue. She gathered all her strength, smiled into his repulsive face and, trying to say something to delay their garden party, replied as closely as she could to his own manner of speaking. "I am sure our time together will be pleasant whether we eat or not, so long as I can feel confident that you take no offence at my unready state of dress."

His reply was another smirk and a low bark that she imagined stood in for a laugh, then he turned with a wave of the arm to the surrounding landscape. "Have you had the time to take in our beautiful countryside?" he asked so politely he sounded almost normal.

"To tell you the truth, duke," she replied. "Is that the proper term? Duke? I'm sorry if it isn't."

He replied. "I am Pule."

"Well, Pule, to tell you the truth, there's been so much going on, I haven't seen all that much of your beautiful countryside. I would really enjoy a long ride."

After fixing her with an almost maniacal stare, he said, "We will soon be at the palace, but I would be more than pleased to take you *home* by a longer route."

Rats! I'm only digging myself in deeper. This joker was more than a match for her. "That would be most enjoyable," she replied.

Soon they were riding along the winding lanes of the royal grounds, the surrounding vegetation growing more lush and varied as they neared the palace. Once in the gardens, they wended their way farther away from the palace itself. Here and there she saw what could be called gazebos except for their large size and varied shapes.

Finally, the horses were drawn to a halt before a gold gilt shelter large enough for a family reunion. Pule stepped down from the cart and turned to hand her down. The page stood near, looking as if he expected to be scolded for doing nothing. But Pule ignored him, leading her along a path of blue roses that caught her attention, and up the steps of the oversized and incredibly ornate gazebo. The benches were covered with cushions so soft she sank down into them. The large table before them was laden with enough food for twenty people. There were no servants and the page and driver had remained with the horses and cart.

Pule gathered an ungainly heap of fruits and pastries onto a platter which he placed in front of her. Well, she would have to eat something. At least that would give her a little time out from talking to him. She took small bites of several dainties, some of which seemed so familiar she wondered if they were leftovers from the passage feast.

Sitting too close, he poured wine for them both, but he was eating and drinking little. She knew what that could mean, although in her former life, it usually indicated a different goal from getting information from her. At least she hoped the more common goal was not his intention. If he did attempt to seduce her, she would have to forget about Kandra's advice to go along with his suggestions. She tried to appear as if her mouth were stuffed with food and tipped the wine glass several times, taking less than she hoped it appeared. Maybe if she were to act half-drunk, he would give up on her.

But he was not deterred. "Is it true, lady," he began. "that you have no recollection whatsoever of how you came here from Laria?"

She shook her head, holding her mouth as if full until she swallowed. "None whatsoever." It was no lie, since she hadn't come from Laria.

He leaned around and looked her full in the eyes. "It is said you were found in the fields by Lorimar's daughter."

"That's right." She nodded vigorously. "That's all I remember. Nothing before that."

He stared at the blue and violet painted floor for a few minutes. "What clothing had you on when you arrived?"

"Just … some exercise … some casual clothes. Kandra has been kind enough to supply me with clothing. She gave me this." She pulled a bit of her skirt outside the cape, trying to continue with trivia. "But it's just an everyday dress, like I mentioned when I first got into …"

"That is of no importance." He cut her off sharply. "It is said that you came here wearing men's clothing."

Poppy stuffed a few of what looked like olives into her mouth, then pretended to choke on them. After a little time to think, she answered, "I do have one vague memory—of a brother. Perhaps he allowed me to wear his garments to play games." She shrugged and gave him what she hoped was a helpless look. She had to stop this kind of interrogation, or stall it until she could get some direction from Lorimar. "I just don't remember anything very clearly. My mind is just … boggled."

"*Boggled?*" He repeated disdainfully. "A Larian word?"

Poppy nodded.

Pule reached for the nearest bottle of wine. "No more questions," he assured her in a suddenly conciliatory tone. "It was my purpose to show you a pleasant day, my dear, never to place you in discomfort." He poured more wine into both of their glasses.

Poppy gave no protest, although she had no intention of drinking much of it. It was probably just his next ploy. She brought the glass to her lips a couple of times while taking in very little of the fluid. *Too bad it tastes so good.*

Pule didn't seem to notice. His restrain abandoned, he now finished off one glass and poured himself another, holding the bottle toward hers with a questioning lift of eyebrows, putting it down again when she shook her head.

Let him get drunk, she thought. Maybe he'd be the one to mess up and reveal his true purpose in harassing her like this. Even better, maybe he'd fall asleep and she'd be able to sneak over to the cart and ask the driver to take her home.

But her detestable host seemed even wider awake after two more glasses of wine. While he went some distance down the long table to get another bottle, she held her glass over the side of the open structure and poured its contents onto the ground; then she let him fill it again from the new bottle.

"Your dancing last night was more than delightful," he said, sliding up against her, slopping wine from his brimming glass. She hitched herself away, pulling her cloak close as if she were only worried about the garment. Then said, "Kandra lent me this lovely cloak. I'd hate to take it back stained." No use insulting him. The 'pleasant' side of his nature was scary enough.

"My most sincere apologies, lady." He performed a slight bow that caused more of the liquid to spill from the glass, giving her an excuse to edge over a little further. "But I can assure you that the house in which you are being entertained can well afford fine clothing."

"Apparently," she replied noncommitally.

"Indeed they can," he repeated. "In point of fact, Lorimar, a foreign-born *personage* (he pronounced the word with contempt), has risen to a state of considerable honor in Halderwold."

"Yes," she said. It was her turn to pump him. "But I am under the impression that all Larians are well-respected here."

His features twisted themselves into a sneer that remained on his face for some time. "By *some*, of a certainty. But there are others in this society … there are others not so inclined to fall down and worship the *royals* and their *cortege*."

"But are you not part of that *cortege*, Pule?" Poppy wasn't surprised by his attitude, though she hadn't expected him to share it so readily with a Larian. Of course by now he had begun to look and sound quite drunk. She sat quietly feigning interest in his conversation. Let him spill the beans—it might provide her with some useful information to carry back to Lorimar.

Then maybe this *date from hell* wouldn't have been all for nothing.

Her attention was rewarded when he spat out, "*Laria!* Is the whole planet not Lara? Is Halderwoldian soil not every bit as blue as Larian?" He leaned over and jutted his face repugnantly close to hers. She forced herself not to shrink away as he continued, "Tell me, lady! You, who have so lately come to our fair land. Are we not as good as the *Larians?*"

"Every bit as good," she assured him, then added quickly, "Though I lack memory of my past, I cannot imagine being more congenially welcomed and considerately taken care of. And I don't mean just the house where I'm staying. I mean everyone I've met …"

He interrupted her to agree, "There is *nothing* wrong with Halderwald! We have a noble history and a code of purposeful endeavor. What do we want with foreigners coming here—ordering our society?"

"But I was told no foreigners have come her for a whole generation," Poppy dared to interject. "And what changes would you like to see here?" Now she baited him. "It all seems quite peaceful and … *orderly* as it is now."

Forgetting his courtly manners completely, he spat on the floor. "It is orderly as *they* have ordered it! Perhaps it is time for a *new* order to be established!"

"Perhaps it is," she replied calmly. Then, feigning a huge yawn, she continued in the Halderwoldian manner of speaking. "Your conversation is captivating, Pule—even enlightening. But I am afraid the exertions of last evening, after several days of helping the ladies with the extensive preparations for the children's passage, and then the storm—which I am not accustomed to, have left me completely exhausted. I dream of nothing more than relaxing in the bath and sleeping through a whole night with neither fears nor concerns." She looked him fully in the eyes. "Would you be kind enough to take me home?"

The leer that crossed his features at the mention of her bath, soon passed. "That house is not your home, lady," he said peevishly, though he put his glass on the table and rose unsteadily, offering his arm. "But, being a gentleman, I will accommodate you."

"Thank you, Pule." She jumped to her feet before he could change his mind. *Gentleman. A blistering misnomer, if I ever heard one.*

Through most of the ride home, the duke muttered to himself. Stuff about the unfairness of positions of birth and the misconceptions of the body politic. The ravings of a revolutionary or madman—or as close as she ever wanted to come. After he allowed her to be handed down from the cart by the page, who gave her a sympathetic glance, she was through the arched doorway and, not wanting to stop in the outer room, headed straight through the dining room and into the innermost part of the house. In the kitchen, where the faces of the women were raised from evening meal preparations in surprise, then relief, Poppy felt a rush of homey comfort.

Cherry had already bathed, so Poppy took a quick dip, furiously scrubbed her skin with a ribbed-knit cloth to scour away her date with Pule, then hurrying out of the water in apprehension of Lorimar's sudden appearance. Safely dried and dressed, she went back to the kitchen. All was ready for supper, the women told her, since the leftover passage food now had to be used up. They had told Lorimar of her adventure of today, they said, and he was up in his study waiting to hear about it from her. And please tell him supper was ready.

Feeling a nearly desperate desire to rest instead, Poppy reluctantly climbed the stairs. Entering the anteroom of his study, hoping he would be busy peering through a telescope in the large room to give her a few minutes to unwind, she sank quietly down onto the sofa—the one she had slept on. After her trek into the depths of Hesh's realm and her adventures with the royals, everything in this house was beginning to feel as comforting as an old sweat suit.

As she sat staring at the geometric shapes in the carpet's pattern, her appreciation took on a more serious dimension. What if Pule or one of his friends (she assumed he must have some; he could be very ingratiating when he wanted to) had discovered her on her arrival here instead of Cherry? When a shadow fell across the floor, she was glad to drop that thought and look up at Lorimar in the doorway, backed by the slanting late sunlight from his room full of windows.

"Good evening, Poppy," he said. "I regret having had to leave so early this morning. Had I known what was to befall you, I would have taken some measure …"

She waved a hand to dismiss his concern. "Who could have known? Anyway I think it all turned out for the better." She pulled herself into a straighter position as he sat down in a chair facing her. "In fact, I think you may be interested in what went down."

"What went down?" His forehead creased. "Down where?"

"Sorry, I'll just tell you what happened." After mentioning that Hesh had already warned her of the duke's notoriety, she told him of the day's conversation, including the alcohol consumed. Her host listened with a worried expression.

"I had no idea the knave had become so open about his divisive inclinations," He ran his fingers down the length of his hair.

"Well, like I said," Poppy reiterated. "I think the gallon of wine he drank had a lot to do with his talkativeness."

Lorimar shook his head. "Pulc has been drinking more than called for by the occasion for years, but I have never heard of his airing such treasonous fulminations, and to a stranger—and a member of my household!" He rose and began pacing in a circle. "It is quite disturbing. But you are right. It was a good thing for you to go with him today." He stopped in front of her and leaned forward to look into her eyes. "I am proud of your handling of the situation, Poppy. This day must have been a drawn-out misery for you."

She sighed. "You can say that again."

With a tilt of the head that indicated he thought it unnecessary to repeat himself, he reached out a hand to help her up from the deep cushions. "Let us go down to our meal."

Gladly. Poppy took his hand, but let it slide from hers as soon as she was on her feet.

At the table, Kandra surprised her with a scant cup of vigorwart. Poppy raised the cup in a toast. "To a lousy day that, after all, hasn't ended half bad."

The others cast puzzled glances at her, then lowered their eyes to their supper plates.

The next day, to Poppy's great relief, was to be spent quietly with the other women. Malina came early and took over the kitchen work. The girl still called her 'lady,' even when Poppy was functioning more like a kitchen aid under her. Cherry told Malina not to bother tidying up the storm room. She and her friends would restore it to proper organization later. Poppy resolved to be in there with the girls; guessing that their true purpose might be to shut themselves up and let off a little steam after behaving like old ladies for two whole days now.

Before leaving, Lorimar called Poppy into a room on the second floor that she had never seen before. It was full of furniture, obviously where those extra beds came from at a minute's notice. In a clear space, they sat on two kitchen type chairs that he had pulled close together—a little too close for her comfort. Her eyes rested on the cold fireplace as she waited for him to speak. When he did not, she looked at him. He seemed to be studying the floor, pre-selecting his words carefully. Finally he looked at her and told her she would begin her wise training immediately, though not today.

"Tomorrow, you will come with me to the Wise House. You have much to learn, and I think also much to contribute."

She couldn't think what her contribution would be—until she learned something; but if the Wise House was safe from surprise visits from Pule, that was where she wanted to be; the sooner the better. And it was a pretty interesting place from what she had seen so far. Her wise training intrigued her, and she was glad Lorimar seemed to think she was qualified even though he knew she wasn't a Larian. Maybe she would actually learn to read their arcane script, then she could learn things about this civilization without waiting for small bits of information from anyone who would take the time and trouble to instruct her. Or asking what must sound to them to be pretty stupid questions, judging from the amused and patient replies she sometimes received, even from the young girls. Maybe they'd let her teach some of the classes later. After all, she *was* a teacher, not just a clown. Those skills were best forgotten here, anyway, considering her prospects of a once-a-year gig. And there didn't seem much to do around the house anymore, with the busyness over the passage all behind.

Most important, if becoming a wise one would give her some influence with the government to make changes in the sentencing of those kids to years of underground drudgery, no work or study would be too strenuous. She nodded eagerly. "I really look forward to that," she told Lorimar. "Being useful, if I can. I'm ready to go today, if you want."

He shook his head, looking down again. "Not yet. There is more to be considered." After a long pause, he looked at her again and continued. "I have kept you as safe as possible up until now. However, with the information you have given me about Pule's overweening dissatisfaction, and his attraction to you—the one thing for which I hold him blameless—we should not linger over what must next be done."

"What's that, Lorimar?"

He reached out and took her hand, looking earnestly into her eyes. "You must become my wife as soon as possible. I have made my offer to you, and though you have not countered, I am willing to take you … on trust."

Involuntarily, Poppy jerked her hand back and jumped to her feet, then hoped he had not taken her shocked reaction as an insult. "It … it's not that I don't *like* you or anything, Lorimar," she stammered. "I mean … I think you're a very nice man, and quite handsome and generous to a fault, and …"

"None of that has any bearing on your safety," he interrupted calmly, standing to face her. "Which is the present issue. But we will speak more of it this evening. Now I must go." He headed toward the door, turning, before he went out, to add, "And you must think carefully about our situation."

"I will," she promised. In fact she would obviously be able to think of little else. "Rats!" she muttered, after he had gone. "Some relaxing day *this* turned out to be. And I thought the excitement was all over for a few days."

CHAPTER 12

Slowly, she made her way back to the kitchen to see if Malina needed any more help. Seeming to sense her desperation to be busy, Malina set her to dusting some already clean shelves. Not overly busy, Poppy sought some diversion from her racing thoughts. "How old are you, Malina?" she asked.

"Twenty," came the calm reply.

"And you've been doing this kind of work since you were thirteen?"

"Of course," the maid replied good-naturedly. "What other kind would I do?"

"Well, you're so pretty, I'm surprised you're not married by now. Or maybe you are. Though it's none of my business," Poppy hurriedly added. Maybe it was an impolite question.

But Malina smiled, sadly. "My betrothed was a boy of high spirits," she said slowly. "He was … detained. But he will come back to me in time."

"I … didn't mean to be unkind, Malina."

"I know that, lady." Malina smiled again and went on with her sweeping.

And Poppy kept her mouth shut and dusted. When Malina left, she went upstairs and out onto the balcony off Cherry's bedroom. Here she could sit with her feet up on another chair and look at the sky, and no one could see her. She nearly jumped for joy when, in the afternoon she heard voices in the bedroom. Deema and Kellith had come. Poppy went into the bedroom and saw the bathing towels the girls were holding. "Can I bathe with you?" she asked.

"Of course, Poppy," Cherry replied. "I fully intended to ask you." Then lowering her voice, "But we are not going directly to bathe. We are going first to the storm room. I must check to see that all is put in order after the passage festival—and the storm."

"Well, can I come?" Poppy stood waiting like a child.

"Of course."

With new dignity, Cherry found wraps which she offered to the others. "It is sometimes cool in the center of the house when there is no fire in there, and these can be used after our bathing as well." They all followed her downstairs and through the corridors to the storm room, which she unlocked with a huge key and locked again once they were inside.

Everything was neat in the room. Perhaps Malina had read Cherry's 'coded' message and tidied the room up anyway. The girls immediately began kicking off their sandals and doing little jigs, each of her own fashion, as they threw their arms around each other and let out high-pitched giggles and shrieks. Grinning widely, Cherry looked around at Poppy and beckoned her to join their raucous group hug. She went to them gladly, although she couldn't call up the spontaneous dance steps, nor the giggle.

"It is *over!*" Kellith cried. "It is all over! Now we can be ourselves again."

"Not all the time," Cherry reminded her. "But right now we can!" She gave a leap into the air and fell sprawling on the nearest sofa, her shawl trailing on the floor. Her friends followed, letting off a huge, collective sigh of relief as they landed in sprawling positions beside her.

Poppy wished she could join them, but relief was not among her confused feelings. Even though these girls were forced into a too-early maturity, she would gladly have traded places with any one of them. At least they understood what was in store for them.

To Poppy, it seemed her major troubles were just beginning, and she had no idea where they might lead. Lorimar had spoken of her *safety*. How severe could the threat be? Would Pule try to kidnap her? Have her imprisoned or killed? Oh, this was all so *bizarre,* especially since she wasn't even *really here!* And there was no such place as Halderwold.

The girls stares brought her back. "Are you well, lady?" Deema asked.

"Will you not rejoice with us?" said Kellith.

Poppy tried to shake off her self-absorption. "I'm sorry," she told them. The three of them had all landed on the same sofa and she looked around for a place to sit facing them, found a chair nearby. It was time to tell Deema about her sister, now that the excitement of the passage was over.

"I've been to a very strange part of your city," she told the girls. "A place I will never forget. And I have to tell you about it, especially you, Deema."

Deema sat up attentively, all frivolity melting away.

"I was taken deep underground—under the palace—to wait out the storm."

She had hardly uttered the words, when Deema gasped and whispered, "My *sister.*"

"Yes. Your sister. Nona."

"You have seen her?" The girl learned forward eagerly.

"I have, and spoken with her."

"Is … is she well, lady?"

"As well as can be expected, dear." Poppy forgot her own problems as she noticed the pallor that crept over the girl's brown face. "Oh, she's fine. Not sick or anything," she added hastily. "And she gave me something beautiful for you. Something she made, but I'll have to go get it. It's up in the bedroom. And she asked me if you and all her family were well, especially Sil. I told her you were. I'll go get the gift she sent."

They all trouped back up to the bedroom, where Poppy opened a drawer and unwrapped the silver clasp from it's place where she had wound it up inside a scarf.

"This is what Nona does," she told Deema, whose hand trembled as she reached out for the piece of jewelry. "I am told she is extremely skilled at her work." She paused to let the girl hold it, to run a finger over it, then lift her hand to brush away her sudden tears. The others watched in silent commiseration.

"Nona was my attendant for two nights," Poppy continued. "She took very good care of me—better than I needed. She had dinner with us. Her warden—watcher, is a very kind man. And she asked about all of you. I guess I told you that."

"What … what is her life like?" Deema's wide dark eyes told Poppy that anything less than the truth would be obvious.

Poppy hesitated. "Well, of course it's dark down there. I mean, they have lights to work by, of course, but … well, there's no sunlight. But everyone is busy. Not hard work, just crafts like this. And they all seem quite … absorbed in their work." She looked around at the faces that showed no sign of cheering up. "I'm sure she'll still be well when she comes back to you."

Deema finally let out a loud sob, sniffed, took the handkerchief Cherry handed her, and blew her nose. "Our mother …" she blew her nose again. "Our mother is not well. She may never see Nona again." The girl then dissolved in tears. The others put their arms around her.

Poppy felt angry. Angrier, she thought, than she had ever felt in her life. "I'll tell you what, girls," she declared staunchly. "I start training tomorrow as a wise one. And I intend to try and change these laws about sending young people down there for having a good time! I kid you not. I swear, anything I can do ..."

The girls were all staring at her in alarm. "Poppy, no!" Cherry left Deema to rush over to her. Taking her in her arms, she whispered, "Hush. Please hush! I worry about you so. Be quiet now. We will speak of this to my father when he comes home. He will instruct us."

Yeah, like he's already instructed me, and I don't much care for his instructions. Poppy patted Cherry on the shoulder. "Okay, okay. Don't worry."

Whether the girls had intended to stay the night or not, Poppy didn't know. Deema was eager to show the clasp to her family and tell them it had come from Nona, so the two guests left immediately. Poppy and Cherry decided they were clean enough, and foregoing the bathing room, went down to help with the evening meal.

Throughout supper, Poppy avoided eye contact with Lorimar. He and Kandra spoke mainly of the 'righting' after the storm while she and Cherry ate quietly. But when she rose to help carry the dishes back to the kitchen, he was beside her. "We may talk now," he said. "Please come."

She followed him up the stairs to the now familiar anteroom to his study. There was a fire burning here tonight. The air, since the storm, had turned cooler, and the flickering light would have provided a cozy atmosphere were it not for the topic of conversation she knew was before them. Again Poppy chose the sofa and Lorimar seated himself in the chair facing her.

He came right to the point. "Have you an answer for me, Poppy?"

She looked into the fire for a minute. Finally, she faced him and said, "I ... I'm so confused, Lorimar. I mean, I'm not even ... of your *world*."

"You are here," he answered matter-of-factly. "And you must be kept safe. And honored as a guest and a wise one, obviously the correct office for you."

"I do want to be a wise one," she said, looking at him a bit dolefully. "But I hope you realize I'm not really all that wise. I don't have any of these *intuitive* talents you speak of. As for my safety, I still don't see why I can't just live here as part of your family, the way I've been doing. If I'm not here during the day, Pule can't come and take me off in his cart. And it isn't fair to you to have to marry me. You don't even know where I'm from and I can't tell you because I don't know how I got here from there."

"Poppy, it is the only way," he insisted quietly.

"Of course you know it's nothing personal or anything ..." she went on.

He sighed. "I know, I know. I am handsome and generous and exceptional in all ways." His smile was without humor. "And I apologize for forcing your hand in this matter, but I am certain that Pule will make an offer to you and we must do what we can to avoid it. After the offer has been made, it will be much more difficult to mend the situation."

"You mean … an offer of *marriage?*"

"Assuredly."

"You're *kidding!*"

He seemed to guess the meaning of her word. "I am completely serious. I have heard rumors, but even without gathered information, it is the most obvious of conclusions. Pule attempted to join with a Larian when he was but a boy, and he is now, as you may have noticed, of a generation before you, several years older than Vran. It would enhance his status greatly to join with you, and he is a very ambitious man. Now, since there have been no single Larian women in Halderwold in many years—you are prize game. His courting of you is not without determined purpose."

"Courting?" Poppy said weakly. It had seemed the creep had only been bent on getting information out of her. "The dancing, and the picnic yesterday—he's been *courting* me?"

"Yes, of course."

Poppy rose to her feet and stood staring into the fire for a few minutes while Lorimar sat wordlessly. Finally, she turned back to him. "It still doesn't make it fair that you should have to marry a woman … from nowhere."

That rueful smile again as he looked up at her. "And what of fairness to *you*, fair one? You are being careful not to speak of that."

Poppy came back to her chair. "And anyway," she began with new energy. "Is it written somewhere that I can't say '*no*' if Pule asks me to marry him?"

Lorimar gave her a pitying glance and shook his head. "It is not written, but all who know Pule would advise you not to reject him. It could bring dire consequences."

"You mean … he might have me … *killed?*"

Lorimar paused before he answered matter-of-factly. "He might. Or worse. But none could ever prove it his doing."

Poppy sighed deeply. "I see. And just when I was getting to like it here."

"I understand." Lorimar rose from his chair. "But it is your decision. I have advised you to the best of my ability, and … made my offer." He strode across the room and went out the door.

Oh, dear. I've insulted him. Poppy nearly jumped up and went after him, but what would she say except, 'Okay, I'll be happy to marry you.' But she couldn't.

She dropped her face into her hands. *There must be some other way out of this debacle.*

But she could think of none. After a wash-up and a tooth-brushing with one of the things that looked like tiny, stiff pastry brushes, Poppy went to bed. Cherry hadn't come up, and Poppy took advantage of the silence to try sorting out her feelings. Her thoughts seemed past being sorted, her mind completely flummoxed.

She would take a different tack. Lorimar, in his unquestionable wisdom, had stated succinctly, 'You are here.' Yes, she was here, and even though she dreamed constantly of being back home, what if it never happened? What if this was to be her life from now on? How did she feel about Lorimar? Well, she appreciated, admired and liked him. But no, she didn't really feel like marrying him.

But what if Pule did manage to trap her? Well, she just wouldn't let that happen. Like the women of past centuries on earth who married for security or status, or because that was the only avenue open, if it came down to it, she would definitely take the best alternative—and that would of course be Lorimar. And she did want to become a wise one. She couldn't hang around all day helping the maid, who didn't even need help, when she could be doing something interesting, and hopefully useful.

She sighed so loudly she was glad Cherry was not here to ask what the matter was. Then she brightened. Maybe if she just didn't answer Lorimar's 'offer,' he wouldn't mention it again. And maybe he was overly anxious about Pule; and if she kept busy and out of the duke's way, his interest in her would all blow over.

She tried to fall asleep, but, even with things sorted to some degree, and her immediate tack decided on, she still felt extremely unsettled. To bring a modicum of peace, she revisited the dreams of Aunt Holly looking down on her. Aunt Holly had been her main childhood caretaker and companion, had often put her to bed and told her funny stories, while her parents, just home from work, ate their late dinner.

Then she shifted to her mother—her mom, the busy dentist. Once again, she was sitting in the dentist chair, enjoying every minute of it. Like no other kid she'd known, she had loved her dental checkups. Those were the only times she'd felt her mother's full attention. Her mom never hurt her. She had kept her teeth strong and white and perfect, something she appreciated much more since she'd become a young lady. She could still hear her mom murmuring as she worked, "Yes. Good. Very good. You're a good girl, Paige. You haven't ruined your teeth with candy or soda. You've been brushing and flossing, I can tell. Now, what is that? Oh, just something you missed this morning, young lady. Take more time when you brush tonight. You have to get in there under the gum, sweetie."

Then suddenly, she saw her mom really looking down on her, more worried than she had ever looked about her teeth. Poppy bolted upright, awake in the dim lamp light from the corner. *Just another one of those dreams.* But so real, just like the ones about Aunt Holly, though she had probably brought this one on by her concentration. She was rubbing her face with her hands when Cherry came in.

"Are you unwell, Poppy?"

"I'm fine." Poppy lay down and pulled the covers up to her chin. "I'm just having a little trouble getting to sleep."

"I will put the light out," the girl said. "As soon as I undress."

"No problem," Poppy muttered pulling the sheet up over her face.

Cherry was soon in the other bed, and Poppy was feigning sleep, when Cherry murmured softly, "I know about your dilemma."

What did she know? "What dilemma?"

"Your problem with the Duke Pule and my father's offer of marriage. I have known about that for some time."

How could she have known about it for some time when it only happened today?

As if replying to Poppy's unasked question, Cherry continued, "Father tells me the things I need to know, particularly now, since I am an adult, but even before, when my passage was approaching."

"That's nice." Poppy didn't really know what to say. She wanted to burrow deeper under the covers and be left alone. Her reluctance to marry the girl's father might be taken by her as lack of appreciation, and they had been such good friends up until now.

"I merely wish to tell you how I feel," Cherry said; then, without waiting for a reply, she continued, "My mother, Isanda, a beautiful Halderwoldian not much older than I am now—I have been told—died a short time after I was born. I never knew her, nor of course have I seen any likeness of her, but I have been content and well cared for by my father and grandmother."

Poppy uncovered her head, waiting for the girl's conclusion.

"You have been a good friend to me, Poppy, and I would be more than proud to call you 'Mother.'"

"Thank you, dear," was all Poppy could say. She sniffed back sudden, unexpected tears, burrowed back under the covers and waited for sleep.

In the morning, upon Lorimar's rather stiff invitation, Poppy quietly prepared to accompany him. They took a cart up the hill, and she looked around in surprise when they passed the Wise House. "Aren't we heading there?" She inclined her head toward the tall structure as she looked directly at him for the first time since their journey had begun.

"Later," he replied. "First, your education in our laws must continue." He looked at her too, with a seriousness that made something tighten up inside. "As you have probably guessed, my purpose in taking you to Hesh was not only shelter from the storm."

"Well, I've heard that storm wasn't all that severe, but you couldn't have known beforehand?"

"No."

"And yes," she continued. "Naturally, I figured you wanted to show me the consequences of 'undue jocularity.' Well, I sure got it. An explanation couldn't have been half as effective as an actual tour of that … underworld. I guess I should thank you."

"No need. It is a necessary part of your training."

She was relieved that her training hadn't been put on hold until she accepted or rejected his proposal; and, even though she had now decided to accept, if pressed, she would wait until she absolutely had to.

"It's so beautiful," she said, looking around. They were finally traveling over the higher land, through the grainfields and vineyards that he had mentioned.

"Yes," he answered, with a sigh so intense she wondered if his low mood was solely from her hesitation to become his wife. Why he should be depressed over her, she couldn't quite understand. After all, he had made it pretty clear that his main reason for proposing was concern for her safety, and not because of any deep feelings for her. Though looking up at the topmost balcony of the Wise House as they passed had brought back the memory of his near embrace on that first visit. He must have felt some attraction to her from the beginning.

The clatter of hooves slowed and the driver reigned the horse into a turn down a narrow lane heading into the woods. Feeling too stubborn to ask her nearly silent companion, Poppy craned her neck to see anything that would indicate where they might be heading. She saw nothing but trees for at least a couple of miles, then they came into a clearing. It was more than a clearing. It was a large, completely flat area with a huge, very plain one-story stone building at the center. She could contain her curiosity no longer. "What is it?"

"You will see." He still sounded low in spirits as he gathered his cloak to climb down from the cart. He handed her down as politely as ever, offering his arm before they set off toward an entry in the low structure. He was greeted smartly by two guards in the doorway, who quickly stepped aside to let them enter. Their steps were the only sound echoing along the first couple of corridors. It was almost like the passageways under the palace, although these were on ground level.

Finally, they arrived at a large kitchen where half a dozen people were preparing food. A man with the demeanor of a head chef approached and greeted them cheerfully with the usual small bow, "An honor, Wise Lorimar."

"Likewise," Lorimar replied with a nod. He turned to Poppy. "Lady Poppy, this is Bram, the kitchen overseer."

Bram bowed again. "An honor, lady. We have heard of you."

"Nice to meet you, Bram." Poppy tried to imitate the nod that Lorimar executed so gracefully." Then she glanced at Lorimar, hoping for some explanation.

Instead of returning her glance, Lorimar addressed Bram again, "But you are busy. We will not take up your time."

Bram simply bowed again and turned back to his workers, who stood staring at the visitors, waving a hand to set them back to their tasks. With no explanation, Lorimar led Poppy out of the kitchen and down another empty corridor. She looked for a dining room near the kitchen, but there was none that she could see except a small room with about six medium sized tables, and the few who were sitting there drinking something wore guards' uniforms.

"This way," Lorimar turned another dimly-lit corner. There was nothing along the way but some small sleeping rooms—they couldn't even be called bedrooms—they were so simple.

Poppy was growing exasperated. "Okay, I give up. Who lives here?"

"Just the guards," he answered.

She stopped, letting go of his arm. "What is this, a labyrinth? What is it for? Lorimar, I've had just about enough *mystery theater* for today."

He stopped and turned to face her. "It is a prison," he said flatly.

"A ... where are the cells? Those rooms we just passed had the doors open. And that was an awfully small dining room. For that many cooks, there should be hundreds of inmates ..."

"Only the guards live here," he told her soberly. "The errant ones live below."

Her heart plunged like a sinking rock. "Oh God, no. Not another dungeon!"

Lorimar nodded.

"Well, who have they got locked up here? Mothers who let their babies gurgle?" She immediately thought better of her sarcasm and gave him an apologetic look. "The older prisoners?"

"Many of these are ones who already paid their time in the workshops beneath the palace, and were still unable or unwilling to stabilize themselves after being set free. So they are sent here for life."

Poppy was speechless, her throat swelling larger than she could swallow it down. After a moment, she was able to ask weakly, "You mean these people were still … jocular *after* they got out of that sweatshop under the palace?"

"Some are weak and unable to comply with the laws," he replied. "But some are simply … unwilling." He looked wistfully down the corridor. "Experiences may alter a prisoner's very *desire* to comply."

She thought a moment. "You mean they get rebellious."

"You are perceptive. That would describe a certain unfortunate state of mind."

"That happens," Poppy said quietly. "Even in my world." The last was whispered. She thought of Nona and her hope of reuniting with her family after six more years. But that girl would be able to handle it—she didn't have a rebellious bone in her body.

Poppy had realized by now that her visit to that underworld had suspended her natural tendency to think in comic terms. In fact, that visit, seeing what Cherry and her friends had gone through, plus the dilemma of Lorimar's proposal, with the addition of Pule to the mix, had probably wrecked her sense of humor for life. *And, under the circumstances, that can only be considered a blessing.* But she didn't feel blessed. She felt desperate. Not for herself alone, but for all the citizens of Halderwold, especially those young denizens of the darkness far beneath the brilliant skies and flowering fields.

They continued walking, passed a couple of guards leaning against a wall. "Lice? Good for them," one was saying. "Keeps them busy."

With a shudder, Poppy forced her mind back to the business at hand. Much as she didn't want to deal with it, she could never hope to work for change unless she knew all about these present laws and punishments. "And where are the real criminals? I mean people who steal or murder or …"

"The transgressors of the age-old laws are here also," Lorimar explained. "Not in such benevolent charge as Hesh's. Those are only the young ones who fail to manage themselves after their passage."

"And is this the next punishment after the prison under the palace? The kids who fall back into ... *jocularity* get thrown in here with thieves and murderers?"

Lorimar nodded. "This is the final incarceration."

"Doesn't anyone get a *third* chance?" Poppy managed to keep her voice low, though she was screaming inside. Don't they ever get a review for parole?"

"All those convicted, except those you call 'the real criminals,' are allowed a choice. They may come here ... or be exiled to the swamp."

Poppy thought for a moment. "But why do they have to go to the swamp? Why couldn't they just take some other direction?"

He looked at her almost in pity. "The River Halder, which flows from the mountains, sustains our land. From the river and its tributaries, we irrigate the fields when rainfall in insufficient. The forest, which nearly surrounds Halderwold, is backed by the mountains in part, the rest is bordered by the sea. The mountains are impassable, full of steep cliffs and low, narrow rivers, except for the River Dystopia, which runs to the sea through a distant part of the forest, a misty, untraversable area. To say nothing of predatory animals. So only the flatland swamp is left." His voice trailed off.

"Can't they live in the forest—toward this side, where the passage children spent the night?"

He shook his head. "Once exiled, one must not linger. Even if one were to survive there, they would eventually be found and brought back."

"Well, what about Laria. Why can't they go there? And why don't the Larians come here anymore?"

Lorimar stopped walking to explain. "To travel to Laria, or from Laria to Halderwold, one must pass through the swamp. In the old days, there were wayfarer's shelters, tended by those who chose a near hermit existence. The trip was nevertheless a grueling journey, as I remember from my childhood. Since no Larians have come here in many years, it is assumed that the swamp is now either uninhabitable, or peopled by convicts from Halderwold, who may be living a desperate existence, if indeed any live at all. Very few desire to make the journey there to find out exactly what kind of place it has become."

"And those who have gone?"

He began walking again. "None have returned."

Poppy heaved a sigh. "Well, what do they make—these people below here?"

"Nothing."

"Nothing? What do they do?"

"They are given nothing to do," he replied in a monotone, resuming his stride. "Nothing to read. They are allowed very little light."

Poppy was speechless for several moments. Finally she asked in a small voice, "And they choose *this* over taking their chances in the swamp?"

"Some choose the swamp," was the reply. "But most choose to remain with companions of their own kind. Here they are at least housed and fed."

"Yes, they sure are *housed*." *The devil you know is better than the devil you don't know.*

Poppy had no more questions, except, "Will this be my only lesson for today? I ... don't think I could handle any more. And ... we're not going *down there*, are we?"

Lorimar shook his head, and offered his arm. She took it and went meekly back to the waiting cart, trying not to think about that overheard remark about lice.

On the ride back, she asked just how much the girls knew about the punishments for jocularity, and he explained that part of their passage night in the forest was passed in instruction in the finer legalities. Young children were of course taught the importance of good behavior as they grew up, were allowed to follow their natural inclinations to a certain extent, except that they must not carry on any silliness in public. But it was presented as a matter of good manners so as not to frighten them into 'unsoundness' or 'melancholia.' It was up to the adults caring for the children to keep them safe.

"That was the error in your entertaining the children on the street the night you came to us," he explained. "Your transgression, according to our law, is called 'inciting to merriment.'"

"I figured it was something like that," she replied sourly. "After I came to an understanding of the ... customs. What I can't understand is why you people are allowed to drink. Doesn't that effect some 'inciting'?"

"Indeed it can," Lorimar agreed. "There are more than a few beneath us who have been unfit for 'circumspect imbibing.' However, the first offence is treated with leniency, a month's work without pay. After the second, the subject is thereafter forbidden to drink wine at all. After the third ..."

"Pule drank enough on that picnic to intoxicate the whole town."

"Pule is Pule." He sounded as if he were speaking through clenched teeth.

CHAPTER 13

The rest of her day was spent familiarizing herself with the organization of the Wise House. It was hard to keep her mind on it.

Later, in the bath with the girls, Poppy had little to add to the conversation. She came out of her blue funk to realize the girls were splashing her.

"You are entranced, lady," Kellith said. "Wake up before you sink and drown."

The girls no longer giggled in the bath. Even though this lower area had no windows, prudence was the rule now, except in the storm room. When they climbed out of the water and put on wraps, Cherry told her, "Kandra has made you a new dress. Will you wear it to supper?"

"Of course," Poppy replied absently. "I'd be honored."

"Then come and see it." Cherry ran ahead of the others. When they reached the second floor, she called back, "Grandmother was sewing in my father's study. There is so much light there. I believe she left it in there."

The others followed her into the anteroom, then beyond, into the room with the many windows and telescopes. Poppy had seen no clothing in either room. She was following Deema toward the end of the room where the bookcases lined the wall, when she felt a sharp tug on her wrap. As she turned around, it was yanked completely off and the girls were making for the door, Cherry with her towel.

"What the *hell*?" she sputtered, starting after them, but they fled through the heavy door to the anteroom and slammed it shut. And she was unable to push it open. Confused and frustrated, she looked around for something to put on. What if Lorimar decided to come up here and check out a couple of stars before supper? Had these girls taken leave of their senses? Was this what that stupid *passage* had done to them? If this was some new way of having fun—letting loose without actually laughing, well, she didn't see any humor in it. They were supposed to be her friends.

There was nothing made of cloth in the whole room except some of the book bindings. Everything was wood, paper or metal. She backed up against the bookshelves, as far from the windows as possible, even though she was on the third floor of the house.

She was cold and angry when she finally heard them coming back. That dress would feel good, no matter what it looked like. She'd better stifle her temper until she had it on, she told herself, in case these addled teenagers decided to continue the fun by keeping it from her for a while. She moved eagerly toward the door as it opened.

And Lorimar entered.

Her first impulse was to cover her private areas with her hands, but caught herself before doing anything so childish. There was nowhere to go, nothing to get behind—but her pride as a mature woman would not allow her to act like a *demure damsel.* There was nothing to do but face him, and explain.

I don't know what in hell's come over your daughter! She ran off with my towel and left me here! It was a moment before she realized that none of the words had come out of her mouth. She was standing there as tongue-tied as the *damsel* she wouldn't allow herself to be.

More shocking still, Lorimar took a step toward her, gasped, "You are *beautiful*, Poppy," and went down on his knees! Reaching for and grasping her hand, he brought it against his lips and held it there for a long moment, his eyes closed.

She waited, too bewildered to pull her hand away. *At least he's not* looking *at me right now, and anyway it's not the* first *time.* There was no forgetting that episode in the bath. But there she'd had the water to hunker down into. Her tremendous shiver seemed to bring him back to his senses. He let go of her hand and rose to his feet, then turned immediately and went out the door.

What in the name of sanity was that all about? Puzzlement had taken over her mind when the girls appeared in the doorway, Cherry in the lead, and walked toward her with a rose-colored dress over her arm and a serious look on her face.

Deema stepped in front of Cherry, holding up a white garment. "May I help you with your shift, lady?"

Much as she tried to control it, Poppy's voice came out an angry croak. "Yes, you certainly may!" She held up her arms to allow the girl to pull the garment down over the body.

Then Cherry stepped forward with the rose-colored dress. "Grandmother hopes you will like this," she said as if nothing were amiss.

Again, Poppy slid her arms into the welcome material, this time without a reply. Just to be clothed—nothing else mattered until that was accomplished.

Kellith had brought sandals. With a "May I, lady?" the girl knelt to put them on her feet.

Poppy pushed her feet into the sandals wordlessly, not wanting to hear her own strange, croaky voice again. The sandals on, she swept past the girls, out the door, through the anteroom (Lorimar was nowhere in sight) and down the stairs to the supper table. By then she was fully realizing how completely dependent she was on this family; much as she had every right to, it wouldn't be in her own best interest to quarrel or sulk. She sat down and tried to act normal.

But even Kandra was acting strangely. Sitting at the table, the older woman's face was extremely pink, and her expression—almost beatific. Had she been indulging in the precious vigorwort that she doled out so stingily to others? Lorimar came to the table shining as if he had just scrubbed his face and wet his hair. Cherry came in quietly, almost shyly—the others still with her. They all took places at the table. After a cursory glance, Poppy ignored them all, except to remark stiffly to Kandra, "The dress fits very well. Thank you for making it for me."

"It was my pleasure." Kandra half-bowed and handed her the first serving of the choicest dish, something that seemed to be chicken in pink cheese sauce. "I will set about immediately making another, more ornamental one."

Poppy had no time to try and figure out what her hostess was talking about. Everyone at the table was offering her the various dishes before they had taken any themselves, probably to make up for that heartless prank upstairs. There were at least three times as many dishes as at their usual supper table. Kandra must be still trying to use up the leftover passage food.

She accepted them all, piled her plate high and stuffed her mouth, so she wouldn't have to talk. After what the girls had done, she didn't wonder that they were trying to be nice; but that didn't account for the glow they all seemed to exude—even Deema and Kellith. As if it were some joyous occasion. Did rotten tricks take the place of jokes for these people? If they did, well, that was really sick. And if they thought good treatment at the table would make up for such humiliating abuse, they were sorely mistaken; she had no intention of becoming the regular butt of their jaded humor. Yet there was clearly nothing she could do about it except demonstrate by her coolness how upset she was.

After supper, Poppy rose and began gathering up the dishes. Malina always disappeared as soon as the meal was prepared.

"No, no." Kandra pushed her hand so hard she almost dropped the bowls she had gathered. "Not tonight. You must rest."

Poppy shrugged. The girls were picking up dishes from the table; surely the four of them could handle it, and she was just as happy to get away. But Kandra stopped her on her way toward the stairs with a smile and the remark, "We are all so immensely pleased."

Completely bewildered, but not wanting to go to the bedroom in case the girls should come up, Poppy headed back to the anteroom of Lorimar's study and sank down on the sofa, wishing she could read the books on his shelves. Learning to read was something she looked forward to eagerly—it would open up a whole new avenue for passing the time. Especially if she weren't talking to the other people in the house.

She had never been one for watching a lot of television, but it would be a welcome diversion right now as she sat alone, forlorn and vexed by her host family's treatment. All the excitement of preparations for the passage had kept everyone busy since her arrival here, but now she wondered how these people got through the long evenings. If they even wanted to indulge in light conversation, they must have to shut themselves in the storm room in case someone inadvertently came out with something amusing.

Settling back on the cushions, she tried figuring out the logic behind the events and comments of the past two hours, but it was hopeless. First the girls act completely out of character—they had been so kind to her up until now. And Lorimar, after his shocking demonstration in the bathing room the other day, behaves like a neurotic virgin teenager on seeing her naked! And Kandra gazes at her all through supper as if she were an ikon to be worshiped, promising her an 'ornamental dress.' What was it all about?

"Aunt Holly, help me." She heard own voice as if in supplication, burying her face in her hands.

Lorimar didn't come into his study all evening, and Poppy finally settled down, glad of the privacy. She was not going to sleep with those girls tonight. Why had she never asked for her own bedroom? There must be considerable unused space in this house. Even if the custom here required a guest to share your bedchamber, probably if she asked …

Daylight found her under a warm throw spread over her by unseen hands, but ambivalent to the day ahead. On one hand, she was eager to continue her wise training—surely she had been shown the worst of the Halderwold legal system; on the other, she dreaded being with Lorimar, both admiring him and wanting to hide from him. Pulling herself together, as usual, she smoothed out her new dress as best she could and went to breach of fast. Lorimar appeared in the dining room before she had finished.

"We must continue with your training," was all he said.

"I'm ready." She jumped up from her chair, drained the last of her coffee, set the cup down and reached for her cape. A plain dark blue one Cherry had given her.

Settled in the cart with Lorimar, she prepared herself to be 'all business.' After all, she was training for one of the most respected jobs in town, and Lorimar was acting quite normal; she was grateful for that.

"Well," she began, drawing in a breath and letting it out as if some laborious task had been finished. "I guess we'll be getting on to some nitty-gritty today."

He gave her that 'foreign language' glance.

"That just means the basic information," she explained. "Stuff I'll be needing to know to learn my job."

"We are not yet ready for *nitty-gritty*," he said. "But we will spend the day at the Wise House."

"Good." *No more dungeons, please and thank you.*

When he offered no further information, she asked, "Will I begin learning to read?"

"Not today. Your have more to understand of our system. In order to behave appropriately."

Talk about behaving inappropriately! And it hasn't been me. *Except for a few uncalled for remarks ...* But that was all over now. She didn't even feel the urge to joke anymore. The well of wit was dry—and who was she becoming? *Someone who might survive here.*

She soon learned that Lorimar was not insulting her personal behavior. On their arrival at the ground floor of the Wise House, Poppy was eager to look in on the children's classes, to see if their version of a schoolroom had any resemblance to those in which she had spent so many hours both as pupil and teacher.

But, looking at her sternly, Lorimar said, "Our tour of this structure is unfinished. And now, I grieve to say, we must complete your familiarity with the place where you will be spending most of your time from now on."

He grieves *to say?* A sick feeling started at the bottom of her stomach and shot up into her throat. Stifling the many questions that began forming in her mind, she said, "I thought we went through every floor, right up to the roof."

He looked like a man who was about to break the news of the death of a relative. "But we have not gone *under* the building."

Poppy's head dropped into her hands. "Oh, God, no. Not another *dungeon!*"

"Not exactly," he hedged. "But come. It must be dealt with. This is your duty now. Or as you say, your *job.*"

She filled her chest with air. "Yes, it's my job. And I intend to do it. But what more can there be to incarcerate a person for? We've already covered jocularity and multiple offences, along with the old run-of-the-mill crimes like theft and murder."

"This is not a prison," he told her. "It is a safe house. A place where confounded ones are sheltered from storms and ridicule and harm. Our system includes compassionate care-taking as well as punishment."

"Well, I'm glad to hear *that.*" Poppy drew herself up as if she were literally 'pulling herself together.' "Just tell me, Lorimar. After this, will I begin learning—like how to read your books and see what you look at through the telescopes and stuff like that?"

He almost smiled. "Straightaway."

"Okay, then. Lead the way, *nashu.*"

He took her hand and headed down a nearby staircase. The first floor beneath ground level seemed to be all storage rooms. "Safe from the storms," he told her as she was led in and out of many rooms full of books, crocks of food and all kinds of manufactured goods—materials, dishes and tools. She was intrigued by a back room containing a couple of very dusty antique printing presses and asked why they were not being used. The books she had glanced inside seemed to have all been laboriously printed by hand.

"The press has not been *forbidden,*" he told her. "So they did not have to be destroyed. But to avoid tempting the young to begin some dangerous dissemination of ideas, they have been abandoned for the time being."

"And that time being has been six generations?"

He nodded. "Nearly."

"The underground press," she muttered.

Lorimar appeared to ignore her remark.

"What do you make paper out of?" she wondered out loud.

What people wrote on had always been one of her trivia fascinations. From stone to clay tablets to the ancient papyrus made from reeds. From the drawings on birch bark and skins by the Native Americans, to the linen paper of the Europeans, to the paper made from pulpwood of modern times. It was just one of those things that popped into her mind.

"There is a paper mill beyond the vineyards," he told her. "On the river, out toward the forest. We use candic, a soft wood that splinters easily, and so the workers must be well-trained. Now we will concentrate on the activities within the house."

But this tour of supplies was cursory. She was whisked in and out of what seemed like dozens of large rooms. Finally, they were descending another wide stairway, and the next corridor was dim and quiet. Poppy dreaded arriving at their destination. This had to be an insane asylum. The *confounded* ones, he had said. No prison, but a place of care-taking. *Yeah, but he called Hesh's domain a 'workshop.'*

"Again, we will begin in the kitchen." Lorimar placed his hand lightly on the small of her back to guide her along a narrow, dimly lit hallway. She almost stiffened at his touch, but reminded herself to concentrate on the business at hand.

This kitchen, when they arrived, was very much like the one they had visited yesterday, except that the aromas were much more appealing. "Do they serve the same food in all these … places of detainment?" She asked.

"Not exactly," was Lorimar's again hesitant reply. "The young people in Hesh's charge are fed quite well. After all, they are young and expected to return to their lives and have families. (She realized she hadn't been shown the kitchen or dining area in Hesh's prison, and she welcomed this information.) The food here is prepared with a calming effect in mind; and the food in the prison we visited yesterday …" He rubbed his thumb up and down the middle of his forehead. "Well, those people will have no future among us, so they are fed … not the choicest of our produce." He looked apologetic at Poppy's expression of disgust.

"Also," Lorimar continued. "The people in the terminal prison have no dining room. The workers in the kitchen never go down where they live."

"How do they serve the food?"

"It is lowered through an opening in the floor, by a system of ropes and a moving shelf."

"Don't any of those prisoners ever try to ride back up on that dumb waiter ... shelf?" she asked in an acerbic tone.

"It has been attempted," he replied briefly. "To no avail."

Again, Lorimar was greeted warmly and respectfully by the chef, who was introduced to Poppy as Vandar. "So you are the Larian who has made her way to our city," he said pleasantly with the customary small bow and hand gesture. "What an honor to meet you, lady."

"Lady Poppy will be here in the Wise House daily," Lorimar told him. And will give you a list of her favorite foods. She begins her training today."

"Oh, upon your own time, lady." The chef bowed again. "I and all the kitchen staff will do our best to prepare meals appealing to your taste."

Poppy glanced at Lorimar. "It'll just be lun ... the mid-day meal here, won't it? We'll still go home for supper?"

"Of course. But Vandar enjoys providing us with a mid-day meal conducive to another half day of mental labor."

"Oh. Well, that works for me." Poppy gave the chef a friendly smile, which he and his surrounding workers returned with a round of bowing.

Poppy was eager to get to the business at hand, and get it over with. She gave Lorimar what she hoped was a nudging look. He responded by taking his leave of Vandar and leading the way back into the corridor and along an empty stretch where once again the only sound was the echo of their footsteps. Guards stood silent at intervals along the way.

Soon, she began to hear sounds. Weird, blood-chilling sounds. Sounds of hopeless weeping, humorless out-of-control laughter, even horrified screams. She grasped Lorimar's arm and pulled to slow him down.

He looked at her with sympathy. "It must be faced," he said gently. "I am sorry." And pulled her along until the noise became nearly deafening, even through a heavy wooden door they were passing.

"We ... we're not ... going in there, are we?" she asked him.

"Only where I know we will be safe," he replied. "You must trust me."

She tried, hanging on to his arm with taught knuckles. They stopped before a door that emitted no great noise and a guard came immediately to unlock it for them. "How is Arn today?" Lorimar asked him.

"The same, sir," was the short reply.

"And Cresda?"

"She seems well. Unchanged." The guard unbolted the door.

With a nod, Lorimar pushed the heavy door open and stepped slowly inside. Poppy followed him but paused, chilled by a peal of berserk laughter that erupted from a woman seated alone in the corner who, with her head thrown back, continued to laugh wildly until Lorimar approached her and said, "Cresda, it is Lorimar, and this is Poppy. We have come to visit you."

Then turning to Poppy, he motioned her forward. She came on reluctant legs, suddenly struck by the irony of after years of making part of her living emulating the daft, to be now, for the first time, actually meeting them. And it wasn't the least bit funny.

"How … are you, Cresda?" She said shyly. The woman lifted a shaky hand to brush back a mop of wild, white hair and looked at her, then threw her head back and went into another peal of horrible laughter. Lorimar stood by her, placing his hand on her shoulder. "Quiet, lady," he urged gently. "You have guests. Look at us. We have come to see you."

The woman stopped laughing and used both hands to put back her hair. "Come closer, girl," she said in a gravelly voice. "Do I know you?"

Reluctantly, Poppy drew near, then saw that the old woman was looking at her with large, blue eyes. *Is this what eventually happens to outsiders when they are forced to stay in this land?*

But Cresda had noticed her eyes too. "From Laria!" she gasped. "How came you, girl? When?"

"Just recently," Lorimar answered for her. "But she cannot go back. There is still no going back, Cresda."

The woman dropped her head and, after a moment of quiet, threw it back in another, even more chilling burst of humor. "No way back!" She shrieked. "No way out!"

"We had best leave her alone." Lorimar spoke into Poppy's ear. He then took her arm and guided her toward another part of the room.

Poppy stopped him before they could approach anyone else. "How can she laugh like that," she asked, "and not be put into that … other prison?"

"The confounded ones may laugh down here," he answered simply. "She did no breach of the law while amongst the Halderwoldians, and therefore was not accused of criminal jocularity. And besides," he added dryly. "Cresda was prominent among the wise ones—in her day."

A chill that crept down her spine kept Poppy from asking anything further. Her attention was immediately taken by the old man they were approaching, withered and thin with a shock of beautiful white hair falling over his brow.

"And how are you today, Arn?" Lorimar asked gently.

Arn didn't flick an eyebrow. He sat as still as before, staring before him. Poppy stepped up beside Lorimar. The old man's dull eyes rested vacantly on her, then suddenly sparked to life, and a trembling hand reached out to her. "*Marion!*" he cried in a cracked voice. "Marion. You've *come back* for me. At last. At *last!*"

Nearly in panic, Poppy looked to Lorimar for guidance. Should she encourage this poor man in his delusion, or just back away? Lorimar motioned her forward. She stepped closer and took the dry hand in hers, forcing herself to look into the dark pools that were his eyes. "How have you been, Arn?" she asked in as normal a voice as she could manage.

"Oh, Marion." The old man grasped her hand with strength belying his appearance. "My darling, I have never given up hope. I have never forgotten the wonderful times we had in … that place. The beautiful place full of music—laughter. Oh, Marion, you have come. I would know you anywhere by your bright hair. And it is even lovelier now. You have let it grow so long."

Her hand still in Arn's surprisingly strong grasp, Poppy looked helplessly at Lorimar.

"He has not spoken," Lorimar whispered. "For nearly ten years. Nor seemed to recognize anyone, though I have continued to speak to him each time I come down here."

"You're a good therapist," Poppy said, realizing from his glance that he had no idea what the word meant. She remembered that Cherry had told her when they first met that Kandra was a *mender*. "A good mender," she corrected herself.

Lorimar nodded, then turned back to Arn. "How long have you waited for Marion, Arn?"

"Oh, a long time," the old man muttered. "So long. Since I was a young man. Remember how young we were, Marion?" He squeezed her hand so tightly she fought the urge to drag it from his grasp. "Losvaygos," he rasped, looking deep into her eyes. "That was the place. The place that was like … the abode of the Unbounded One."

"Settle down." Lorimar's command was firm but gentle, as he removed the old man's hand from Poppy's. "Everything is all right now, Arn. Marion is going to stay here with us. You will see her again."

"Soon?"

The one word, in his cracked, old voice expressed such desperation Poppy wanted to cry. "Yes, I'll come back soon, Arn. I'll visit you. Don't … don't give up hope."

"I never gave up hope, my darling. Now you are back and you will take me away with you, and we will never come back here." He was gasping for breath.

"Rest, Arn." Said Lorimar. "You will see Marion again. But we must go now."

His dark eyes followed Poppy as she turned away. "Losveygos," she heard him mutter as she walked away.

"Can we go back up now?" She cast Lorimar what she hoped was a pleading look. Surely they were not going to visit all the people sitting around this large room.

"Yes. It is enough for today." He offered his arm, which she took, trying not to look at the others faces, singing, crying, laughing, or just staring.

Back on the first floor, she got a detailed tour of the areas where she would be spending most of her time, though it was obvious to her that he was finding it as difficult as she was to concentrate on the more routine tasks to be taken on.

At noon, at one of the polished tables among the bookshelves, their meal was served. It was a nice atmosphere, redolent of Poppy's favorite bookstore/coffee shop back home. But her appetite wouldn't kick in. She attempted to pick at the food, but gave up when she noticed Lorimar staring straight ahead, holding an uneaten roll in his hand as if he didn't even know it was there.

Keeping her voice low, not to be overheard by those at the other tables (men and women also in training, scribes, and some who worked in the Wise House as teachers and craft instructors), she sidled toward him. "That man … Arn?"

"Yes?" Even as he replied, his look was vacant.

"You know, Marion is a common name in … my world."

His attention now riveted on her, she added. "And they went to Las Vegas. *That's what he was saying!* It's a city of entertainment—and it *is* full of music and laughter. All the time. Lorimar, Arn has been to earth."

"I realize that," was his quiet reply.

"That's … the name of my … planet." She wondered if he actually knew what she was saying.

He did. "Cherry told me your name for Lara some time ago. And we—particularly you—will have more conversations with Arn."

Poppy nodded. *I certainly will. Maybe he can tell me how to get home.*

"And … I wish you to know," Lorimar continued. He dropped his hands from the table and looked at her with pain in his eyes. "Cresda is my mother."

Her hand went instinctively to his arm. "Oh, Lorimar."

"One thing more. Cherry thinks her grandmother is dead. I … thought it would be easier for her." He took a deep breath and looked back at his plate. "We must eat. There is much more work to be done today."

The rest of the work day was easy compared with the first few hours. Going over class schedules and, except for learning to read, what she considered graduate studies in wise training, though she was told very little of what would actually be studied since only those enrolled in the courses became familiar with the subject matter.

It was dark when they rode home, and Poppy was not prepared for Kandra's announcement that she'd had 'a visitor this morning.'

"Who …" Poppy began. With all the pressure of the day, she had nearly forgotten about the duke. But he had not forgotten her. He had arrived a mere half hour after she'd left, in his overly decorated, canopied cart, Kandra related, prepared to take her on another outing.

Dropping onto the cushions of a basket weave chair, Poppy sighed. "Well, I hope he realizes I'm *busy* from now on."

"It will not be that simple," Lorimar began, but Kandra, uncharacteristically, and with a dismissive wave of both hands, interrupted him. "Oh, I told him. I told him of the joining. He should not come here again."

Lorimar glanced down at Poppy. Uneasily, she thought.

"The … what?" she asked Kandra, who stood, again uncharacteristically, in a self-possessed posture, her hands on her hips and a smile on her face.

"The joining," she repeated cheerfully. "And I must show you your gown, Poppy. I have worked all day on it." Then, restrained by Lorimar's hand on her arm, and his gentle, "Not now, Mother. We are both tired and hungry," she turned from Poppy to look up at him. "Oh, then I'll bring the food," she said, and, taking on a more accommodating manner, briskly left the room.

Almost immediately, Cherry came in with a steaming stew and placed the dish in the middle of the table, already set with those blue earthernware—or *laraware*—bowls that Poppy liked, and Kandra brought something like a cross between pita bread and scones. Their drink was grape-flavored tea, and the conversation at the table was scant, Kandra and Cherry glancing up from their meal as if uncertain what to say, Lorimar serious, nearly sullen.

Only Poppy, feeling, at least for now, out of Pule's reach, glad that the worst part of her introduction to wise training had to be over, and excited by the hope of making contract with earth through some information that might be gleaned from Arn, indulged her hunger.

After the meal, Lorimar went upstairs, presumably to his study. Cherry invited Poppy to her bedroom as if the bizarre events of the previous night had never happened, and Poppy was too weary to choose tonight to ask for another sleeping arrangement.

Cherry was quiet tonight. She wanted to hear what it was like to begin wise training. Poppy wondered how much she should tell her, everything here seemed so secret, but Lorimar had given her no precautions. Cherry already knew of the young people's prison, but how much she had been told of the criminal's dungeon or the insane asylum, Poppy had no idea. So she spoke of her bewilderment at all she would be required to learn, beginning with no understanding of the script in the books.

"I can read the books," Cherry's voice came from her bed with a new tone of sulky yearning. "But I will never be allowed to learn the things you will be taught."

"Why not?" Poppy asked. "Your father is a wise one. You're half Larian. Why can't you be a wise one, Cherry?"

Cherry snorted as if her companion were a five-year-old. "My ancestry does not preclude me," she said with a hint of condescension. "Halderwold had wise ones before the Larians ever came here, but because those from Laria demonstrated greater *knowing* than we, they became highly esteemed and most often chosen for the Wise House. We can still become wise ones, but I was examined years ago, and I possess none of the proclivities of my father or his mother. Had I inherited Larian ways of knowing, I would have been allowed to attempt the training." She sighed. "But I did not."

"Well, that stinks," Poppy said. "I should think they could train you to help in some way. There are many different jobs at the Wise house—scribes, teachers. Heaven knows I don't have ..." She stopped short of saying she had no intuitive talents, since it was assumed by most people that she had these abilities simply because she was Larian. Of course Cherry must know by now that she wasn't, though she had never mentioned it. So the girl certainly couldn't be blamed for a little resentment.

Could this attitude have been the secret ingredient in Cherry's deviant behavior of last evening? Poppy realized she had been so concentrated on her own needs, which were many: becoming a wise one in the hope of making a difference in the present system, learning anything that might lead to getting home again, steering clear of 'Pule the Poison,' as she had begun to think of him, that she had probably not given her friend the support she must need in her radical life change.

"I could sure use your help in learning to read," she told Cherry. "It's as if I'm a little kid just starting with this stuff."

"Oh, I would be most happy to help you." Cherry's voice resumed a touch of her old cheerfulness.

"Then I'll count on you," Poppy yawned. And sleep soon claimed them both.

CHAPTER 14

Poppy awoke early, eager to continue her new schooling. Surely she had already seen the bottom of the barrel. *The pits.* Lorimar's hitting her with the prison system right off the bat had created in her a profound sense of mission; she had seen the worst elements of the government she would be working for and trying to improve. And he hadn't said a word all day yesterday about getting married. What a relief to think *that* had blown over! She dressed and went downstairs without waiting for Cherry to wake up. The best plan, until Pule got it through his messed-up head that she was unavailable for day-long rambles and gazebo extravaganzas, was to be out of the house early in the mornings.

Lorimar was up, ready to leave for the Wise House, and Malina had their early meal ready. Kandra wasn't around; maybe she was still asleep too. Good. At last Poppy felt she was doing something to steadily earn her keep here.

As she had hoped, today was mostly introductions to routine: the classes (she observed a gym class that got the blood bouncing in her veins, just watching), her first lesson in the Larian alphabet, which the Halderwoldians had come to use as well, since they had been using a more limited one when the Larians first came.

And she had been taken on another trip—a pleasant one this time, to meet the overseers of the vineyards. Goric, the head manager of the bottling area, had given her a generous sample of their blue-grape wine; and Belda, the overseer of one of the largest grape-pressing areas (and an Amazon of the old stripe if ever there was one), had proudly shown them some newly planted grape arbors that were growing bountifully, and several huge vats where the grapes were 'trounced.' Another long day, but a pleasant one this time.

When they arrived at home, supper had been prepared for some time. "We will move supper hour until a later time," Kandra said to no one in particular, but Lorimar replied quietly, "That would be appreciated, Mother." Kandra nodded and bustled out of the room.

The food was still delicious, as usual. After they had finished all but tea, Kandra approached Lorimar cautiously. "May I impose upon Poppy for a fitting of her gown?"

Looking at Poppy, he asked in a voice that betrayed forced casualness, "Have you the energy to stand for the dressmakers tonight?"

"I can stand for the dressmakers." She repeated the unfamiliar phrasing. "But I'd really love a short soak in the bathing room first, after two days of just sponging."

"What is '*sponging*,' Poppy?" Cherry began, but Lorimar's glance silenced her. "Of course," he said. "I am sorry I had not realized. I myself was in the bath before daylight. Please go down and bathe at your leisure. Perhaps Cherry will attend you."

"Thanks." Poppy looked at Cherry, hoping for her company. The girl nodded amiably.

Soon the two of them were in the bath. "I bathed this afternoon," Cherry said. "All alone. But I like it much better with companions, especially you, Poppy."

"Gee, thanks, Cherry." Poppy was luxuriating in the tepid water. It had been three days since she'd been down here. Apparently Lorimar hadn't noticed how grubby his new student was becoming. Well, now she was beginning to realize just how much the man had on his mind.

Kandra was waiting for Poppy in a room she had never seen before, along with three dressmakers and what appeared to be reams of sky-blue silky material. Cherry had brought her up here to the third floor after their bath, and now sat on a stool watching the women arrange the material around Poppy's figure.

Poppy tried to be patient. This dress must be for some ceremonial initiation into the wise ones, but all the fuss seemed unnecessary. Without moving her body, Poppy turned her head toward Kandra. "Why a new gown when you have so many lovely ones upstairs? Couldn't we just go pick out another, like we did for the passage?"

A collective gasp came from the women working on her dress, and Kandra replied, "Not for a *joining*, lady. You must wear a gown that no one before you has worn, and it must be this particular shade of blue."

"*Joining?*" Poppy asked. "You mean my joining the wise ones, right?"

Kandra looked bewildered. "Well, that will be a joining of sorts, but the gown is, of course, for your *essential joining.*"

Poppy stood looking from one woman to another. All hands had become still, all eyes upon her. Cherry whispered, "*Lady Poppy,*" and Kandra began fanning herself with a piece of material; then, addressing the seamstresses, she said abruptly, "That will be all for tonight. Your work so far is very good. Please come back tomorrow."

Without a word, the women gathered up their sewing bags and left. Poppy, still standing with many pieces of silk pinned around her, asked in a small voice. "How do I ... get out of this?"

Kandra soon had the material rescued and arranged wrinkle-free over a chair. "We will talk." She looked at Poppy, red and flustered, then brushing at her hair, she added, "but perhaps tomorrow."

Cherry had risen and walked toward the door, and now looked toward Poppy, who was glad to follow her out of the room. "What was that all about?" she whispered as they walked down a corridor.

"Do you not ...?" Cherry began in a frustrated tone. "Are you not anticipating ...?" The girl gave up until they were in the bedroom. Then, sitting on her narrow bed, facing Poppy who had slumped down on the other, she assumed a very serious demeanor. "Poppy, are you not happy to become wife to my father? Do you not consider it an honor as well as a momentous event?"

Poppy answered slowly, "Well, he did ask me, as you know, but I haven't given him an answer. And that, I should think he must realize, means I'm not ... *ready* to answer." She studied the girl's sober expression. "*Doesn't* it?"

"Lady," Cherry said formally. "My father gave you his offer some time ago. And even though my friends and I saw the need to urge you toward a counter-offer, our interference did not nullify the effect of betrothal, since you, after all, accepted his obeisance."

"*Obeisance?*" Poppy repeated stupidly, her mind grinding to a halt.

"Indeed. He knelt before your nakedness, accepting you wholly." She glanced away. "And you accepted his gestures. I am sorry. My friends and I watched, which I know was not polite, but does not render the ritual uneffective."

Poppy found herself standing. "Cherry, what in the wacky hell are you talking about?"

Cherry stood and faced her. "I speak of my father's offer of joining—in the bathing room some days ago—and your counter offer in his study."

Poppy pressed her hands to her temples. "*Joining!* Wait! That means *marriage*, doesn't it? Now I get it! But Lorimar didn't make any offer of marriage in the bathing room. It was just three days ago … in a room full of furniture. And then that same night in the anteroom of his study—the night after I had to spend the day with Pule. He explained that Pule would try to marry me, might even harm me if I refused him. So, as he saw it, the safest thing for me would be to marry him. It wasn't *romantic* or anything …" she finished lamely.

Cherry was slowly shaking her head. "His offer, Poppy, was before the passage. The day he showed himself to you in the bathing room."

Poppy felt her face flame. "Your father … told you about *that?*"

Cherry nodded soberly. "Of course. I am his only child. Whom he marries will certainly be of concern to me."

"Are you *serious?*" Poppy practically shrieked at the girl. "What could that little … *lesson in anatomy* have to do with *marrying* someone? You'd think he would have spoken to me first if he was thinking about marrying me, instead of telling you about his … *exhibitionism* in the bath!"

"My father does no *exhibitionism!*" the girl cried. "Whatever that means. He is the *nashu*. You should feel *honored*. After all," She lowered her voice. "We in this house all know you are no *Larian*. But my father has offered to take you anyway. In fact, he told me he offered to take you *on trust*, even before your counter offer."

"Why do you keep talking about *offers and counter offers?*" Poppy was completely frustrated. "I had no idea a skinny dip was an offer of marriage—and I never gave him any counter offer! And what's a counter offer to a marriage proposal, anyway? You either say *yes* or you say *no*. And I tell you no answer at all means *no!* And what's this taking me *on trust* supposed to mean? I swear I don't have the slightest idea what you're talking about, Cherry."

Cherry drew a deep breath and spoke in a calmer tone. "As I have already explained, it is not common practice for my friends and I to interfere, but you clearly needed help. You are so … retiring. That is why we carried your clothing away—only to help you. And it does not detract from your counter offer in any way," she added quickly. "Because you *accepted* his obeisance—his kneeling before you, and his physical touch while you were naked."

"Good Lord," Poppy said.

"And taking someone *on trust*," Cherry continued, "is to marry them without fully viewing their body to be assured that it is free of malformations and carbuncles."

Carbuncles? Poppy stumbled backward until her legs struck the bed, and sat down hard, dropping her head into her hands. "That dress. It's a ... *wedding* dress, isn't it?"

"Wedding?" Cherry said. "That would be the same as *joining*, would it not?"

Poppy nodded without lifting her head.

Cherry sat down on her bed. "The joining ceremony is to be held in two days." All firmness disappeared from her voice, and in a childish whimper, she asked, "Will you not rejoice to become my mother, Poppy?"

Poppy looked at the girl, moved over and put her arms around her, burying her face in the wavy, black hair that smelled of lilacs. And Cherry hugged her back. They sat wordless for several minutes, until Poppy sniffed loudly and said, "Cherry, I couldn't ask for a better daughter than you."

The girl drew back to look into her face, "Then you will rejoice?"

Poppy sniffed again, swallowed, and nodded. "I will rejoice."

There was no help for it. With the problem of Pule hanging over her like dragon's breath, the necessity of her close association with Lorimar in her wise training, nowhere else to live, her very life perhaps depending on their keeping the secret of her origin, her fondness for Cherry and Kandra, finding out she had already unwittingly become engaged—and no direction home. Unless she wanted to head for the swamp, she was getting married! In two days.

How she tried to contact Aunt Holly that night. Her mother, her father, she talked to each one, only to wake up in the same bed beside the sleeping Cherry. Well, she told herself, in the cold, bright light of day, Lorimar was a kind, prosperous, good-looking, intelligent, man. A girl could do a lot worse. *Ah, wonderful, I'm coping.*

Her coping mechanism in operation, Poppy applied herself diligently that day to her first lesson in the rudiments of the Larian alphabet. Lorimar seemed pleased with her efforts and her progress. At lunchtime, he sat watching her pick at her food. "If you do not like this fare, they will bring you something else," he said. "In fact, the cook waits for your list of favorites."

"What? Oh, the food. No, everything's delicious, as usual."

"You are not eating as heartily as usual."

"I'm just ... letting those letters run through my head. I've given myself a time limit. I should be able to read and write sentences in, say, two weeks?"

"There is no need for a time definition," he said quietly. "Particularly one so ambitious. Your diligence will surely bring you into Larian proficiency at a suitable pace."

"Well, I just want to get there." She let her hands drop to her lap and faced him. "I want to be able to read all these books and learn the laws, and get to the point where I can contribute ..." She stopped and looked into his eyes. "And I want you to know I'm looking forward to our *joining* day after tomorrow."

There. She had it out. It was settled that he knew she understood.

He continued to look at her intently for a minute. "But do you wish it, Poppy?" His tone seemed to convey a considerable degree of hurt.

"Yes, I wish it," she replied, forcing herself to continue looking him in the eyes.

His hand closed warmly over hers and his voice expressed great relief. "Then it is settled. And none too soon. Day after tomorrow comes quickly upon us."

"Yes, it does." She picked up her spoon and ate the rest of her fish chowder. At least that's what it tasted like.

The next day Lorimar took her to the Wise House, but told her before they left, "Brides are not required to work at all on the day before joining, but I prefer to keep you with me until ... after tomorrow.".

"Well, I don't want to be here waiting for any surprise visits from Pule," was her firm rejoinder.

He nodded, opening the door and stepping back for her to precede him. "You will come, but I will not allow you to exhaust yourself."

Poppy forced a smile. "This has to be the first time I've ever had anyone prevent me from overwork in my life. Do you know I had two jobs and school all at once before ... before I came here."

His hand on her shoulder gently reminded her not to speak freely of her prior world, especially so near the street.

The day passed swiftly, if more leisurely. She was getting married tomorrow. Actually getting *married*. Even if this were a dream, nothing could be more real.

Arriving home earlier than usual, several ladies, along with Kandra and Cherry, were waiting for her to eat supper and come to the third floor room where they had carefully laid out clothing, skin lotions, and jewels. Asking her several times whether she was pleased with everything, they finally seemed assured that she was satisfied with their efforts. The other ladies—*five* of them—were sleeping here to help dress her in the morning, and attend her at her joining.

Kandra dismissed them all before turning to Poppy. "Now we speak of the rituals for the morrow," she said. "Cherry may stay. She too will need this knowledge in the near future."

Cherry sat quietly, her eyes bright with interest, as Kandra spoke. "We will begin early to dress you. It is better that you eat lightly in the morning in case of stomach uncertainty. Also, as you know, the dress has a fitted waist." Ignoring Poppy's nodding in agreement, she continued, "We will leave the house at the fullness of the morning sun and proceed to the Wise House. A cart, of course, will be waiting to take us there. Lorimar will arrive before you by a different conveyance. The ceremony will take place on the topmost area where we held the passage ball, but your attendants, including Cherry, will meet you at the outer entrance." She paused just long enough for Poppy and Cherry to exchange a look of one accord.

"There will be music—orchestras on the upper terrace which you will hear before you mount the stairways. As you reach the upper terrace, take no alarm at the many round objects floating toward you through the air. They are called 'fairblows' and are but airy baubles full of feathers and other light but messy substances meant for gaiety but a nuisance to the women who later clean up the ones that break."

She paused again to rearrange her sour expression at the mention of the cleaning into one of pleasantry. Poppy was sure Kandra wouldn't be doing any of the cleaning up, but it was nice of her to think of those who would. Yes, Kandra was a nice lady. A girl could do a lot worse for an almost mother-in-law.

"When the fairblows are landing on and around you," Kandra continued. "Do not distress yourself if any of them should land upon you and break."

"What if they do?" Poppy interrupted.

"As I said, they are sometimes filled with messy substances. It is expected."

"You mean, after all the trouble you and the dressmakers have gone to …"

"It is *expected*," Kandra repeated with a note of impatience, then continued. "I am sorry—there is yet much to be done. Lorimar will be waiting on the other side of the rooftop and will then take his place beside you. The second manicule will come before the two of you …"

"The second *what?*" Poppy interrupted again. Cherry stifled a giggle.

"The second manicule," Kandra repeated in a now slightly peevish tone. "A magistrate who is also a wise one—the next in status below the nashu. The nashu cannot be expected to join himself to you."

"Funny I haven't heard of these *manicules* at the Wise House," Poppy mused.

"His importance comes to the fore only when the nashu is unable to perform his duties," Kandra almost snapped. "There has been no other occasion since you have been with us to revert to the second manicule."

"No problem," Poppy muttered, noticing Cherry press a hand over her mouth.

More details were set forth than Poppy had the focus to memorize. Suddenly she felt very tired. Kandra noticed and assured her that there would be plenty of helpers on the scene tomorrow to guide her every move.

The instructions finally at an end, Poppy was longing for her last night alone in her little bed in Cherry's room, pushing thoughts of the next night from her mind.

After she had crawled into bed, Cherry came and kissed her. "This is the last time I will say, *Good night, Poppy,*" the girl said happily. "Tomorrow it will be, *Good night, Mother.*"

"And won't that be lovely, dear," Poppy murmured, returning the kiss. Then she squirmed down under the covers, sent one last plea to Aunt Holly, her mother, father, even called mentally on Allister and Tremain, to rescue her, before giving way to her weariness.

The morning came. She was still here and it was really going to happen. She ate a small roll with jam, drank one cup of coffee, and presented herself to her ladies. They gave her a sponge bath and took two hours to dress her and her hair. Poppy was totally compliant; the die was cast.

In her gorgeous sky-blue gown, almost every spot of her exposed skin sparkling with blue diamonds, and a cluster of bluets on her wrist that Cherry had picked early this morning, she rode quietly to the Wise House and followed all Kandra's directions in mounting the stairways, aided every step of the way by the several ladies whose faces beamed as if they were taking part in the marriage of the century. Well, maybe they were, in Halderwold—the long-widowed nashu and the first Larian to come in a lifetime. Poppy put all thoughts from her mind except the instructions she had received. Step by step, she must do it all correctly. This was no occasion for stumbling or bumbling.

It seemed like a mile of steps, with the others making a real business of tending her flowing skirt, before she reached the upper terrace. Her mind was like another person talking to her: *How beautiful the sky is. And all the flowers they've put around. Just as if it were a real wedding. Better try to enjoy it. It may be the only one I'll ever have. Don't lose it now, kid. We've got to get through this. Who's 'we?' Stop it. Pay attention!*

Standing where she had been placed, looking across the wide sweep of terrace, she saw Lorimar standing at the other side in a shining white robe and beautiful lavender cape that rippled back from his shoulders in the breeze. Something like a silver coronet encircled his hair, another, a gold one in his hand. Was that one for her? He *did* look splendid, and now he was coming slowly toward her.

That was when all the round things—the fairblows—began to appear in the air. Dozens of them. They came drifting down all around her out of the blue sky as she waited for Lorimar, hoping none would land on her and break. Not now, before the ceremony. A blue one touched her shoulder and rolled down her arm like a sturdy bubble, a yellow one landed right on her chest and tumbled down the front of her dress. She barely felt it. A purple one was coming right toward her forehead. She closed her eyes, waiting for its soft landing.

CHAPTER 15

She opened her eyes and looked straight into Kandra's brown ones.

"Oh, praises be!" The woman exclaimed. "My darling, you're *awake!*"

"I … seem to be," Paige stammered. After a breath, she realized she was looking at a pale green wall. "What happened?" she asked weakly. "Did that fairblow knock me out?"

The other face hovered. "That *what* dear?"

She twisted her neck to look around her. "What is this place? Why is everything so … green?"

"It's a hospital room, sweetie," Aunt Holly told her gently. "You fell at the gym. Remember?"

"A … hospital room?" Paige made a lunge to sit up, but Holly's hand on her collar bone pressed her firmly down again.

"Not so fast, dear. You'll get dizzy or something."

Page lay back, but swivelled her head to take in the room. "It is! It's a hospital room. I'm *home*. I'm really home!" She looked into her aunt's eyes again. "I am, aren't I?"

"Well, you will be soon, I hope," her aunt said, kissing her. "And I'm so happy I don't know what to say!"

"Mom? Dad?" Paige murmured.

"I'll go call them right now," Aunt Holly said briskly. "No, I won't. I won't leave your side. *Nurse! Aid! Someone!* I need someone to make a phone call!" she turned and yelled at the open door.

A young nurse appeared and took a slip of paper from Holly. "Welcome back!" she said to Paige.

"Never mind that!" Holly flapped a hand at her. "Just make the call and tell the doctor, and then you two can chew the fat. Okay?"

The nurse nodded and hurried off.

Paige was surrounded all of a sudden with people who wanted her to see if she could sit up, drink, eat, tell them what day and what year it was, and who Aunt Holly and the president were.

Overwhelmed, she answered curtly, "Of course I know who she is. She's my Aunt Holly, and she's also the President of the United States. Now buzz off!"

"You're okay, Honey," Holly told her gaily. "Get rid of 'em all."

"Oh, Aunt Holly." Paige reached for her aunt's hand which was already caressing her cheek. "Isn't it wonderful? I don't have to get married!"

"I hope not, dear," Holly replied. "But that's not why you're in here. You had a concussion, not a *miscarriage!*"

Paige felt her aunt's quirky humor fill her with comfort. "Don't say anything like that in front of Mom, Aunt Holly. She wouldn't think it was funny."

"Wouldn't think of it," her aunt assured her, tucking in the already binding covers.

Her parents were soon by her bedside. They had, for the first time since she had been unconscious, they told her, gone out for a real meal. Paige basked in the warm attention as the three of them swarmed around her—like her seventh birthday all over again. Two days, she had been out, they told her. Two days, in which she had lived … what? A couple of weeks? And so much had happened. And she mustn't speak a word of it, she knew. Not unless she wanted to be kept here for 'observation.'

And she wanted to go home. Home to her own apartment, her own bed, her own clothes, back to school and work. Thoughts of seeing her fellow clowns, and even Allister, now flowed warm and welcome into her mind.

Yet all this seemed as unreal as Halderwold had at first. Being back here so abruptly, Lorimar and Cherry and Kandra, and all those people and their world vanished like a fading dream—yet not like a dream, and not fading. That world had been a place as real as this. Being called 'Paige' even sounded strange to her ears now.

She shook her head, trying to dislodge the faces of her Halderwoldian friends from her mind. She would never see them again. She must let them fade, command them even, if they lingered. "I want to go home," she said.

"Of course, dear," her mother told her, brushing back her hair. "Dr. Blanchard just needs to run a few tests."

"I'm fine." Paige made another move to sit up but her father's hand on her shoulder gently pushed her down. "Lie still, sport," he said with gruff gentleness. "You're awake and you're rational. Everything else will fall into place."

"I don't think falling in place is a good metaphor for the occasion, John," Holly quipped.

"Don't be a flippant, smart-ass, Holly," he replied without even glancing at his sister. "That doesn't suit the occasion either."

"Now don't start," her mother snapped. "Just—both of you—shut your mouths for a change."

Holly's deep, impish chuckle preceded her next remark. "I thought you were in the habit of urging people to keep their mouths open, Rose."

Rose shot her sister-in-law a warning look and let out an impatient breath as the doctor entered the room.

They all waited in attentive silence for his remarks. He did want to keep Paige for another day.

"I'd rather go home," Paige protested. "Can't I just come back in a day or two for a checkup?"

"I'd really rather keep you here," he insisted. "In case of a relapse. Just for one more day."

"A ... relapse," Paige repeated. "You mean I might go back to ... where I was?"

"It's unlikely," the doctor said matter-of-factly. "But possible."

"I'm staying in her apartment," Holly said. "I can watch ..." only to be interrupted by John. "We have a room just across the boulevard. I think she should stay here."

"Okay, I'll stay here, Doctor Blanchard," Paige agreed. If they were only going to argue about it. "For one more day. And ... could you give me something to keep me from going back to ... sleep?"

"No. Not if you're comfortable. Medication would only mask any tendency for you to lapse into unconsciousness."

"She'll stay here," Rose declared flatly. "And no medication."

Paige did doze off after her poached egg and toast dinner, even though she kept the television on, fighting sleep. Waking with the first light, she glanced around and spoke with relief to herself, "It's *green*. I'm still here."

"You go home today," a brisk voice told her. An aid came around to stand beside her. "But first, breakfast. Are you hungry?"

"Yes, I am, actually," Paige replied. "But I had an egg for dinner last night. Do you have anything else?"

"How about an English muffin with jam? Or toast, oatmeal, cereal? We've got everything."

Paige squirmed to feel her body in the bed, to make it real, and yawned. "English muffin ... with blueberry jam. And ... do you have *real* coffee?"

"Of course we do." The girl laughed and left the room.

After breakfast came the routine wash-up, blood pressure, temperature, and a few unexplained machinations by the medical staff. Then a couple of hours alone, when she forced herself to concentrate on her surroundings. *I will not even think of Halderwold. It doesn't exist. It's pure fantasy.*

But when you resolve not to think of an elephant, what comes marching before your mind's eye but a whole herd of elephants. Paige got up. She'd already been to the bathroom twice on her own. There was no reason she couldn't stroll around a little, get oriented. She put on the limp bathrobe and the mules she found in the small closet, and sauntered out the door and down the hall.

She felt almost normal; much the same as if she'd slept in after several days of overwork. Pausing at the end of a corridor at the top of a stairwell to look out a large window, she peered down one story on a scene of misty drizzle, the few walkers below hurrying along in dull raincoats. But it was home. Her own ... planet? Dimension? She closed her eyes and gave her head a shake. *I will not think like that. I'm home. The weirdness is over!*

She opened her eyes and looked down again on a group of earthlings coming across the street. A man stepped up onto the curb and glanced up at the building. Her heart jumped. *Lorimar!* He was wearing a long, dark cloak and wide-brimmed hat, but his face had been clearly visible when he had looked up. *I must speak to him! I have to know how he got here. Is he looking for me? My God, if that world is leaking into this one....*

Trying not to move so fast as to draw attention from the few nurses and aids traveling the corridors, she made it down the stairwell, judged the direction he had been heading in from where she was, and walked toward what turned out to be the main entrance lobby. A few people sat on the sofas, speaking in low tones, reading, staring into space. But there was no Lorimar.

"Miss, are you looking for someone?" She looked to her left to see three women at the admitting desk all looking at her. One got up and came toward her. "Can I help you, dear? Shouldn't you be on your own floor?"

"Did a man just come through here in a long dark cloak and ..."

The woman slipped her arm through hers firmly, as another got up and came quickly over to take the other. "We'll get you back to bed, honey. What's your name?"

Paige tried to shake them off. "Paige Nelson, and I'm perfectly all right. I can walk by myself."

"Don't worry, we get paid to do this," one of the women said with obviously faked lightness as she exchanged glances with the woman still at the desk.

"Sure, honey," the other said. "We'll have you back in your own room in no time. Do you know what floor you're on?"

Paige flung herself out of their hands. "I'm going. I'm going. "Don't worry about me!"

She was halfway down the corridor leading back to the stairwell, when two male aids came out of nowhere; each took one of her arms and escorted her back to her room, stanchly resisting her efforts to break away.

"This is all *crazy!*" she told them as they deposited her into bed and tucked the covers around her. "I was just walking around minding my own business. I saw someone I knew coming toward the front entrance and I went out there to meet him."

"The guy in the long black cloak," one said with a smile.

"I didn't say *black*," she snapped. "I said *dark!*"

"Well, if he came to see you," the other told her as if speaking to a child. "He'll find your room. And you want to be here when he comes, so be a good girl and stay in bed now. Okay?"

She heaved a sigh and yanked the covers up to her chin. "You guys are clueless."

"We're not claiming to be geniuses," the first one said as they turned to leave. She heard chuckles as soon as they were through the door.

She was back in bed just in time. In less than five minutes, Aunt Holly came bustling in, followed by her parents. "Feel like getting up?" her father asked.

"I've already been." She tried to sound casual. *God, that was stupid, going downstairs like that. Now they'll think I'm nuts or something—and I'm not so sure myself. Let's hope I'm out of here before word gets to Dr. Blanchard.* "I walked down the hall, even down the stairs. I'm fine."

"Great," John said. "Now, another once over by the doctor and we should be taking our little girl home."

"Home from the hospital," Rose chirped in a singsong voice. "Just like the day she was born."

"Well, I don't think you'll be able to carry me this time, Mom."

Soon Dr. Blanchard came. "How's my girl?"

"She's fine, Doctor," Paige said, as bright and chipper as she could manage. "Ready to go home."

"Well, we'll just take a look …"

The same tests, blood pressure, the gamut. "I'm fine, right?"

"You seem to be." He paused. "Your concussion was mild. I'm surprised you've been unconscious as long as you have."

"Well, I'm awake now, and I feel pretty normal. So I can go, right?"

"Probably. But what's this I hear about your jaunt downstairs looking for a man in a black cloak?"

"Oh, for heaven's sake." Paige turned her head from side to side to express disgust, while her three relatives' mouths fell open. "They've taken it all out of context. I felt like walking. I saw someone I knew out the window, coming toward the building, and I went down to see if he was coming in the front entrance. Then the ladies at the desk panicked—for no reason. And I guess they called the aids who escorted me back to bed. Totally unnecessarily."

The doctor looked at her. "But what about the long, black cloak?"

"Oh, he had on a dark coat or something. Maybe it was a bit long. I didn't get a really good look at him."

"But you say you knew him."

Paige look pleadingly into the doctor's eyes. "Doctor, can I go home? This is all nonsense. A misunderstanding."

"Well," the doctor said slowly. "You do seem to check out …"

"I'll vouch for her, Doctor," Holly said loudly. "I can stay with her as long as necessary. I'll watch her …"

"This isn't the city court," Dr. Blanchard cut in dryly. "I'm not worried that she's going back to her dark-cloaked gang or anything. I just want to be sure she's back to normal, physically and …"

"*Mentally.*" Paige finished for him. "Doctor, this isn't a mental institution either, and I'm ready to go home. Can't we just … finish the paperwork or whatever it takes?"

"Of course," he replied after a pause. "I'll go sign you out." He took in the others with a sweeping glance. "And good luck. Call me if you need to."

Hand shakes all around, and he was gone. Paige was up and into the bathroom to put on the clothes Holly had brought two days ago. She paused after peeking into another bag that held the orange sweat pants and colorful sweater she had been wearing the day she passed out and found herself thinking, *How did they get here?* It seemed such a long time since Cherry had hidden them away. She closed the bag and carried it with her as she went back to join the others.

They left the room and Paige headed down the corridor toward the stairwell, but her father caught her arm. "We'll take the elevator," he said, tugging her in the opposite direction.

"But, Dad, it's just one floor," she protested.

"Just the same," was his noncommittal reply. Knowing he just wanted to get her out of the building the fastest way possible, she acquiesced and went with the others past the 'Elevator' arrow, and around a corner.

Waiting for the elevator, she noticed the sign over the door at the end of the corridor: 'Children's Unit.' There was something she was supposed to do. Of course. It all came back. The birthday party—Hanna and … Mollie. Yes, the little girl, Mollie, in the hospital with only a monthly visit from her mother. She had promised to visit her. A long time ago she had promised and she hadn't done it. No, not a long time ago, just a few days. But it seemed a long time. Slipping out of her father's relaxed hold, she headed for the door to the unit.

She was inside before the others caught up with her. "Do you have a patient here, a little girl named Mollie?" she asked the nurse at the desk.

"Why, yes. We have a Mollie Sanders. Are you a relative?"

"I'm a friend," Paige told her. "I promised to visit her. I know it isn't visiting hours yet, but could I speak to her for just one minute?"

"Well, she is having a pretty good day," the woman replied thoughtfully. "I don't see what harm it could do." Glancing up at Paige, she added, "She's the last one on your right before the second window. Poor kid doesn't get many visitors. Her family lives in Wyoming."

Paige's relatives were behind her now. Without turning, she moved quickly down the row of beds. Approaching a little girl with dark bangs cut just above two big, sad brown eyes that looked at her inquiringly.

"Are you Mollie?"

The girl nodded. Paige put out her hand. "I'm Paige. A friend of your friend, Hanna. She told me you might like an extra visitor."

The sad eyes brightened and a smile appeared beneath them. She put her small hand in Paige's and weakly accepted a handshake. "My Mommy lives far away. Out west."

"I know," Paige told her. "Hanna told me. And I came to tell you that I know a clown who wants to visit you. Would like a visit from a clown?"

Now a real grin spread over the small face. "Oh, I'd *love* a visit from a clown. What's his name?"

"It's a *her*. And her name is *Poppy*. I can't stay very long right now, but I'll be sure to tell Poppy you want to see her, and I think Hanna will be able to come with her."

"*Super!* When can they come? Can they come tonight?"

"Not tonight, but soon. As soon as I talk to her and find out when Hanna can come."

"Okay." The girl settled back on her pillow, her wan face now full of hope.

"Okay. I … they'll be seeing you. And … I hope you get well soon." She had forgotten to find out what Mollie's illness was.

"I will," Mollie assured her.

The nurse at the desk had kept the others near the door. "Just remembered a promise I made," Paige explained when she reached them. She turned to the nurse and asked if she could visit Mollie as a clown.

"I think that would be very nice," the nurse replied. "In fact, I'm sure all the children here would enjoy it. So long as it's between seven and eight in the evening."

"Great. I'll call before I come. There'll be one more little girl with me. A friend of Mollie's."

Finally, they were all on the elevator, all unusually silent.

"It was a birthday party the other night," Paige explained. "One of the kids told me about Mollie. Her mother lives in Wyoming and can only visit once a month. The kid's lonely, so I'm going to visit her—and the whole ward—as Poppy the Clown."

"That sounds wonderful," Holly said.

The others looked relieved. Until they stepped off the elevator on the first floor and Paige gasped. Passing, was a man who seemed to recognize her. On second glance, he stopped. "Miss Nelson?"

"Of course!" Paige exclaimed.

"Well, of course," the man said, shifting from one foot to the other with an air of discomfort. "I mean, I was pretty sure …"

"I meant …" Paige stammered. "I meant … of course *you're* Tremain Tate!"

"Well, yes, of course that's true too," Tremain replied.

John reached an arm around his daughter and held out his hand. "I'm John Nelson, Paige's father. She took a spill a couple of days ago but she's going to be fine. Nice to meet you, Mr. Tate."

Tremain pumped John's hand as if he were glad of something to do. "I'm so sorry to hear that." He turned back to Paige. "I hope you're recovered enough to continue teaching."

"I'm fine," she said. Why was he wearing a raincoat a mile too long? He must have borrowed it. The dark hat was in his hand, and he *did* look awfully like Lorimar now that he was being serious. "I'll be back at school the next time they call me."

"Great," he said without enthusiasm, and after a nod at the other women, turned and hurried away.

Paige expected a 'Well, what was *that* all about?' that never came.

Soon they were all in her apartment, eating pizza at her little kitchen table.

"That noise about a man in a cloak?" John asked finally. "Was it Mr. Tate in his long coat you saw through the window?"

"Yes, it was him," Paid replied, chewing. "He teaches at the high school. A stupid mistake."

He shrugged and let out a breath. "Something like that could happen to anyone, looking through that rain." He reached over and gave her a pat on the shoulder. "The only thing that matters is that you're all right."

"That's what I would think." Paige replied.

"And I," Rose agreed. "Absolutely."

"Ditto me," Holly said, but her eyes held a question Paige knew would not rest unanswered.

Rose had a root canal scheduled for the next morning, and the patient had been in some pain. After reassuring her mother several times that she felt fine and would be all right, especially since Aunt Holly was staying for a day or two, Paige said goodbye to her parents. "Be sure to call us if you feel the least bit funny," Rose called back as they went off through the mist to their parking place.

"I'm a *clown*, Mom," Paige yelled, waving. "I'm supposed to feel funny." *But I don't.*

Paige and Holly climbed back up the steps to her apartment. She had volunteered to clown for the kids in Mollie's ward—but now she realized her need for some kind of attitude adjustment to get back into clowning mode. It was a promise; it had to be done. Surely Aunt Holly would help lift her out of her bland mood.

Settled in her own small living room, she looked at her aunt, trying to rediscover the comical traits she had always found so endearing: the wild, too-red dyed hair, the overdone makeup, the dumpy but nimble body, the large, expressive brown eyes that usually sparkled with wit. But the woman sitting facing her now suddenly appeared a flabby soul, pathetically fighting age, eyeing her with a curious, concerned look in a pair of eyes surrounded by new wrinkles.

Holly finished her ginger ale and set the glass down on the coaster with a thump. "All right now, my darling," she said, looking straight and earnestly at her niece. "What really happened?"

"I ... passed out, Aunt Holly." Paige tried to sound confused by the question. "I had a concussion. At least that's what you've all been telling me. What more is there to say?"

"Just that there seems to be more," her aunt replied in a 'you're-not-getting-off-the-hook-so-easily' tone of voice. "You're not the same. You act as if you've been away for months. And what's the deal with that Mr. Tate?"

"I told you; he's a teacher at the high school." Paige tried to sound nonchalant. "I hardly know him."

"Now, there's more to *that* story!" Holly said, her head tilting sideways.

Paige thought she saw a way out. "Yeah, there is, actually. You see, he made fun of me one day when he caught me trying on his hat. So I kind of ... hate him."

"Huh!" Holly barked. "And you've always been one to follow men you hardly know around, trying on their hats!"

Paige felt her face warming. "Oh, Aunt Holly! I'm telling you the unvarnished truth. You see, it was that Allister Cormick, my clown school instructor. He had just humiliated me something wicked about not having found my hat ..."

"And you mistook that man's hat for the one you lost." Holly had this way of making a statement that let you know she didn't believe a word of it.

Paige pouted. "C'mon, let me tell you. I won't if you're going to interrupt."

"Sorry, dear. I won't emit another syllable."

Paige pulled her feet up and wiggled into the corner, comfortably settling into her familiar position on this sofa from her childhood that her parents had given her when she moved in here. Then she spun the tale of the wild hat class, then the unsettling run-in with the owner of the soft cap by the high school closet. Holly was cackling uncontrollably by the time she'd finished. And, to Paige, she had become her old, dear self again. Not all that dumpy or wrinkled after all.

"You mustn't let male teasing get to you like that." Holly dabbed at the corner of her eye with her napkin. "He probably *likes* you. And he *is* a good-looking guy. Is he single?"

"Oh, Holly!"

"Well, you *are* in your mid-twenties, my dear. Don't you ever think of getting married?"

Paige held up her fingers, ticking them off one by one. "I've got a job as a teacher, a job—no, a *business* as a clown, classes with a madman, workouts that would leave Governor Arnold panting, and a concussion to get over. I don't have a lot of time to think." *And worrying about Lorimar and his family—and whether I'm crazy or not. And this is the first major upset of my life I can't share with you.*

Holly smirked. "Romance comes when you least expect it; and it's like a new baby—it makes room for itself in your life."

Paige's answer was another sigh. She *was* feeling better, though. *I knew a dose of her medicine would help me get back on track. She's a real ... mender.* "I don't think I'll be wanting any dinner after that pizza," she said. "How about you Aunt Holly?"

"Dinner, shminner, girl. You got any booze?"

"Merlot."

"That'll do fine." Holly was on her feet. "Don't get up, dear. You rest."

"Bottom shelf in the refrigerator door. Two glasses."

Paige stretched her legs. *What I could really use is a cup of vigorwart. Yup. I'm crazy.*

Two days later Paige, with Hanna and her mother, went to visit Mollie in her ward.

"Nothing too exciting," the head nurse warned rather severely. "These children need to go to sleep after you've gone. They are unwell."

Paige had an impulse to say, 'Duh. You mean that's why they're in here?' But she didn't. In fact, it didn't even seem funny after she thought about it for a second. It was just fresh, even unkind, to a probably overworked woman, concerned about her small patients.

Paige—Poppy once more—did a few standard tricks and a few original goofs. Poor Mollie looked so sick and forlorn, even as she sat propped up on her pillows giggling, Poppy had trouble keeping up her patter of nonsense. Twice she felt tears jump into her eyes. *Not very professional tonight,* she scolded herself. Finally, she said goodnight and left the hospital as soon as they could pry Hanna away from her friend.

Who am I? Paige wondered, climbing wearily up the stairs to her apartment. *I've lost something. I've lost … I've lost … the* soul *of a clown.*

Holly was still there, planning to leave in the morning. She took one look at Paige and said, "You shouldn't have gone back to work so soon. You look exhausted."

"I'm not exhausted." Paige slumped down on a kitchen chair and tossed her wig on the table. "I'm just … not in the groove." She looked up helplessly at her aunt. "I'm not *funny* anymore, Aunt Holly. I mean, the kids laughed and everything, but I don't *feel* funny, and I don't know if I can get it back. Maybe I should just … drop out of clown school. Maybe it's not worth the money. Or the abuse."

Holly hovered over her niece, hands on her hips. "I don't want to hear you talk like that, Paige. I mean, you don't *have* to be a clown. You're already a high school teacher, and if your clowning was just an adolescent thing … But it just doesn't seem right. It comes so naturally to you—taking after *me* of course, like John always says." She gave a quick laugh. "God knows, you certainly didn't inherited your sense of humor from your *mother!*"

"Holly …"

"God love her," Holly continued. "She is what she is, and nothing less than a ministering angel to those poor people with the toothache, but …"

By now Paige was giggling tiredly, her chin propped up on her hands. "Aunt Holly, you can come up with the most *compassionate* insults."

"Never mind my compassion," Holly went on. "It's there when it's needed. We're talking about *you*. You've had a fall and two days unconscious. I know it's been three days since you woke up but who knows what side-effects could linger. All I'm saying is don't make any hasty decisions."

"Actually, I don't feel capable of making *any* decisions." Paige let her head drop down on her arm.

"Well, it sounded like one in the making, and I think you should wait. Go back to school, and to work when they call you. But try and take it easier than you did. And for heaven's sake don't go to the gym for a while. Not until you're feeling like your old self. Promise me that." She put her hand under Paige's chin and pulled her face up.

"I promise," Paige told her with her mouth squished between Holly's fngers. "And that's the easiest promise I've ever made, the way I'm feeling right now."

"Good. And I believe you. Now get that glop off your face and go to bed. Can I fix you some cocoa or something?"

"That would be nice. Just like when I was nine." Paige dragged herself up from her chair and headed for the bathroom. "I'll wash and get undressed while you're heating it." Then she turned back on her way out of the kitchen. "And don't think I don't appreciate your concern and ... companionship, Aunt Holly."

"Oh, we don't think anything like that, dear," her aunt said, searching in the cupboard. "Where do you keep those packages of cocoa?"

"Second shelf, behind the soy sauce and garlic powder."

CHAPTER 16

What Paige still couldn't understand, what kept her in bed after waking in the morning knowing she had several days of clown school to catch up on, was her low spirits. In that other reality—it was a reality—she had thought she'd be happy to see people she didn't even like just to be back in this familiar world. The world she considered the real one.

But she woke up in the mornings wondering what had knocked her out at her wedding? Who had shot that heavy projectile disguised as a balloon? Was Pule behind it? Was there a battle or a revolt going on right now in Halderwold? Were Lorimar and Cherry and Kandra in danger or even injured ... or? If not, did they miss her? Did Lorimar actually love her? Had he claimed to want to marry her for her own safety to avoid admitting his love? Or was he still in love with the dark beauty, Isanda, the wife of his youth? Cherry loved her, but she had other friends, and would be finding a sweetheart soon.

With a groan, she forced herself up. *When I was there, I kept telling myself it wasn't real; now I worry about them all as if it were the only place that is real.* How did you handle two worlds at once? Where was the joy she should be feeling—the relief at being home? The joy she had felt in the hospital hadn't lasted. This transition was almost as tough as adjusting to her bizarre life in Halderwold.

She found her robe and made her way into the bathroom. Aunt Holly would be leaving, and she needed a bright and proper face to say goodbye, or she might report to her parents that Paige still wasn't herself, or worse, decide to stay. As much as she enjoyed her aunt's company, she had things to cope with. Things that could only be untangled in alone time, if they could be untangled at all.

Holly left, with an aspect of unease. "You're sure you're ready to be alone?" she asked for the third time, standing outside the door, suitcase in hand.

Paige tried for a light tone, shading her eyes with her hand and scanning the horizon. "I see no buzzards circling, nor any wolverines peering from the hedges, waiting to get me by myself." Her jest failed miserably, and Holly swung her bag back toward the door. "Maybe I should stay one more night."

Paige actually barred her way. "And just maybe you should get back to your own life and your garden, and your dress shop before your customers turn to the larger chain stores."

"Well!" Holly bristled. "If you're so eager to get rid of me."

Paige put her arms around her aunt's neck. "You know that I know I can count on you, Aunt Holly. But I've taken up enough of your time. And I've got a schedule to get back into—today." She let her arms slide down to look at her watch. "I'm due in class in about ninety minutes."

"You're teaching this morning?"

"Nope. Back to clown school. Got to pick up my life, and so do you."

Holly stood for a minute as if undecided. "Well, I'm not going to force my little old, boring self on you."

"Nor I on you." Paige gave her a peck on the cheek. "If I need you, Kandra—Aunt Holly. I'll let you know without hesitation."

Holly shot her a sharp look; hesitated, then turned to leave. "Just make sure you do. The minute you need me."

Finally, she was gone. Paige felt nasty and ungrateful about shoving her off like that, but no help was going to come from keeping her here. Her mental mix-up was her own to sort out, and Holly did have a busy life of her own. Her staying longer would only be a waste of time for both of them. She'd do something really nice for her aunt after she got herself back together. Something really nice.

She was early to class; wanting to avoid a room full of people turning to stare when she entered. They all looked at her anyway as they arrived, but at least not all at once. A few asked how she was, and she said simply, "Fine."

Sue Gates, after she had inquired and received the same short reply, sat down beside her. "You were so upset the last time I saw you. I've been wondering if that's why you fell."

Paige managed a smile. "I'm fine now, Sue. Thanks for asking."

Sue left her alone then, except for an occasional glance throughout the class, which was uneventful. Allister was enjoying—or the class was enjoying—one of his calmer days. He nodded in Paige's direction, told her they were glad to have her back 'unmaimed' after her 'episode.'

"Thank you," she replied, looking down. And that was that. He did not mention hats.

The class was about salvaging an act going downhill because it was unsuited to the audience. If he only knew the type of audience she'd performed for lately. But no. She hadn't. Not *really*. Damn it, what was real and what wasn't? She shook off her diverting thoughts, forced herself to concentrate on the class, and got through without mishap or embarrassment. She had that to be thankful for, she told herself, driving home. Now, getting back into the routine of school was behind her; she didn't have that to dread anymore. But she felt worn out after just a half-day of her old busyness.

Then the school administrator called and asked her to teach two classes the next afternoon. She groaned a little after hanging up the phone. *But maybe that's exactly what I need. To fill my head with my old life—my* real *life again, and let this other stuff just go* … If it would. Surely it would. The next day, she'd be back on her full schedule, except for the gym. She hadn't had the nerve to go back to her workout routine yet, though it would be necessary for good clowning. But there was time.

Her mother must have been thinking the same thing. She called in the evening for reassurance that Paige was all right after her first day back at school, and Paige told her she was *fine*. The word she had settled on to describe her condition to everyone who asked. "And I'll be teaching two classes tomorrow. No time to play the invalid."

"You know, there's something I've been wanting to speak to you about, dear," Rose said cautiously. Paige knew what was coming—this wasn't the first time. "Do you really need to be a clown any longer? I mean, I understand it was lots of fun when you were a girl, but now you're a high school teacher and that's a good career and I'm proud of you. Wouldn't it be better all around if you just concentrated on that? You're getting along so well with the Gifford High faculty, I'm sure they'd consider you for full time if you apply. Or have you applied already?"

"No, Mom, I haven't. And we've been all though this before. Lots of people have dual careers, especially if one of them is show business. Then the other one is for steady income."

"Well, steady income sounds like the thing to me," Rose pursued. "And it seems to me if you gave more of your time to it, well, then you'd have time to spend with … adults, like eligible young men …"

"Enough, Mom. I'll get married when fate brings the right man around. You wouldn't want me to marry just anyone, would you?"

"Of *course* not," Rose practically spit into the telephone. "But you have to put yourself in places where fate can work with you."

Paige was lying down on the sofa now, holding the telephone like a heavy tool. "I go places, Mom. I meet people."

"Well, the next time you meet a nice young man, don't tell him you're a clown. Start with the teaching."

"I do that anyway."

"And, by the way, that Mr. Tate looks like a nice man. Is he married?"

"I don't know, Mom."

"All right, dear. Just one more thing. Why did you call Holly '*Sandra*' when she was leaving?"

"What? I didn't."

"She says you did. She's worried. So am I."

The giggle that rose in Paige's throat was a symptom of utter exhaustion. She hadn't experienced such fatigue since she'd had that lingering flu two years ago.

"I don't see anything funny about this situation, Paige." Her mother assumed a scolding tone.

"Mom, there's no … *situation*. I don't know what I said that could've sounded like … what she thought she heard. Right now, I'm just … *really tired*. You'd think being out for two days would leave a person rested, but …"

"That's not real rest, having a concussion—you still need rest to heal. You're not going out again tonight, are you?"

"No. Who would I go out with, Mom? I *never* meet any men."

"Now, don't be smart. I want you to heal, that's all. You do sound exhausted. Remember when you were around eleven and you used to get hysterical and laugh at nothing when you were tired?"

"Yeah, I remember. And you'd send me to bed. Please do that now."

"Go to bed."

"I will. Just as soon as I brush my teeth. And floss."

"Good girl. Good night then."

"Night, Mom."

It *was* kind of nice, her mother showing such concern. But she had lost it, calling Holly 'Kandra.' She'd hoped the slip-up had gone unnoticed, but no such luck with Aunt Holly. That woman was a shrewdy.

She did sleep, and morning found her feeling almost normal. A morning of clown school and a whole afternoon of teaching. *That should get me back on track.* Paige went out to face a full day in Gifford, New York. U.S.A. Then remembering how she and her friends used to address notes to each other in grade five, she added, 'Planet Earth, Solar System, Universe.'

Class went okay. Allister was still cool, talking about handling the occasional child who became frightened and cried. That had never happened to Paige yet. She didn't think her kind of clowning could be threatening to any child, but a couple of the guys in the class said it had happened to them.

Allister told them that tomorrow they'd be talking about 'sophisticated children,' kids who had been so overwhelmed with entertainment all their lives, they already had a taste for 'high-end humor.' Oh, God, if only they could have seen her rare, appreciative, 'unsophisticated' audiences in Halderwold. If only she could tell them about it. *Time to re-zone the thinking. Back to the real world, kid.*

Alone again in the high school cafeteria, she couldn't resist a peek into the closet to see if *that hat* was still there. It was, and there wasn't enough money in the whole town to bribe her into touching it again. She also noticed a rain coat—*the* raincoat hanging in the closet. A very long, dark blue coat. It must belong to that seven foot coach of the boys' basketball team. She was standing looking into the closet when the outside door opened and footsteps indicated someone had entered the room.

"Not eyeing my hat again, Miss Nelson?"

She turned to face the man she knew would be standing there, mocking her. Only he wasn't. Tremain was there, but his expression was sober, apologetic. "I didn't intend to upset you the other day," he said mildly. "I just have this notion that humor can sometimes get you through an awkward moment better than good breeding." Then after a pause, "I'm glad you've recovered from your accident at the gym."

"I'm okay," she replied. "And ... thanks for your good wishes."

He nodded.

"And I can explain the hat thing." She couldn't resist straightening it out. "I'm a clown, you see. I mean, in addition to teaching, I entertain small children as Poppy the clown. I go to clown school—Cormick's, here in town—and he says a clown has to find her hat, so I ... sort of got into the habit of checking out every hat I see. But I shouldn't have been fooling around with one that didn't belong to me, or to someone I don't know."

"But you do know me. I'm Tremain Tate."

"Yes. I know who you are."

"Well, then you know me."

"Okay, and I apologize for messing with your hat."

"Really, it's perfectly all right. I was just trying to be … light-hearted." He gave a small, self-conscious laugh. "I guess I consider myself a clown of sorts too. At least an amateur comic."

After a silence from her, he added, "But not a very funny one."

She closed the closet door. "I guess I got a sampling of *that*."

"Sorry." He lowered his head and rolled his eyes up at her like a little boy. "Some of my students laugh at me."

She felt herself relax a little. "Actually, it *was* sort of funny, I mean after the fact. I guess I just didn't appreciate being the butt of your wit at the time. I'm so used to being the one dishing out the nonsense."

He looked at her, all taunting gone from his expression. "Where did you lose your hat, anyway?"

"Oh, it's not anything like that. You see, a clown's hat is kind of a … signature. Like a trade mark. It's supposed to express your clowning style … your clown persona." She sighed. "For some reason, I'm having one heck of a time even figuring out what kind of a clown I *am*. Maybe if I knew, I'd know what kind of hat would suit me."

"Hmm." He was thinking. "Maybe I could help … if I were to see you perform. Got any gigs in the near future that I could attend?"

She laughed. "I mostly do birthday parties for pre-schoolers. I don't think you'd fit in."

"I have friends in low places," he replied with a smile, holding a hand out about three feet off the floor. "I mean age-wise, as well as the other. My friend—the man I was visiting at the hospital the other day, has two little kids. Maybe one of them is due for a birthday party soon. I'll ask. The least I can do after shaking you up the other day is promote your business."

Paige wished she could tell him the little teasing scenario he'd put her through had paled to nearly nothing after all she'd experienced since. "Please don't worry about it. It's my business to be laughed at." For some reason it seemed important now that he think her sophisticated—too mature to be troubled by that kind of nonsense.

"And by the way," he said, as she began to walk away. "I had to borrow a coat the other day to go to the hospital in the rain, so my offer to lend you my hat still stands. It's one of the ways we teachers support each other here at Gifford High."

"Thanks," she said. "And let me know if any of your little friends needs a clown for their birthday party."

He said he would.

Driving home, she realized she was feeling better. Her anxiety had diminished, her energy-depleted cells seemed to be filling up, mathematics and clown school material were again occupying her head, and she was beginning to feel at home in this world again. Putting her mind back on work and studies left little time to entertain constant worry over Lorimar and his family. They were fading further and further into the world of dreams, and she was glad to let them.

A few days later, she met Tremain in the hall again. They greeted each other, then he said, "By the way, my friend's little boy will be four next Tuesday. You available for a party? I want to give it to him for a birthday gift." He raised his hands in a helpless gesture and rolled his eyes upward. "Who knows what to give a boy who's got more toys than a toy store?"

"I could do a party Tuesday," Paige replied. "If I don't have to teach, there'll just be my clown class, so I should still be in character by late afternoon."

"Great." He searched his pockets. "I thought I had my address book, but ... tell you what. "I'll get his mother's work number so you can call her directly. Her name is Gracie Mack. Will you be teaching again this week so I can give it to you?"

She shrugged. "I never know until they call me."

"Then ... would you care to give me your number, so I can give it to her ... or I could call you and give you hers, or ..."

She tried not to smile as she opened her purse. She'd seen better feigning jobs done by eighteen-year-olds. "Here's my Poppy the Clown card. Gracie can call me. Tell her to leave a message if I'm not home, and I'll get right back to her."

"Great." He stood looking at the card. Then he kind of waved it in the air before plunging it into his coat pocket. "Then I'll see you ..."

"Around," she finished for him. "I've got a class right now." She walked away amused at his sudden descent into adolescent uncertainty. Where was the suave, heartless comic who had mocked her before the closet mirror? It felt a little wicked, letting him tread water like that before pulling him out—and enjoying it throughly—but he'd had it coming.

She didn't teach again by Tuesday. She visited Mollie and her ward-mates once more, and concentrated on her clown classes, and some new promotional material she'd left at the printers before her fall. Gracie had called and arranged for the party at six o'clock.

Paige had plenty of time to plan her act, get into her costume, and get to the Mack's early. As children began to arrive, a tall figure appeared among them.

"So, this is Poppy the Clown," Tremain said with a grin. "Since this is my gift to Timmy, I thought it would be appropriate for me to attend the shindig."

Damn. He's grabbed the upper hand again. She was uncomfortable performing before adults unless they were parents of her audience. So long as the kids enjoyed themselves, the parents were happy.

"You'll probably end up sending me a bill for an hour of boredom." She turned to press the start button on her record player. Soon the room rocked with exaggeratedly cheerful music; she cranked up the volume to a level preclusive of conversation. Tremain took an adult-sized chair at the back of the room.

The party went well. She was learning to enter a level of concentration that blocked out interference, which Allister insisted was necessary to successful clowning.

When it was over, she began gathering up her props, hoping to get out the door while Tremain was still talking to the kids. He could settle up with her the next time she saw him in school. Talking to him in her costume made her feel like … well, like a *clown.*

But he was by her side. "Can't let you forget your remuneration."

"Next time you see me …" she began.

But he already had her record player under his a arm. "I'll work off part of your fee," he said, picking up a plastic bag with the other hand. "Ahh, bells and whistles. Tools of the trade."

She turned and headed into the kitchen to find Gracie and say good night. Her hostess expressed great satisfaction with her performance and offered her a tip, which she refused. By the time she left the house, Tremain was standing by her car, ready to load the things he had carried out.

"I should have asked for your key. I could have had everything packed. You must be exhausted after that workout."

"That's why I frequent the gym," she said dryly, unlocking the car. "And conk out for days at a time."

"Well, let's hope that doesn't happen again." He piled her props into the back seat.

"That goes without saying. Goodnight and thanks for the gig."

She got into the car and started it. He was still standing outside, so she let down the window. *Can't just drive off and leave him standing there.* "Well, goodnight," she said. "Thanks for carrying stuff."

"My pleasure." He fished a check out of his coat pocket. "And here is your paycheck. The help was a perk. And … there's more if you'll accept it."

She took the check. "What?"

"I'd like to take you to dinner."

She let out an unladylike snort, followed by an undignified giggle.

"Well, I didn't mean tonight," he said, laughing. "I mean, not right now anyway. Unless you want to go home and change and …"

"I'll take a rain check." She shifted into drive. Her annoyance with him was melting. "Or a clown check, hat check, whatever."

"I'll call you," he said. "You'll be my hat check girl."

"Sure." They were both grinning as she drove away.

Saturday night he took her to a new restaurant. They had Zinfandel, artichoke and green bean salad, salmon with pineapple salsa and couscous.

"I haven't eaten anything that took more than ten minutes to prepare in weeks," Tremain remarked, offering her the plate of crusty rolls.

Paige took a second roll and started to claim the same experience, then suddenly remembered the laborious and lengthy passage food preparations. But of course that didn't count. It occurred to her that she hadn't been dwelling on Halderwold and its people so much lately. And that had to be good. *One world at a time.* Someone important had said that. She turned her attention completely to her dinner and her companion, and asked him what he had studied in college.

"I majored in English," he told her. "And I did a few courses in psychology, but my fascination was literary criticism."

"Why did you find that so fascinating?" She asked, picturing a bunch of old fogies analyzing the words of people who were already dead and could never confirm their interpretations. "I took a lot of math, so I suppose I'm deficient in—what do they call it? Deep reading?"

"Well, it was literary history that really grabbed me." He took a fork full of couscous and chewed thoughtfully. "The Middle Ages. I found the carnival literature such an insight into the psychology of repression."

She almost physically felt her ears prick up. "That does sound interesting."

With that encouragement, he continued. "Well, the leaders—the church leaders in particular; they were the true leaders—understood that being on the bottom all the time could result in explosions of resentment and anger by the peasants and low level workers. Could lead to crimes—even revolution. So they gave them carnivals and feast days. Quite a few every year. Sometimes for several days in a row the lower classes were allowed to make fun of their betters. Dress like them, ape them in their manners and speech, mock them in public as much as they felt like. Have you ever heard of 'The Feast of Fools?'"

She laughed. "Isn't that what we're having now?"

"Our own version." He took on a mock professorial manner. "But I speak literarily."

"I may have," she said. "But I thought it was just an expression from some old movie."

"It was sort of a game, but a serious one, and it went on inside the churches. The people, including the workers and peasants, would elect a 'King of Revels,' to preside over the worship rituals, which would all be crazy stuff, making fun of the regular church services."

"No kidding! They let the peasants do things like that?"

"The church actually sponsored it. And it wasn't just the poor people and workers. Brothers in the abbeys did it too. They'd choose a 'Lord of Misrule' and parody all their regular rites and activities. It took the pressure off for a while."

"Yes," she said thoughtfully. "I can see how it would. Sort of like 'mental health days.'"

"Actually, better—more structured and social. People got together and worked out their tensions having fun. And their games were directly related to their problems."

"That would be great therapy," she agreed.

"It was. And they were all in it together. No danger of getting fired when the boss walks in on you spoofing him."

She spiked a green bean with her fork and bit slowly into its pungent crispness. "I never got into that kind of history. I was so bored with those battles and strings of rulers with the same name."

"I understand that completely," he said. "You'd probably find my kind of history a surprise. I'll lend you my favorite book if you're interested."

She nodded. "I am. Definitely."

Dessert was a fig tart with whipped cream for him, and for her (she decided to cut down on the calories), lemon yogurt mousse, accompanied by more talk about humor as therapy.

They had gone out late, sat in the restaurant talking until near closing, and got home close to midnight. She didn't ask him up, and he didn't hint for an invitation. The evening had gone much better than she'd expected.

A birthday party claimed Sunday afternoon. Tremain called in the evening to chat, and remembered to bring the book to her at school on Monday. They spoke frequently, ate lunch together when she was at school, and finally, she made dinner for him in her apartment.

Sometimes she drifted, jolting back to find herself startled by his light-hearted ways, then realized she was half-consciously comparing him with the duty-burdened Lorimar. Try as she might to forget the Halderwoldians, scraps of dreams, real as day, drew her back to them. It was something that would have to wear itself out over time, she decided.

She threw herself into her present life: clown classes, gym workouts renewed, carefully, visits to the children's ward. She had become acquainted with several children there, and went to see them sometimes as Paige. Her party business was thriving, probably because of the new balloons with her name and phone number that she passed out to all the children at the parties.

She was teaching more often, frequently rushing home from school to get into costume for a party. Even tutoring Cheryl in algebra she wouldn't need until college, but the girl was eager for a head start and seemed to enjoy being with someone who would talk about math. Sometimes, going over problems with her enthusiastic student, Paige would stop and look into the discomfort rising in her chest only to recognize it as an ache for Cherry, her youth and mental acuity probably soon to be tethered to teenage motherhood, with no prospect of 'going back to school' when the children were older. Something now available to girls in the lowest income brackets here.

And her mother was so happy about Tremain. Both her parents and Aunt Holly had met him and approved heartily—too heartily. Enough to cause Paige considerable embarrassment since nothing ultra serious was happening between the two of them yet. They had enjoyed some good meals and some great discussions, particularly about medieval mental health, a subject she nearly harassed him to tell her more about, and he seemed to enjoy dipping into his reservoir of information on the subject. If she had been familiar with this period of European history before her tumble, she'd have wondered if her mind had created Halderwold from the material. But she couldn't recall ever reading or hearing about it before Tremain.

CHAPTER 17

On a beautiful Saturday morning, it was Paige's turn to take an elderly neighbor shopping, a grandmother who had hired Paige for a beautiful party for her twin granddaughters' seventh birthday. Ethel Parker was a lovely, old-fashioned person who gave her granddaughters sweet little dresses with aprons (aprons!) and doll buggies. And she had asked that all the girls at the party wear party dresses. They had, and obviously enjoyed looking pretty. Ethel had suffered a slight stroke and was no longer able to drive, so Paige took her turn among the neighbors on the block, driving her on her weekly trip to the supermarket.

Today, to make Ethel's shopping trip as pleasant as possible, Paige wore an ankle-length skirt and a blouse with sleeves; it was a cool day anyway. And Ethel told her over and over how beautiful and *demure* she looked. Coming from Ethel, she knew 'demure' was the highest of compliments.

The shopping trip over, and the rest of the day open to anything she felt like doing, Paige stood beside her car wondering what that would be. The inside of her apartment had no appeal with the blue October sky inviting her back to the open road. On a sudden impulse, without even changing her clothes, she brought her bicycle out of its place in the hallway, jumped on, and tucking her skirt underneath her on the seat, took off down the street. Before she knew it, she was out of town, heading down a road that passed a lovely pond surrounded by bushes with clouds of red berries.

She wasn't the only one to take advantage of the day and the scenery. As she approached the pond, a string of motorcycles came up the road toward her, mostly two by two. Some of the women waved to her from their perches behind the drivers as they passed; some of the men waved. Paige waived back, keeping a tight grip on her handlebars with the other hand. This many motor-cycles at once made her nervous.

A car came up behind her and slowed, looking for a chance to pass. She would have moved off the road had the gravel on the side not appeared to be loose; but she could now see the end of the motorcycles, so she held her ground. The car would be able to pass in a few seconds and all would be peace-ful again. But the car pulled out around her as the last motorcycle, a single, was passing. Then around the curve behind it came four more, and the driver of the car pulled back too soon.

Too soon for the bicycle behind it. Paige yanked her bike off the road and skidded in the gravel. Just when she seemed to be righting herself, the front wheel hit a clump of grass while the back skidded around toward the road. She saw the grassy slope and the pond and the red berries coming up to meet her.

The first thing she saw when she opened her eyes were the bluets, growing tiny and sweet in front of her face. Then, before she could look around, think of trying to get up or even lift her head, a sharp prod jarred the middle of her back, accompanied by a gruff command, "Up you! No naps before the grapes are finished!"

"Stop it!" Paige gasped, before she found the strength to sit up. But another prod landed on a kidney. Finally, she was able to twist her body around enough to view her tormentor, one of the most muscular women she had ever seen, armed with a wooden rake that hovered menacingly above her.

"Back to the grapes!" The woman shook the rake over her threateningly.

Dizzily, Paige dragged herself into a sitting position and looked around to find herself in the middle of a small, grassy area in—what had to be a vineyard. Grape arbors bordered the area on all sides. Several great vats sat in the middle, over the sides of which she could see heads bobbing up and down.

"Get back to your vat!" the woman bellowed. "Or you'll have more than blue feet to show for your day."

"I ... I don't think I belong here." Paige strained to find strength to get to her feet. She'd made it onto her knees when a husky arm encircle her waist and actually lifted her to her feet.

"Come on, now. Rest time is over." The woman half-dragged her toward the nearest vat.

"So you caught another lazy one, Belda," said one of the men lifting the buckets of grapes outside the vat.

Belda tightened her grip painfully on Paige's rib cage. "Up the steps or I'll toss you in from down here!"

Hand over hand on the rough wood, Paige called up all her strength to clamber up the steps, catching herself twice from tumbling over the side. Belda was close behind, and as soon as she reached the top, delivered a firm shove that sent her flying into a sea of mushy grapes. It was either scramble to her feet or drown in grape juice.

Somehow, for the next two hours, she managed to keep her feet moving. The sun was going down and the work day would soon be over. The sunset took on Halderwoldian hues, and she now remembered Belda, the woman who had shown the vineyards to Poppy and Lorimar, bowing and fawning before her betters. Well, at least she knew people here. The very thought of finding herself in another strange world, dealing with new rules and manners was more overwhelming than she could even entertain.

Finally, a loud whistle blew. Or rather several whistles held by overseers blew at the same time. "Time to quit for the day!" The call circled round the vineyard and the treaders in the vat scrambled toward the steps, climbed up the inside and down the outside to the ground. Paige was the last to make it out. No one paid her much attention; and they had nearly all hurried away from the area by the time she reached the ground. She crawled under the steps and sat with her back against a rough pole, hoping they would all leave without noticing her. She had to recover from her exhaustion enough to think what to do next.

Not much time seemed to pass before the sun set and darkness began closing in, thick and palpable. She welcomed the dark as a cover while she figured out where she was and what to do next. Then she saw the moon coming up. A nearly full blue moon. As soon as she gathered enough strength, she'd get up and somehow find her way by moonlight into the city and Lorimar's house. She was lucky she'd just happened to go biking in a skirt instead of shorts.

Finally the bluish moonlight, nearly as light as a winter night on earth, spread over the landscape; and Paige, her yellow blouse and skirt died purple, dragged herself out from under the steps and looked around, trying to decide on directions. *Let's see, I think the moon rose from that direction when I saw it from the top of the Wise House, and that was—over that way from the city, and it was waning, and I have to be out on the side—yes—over on the other side of the Wise House, where Lorimar took me out to the vineyards.*

She gave up on directions by the moon, but finding the road was easy once she got her legs moving. Just going down the hill in the same direction the others had taken, it soon lay below her, a pale ribbon winding down a hill. And she hadn't gone many steps down the road when she heard a cart approaching from behind. Her first instinct was to hide in the bushes, but then she realized she was dressed okay this time. The stains wouldn't be too noticeable in the semi-darkness. She had no coins to offer, but maybe they'd give her a ride anyway.

The cart pulled up beside her and stopped and she had the full attention of three men, a driver on a wide front seat, and two men in the back.

"Would you prefer to ride, lady?" one of the men in the back seat asked in a mockingly polite tone. When she looked up, they all sat there grinning and she studied them as well as she could in the dim light. Better to walk than get in with men who might be up to no good. But it was an open cart, and her whole body ached awfully.

The elderly driver slid over to her side of the cart and held out a hand. "Nothing to fear, woman. They are just having a bit of sport."

Then she understood. Of course they took her for a worker, or maybe even a prostitute, and had called her 'lady' to tease her. Well, she could take a little joshing in exchange for a load off her miserable feet. They were probably okay. She clasped the driver's hand and hoisted herself up on the wooden step and into the front seat beside him. "I just need to get into the city," she told him.

"And we are heading there straightaway," the driver said, shaking the reigns.

"Welcome on board," one of the gallants in the back seat said.

"We will take you anywhere you wish, lady," the original speaker added, with a note of raucous disrespect in his tone.

Paige turned around to get a good look at the men, in case she should ever run into them again. Her face was in full moonlight as she said, "I appreciate your kindness."

Silence for a moment, then one of the men gasped, "*Lady!* I beg your pardon. I assumed you were a worker from the vineyard."

The other bowed and held his hands out in the Halderwoldian greeting. "I also beg your pardon, lady. Please allow us to take you to the door of your destination."

She looked them directly in the eyes. They were young, just boys having a little joke. And they had seen her eyes. Good. "I am bound for the house of Lorimar, the nashu of the Wise House," she told them primly.

The men exchanged glances. "Of course, lady," one of them said. "That is not at all out of our way." The other simply nodded his agreement.

They rode in silence for a few minutes until Paige, deciding it could only be to her advantage to have as many friendly acquaintances here as possible, turned to them again and said, "I am Poppy, a wise one in training."

"Of course you are," one said, bowing again.

"Naturally," the other added with a decorous nod. Neither of them gave her his name.

The driver had speeded up the pair of horses to a brisk canter, and as they rounded a turn in the road that came out on top of a hill, she saw the Wise House and the city below, all the buildings shining bluish in the moonlight. He had to reign the horses back as they traveled down the hill, but in a very short time, they were clip-clopping along the narrow streets, then the familiar street approaching Lorimar's house. For some reason, the driver pulled up several yards short of the house. Turning to Poppy, he said, "I will escort you from here, lady."

"Oh, that's not necessary at all," she told him. "I know the way perfectly."

He didn't argue. "We will at least wait here until we know you are safely at the house," one of the men in the back seat said.

"I'd appreciate that," Poppy said, as she rose to step down. One of the men from the back was already on the ground to hand her down.

"Thanks very much," she said, as he politely held her by the hand and elbow. "I'll be fine from here."

"Good morrow, lady," they all said.

"Good morrow." She hurried down the last few yards to Lorimar's house. Pausing in front, she could see a dim light in the vestibule. The door that had stood open most of the time when she was last here was now closed. She stood wondering if she should knock or just step inside, when her hunger and fatigue brought the sudden memory of *vigorwort*. Surely her absence and her distressed appearance would rate a cup. She pushed the heavy door, and it opened easily. She stepped gingerly inside the vestibule, closed the door behind her, then paused as she heard voices. A child's voice—a young child babbling, then a soothing woman's voice.

"There, there, Alvar. No more berries. Time for bed now." The voice sounded like Cherry's. Poppy moved toward the open inner door that led to the dining area and peered inside.

The young mother looked up, startled, then jumped from her chair, her mouth opened but no sound issuing from it. She held a child about a year old in her arms. Cherry stood in stunned silence, then took a couple of steps toward her unexpected guest. "Poppy? Yes. Why yes, it is *you!*"

"Yes, it's me, Cherry," Poppy said, moving into the room. "Whose baby is that?"

After staring at her guest for another minute, Cherry said, "Well, it has been two years since you … disappeared. I have married and.this is my son, Alvar. Is he not beautiful?" She held the little boy out toward Poppy..

"Yes, he surely is." Poppy replied, nervously moving into the room. "But I was only gone for a few *weeks!* Oh." She remembered how her time here before had lengthened into weeks, while at home she had been unconscious for only a couple of days. "How is …" She was afraid to ask. "Everyone?"

"We are well," Cherry replied. "Kandra is … well, and father … is well also. He is not yet home from the Wise House. Much more of his time has been claimed of late by his duties there."

Poppy went over to her. "You don't look … I mean, I hope you're happy, Cherry. I just never thought you'd be getting married so *soon*. Is your husband here?"

Cherry shook her head. "He is with the guardsmen. Outside the city." She suddenly seemed to read Poppy's concern. "Vade is a good man, Poppy. And of course I am happy. What else would I do but marry?" She paused to hitch the baby up onto her shoulder. "But we have had occasion to fear since you left." Then she broke off and went to put her son down between two large cushions on a sofa. "But let me go and tell grandmother you are here. And please sit. You are tired and perhaps hungry. And why are you completely stained with … well, I can smell grape juice."

Poppy went to the sofa and sat down beside the baby with a huge sigh. "I'll tell you all about it, but I'm more concerned right now with what's been going on here. Yes, please get Kandra. I'll watch the baby," she added when she saw Cherry pause to glance back at her son.

When Kandra came rushing through the inner door, Poppy gasped at the change in her appearance. *My God, she's aged ten years!* Poppy stood up and moved into Kandra's open arms. The older woman cried a little as she embraced her friend. Cherry joined the circle and put her arm around Poppy too.

"We have missed you greatly, Poppy," Kandra sniffed. "But Lorimar instructed me not to mention you or ask where you had gone."

"Yes, that's better left unquestioned," Poppy replied, forgetting her fatigue in sympathy for the older woman's fragility. "Come sit down, Kandra. We'll talk."

The all sat. Cherry closed the door to the vestibule, then picked up her baby and sat in a chair, while Poppy and Kandra sat side by side on the sofa. Kandra clung to Poppy's hands with a disturbing desperation.

With a squeeze that Poppy meant to be reassuring, she said, "Okay, just tell me what's been going on here. And start at the beginning. It seems I've been away much longer than I realized."

A huge sigh preceded Kandra's words. Cherry had tucked Alvar into the large chair, and, sitting in front of him, leaned forward to be part of the conversation, though waiting respectfully for her grandmother to lead.

"Things have not been well here," Kandra began, her voice beginning to tremble. The king—Vran—has fallen ill."

"Do they know what's wrong with him?" Poppy asked.

Kandra shook her head slowly, hopelessly. "No one can tell. The royal diviners have performed every ritual of quest, and the royal menders have given him every healing herb known to them, still he languishes."

"Aren't you a healer, Kandra?" Poppy asked. "I mean, when I first met Cherry, she told me you were a … a *mender* of people. That you used herbs and soup and wine … wasn't that it?" She glanced at Cherry. "And there was something else … what was it? Oh, yes. *Quietness.* Couldn't you do something for Vran with … that kind of medicine?"

Kandra raised her hands and let them drop onto her lap. "I believe the menders have sat with him in all rites of quietude known to them, and his caretakers will let no one else near him. Avive cares for him day and night."

"But why?" Poppy asked. "I thought this family was really close to the king and queen."

"We *were*," Cherry put in.

"Yes, we were," Kandra agreed in a doleful tone. "But as I said, Avive has no way of knowing whom to trust. And, alas, she had chosen to trust no one. Not even Lorimar, though he has given her no reason to doubt him."

"But what has happened?" Poppy asked. "How did things get like this?"

Cherry slid nearer the edge of her seat and leaned forward as if the walls had ears. "It is *Pule*, Poppy. He has somehow convinced Avive that everyone is against the king, that no one can be trusted … except himself. Though it is hard to imagine that she actually trusts *him*."

Wouldn't you know it. Her old problem admirer. "But I thought everyone knew that Pule was a … *scoundrel*," she said. "How can Avive have been duped by him?"

"She may not be," Kandra said. "But he interferes in no way with her care of Vran, which is her only concern. What we fear most is the rumor that he has convinced her that, should Vran die, he would be the proper regent for Var, the six-year-old prince, until he is old enough to take the crown."

"Oh, my *God!*" Poppy breathed. "I thought everyone knew that man was … *bad news.*" She looked from one woman to the other. "Can't Lorimar talk to her?"

Both women were shaking their heads slowly. "No one can," Kandra replied. "Except for a few servants, she spends all her time with Vran and her children, and Pule has arranged that everyone else be kept away. Avive is so consumed by her husband's illness, she has allowed that *blackguard* to run the palace." Seeming to gain energy with her accounting, she went on, "The Wise House barely exists. The position of advisement to the crown that the wise ones have exercised these many years has been so restricted it has nearly vanished."

"How could this have happened?" Poppy sat astonished.

"Need you ask?" Cherry, replied in her new, mature tone. "Pule has been about the task for years, turning the constituents of the palace against the king's authority and the traditional office of the wise ones." She paused, glancing toward the closed door, then continued in a low voice, "My grief has been to see my father bowed down within himself for a long time now—not the same man he was when I was a child. The possibility of this turn of events has been on his mind, I think, for a long time. He is wise."

"And so are you, Cherry," Poppy told her softly. "I've known that for a long time, too."

"I am a mother now," the younger woman replied. "That is my office. I will never have a place in the Wise House, even if that would do any good now."

"Wasn't Lorimar's mother a mother?" Poppy asked.

"Of course, but as I explained to you long ago, I lack the natural abilities."

"Well, I still think your natural good sense should count for something," Poppy said.

"Besides," Cherry added. "I have of late been occupied with learning the mender's trade from grandmother, and she claims I do have natural talent for that." She glanced at Kandra.

"Indeed, I believe it to be her true calling," her grandmother affirmed.

Poppy nodded. What right had she to be telling Cherry what to do anyway?

"But speaking of Lorimar's mother," Kandra said sadly. "She has passed on to the Unbounded One. That is another sadness for Lorimar. I think he always held hope that she might one day dwell with us again."

"Oh, Kandra." Poppy reached for her hand again, then glanced at Cherry, recalling that Lorimar had told her Cherry believed his mother to be dead.

"I know," the girl said quietly. "It is well that I did not know as a child."

There were sounds of someone entering the vestibule. The three women looked up and Cherry rose to go to the door, as Kandra moved to take her place in front of the sleeping child.

Poppy sat nervously, feeling guilty of something—as if she had purposely abandoned these people two years ago, leaving Lorimar 'at the altar.' Not that her presence here would have made much difference, from what she had heard. She rose to face the man she had very nearly married.

He was changed too, although more handsome, she thought, in a mature way. New forehead creases lent a look of knowing more than he cared to, and the added silver in his hair shone with senatorial dignity. Cherry had probably gone to the vestibule to let him know who was inside.

"My lady," he said, showing no surprise or emotion as his eyes met Poppy's.

"Lorimar," Poppy began, but she hardly knew what to say. "I didn't leave ... *on purpose.*"

He offered a flicker of a smile and held out his hands in formal greeting. "I know that, of course," he said simply, which seemed to put all three women at ease. Kandra went to the kitchen to bring food, and Cherry picked up her sleeping baby and went to put him to bed, leaving her father alone with his unexpected guest.

He gestured toward the sofa, "Sit, lady."

"Please don't call me that." She plopped back down in the spot where she had been sitting, and he sat beside her, but not close. "Lorimar, I'm so sorry to hear about your mother."

He nodded. "Thank you, but perhaps it was for the best. Arn has passed also." Then without waiting for further comment from her, he said, "The fairblow that struck you contained stones."

"The ... oh, you mean that balloon thing that knocked me out. I figured it must have had something like that in it."

"The archer who shot it was discovered," he continued.

"What ... happened to him?" She was afraid to ask.

"He is serving an appropriate sentence," Lorimar replied evasively. "However, the true propagator remains unpunished."

"And do you know who that is?"

"None other than your old friend and suitor," he told her with a rueful smile.

Poppy waited for more, but when Lorimar sat staring at the carpet, she said simply, "Pule."

He nodded, and sat silent, looking weary. Soon Kandra appeared with a tray of food and drink for both of them, and they followed her to the table. There was no vigorwort, Poppy noted at once. They had probably used their stores of it up themselves, with all they'd been going through.

Even though she and Cherry had eaten earlier with the baby, Kandra sat with them at the table, filling in the details that Lorimar left out in his telling of the events of the past two years. After their near-joining, Poppy had been placed unconscious in a covered cart to be carried home, but was found neither in the cart nor anywhere else when they arrived. Lorimar, as the nashu, and also in his own personal interest, had launched an investigation into the stone-filled fairblow and who had shot it. The search had not been difficult. A young man called Fridon, a close friend and supporter of Pule in all his machinations, and also a superb archer, was fingered and confessed without much ado. Lorimar's opinion was that Pule had ordered him to confess to put a speedy end to the investigation.

"Fridon affirmed at his trial that 'the young woman was an outlander and an interloper, and deserved no better treatment,'" Kandra added in an acerbic tone.

"Well, that *is* partly true," Poppy admitted.

"Nevertheless," Lorimar continued, "it has been the custom here for generations to honor Larians. And anyone, even the nashu—even the king—may join with a woman of his own choosing."

"That's reasonable too," Poppy agreed between bites of crunchy bread. In spite of all the stress, hard work had created a hearty appetite.

"And attempting to murder a bride on her joining walk is not allowed under our laws," Lorimar pronounced, as if that were not self-evident, Poppy thought. "Though she be facing the humblest grape-trouncer in the land," he finished.

Tell me about grape-trouncing! Poppy gave her head a shake to try and rid it of the rigors of her day, then glanced down at her purple-stained outfit in the light of the table lamp.

Kandra noticed, and gave her a cursory glance as well. "What has happened to you since your arrival here?"

"I landed here this afternoon, in a vineyard," she explained. "And that huge woman named Belda thought I was supposed to be stomping on grapes and threw me into a vat."

A flicker of amusement passed briefly over both faces, then Lorimar assumed a serious expression and murmured, "Belda will answer."

"Oh, please forget it. I don't think she knew any better ..." Poppy began to defend the woman lest she be imprisoned or something for her misjudgement.

Kandra just sighed, "Belda," and quickly resumed her former serious expression. "I will dress you at once."

"First we must finish our conversation," Lorimar said gently. "And our supper. Better to wait until morning, mother."

His mother-in-law rose from the table. "I will prepare a bed then."

After she had gone, Lorimar looked Poppy in the eyes. "I admit I am at a loss to know how to greet you, Poppy."

"Well, I'm at the same loss," Poppy replied, feeling suddenly shy now that the two of them were alone together. "But I would like you to know that, in my time, I have been home for only a few weeks, and I haven't ... gotten married or anything."

The forlorn smile appeared again. "Then I will not congratulate you. Perhaps I should offer my sympathy that you have found yourself among us again."

"Don't talk like that!" Poppy exclaimed. "You have no idea how I missed you ... all." The last word was added after a pause.

"We missed you as well, lady," he replied in a formal manner that suggested restraint.

Wordlessly, Poppy ransacked her mind for the proper way to talk to him. Dealing with a man from another world who might, or might not, love you hadn't been covered in charm school. Of course she remembered more from clown school than from charm school, and that didn't apply here at all.

When she said nothing, Lorimar continued, "Since there is no way of knowing how long you ... may be with us, it is difficult to know how to speak with you. There may be no reason to draw you into our difficulties."

"Well, I want to hear them, why don't you start by telling me what the situation is," she suggested. "Cherry and Kandra told me the whole realm is living in fear. Maybe I can help in some way."

"I will tell you all," he said. "But to include you in any plans we might formulate could be a mistake since you may ... disappear at any time." He glanced at her apologetically. "I mean no offence to your intentions or your concern for us, but I feel we must be forthright with each other."

"Oh, I couldn't agree more," Poppy replied quickly. "And I realize the ... possibility of my not being able to follow through. But I'm really concerned. And you know, sometimes just talking about things can help."

He nodded. "Possibly. In fact, I think speaking with you can only be encouraging, since it has become so difficult to know whom to trust."

"Good." Poppy was intrigued. "What plans do you have?"

He looked thoughtful for a moment before answering, "None worthy of putting into play immediately, but somehow we must deliver Vran from the danger he is in, hope that he recovers from his illness, and in any happenstance, rid Halderwold of the dangerous influence and power of Duke Pule."

"Pule the Poison," she muttered. Then, "Well, for all we know, I could be here for a while, and I'll do anything I can as long as I'm here. Got any ideas on how we could go about something like that?"

Lorimar sighed and shook his head. "It is all rather overwhelming. But of course I did not know you were coming."

Poppy shrugged. "Neither did I, but now that I'm here, maybe we can come up with something." She brightened. "Maybe Pule will still like me. If I pretend I like him, maybe I can get some information about any schemes he's hatching."

Lorimar shot her a look and replied as if to an adolescent daughter. "Poppy, a man who attempted to have you murdered is not one I would wish you to consort with; nor, I think, one who would be wont to share his secrets with you."

"You've got a point there," Poppy had to admit. "But there must be some way we can get ahead of that creep. He's not all that smart, you know. I talked with him enough to know that. We've got to think hard."

"Tomorrow," he said, rising from the table, then added with no attempt to cover his chagrin, "Do you remember where Kandra's room is?"

"I can find it," Poppy said softly, looking toward the doorway that led to the stairs. By now they would have been sharing a bed for two years, she couldn't help thinking as she went up the stairs. Maybe they'd even have a baby. She wasn't sure how she felt about that, but one thing was sure: life was strange, even when it wasn't even your real life.

Poppy's head, on awakening, was full of concern for Halderwold, almost as if she'd never been away. It was an early conference the four of them held at their breach of fast table. Cherry seemed as overjoyed as circumstances would allow at having her friend back, though clearly mixed with anxiety over her possible disappearance; Lorimar was trying to create some plan for discovering Pule's intentions, or at least some strategy on which to build a plan. Poppy was eager to help, and she might be useful, he agreed, but he would not consider putting her directly in harm's way.

Kandra reminded them that the first concern was the king's illness. "I am vexed by my helplessness in this matter," she told the others. "Somehow, I must get close enough to try and find out what ails him. Until we know whether or not he can be mended, how can we predict the future for any of us?"

"Grandmother's vexation is foremost," Cherry put in. "Whether we are to have a king or not is the beginning of our dilemma."

"That girl's got it on the ball," Poppy said.

The others cast brief, quizzical glances her way, and Lorimar rubbed the back of his neck under the long hair he now wore bound in a pony tail. "I live with deep-thinking women," he remarked. "So where do we begin, ladies? No one is allowed near Vran. Pule has completely taken charge of the palace staff. He has men like stanchions around the royal apartments, and Avive pays no attention to anything save the condition of her husband.

"Then that is where we must begin," Kandra said. "And *I* care for him as well. Vran has been a good friend as well as a good king. Somehow, I must be allowed to approach him and perform a palpleth."

"There is no *chance* …" Lorimar began, but he was interrupted by his fifteen-year-old, wise-woman daughter. "Father, there must be ways to get into the palace. Couldn't one of us appear at the palace as a laborer in need of a post?" She gave a small, stifled giggle that reminded Poppy of the old Cherry. "You remember how Lady Poppy looked last night after trouncing grapes?"

"Not much like any kind of lady," Poppy said.

"It is true," Kandra said thoughtfully. "The palace hires day laborers. Cleaners and cooks' helpers …"

"And laundresses," Cherry added. "I will dress in poor clothing and approach one of the back doors …"

"No *way!*" Poppy butted in. "There could be someone there who knows you. That sounds like a job for a person who hasn't been seen around here for a couple of years."

Lorimar's eyes took on an intensity. "But what if Pule should notice you, Poppy? He would remember you, I am sure."

"What would the duke be doing around a … scullery maid or laundress?" Poppy asked.

All three of the others let out a synchronized "Huh!"

"The duke has been known to pay inordinate attention to female palace workers from the scullery maids up to the royal protocol reminder," Lorimar said.

"I think I can pull it off." Poppy was not to be deterred. "Those yokels who gave me a ride down here from the vineyard last night thought I was a real grape-trouncer. They poked all kinds of fun at me until I looked them in the eyes."

"You looked them in the eyes?" Lorimar said, concerned. "Were they … any of your former acquaintances?"

"No. Never saw any of them before. But I told them who I am."

"Then I am even more loath to put you in any kind of jeopardy."

"Well, this is the only workable plan we've got, isn't it?" Poppy insisted. "Unless we can come up with a better one fast, I'm off to the palace. There's no time to waste."

The others looked at each other, then back at their guest. "Then it's settled," she said. "Help me get me dressed up like an out-of-work laundress or something, and I'll go apply for my new job."

Reluctantly, Lorimar left for the Wise House, and the women ransacked their rag closet for cast-off dresses they had planned to tear and up and use for cleaning cloths. Before long, Poppy's hair was wrapped in a ragged grey scarf, her dress a faded rust-colored, too-large knit dress with parts of the hem hanging raveled and uneven. Poppy concocted an eyelash and eyebrow stain from blueberry juice and a small amount of ground burnt herb. They smudged her bright hairline with the same mixture. "Try not to let anyone see your eyes," Kandra warned her. "Most lower servants rarely look their betters in the eye anyway."

Wrapped in a shabby cloak with a hood, bread, cheese and a little money in her pocket, Poppy went off to hire a cart that would take her out of the city and within a quarter-mile of the palace. She paid the inattentive young driver his fee, climbed down with no offer of help from him, and began walking in the direction of the palace in her nearly worn-out sandals.

CHAPTER 18

Landing a job at the palace was easier than she had expected. The guard made her wait outside a rear door until he went inside and came back with a flustered middle-aged woman who turned out to be the overseer of the laundry.

"Come right in here, girl; everything is behind schedule." The woman huffed and muttered as she led Poppy into an enormous area where great tubs of hot water filled the room with steam like a smoke screen. "The work has not been getting done on time. The king must have clean bedding twice a day now. The queen demands it, and all is behind!"

"Where do I start, lady?" Poppy asked, keeping her head bowed.

"Oh, I am hardly a *lady*!" the woman gave another huff that came dangerously close to a laugh. "I am a *missus,* but so are the other overseers, so you may call me Etral." She picked a long wooden pole from a rack and handed it to Poppy with the simple instruction, "Take this and lift all the clothes out of that vat and put them into the cold rinse in that tub over there. Then you must wring them all out carefully, but mind you, girl, not until you have stirred them enough to make sure they are well rinsed."

Poppy took the pole. "I can do that, Etral."

"Good. I will come by later to see if you are doing a good job. What is your name, girl?"

Poppy hesitated. The women at home had forgotten to give her a name. She racked her memory for a Halderwoldian name, but aside from *Kandra, Cherry* and *Avive*, the only name she could remember on the spot was "Belda."

"*Belda?*" Etral repeated with a low snort. "I did not think anyone else went by *that* name." Then she whirled around, peering through the steam in all directions, sighed loudly, and said in a sort of stifled wail, "Now I must go and find someone to do *Serica's* work. *Again!*"

Poppy proceeded to fish the items of clothing out of the hot water, realizing the steam would most certainly set her eye-makeup running, but probably no one would notice or care. Just in case, she picked up the hem of her skirt and wiped her eyes as well as she could without a mirror. The other four or five women that she could see were moving through a robot-like routine that was broken only by their frequent swipes at the sweat running down their faces. However did Serica get away with goofing off on a busy job like this, she wondered. And why would Etral go looking for a *replacement* for her, rather than finding Serica herself and dragging her back to do her own work? And why did the overseer seem more frightened than angry at the situation?

It was after the quarter of an hour in which the women were allowed to eat the food they took from their pockets, washed down with cold water from the rinse-spout, that Poppy laid eyes on an attractive young woman she decided must be the prodigal Serica. She was walking almost leisurely beside Etral, who was gesturing frantically toward the laundry tubs as she talked to her obviously uninterested companion. Finally, it seemed Etral had persuaded the girl to do some work, and heaving a huge sigh of annoyance, Serica grabbed a wooden pole from the rack and plunged it moodily into a steaming tub close to where Poppy was working. She worked steadily for a short time, then looked around as if bored. Spotting Poppy, she called, "Who are you?"

"Belda." Poppy kept on working. "What's *your* name?"

"Serica," the girl replied, after shooting Poppy a peculiar look. "From the vineyards?"

"Yes, I did work there." Well, it was no lie.

"I think I have heard of you," Serica said. "But I thought you would be … bigger."

Poppy shrugged, wringing the cold water out of a sheet that seemed to have become twice as long as they had been a few hours ago, and wishing she'd come equipped with a name of her own. "Do not mistake me for Belda the Overseer," she said. "I worked there only as a grape-trouncer."

Her answer seemed to satisfy Serica, who turned back to her vat.

For the rest of the afternoon, Poppy struggled with bedclothes that seemed to gradually become more and more stubborn and hard to manage, probably, she realized, in direct proportion to her growing fatigue. This was hard work, but she kept up as good a pace as she was able, only pausing now and then to give her aching arms a shake, while Serica continued to transfer a few items out of the hot water into the rinse, then dawdle, looking around as if she had lost someone before resuming her leisurely work pace.

Finally a much better-dressed young woman carrying a basket of laundry appeared out of the steam, walked up to Serica as if she had been looking for her in particular, and handed over the basket. Serica nodded to the woman and accepted her burden as if eager for more work. The woman then turned quickly and disappeared in the same direction from which she had come. Serica began lifting each item from the basket into the hot water as if it were sacred. With care she had not shown in her work all day, she stirred them gently then let them soak a few minutes while she went off to return with a tub considerably smaller than the cold water tubs the rest of them used. She poled the new items out of the vat and piled them into the small tub, then picking up a large wooden bucket, she muttered, "got to get some clean water," and set off at a new brisk pace into the steam.

Poppy wondered why she hadn't gone to the nearby spigot all the workers in her area were using. The girl probably just wanted an excuse to take another lengthy break; and it was some time before she returned, laboring under the weight of her full bucket, which she then dumped on the clothing in her small tub.

Etral was passing just then. She paused and sniffed at Serica's tub. "What is this?" she asked.

"Just the king's bedding," Serica replied with a little toss of her head. "You know the queen always sends Mari to me with it."

"I know, and I hope you will rinse them well," Etral replied. "But have you not put too much scent in the rinse?"

"Mari asked me to use more," Serica replied, stirring them slowly. "She said the king becomes a little more enlivened by the scent of lavender blended with bergamot."

The older woman scowled. "Well, if that is what the queen has instructed—but it smells *too* fragrant to me."

"Mari comes to me directly from the queen," Serica said in a haughty tone of finality, continuing her stirring. Etral moved on, her face flushed even more than it had already been from the heat.

The work day was nearing its end when Serica drifted away again, leaving the king's bed things soaking in the peculiar but rather pleasant concoction. Poppy moved over to the tub to breath in the scent. It really wasn't bad. Maybe Kandra would be interested in this rinse. Being an expert on herbs, she was probably already familiar with it. But Etral hadn't known about it, even though laundry was her area of expertise.

She glanced around to make sure no one was watching, then pulled a small item which turned out to be a pillow case from the tub, hurriedly wrung it and wrapped it around a leg under her long dress. Returning to her own tub, she wondered what was going to keep it there, when she remembered a night dress with string ties that she had rinsed an hour or more ago. The nightie was easily retrieved from her tub of finished laundry which the 'clothesline workers' came for at regular intervals. The nightie went off to the clothesline minus a string before Poppy was allowed to leave for the night.

Walking toward the road in a group of day laborers, Poppy realized that even if her dark hairline and eyebrows were smudged or gone altogether, it was unlikely that any of these women had the energy or the interest to lift her head and examine a fellow worker in the twilight that was fast turning to darkness. She dawdled by the roadside until the others had gone, then found a cart to take her home. Happily, the drivers she encountered today, unlike her hosts of last evening, showed no personal interest in her whatsoever.

"What a relief to be back!" Poppy cried as the safety of Lorimar's house enveloped her once more. She realized she had almost said "back home," but there was no time to analyze her misuse of words. Both Cherry and Kandra came on like mother hens, unwrapping her from her cloak with exclamations of the sweaty mess she had become. Cherry practically dragged her to the nearest relief site and sat her on a stool, pealing the damp dress off over her head and tossing it onto a nearby bench. Kandra following with a kettle of hot water from the kitchen. Then they noticed the damp packing tied around her leg.

"You are injured!" Cherry cried, kneeling beside her.

"No. No, I'm not hurt," Poppy told them as Kandra put the kettle down on the stone floor and with a breathless, "What is this?" knelt and began tugging at the string.

"It's just a … Poppy laughed a little, partly because it was going to sound so silly and partly from exhaustion. "It's … one of the king's pillow cases."

"You *stole* one of the king's pillow cases?" Kandra had pulled the cloth from her leg and found no injury. Now she sat back on her heels, staring at her guest in disbelief.

"Well, it was all a little strange," Poppy continued. "You see, there's this girl there. Serica. And she hardly worked at all while all the rest of us worked our butts off, and sweated them off too, in all that steam."

"I believe I know Serica," Cherry murmured.

"Well, the overseer, Etral," Poppy continued. "She seemed to be scared of making Serica do her work. And when she finally did do some work, this woman … Mari, came in with a basket of the king's bedding and gave it to her."

"Mari is the queen's chamber maid," Cherry put in.

"Well, then Serica all of a sudden got a work ethic going," Poppy continued. "She washed the bedding in the hot water, then went off and got a smaller tub with herbs in the water to rinse it. Then Etral came over and had a fit over how strong it smelled until Serica told her the king liked the herbs …"

"What herbs?" Kandra interrupted, pressing the pillow case to her face.

"Well, she said it was lavender and … bergamot."

"Hmm," Kandra sniffed harder with a look of concentration. "But there is more here than lavender and bergamot. Did she mention anything else?"

Poppy shook her head. "No, that's what she said was in the water."

Kandra continued to sniff and stare at the wall as Cherry reached for the other end of the pillow case and pressed it against her nose. "It smells good, grandmother. Perhaps we should use these herbs in our laundry."

"Leave it!" Kandra cried suddenly, giving Cherry a shove that knocked her over onto the floor. "Get away! Poppy, wash your leg at once—in the hot water. As hot as you can stand!"

"Kandra … what?" Poppy jumped to her feet and looked around, trying to remember how to wash in this old-fashioned setup.

"Grandmother, what *is* it?" Cherry shrieked, scrambling to her feet.

"*Fogbane!* Wash, child! Wash at once!"

Cherry picked up the kettle and, after nearly dropping it, shakily poured hot water into a basin. "Surely it will not harm us, merely *touching* it." She grabbed a wash cloth, dipped it in the hot water, then held it out by a corner to her grandmother who had gotten to her feet and stood shaking her hand. But Kandra waved the cloth away. "Wash your own nose! And your hand!"

Cherry rubbed her nose hard with the cloth, then plunged her hand into the hot water with a cry of pain. Then she hurriedly wet the cloth again, lathered it with soap, and turned to Poppy. "Sit down and let me scour your leg. You had that cloth wrapped around it."

"How long?" Kandra asked Poppy, rubbing her own nose and hand with another cloth she had dipped in the water.

"Just a couple of hours," Poppy replied, obediently sitting down again. "It was only a short time before I left that Serica went out and gave me a chance to pull this out of the tub."

"All will be well. Hold out your leg." Kandra had calmed as she took the cloth from Cherry's hand and began vigorously scrubbing Poppy's leg.

"Then we will not die?" Cherry asked, close to tears. "My baby …"

"No, dear," her grandmother said, glancing at the girl with a contrite expression. "Forgive me. I spoke too soon and in too much perturbation. Even though the cloth was wet and the bane has penetrated our skin to some degree, it has not had time to do great harm. Bring me the jar of tamakon leaves from the shelf over the water jug. They will sooth this poor, scalded leg."

"Kandra, how long will this take to kill Vran?" Poppy asked, ignoring her leg now that she felt assured it wasn't going to drop off.

"From bed clothing that has been dried, it will take some time—I do not know how long—of constant application to his skin, but I fear it has been going on for some time already. We had word that he was ailing several weeks ago."

"I'd think stuff like this would be illegal!" Poppy sputtered.

Kandra continued rubbing. "Oh, indeed it is, if I understand your word. Fogbane has been banned for many years. Ever since Konell, the greatest of herbalists, declared it a bane. And it is nearly impossible to obtain, growing only on the foggy banks of the River Dystopia."

Cherry gasped.

Poppy asked, "Where is that river, Kandra?" She vaguely remembered Lorimar including it in her preliminary wise training.

"On a far side of the forest. A queer, misty place." Kandra had taken a handful of dried leaves from the jar Cherry set on the floor and spread them on Poppy's wet leg, then began rubbing them into a paste. "No one goes there."

"Well, I guess someone did," Poppy said.

Kandra looked thoughtful, her hands busily spreading the paste.

"How far is it to the river, grandmother?" Cherry brought a dry cloth and wrapped it around Poppy's leg, keeping the herb paste plastered on her skin. "On the night of my passage, we seemed to go far into the forest, until the leaders were afraid to continue."

Kandra gave a little snort. "Where you were taken was no more than an hour's journey. To reach the River Dystopia would take at least three or four days, through the forest and into the mountains, if one ever reached it at all. I have heard there are streams swift for wading and hillocks steep for climbing, and fog, and wild beasts …"

"What's on the other side of this river?" Poppy asked.

Kandra shrugged. "Nothing I have ever heard of. Before one reaches the river, all is enveloped in fog day and night. When I was a young woman, four men set out carrying a boat, declaring they would reach the river and launch it, but nothing more was ever heard of them."

Poppy thought for a minute. "Isn't there some kind of … antidote for this poison, Kandra?"

The older woman looked puzzled. "Anta dote?"

"Yes, another herb or something to … you know, offset it's effects."

"Oh, an *amender*."

"Yeah. That sounds right."

Kandra sighed. "Alas. The only known amender for fogbane is the moss of the cheroak tree."

"Well, where can we find a cheroak," Poppy pursued. "I'll even climb it for you."

"There are no cheroak trees in Halderwold," Cherry said dully.

"They grew very tall," Kandra explained. "The last was blown down in a storm several years ago. A woman I knew saved some moss and tried to make it grow on a monan tree, but it all died. Since we had not much use for it anyway, fogbane having been banned long ago, no one made any great effort to save the moss."

"*Bummer!*" Poppy muttered.

The women looked at her with blank sadness.

"Doesn't it grow *anywhere* around here?" Poppy could not give up hope. "Maybe a *little* way into the forest or somewhere?"

"Perhaps in the swamp," Kandra replied vacantly. "That is where it came from in the first place. But little does that serve us."

Their conversation was interrupted by Malina, who glanced at Poppy with surprise, but said nothing except that Lorimar had arrived and supper was ready. She disappeared again, and the three of them went to meet him, Poppy with her leg now wrapped and tied securely.

After retrieving her son from the kitchen where Malina had been watching him, and making sure she had left the house, Cherry came back to the dining room. Lorimar merely had time for an inquisitive stare at their flushed and woebegone faces before they began filling him in on the news of the day. Once updated on Poppy's laundry adventures, the women brought in the food and they gathered at the table, where he sat silent for several minutes. "Pule," he said finally. "Pule must be behind this."

"But I see nothing in the day's happenings to duly bear it out," Kandra said. "Mari is Avive's maid. Perhaps she has some grievance of her own."

Lorimar's weary eyes took in the others at the table. "It is no secret that Pule has been ... familiar with Avive's maid, Mari, for some months now."

Kandra gave a shrug. "Well, that is no surprise. Also, it would explain how fogbane could be recognized even though it has been banned for some time."

"How, grandmother?" Cherry asked.

"Konell, who had it banned, was Mari's grandfather. In the absence of the paintings we were formerly allowed—though it is whispered that some menders have kept hidden likenesses—it's appearance is now unknown even to most herbalists. But Mari may have that knowledge."

"What does it look like, Kandra?" Poppy was curious. "How could someone find it by description only?"

"It has a very unusual appearance," Kandra told her. "I remember nearly all the likenesses in my mentor's book—before it was found and taken from her. A reddish brown pointed leaf with a spiny stem. It shows up easily in the mist."

"I wonder where Serica fits into all this," Poppy said thoughtfully. "I'll have to get more acquainted with her and ..."

"That you will not, lady!" Lorimar's hand came down on the table with a slap that made them all jump. "You have put yourself in quite enough danger already. We are fortunate that Pule had no opportunity to see you."

"And you have certainly come home with a trove of information," Kandra added. "To say nothing of a deadly leg-wrapping. I say your work is done."

"But ... we have to do more, and soon," Poppy objected. "The king could be dying right now. And I doubt if Pule would recognize me after all the time that's passed here, especially the way I was dressed, and working in the *laundry*."

"We will take no more unwarranted risks with your safety," Lorimar said in a stilted, rather formal tone that gave Poppy the feeling he was trying to mask his personal concern. "We must find a way to uncover that rogue's maleficence without harm to the innocent."

Poppy sighed. She felt like saying, 'I got nothin.' But that would only bring that stare of puzzlement from the others.

"I must think," he said, getting up from the table and heading for the stairs. He had eaten almost nothing.

The women sat looking at each other for a few minutes, took a few more bites, then got up and carried the dishes to the kitchen.

"Malina gave me a stare in the bath … relief site," Poppy mentioned as she set a stack of bowls down by the sink. "Do you think she remembers me?"

Kandra looked thoughtful for a moment, then replied, "Malina is my brother's child. There is no danger of her disloyalty, and I will speak to her of you tomorrow." Then she surprised the others by putting the kettle on the fire with the announcement, "Vigorwart for all of us."

Poppy slept the sleep of the drained, a warm cloth soaked anew in some healing herb—she'd forgotten what Kandra had called it—wrapped tightly around her leg. She woke early to mull over the present conundrum. There was no help for it, she decided, groaning a little and lifting her arms in an attempt to stretch the soreness out of her shoulders and back. Much as she longed to remain in the comfort and security of the house, she had to go back to the laundry. She waited until Lorimar had gone to tell the women of her intention.

"No, no!" Kandra exclaimed. "All went better than we dared hope yesterday. You must not press your good fortune."

"Someone has to do *something!*" Poppy insisted. "And the only clues we've got so far have come from that laundry."

"Poppy," Cherry said in an uncharacteristic simper. "Do not go. Father has said …"

"Your father is taking too much on himself," Poppy told her firmly. "He needs help. And it'll be just one more day. I promise," she added, seeing the girl hugging her child and rocking back and forth as if to comfort him, or herself. "And don't forget, I was … am a wise one. It's my *job* to help solve problems like this."

Reluctantly, the women helped her dress. "We can skip the makeup today," she told them. "It wasn't half an hour yesterday before it was running into my eyes and I had to wipe it off. It was so steamy you couldn't see in there, and the women were too busy to pay any attention anyway."

"All except for Serica," Cherry put in, kneeling to ravel her hemline a little more.

"Yeah, there's definitely something going on with Serica," Poppy said. "She's got that overseer, Etral, nervous as a rabbit."

"What is a *rabbit*, Poppy?" Cherry's upturned face showed a bit of her old, girlish curiosity.

Poppy smiled. "I'll tell you later. Maybe when I get back we can take a bath—like we used to."

"That would be most pleasant," Cherry replied.

But there was a whole day of hard labor to get through before she could relax in the bathing pool. Poppy hired a cart to the palace again, after walking some distance from Lorimar's house, and again the driver took no particular notice of her. She walked to the palace, recalling the way to the laundry after the guard let her in.

"Good, you're here," said Etral. "Tend that big tub over by the stairs today. I believe it has cooled. You will need to carry hot water from the vat on the fire pit—here is a pail."

Poppy nodded. It seemed too late to say "Good Morning." Then Etral paused before hurrying off, and said, "You did good work yesterday, Belda. I hope you intend to work as hard today. We need to catch up."

"I will do my best," Poppy replied, then took the pail and made her way through the steam over to the almost boiling vat that sat partly over the huge fire pit. She had to mount a three-step set of stairs to dip her pail in the hot water, and climb down gingerly without spilling any on her feet. Safely at her work station, she realized that several more trips to the hot water vat would be necessary, all of which she managed without scalding herself. She was damp to the skin when she finally had her tub full enough and hot enough to accommodate the pile of laundry that had already been dumped into it. Several handfuls from the pail of oily homemade soap that sat nearby made the tubful ready for stirring with her pole.

All morning nothing unusual went on in her area. She wished she had been stationed beside Serica again. She might end up slaving in this steam all day with no new information for her pains. One thing she did take note of was the stairs. And this was the direction from which Mari had come yesterday. She kept an eye on them.

It was after their short lunch break that she spotted Serica, who said, "A pleasant way to pass the day, is it not?"

"Well, one must work to live," Poppy replied cautiously. "Do you not find life so?"

"Yes, I find life very much so," Serica said in a disgusted tone. "And when one is born in a lowly state and plagued with misfortune, things do not improve with ease."

"Then they must be borne," Poppy said.

Serica looked at her more closely. "You worked in the vineyards before?"

"Yes. But I grew tired of being stained blue."

"You are related to the other Belda?"

"Distantly."

Serica sighed. "You may not find being covered with sweat and weary to the bone any more pleasant than being blue."

"It seems a little better so far."

"You will soon grow sick of it,"

"And how long have you worked here in the laundry, Serica?" Poppy asked.

"Oh, too long," the girl sighed again. "I was married, you know, and kept my own home and garden for a few years. Though we had no children, it was a good life; but my husband … he was sent below."

Poppy shivered beneath her sweat. "Jocularity?"

Serica nodded as if she dared not even say the word. "He … was fond of his wine, and spoke in poor judgment when inebriated. And so I am here, laboring in the steam."

After thinking, *but not very hard,* Poppy felt sorry for the girl and admitted to herself that she wouldn't have any great ambition either if she had to labor here day after day with no end in sight. She wanted to tell her she was better off here than her husband, that she had seen the prisons and at least she could leave at night and see the moon, and the sun on her day off; but she could not afford to offer any attempt at comfort that would hint at her own past adventures.

The day wore on, Poppy doing the same things she had done yesterday, Serica working by spells, occasionally wandering by. Etral bustled by several times, nodded at Poppy and seemed to go out of her way to avoid Serica. So long as the girl was making any semblance of working, Etral left her alone.

Again, toward late afternoon, Mari came down the stairs carrying a basket of laundry which she took directly to Serica, even though she had to pass several other laundresses including Poppy. Edging near enough to peer through the steam, Poppy noticed that, after the laundry was handed over, a small cloth packet which Mari took from her bosom was passed from her hand to Serica's, and Serica slipped it quickly into her pocket.

Then, with Mari gone and Serica seeming to undergo a second wind in her labors over the new laundry, Poppy went back to her own work, wondering if she would get a chance to snitch another piece from Serica's tub for further evidence that the poisonous herb was present in the king's bed clothing. Poppy had no idea how court trials were conducted here, but it seemed that an accusation of this magnitude against a man in line for the throne, taking into consideration his ways and means, would require some pretty substantial proof.

Her chance came with a shock. Approaching the fire pit to fetch another pail of hot water, Poppy passed Serica stirring the bedding in the small odoriferous tub. She saw Etral heading toward her, then veering suddenly away to disappear among the huge, steaming tubs in the center of the large room, as a tall, dark-clothed figure approached from the corner where the stairway came down. Serica stopped her work immediately and spoke with the dark figure, standing close with her face turned up into his (it must be a man judging by height).

The conference was over quickly, though Serica appeared to be clinging to his cloak as he turned to leave. He turned back briefly, actually removed her hand from his clothing, then turned and walked back toward the stairs. Serica followed a few steps before he turned again and spoke to her while motioning for her to go back. They seemed to be arguing, then he put his arm around her shoulders and turned her around facing the way back to her tub. Poppy forgot herself and stared, though visibility was poor, and as Serica returned to her work station, the man turned and noticed her.

Coming slowly toward her though the steam, he was finally close enough for her to glimpse his face. Plunging her arms into the nearest rinse tub, she bent her head over it. The man paused beside her. "You are new?"

Without looking up, she nodded, then tugged her scarf forward to make sure her hairline was hidden. He reached out and took her chin in his hand, forcing her face none too gently toward his, though she kept her eyes lowered. "You seem ... familiar."

She turned her head forcefully, freeing her chin, and bent over the tub again. "I am Belda, sir," she said in a soft voice. "From the vineyards. I have been here only two days."

"There are two of you?" he asked.

A shock went through her. So he *did* remember Poppy. But wait, hopefully he meant two Beldas.

"Distantly related, sir," She replied, pulling a sheet from the water and rubbing it vigorously as if trying to removed a stain.

After a pause in which she feared he could hear her heart thumping, he stepped back and said, "Well, enjoy your new occupation. I thought you resembled someone ..." He ran a hand down her back—too far down. "You are as lovely as the vineyard libations."

"Thank you, sir." She kept her head down and gritted her teeth..

Duke Pule wandered off and, daring to glance up, she saw him draw his hand across his forehead and make a motion that suggested flinging sweat away, take a circuitous route around Serica, and disappear toward the stairs in a flurry of dark material and steam.

Too hot for the old boy down here. Good! Maybe he won't come back.

So, Pule *was* in on it. What a surprise.

Serica pouted the rest of the afternoon, plunging her pole angrily into her tub, refusing to speak when Poppy drifted by to mention the day would soon be over. But she left her tub again, long enough for Poppy to grab a small item from the cool rinse water—a handkerchief this time—wring and stuffed it into her pocket, before going back to plunge her hands into her own tub until she felt they were safely rinsed from the herbs that wafted even stronger than yesterday from Serica's deadly concoction.

CHAPTER 19

When Poppy reached home, Kandra nearly pounced on the handkerchief that she turned her pocket inside out to dump onto a plate on the table. The herbalist bent to sniff it carefully, then pronounced it steeped in the same herbs, with the fogbane even stronger. "I will speak to Lorimar when he comes," she told the girls. "Go and take your bath."

"We may pretend we are young again," Cherry said happily as they descended the stone stairs.

"We *are* still young." Poppy smiled at her companion. "Just because you're married shouldn't make you feel *old*."

"I do not feel *old*," Cherry told her. "But I have learned responsibility."

"Well, that's not the worst that could happen to you," Poppy remarked.

The bathing water was barely tepid; it had been hours since the 'stoners' came by to warm it, but that suited Poppy fine after her steamy day. She was glad to cleanse the sweat and ease the aches, and the girls' conversation concluded at once that she would not have to go back to the laundry again. It was clear that Pule was the instigator and perpetrator of the king's illness. Pulling her thoughts back to the present, Poppy had a sudden urge to get out of the water. What if Lorimar should come down and join them, thinking himself still *betrothed* to her? It was probably out of the question, but the thought made her nervous.

"Why are you going so soon?" Cherry asked, as Poppy began climbing out of the pool. "And you have not yet told me what a *rabbit* is."

"Well, I've soaked in wash water and sweat all day," she offered as an excuse. "I'll be shriveled up if I don't dry off soon."

"Very well," Cherry agreed reluctantly. "But it is so nice having you here once more."

Poppy smiled down at her friend from under the towel she had wrapped around her head. "And it's wonderful being with you again, Cherry—all of you. But I hope you realize I have no control over my coming and going ..."

"Yes, I know," Cherry said quietly, and climbed up the steps from the pool. Grabbing another towel and wrapping herself quickly, she exclaimed, "I am so *fat!*"

Poppy laughed. "You're not fat. Under all your new *responsibility*, you're the same girl I met out in the field."

Her friend offered a wan smile. "No, I shall never be that girl again, Poppy. I have gone through my passage, remember? And now have a husband and child, and bear my share of the troubles of the realm. Being the daughter of the nashu, they weigh upon me also."

"You're still my little ray of sunshine." Poppy patted her on the shoulder.

Cherry smiled. "Well, maybe I am. Somewhere on the inside."

"Oh, and a rabbit is a small animal with soft fur, long ears that stand up, and long hind legs that help them to jump. They need to be fast because many of the larger animals like to eat them, poor things. They're so cute people often keep them for pets."

"What is a pet, Poppy?"

"Well, it's an animal that gets to live with people for no useful purpose except ... that they like it for companship and ..." She'd almost said 'amuse-ment.'

"Oh, a *favored*," Cherry said.

"Yes, that says it. Do the people in Halderwold have any favoreds, Cherry?"

"Not many," the girl replied. "Some of the farm people have favored sheep or goats. And some of the very rich have lipkins."

"And what do lipkins look like?"

"Well, they are small with soft fur." She held her hands about a foot apart. "They have ears that stand up." She held her hands standing up on her head. "And stiff whiskers that stand out like this."

"Sounds like a cat."

"Cattle?"

"No. One ... *cattle* would be a cow, wouldn't it? A cat is soft and furry. You can pick it up and sit with it on your lap."

Cherry nodded. "Yes, you can do that with a lipkin. They have beautiful faces—little noses and Larian eyes."

"Why do only the very rich have these lipkins?" Poppy asked.

"Favoreds tend to make people *laugh*," the girl replied as if it should be obvious. "Some rich people have apartments in their houses for their favoreds to dwell in."

Good thing they don't have monkeys here, Poppy thought, but she didn't mention them. It would be too difficult a thing to try and describe.

"Isn't this one of the 'rich people's houses,' Cherry?" Poppy asked gingerly, hoping it wasn't a rude question.

"No, it is the house of a wise one," Cherry replied casually. "More noted for honor than wealth."

Poppy shrugged. "I was just remembering all those lovely jewels upstairs that Kandra was so generous with."

"Oh." Cherry let out a small breath that, Poppy had noticed, frequently stood in for a laugh here. "It is land that is counted as riches. We have only this area along the River Halder that can be irrigated well enough to grow food. The grasslands are vast, but dry, and the forest yields wood and herbs. The mountains provide us plentifully with minerals and jewels, lovely to enhance one's pleasure, but people cannot live on such wares."

What a great value system. Poppy didn't say it aloud, knowing it would not be understood, and there was no more time for explanations. They were already in the bedroom, and she was eager to get dressed and go down to wait for Lorimar. She was glad Cherry seemed to have found their light conversation more refreshing than the bath. Heaven knew the girl needed that.

Lorimar was in the dining room when they came downstairs. Kandra had filled him in on Poppy's disobedience of the day, Pule's visit to Serica, and his conversation with Poppy.

"Let us hope the duke does not remember you," he told Poppy in a dry tone that gave her the definite impression she would have been in for a tongue-lashing had she not come home with some important information.

"I don't think he did," she replied. "I think he just has a habit of checking out any new female he happens across."

Lorimar nodded his agreement. "I have requested a meeting with Avive," he said. "She has ignored my last two requests, but I have sent word that I bear news that may serve to distinguish the nature of Vran's illness. Surely she will see me this time."

"Who is your messenger?" Poppy asked him. Who could be trusted any more, she wondered.

"Why, my scribe, Armal," he replied, adding, "He is a close relative of the queen, so I believe he has a chance of getting my message to her. He returned with only the assurance that the queen would be told of his visit. He will go again in the morning for her answer."

"But will he be able to speak directly to the queen?" Poppy pursued. "Or will he have to go through Mari?"

"Yes, I know." Lorimar ran his hand over his forehead. "But Armal knows he must persist in getting my message to Avive. If he fails, I myself shall go to the palace tomorrow, and I will not be turned aside until I speak with the queen."

Kandra sighed. "I only hope you will not be too late."

Poppy drew in a deep breath. The bath had revived her somewhat from her day of hard work, and the relief of being through with the job brought a feeling of well-being, particularly now that the job included possible visits from Pule. Her temporary comfort was so pleasant it brought guilt. No longer did she feel these people or this place in any way unreal. No matter where or what Halderwold was, or who might consider it imaginary, these people were her friends and their problems were serious. And she cared.

Time dragged the next day as the women waited for word of Lorimar's success in gaining access to the queen. Poppy was glad to rest her sore muscles, and she enjoyed getting acquainted with Alvar, who had, for better or worse, inherited his mother's tendency to giggle. But two or three nervous glances from Kandra reminded her not to encourage him with exciting game-playing.

She switched to singing soothing songs. Old nonsense songs she hoped would mean nothing here. "I'm a little tea pot short and stout," she sang an old English rhyme as she rocked him on her lap. "Here's my handle, here's my spout. Tip me over pour me out."

But the baby kept musical time with his chubby little arms, giggling again with the pleasure of the rhythm, and Poppy noticed Cherry's worried look.

"Cherry, you laughed all the time when I first met you, why can't Alvar?" she asked, after Kandra had gone upstairs to sew in the sunlit observatory.

"Silliness is better tolerated in one's thirteenth year," Cherry said with a wistful smile as if she were an old lady remembering the good times of decades past. Remember the day you came? I had to drag you in from the street, you were unsettling the children so dangerously. I told you then it must not be done in a public place."

"But this isn't a public place. We're home."

"Kandra is anxious." Cherry picked her son up and jiggled him against her shoulder. "Things have changed since you were here, Poppy. If little ones acquire a habit at home, it is all the more difficult to control them in public. Now, we keep children in the laugh … in the *storm* room much more than when I was a child. Besides," she turned to glance toward the door. "His father is due for some hometime today, and the baby gets excited when he sees him, so I must keep him as calm as possible now."

"Oh, I'm going to meet Vade?" Poppy cried. "He's coming home today?"

"Only for a few hours," Cherry replied. "And I am eager too," she added as a pink spot appeared on each cheek.

"Why can't he come home every night, Cherry?" Poppy asked.

"That is not the way the guards work," was the simple answer. "They are required to put in four days and nights each work period. Then they come home for a few hours before another four days and nights. After that they may stay home for three days."

"I still don't understand why they can't come home every night," Poppy pursued. "It can't be more than an hour to and from work. Where does he guard anyway?"

"They are moved around," Cherry said. "I do not know where he is at any given time. It is a new arrangement which Pule has introduced. Father thinks it is to avoid collusion among them. If several men are together for very long, it is conceivable that they might begin to scheme against authority."

"I wonder why Pule would imagine a thing like that happening," Poppy mused sarcastically. "Well, I'll be happy to meet him, Cherry. But who will we tell him I am?"

"Oh, he knows about you," Cherry replied. "But not about your being back. Do not worry though. He knows you are a dear friend of mine, and the family."

Vade came in softly about an hour later. He was already in the room before the women looked up to see him. Alvar had fallen asleep on the sofa, and Cherry slipped away from him quickly but quietly and into her husband's arms for a long embrace. When she turned to introduce them, Poppy faced a skinny boy about sixteen standing bashfully before her, holding out delicate-looking hands in greeting. Even his guard's uniform failed to make him appear completely grown up.

"Hello, Vade." Poppy stood up and returned his hand gesture. "I've been eager to meet you. But not as eager as your wife for you to come home," she added playfully. This brought blushes to the faces of both teenagers, and he acknowledged her greeting with a smile, glancing toward the baby. Then she realized they were trying not to wake him.

"Let me watch Alvar for a little while," she told them with a wave of her hand. "Why don't you two go up on the balcony and take in the scenery for a while?"

With deep blushes and a look of gratitude from each, the children—yes, they were children—were off up the stairs.

Poppy sat down gingerly beside the baby. If she kept really quiet and didn't wake him, the lovers might have as long as an hour to themselves, and these people needed any little joy that could be squeezed out of their present situation. She sat by the sleeping child for over two hours, scouring her brain for ideas to aid the kingdom's dilemma. But she had come up with nothing new when the chubby legs began pumping and Alvar opened his large, dark eyes to take one look at the stranger he no longer seemed to remember, and began to scream.

In no time, Cherry was down the stairs. "I knew his sleep would not last much longer," she said, scooping the baby into her arms. "He is hungry." She sat down, loosened her dress, and sang softly to the baby as he relished his lunch. Vade hadn't come downstairs. "He fell asleep," Cherry explained. "They are not allowed much rest on duty."

Another devious ploy, thought Poppy. Keep them exhausted, then they'll be dreaming of home and rest instead of more energetic projects—like over-throwing their ruler.

When Vade came down the stairs, he took his son into the storm room for a visit before he had to leave and, Poppy hoped, a giggle session for the poor kid. After about half an hour, they emerged and Vade gave the child back to his mother and kissed them both goodbye. "Next time it will be three days," he said to Cherry, who held onto his hand until he had to pull it away from her.

Lorimar finally came home. Avive had agreed to see him, he told the women. He had gone to the palace immediately, and she had assured him, after he had been admitted to the sitting room adjoining Vran's sickroom, that they were completely alone and that he could speak freely with her. Still, as they began their conversation, he had risen and pulled aside some heavy drapes, expecting to find Mari crouched behind them but there was no sign of anyone hiding in the room. So he had told her of their discovery of the poison herb.

"And what did she say?" Kandra leaned forward, her hands clasped at her waist.

"Avive is so weary she does not visibly react in conversation," he said. "But after staring at me for several moments, she leaned back and closed her eyes. Then she looked me in the eyes and said, 'In spite of my warnings, Wise Lorimar, and for my love of Vran, I will trust you again. I see no other choice.'"

"Uniplax be thanked," Kandra breathed. "But what is there to be done? It must be soon ..."

"It will be very soon," he replied briskly. "Vran and Avive and their children arrive here tonight. We must make arrangements to receive them."

Both Poppy and Cherry were immediately on their feet, leaving Alvar alone on the sofa; all three women began to talk at once. "I will go to the third floor guest chambers and make sure the bedding is fresh," Cherry said.

"I'll help," Poppy said. "I know where all the towels and things are stored." That was the first time she'd ever heard of the 'guest chambers' in this house, but she had no time right now to dwell on the possible reasons why she had never been invited to occupy one of them.

Kandra turned in a circle, her hands in the air. "We must prepare for the whole family, and servants. We must send for a maid for Avive. Surely she will not bring Mari ..."

"No," Lorimar said firmly. "I told her servants will be provided by my household. In the interest of security for Vran, all their people should remain at the palace."

"And she agreed to that?"

"Indeed she did. Avive has reached the end of hope and is now ready to trust me with their lives. I should have pressed to see her sooner; but then, I had nothing to tell her until you discovered the fogbane. And before we had the help of ..." He turned to Poppy. "our dear friend."

"Happy to help," Poppy said quickly, turning away. *He doesn't know what to call me.* "Now I'm going upstairs and dig up some towels and soap and stuff."

Cherry had already picked Alvar up and was heading for the stairs. "Just as soon as I put the baby to bed, I will be with you, Poppy," she called back.

All was swiftly made ready, and before three hours had passed, two royal carts arrived. The king was carried in unconscious, wrapped up, Poppy thought, almost like a mummy, and was put to bed by Kandra and Cherry. Avive and the children, the little boy, Var, and his older sister, followed quietly. The men who had driven the royal carts and carried in the king and the supplies were immediately sent back to the palace. Avive had given Lorimar and his house complete charge over her family.

Armel the scribe, hefty a young man with long black hair, had arrived with the royal family, and was to serve as Lorimar's messenger to and from the Wise House while Lorimar remained at home with his guests. The scribe had brought several large volumes, which he carried up to the observatory where he would work while he was in the house.

Poppy wore a head scarf with her hair pinned up under it, kept her distance from the guests, and even from the new help. She had been shocked at the queen's appearance. Like Kandra, the formerly pretty woman had aged severely. There was probably little chance of Avive remembering her anyway, she thought. In fact, it had likely been ages since the queen had given a thought to the red-haired stranger she'd met so briefly two years ago. Still she had kept her eyes averted when Avive passed her, hoping to be thought one of the servants.

And she had stayed out of the way, waiting to be given some task. Kandra and Cherry had taken a long time preparing the king for the night, explaining after they came downstairs that they had stripped and bathed him, then wrapped him completely in new cloths that Kandra had soaked in an herbal mixture as they waited for him to arrive.

The two had gone back upstairs and Poppy now sat before the huge kitchen fireplace, burning the wrapping that had covered Vran when he was carried in. Avive had wrapped him in clean linen as soon as Lorimar told her of the poison, but all the linen in his chambers had no doubt, by that time, been infused with Serica's virulent rinse. The material emitted a peculiar odor as she carefully poked 'every stitch' (as Kandra had forcefully instructed) of the curling edges back into the flames.

Alone, Poppy mused on the other women now in the house. Malina and Cleod, and two other women whom Poppy had never seen before, were already there when Avive and Vran had arrived, and were to remain in the house to help serve them. Loyalty was an issue of course. She remembered Kandra's mentioning that Malina was 'her brother's child.' That made her first cousin to Isanda, Kandra's daughter and Lorimar's wife, who had died so young. Malina was very pretty, and resembled Cherry, though she was several years older, and Poppy assumed that they presented a good idea of what Isanda had looked like. (Of course it didn't matter now what Isanda had looked like. And yet it did.) Cleod seemed obsessed with serving her queen, so her loyalty was unquestioned. The other two, young girls named Jovik and Fral, Kandra had known all their lives and considered them completely trustworthy.

Poppy had agreed with Cherry and Kandra that, if she were recognized by the king or queen, they would say she had been weak and house-ridden since her ill-fated joining day, and had just recently regained enough strength to help with the housework. They had also decided to make the excuse that she was afraid there might be more men in the city who shared the criminal archer's opinion of 'outlanders,' if a further explanation was required. So far, there had been no questions about her from the servants; except that Malina, she was almost sure, had recognized her, though she had said nothing. And Kandra had assured Poppy that she 'would speak' to her. Poppy wondered what she would say.

The whole house finally quieted down for the night and the four servants went to bed in Cherry's old, spacious room.

"Deema and Kellith will come in the morning," Cherry told Poppy before they went to bed, Poppy in Kandra's room, and Cherry in the new bedroom she shared with her baby and husband, when he was home. "I have told them you are here, but to say nothing. They are eager to see you."

It would be nice to see the girls again, Poppy thought as she lay waiting for sleep. She had forgotten to ask Cherry if her friends were married now too. She thought of Nona, Deema's sister, still in her sweatshop below the palace. How many years had she left before coming back to the city? It would be four now. She thought of Hesh, and hoped he was in good health and still the kind care-taker of the young prisoners ... *slaves*. Old friends, they were to her, all of them. She fell asleep wondering how she might manage to visit them again.

The next morning was pandemonium in the house. Everyone, including the extra women, bustled around, taking care of the royal family. Cherry invited Poppy to join her and the children in the storm room. Cherry had already brought breach of fast supplies into the room, and Poppy was glad to eat with the children. How do people entertain royalty? Of course, here in Halderwold, the king and queen seemed much more comfortable to be with than she had expected. Probably easier to be around than most of the important people back in her world, not that she ever expected to find that out by experience.

To Poppy's surprise, Var and Josel were delightful children. Rather than being spoiled and willful, they were the soul of manners and consideration, offering food on the table to the others before taking a second helping.

"Please eat as much as you desire," Cherry kept telling them.

"Father says the king must provide for his people first, even before his own welfare," Var told her, his six-year-old face somber.

"Well, there is enough in the kingdom for us all," Cherry assured him. "Our crops have been bountiful. Please eat, and have no care."

"Mother says we must remember we are here for the people," eight-year-old Josel added, in the same grown-up manner. "If others are miserable, we have failed."

"Well, we are perfectly happy," Poppy joined the conversation. "We all have enough to eat and nice homes to live in, so please don't worry about us. Would you like another pancake?"

"Flatloaf," Cherry corrected her with a grin. She and Poppy exchanged a glance that said how comfortable they both were, being together again.

After eating, Cherry nursed Alvar with a shawl draped discreetly around them both, while Poppy helped the royal children wash their hands in the relief site.

"Now it is time for your studies," Cherry announced after tucking her satisfied and sleepy son between two gigantic pillows on the sofa.

Poppy felt a pang of self-consciousness. "I wish I could help you teach," she whispered to Cherry. "But I only learned a few letters before I ..."

"Why don't you sit down and learn with them?" Cherry suggested.

"Yes!" Poppy jumped at the opportunity. "What will you tell them about ... why I still don't know how to read?"

"Many of the people of Halderwold cannot read," Cherry told her matter-of-factly. "Few of the servants in the palace can. Just keep up your story of being from the vineyards, if they should ask."

Poppy was stunned. "I thought ... when Lorimar showed me the class-rooms in the Wise House, that all the children here went to school."

Cherry was already shaking her head. "Not those whose families have always worked at farming or raising horses ... or making wine .. or...."

"I get it. The peasant class," Poppy said dryly.

Cherry looked as if she wanted to apologize. "My father has always wanted to include more of the children in the school, but many of the parents need them to help with the work."

The children seemed fine with Poppy joining their lessons. Josel had heard the last remarks about schooling. "When I am grown," she announced, "I intend to work to see that all the people, especially the women, shall learn to read. Then they can teach their children, even if they have no time to go to school."

"That's a wonderful idea," Poppy told her. She hoped things worked out so that one of these children inherited their father's job.

About mid-morning Jovik came to take the children for 'an airing' up on the balcony. Soon after they left, Deema and Kellith came into the storm room. Poppy greeted them with eager warmth, and they were as enthusiastic to see her as if she had been a long-lost family member. Kellith was married and four months pregnant, but Deema was still single; needed, she said, to care for the smaller children. "My mother is failing," she told Poppy. "She no longer has the strength to do much work."

"How is Sil?" Poppy asked, truly interested, but mainly to prolong broaching the subject of Nona's remaining four years.

Deema sniffed loudly and seemed to cheer up. "Sil is nearly grown. She helps me greatly in caring for our four younger brothers." Then she looked pleadingly at Poppy. "Is it possible, lady, that you might visit Nona again? To give her greetings from us and tell her our mother still lives?"

Poppy looked at Cherry. "Surely the prison ... the people down there get news of their families?"

But Cherry was shaking her head again. "Hesh receives general news, but sharing it with his charges is not allowed. Your visit with Hesh and your association with one of the detained was very unusual, allowed only because my father deemed it necessary to your wise training."

"Then I can ask him to take be back down there."

"Never!" Cherry's plump face took on a look of alarm. "Poppy, we keep telling you things have changed since you have been here. We no longer enjoy the leniency of Vran's good nature."

"Yes, much has changed since you have been here, lady." It was Kellith who spoke. She had been sitting with a pillow stuffed behind her and her arms wrapped protectively around her belly. "We have not the freedom we once enjoyed."

The sudden, whispered warnings from Cherry that used to stop their conversations short flashed through Poppy's mind. *Good heavens, if that was freedom! If we have to be more careful that we were then ...* She looked at Deema, whose dark eyes held such a pathetic expression of hope, waiting for her answer. "I'll ... see what can be done," Poppy told her.

After the visitors left, Poppy and Cherry were left to do nothing more than join Jovik and the children until supper time approached. Poppy asked to help in the kitchen, but Kandra assured her that the extra women would do all that was needed, along with helping Avive bathe Vran constantly in very warm water and cleansing herbs.

"Has he shown any signs of improvement?" Poppy asked.

"Not as yet," was the reply. "It may take several days for complete skin cleansing, to say nothing of the innards, and for him to fully take the teas we are attempting to urge down his throat."

"Can he swallow?"

"To some small extent, but unknowingly, I believe." Kandra sighed and looked around as if trying to recall some forgotten herb on the shelves that might be an aid to their therapy.

"How soon will we know?"

Kandra shrugged sadly. "We do that which is within our knowledge. Beyond that, it lies with the Unbounded One. The one thing remaining, beyond our physical ministrations, is to perform a palpleth, which we shall do tomorrow morning."

Poppy was curious. "Yes, you mentioned that while Vran was still at home. What is a palpleth, Kandra?"

"It is a quietness ritual, sometimes rendering great insight into the affliction."

"And who does this? Just … *menders*?"

Kandra spoke as if reluctantly. "It is a quiet sitting, concentrating on the healing of the afflicted. It must be guided by a mender, but others join in."

"Oh, I'll be happy to join, Kandra," Poppy said with enthusiasm. "I've been feeling so useless and bored, just trying to keep out of the way. When I was here before, there was so much going on—getting ready for the passage and everything. Then the storm and Hesh and Pule, and my wise training …" She stopped short of mentioning her almost marriage.

Kandra seemed to become nervous; her hands, which had fallen wearily onto her lap, now fluttered about her hair. "I … will think upon it, dear," she said, almost apologetically it seemed to Poppy.

"But what is it?" Poppy pursued, eager to take part in anything that might help Vran. "I can sit quietly." She now realized she was being over eager, like a child. "But of course I'm not a native of Halderwold. If I've spoken out of turn …"

"It is not that," Kandra said hesitantly. "It is merely that … you are still a single woman. No fault of your own, of course."

"A person has to be married to meditate here?" It was out of her mouth before she realized she was being forward, maybe even rude. And Kandra looked so tired. But it didn't make sense, and she had to know why she couldn't be more useful.

Kandra took a deep breath and let it out slowly as she knit her brow as if explaining something difficult. "When a woman births a child, she said carefully, "It changes her. Not until then does she experience putting another's welfare completely before her own—even before her own life, with no misgiving nor resentment. There are exceptions, of course, but I speak of those who have a natural concern for others."

Poppy listened silently.

Perhaps encouraged by her attentiveness, Kandra spoke more easily. "You see, dear, sitting in palpleth, one must become empty of all concerns except the well-being of the person in need of healing. It has been found by menders that women who have born a child are more adept at this kind of concentration than men or childless women."

"Are there exceptions?" Poppy asked humbly.

"Yes, the talent is not exclusively found in mothers, only more readily."

"Will Cherry be allowed to sit in on this palpleth?"

Kandra nodded. "Not only has Cherry become a mother, but she has also shown considerable progress in the mending arts this past year."

"Couldn't I just try?" Poppy asked. "If I stink at it, I could just leave the room, couldn't I? I feel so useless, Kandra."

Kandra was thoughtfully silent for a minute, then looked at Poppy and said gently, "I will ask the others who will sit with me. If they are willing, you may join us. I appreciate ... have always appreciated your willingness to do whatever you can to help us, Poppy, and I do not wish to sound harsh, but remember, it is the king's life that is our concern here, not your ... entertainment."

Poppy was jolted into silence by her hostess's words, until she realized that *entertainment* here could only mean generosity toward a guest, not their amusement.

She also realized it was very probably time for her to show some humility. On her first arrival here, she had been immediately honored as a Larian, which she wasn't, taken into wise training, for which she had no natural talents, and in general, treated like royalty. Had she come to expect this kind of indulgence, when she knew darn well it was by no means her due? True, she had taken more than a few risks in her efforts to help these people, but the decisions had been her own. These people had always shown the utmost concern for her safety.

"I will abide by the decision of your group, Kandra," she said quietly.

"And I will encourage the others to do what they think is fair," Kandra replied with a nod.

CHAPTER 20

Lorimar sat upstairs with Avive throughout the evening, and Poppy went to bed having had no opportunity to ask him about visiting Hesh. Kandra spent the night in the king's room, and Poppy missed having Cherry in the room with her. The other beds made her feel like a college girl left alone in the dorm, too poor to go home for the holidays. But that was good—she needed time to think.

Before sleep claimed her, she had decided not to bother asking Lorimar about her visiting Hesh. He'd been so paranoid about her safety, his reaction would no doubt be as fervently negative as Cherry's. And besides, he didn't have time now to worry about her, what with royal guests, and everyone in the house straining to pull the king back from the claim of death.

But she needed to get back down there, to see Nona and talk to Hesh. She had learned more from Hesh's straightforward and well-informed conversation about the state of the kingdom than from anyone above ground, including Lorimar, who always spoke so cautiously, and was now too busy to talk to her anyway. She couldn't blame him for mentioning nothing about her taking up wise training again, since they both knew she could be gone at any given moment, and the wise ones probably had more important things to do right now than training an 'outlander,' who might disappear again. And maybe she *would* disappear. But still, she had to plan as if she'd be staying, just in case.

And it would be good for her to get away from the house. She had no essential duties, and there was always the caution about someone recognizing her and asking problem questions. Before she slept, she knew what she would do if she were not allowed to join the palpleth. Or what she would at least try to do.

While she was dressing in the morning, Cherry came into the room. "You wish to be part of the palpleth, Poppy?" she asked as if she were surprised.

"Yes, I'd like to do anything I can to help the king … if they'll let me," was Poppy's reply. She had already dressed and was combing her hair, without a mirror; something she still had trouble with. But what difference did it make with a head scarf on anyway? She paused to look at Cherry, wondering if she had anything to tell her.

She did. "The people have agreed to allow you to join."

Poppy hesitated. "Willingly or reluctantly?" God, it was hard to be humble here, after the treatment she had grown accustomed to.

But Cherry grinned. "Willingly, Poppy. Do not fear; you are not being tolerated merely out of a sense of benevolence."

"Okay. But do you know why they've made this decision without even … interviewing me?"

"What is *interviewing*, Poppy?" Cherry asked in her usual frank manner.

"Oh, asking a lot of questions to see if I'm sincere."

Cherry snorted—almost laughed. "Your sincerity has never been at question. It is merely a person's ability to concentrate, and of course their well-wishing for the person who is ill, that is required for a palpleth. And Krandra sent me up to say that you have been accepted." Then she added in her new, mature voice, "And if you really wish to join, you have only to accept their decision."

Poppy smiled. *What would I do without your frankness?* "I get it. Just say 'thanks' and shut up."

Cherry nodded. "We will breach our fast in my room, then go down to the sickroom."

Poppy followed her to the new bedroom. The room was surprisingly small for two people and a baby, with no balcony or window low enough to look out; but of course most of the bedrooms here—the ones she had been in—were large enough for a row of guest beds, so it made sense that a room for newly-weds needed no such extended capacity. It was a cozy room, with rugs in warm brownish pink and a nice blue and maroon hanging on the wall at the head of the bed. She wished she could sleep in here with Cherry when Vade was away, but apparently that was not appropriate or surely Cherry would have invited her.

They ate the simple meal waiting on a small table, with the only two chairs in the room already pulled close to it. The coffee was delicious, as usual, but when Poppy reached for the pitcher to pour herself a second cup, a gentle hand prevented her. "It is better not to partake too readily of a bracing fluid before a palpleth," Cherry told her apologetically. "We may drink more vivor later."

Poppy withdrew her hand. "*Vivor*," she repeated. "You know, I don't believe I ever heard the name of this delicious beverage before. I guess I liked it so much, I didn't need to call it anything. I just thought of it as coffee."

"*Coffee*." Cherry repeated. "A soothing word for a fluid so enhancing."

"And *enhancing* is a mild word for a fluid so … invigorating," Poppy replied.

They both giggled softly. Poppy was relieved to see a glimpse of her carefree old friend in this serious young woman.

Cherry adjusted her shawl. "Now we should join the others."

Eight women and two men had gathered in Vran's room, and sat encircling his bed. Avive was there, Poppy noticed immediately, sitting by her husband's head with eyes closed. One of the men she recognized as Armel, his eyes closed, his arms wrapped within the folds of the grey cape of the wise ones. The other man, an elder with thin white hair and the peaceful expression of one seasoned in reflection. He and one of the women held things that appeared to be musical instruments, but they were silent now. The women seemed to range in age from very old, to another girl about Cherry's age. Some of the eyes opened briefly, then closed again, as Poppy and Cherry entered and took the last two chairs in the circle. Poppy glanced around at the others, tugged her scarf out a little further over her face, and was the last to close her eyes.

She had begun to think this was the palpleth, just sitting quietly. But of course something important had to be going on in the minds of these people. She tried to clear her mind, trying to recall the little she had learned of meditation in the Buddhist section of her course in World Religions in college. Her life had been active, but she'd learned to settle down in the yoga course she took one year when her gym workouts had caused soreness in her back. Her teacher, the most serene woman she'd ever met, would lead the class in a 'positive thinking' mediation at the end of each session. They would mentally go over their bodies, affirming health and fitness for every part. Maybe she could do that now, she thought, only for Vran's body instead of her own.

She was jolted out of her attempt at solo meditation by the voice of Kandra, even though her words were quietly spoken. "Let us all regard the symbol of the Uniplax."

Poppy peeped at a large drawing mounted on the wall which she hadn't noticed upon coming into the room, having been so interested in the people sitting here. It was the same symbol as that engraved on Lorimar's clasp. Lines that seemed to form circles on the outside of the figure, but melded into swirls toward the center of the pattern until they couldn't be separated by the eye. Along with the others, she stared at it, then following Kandra's gentle instructions, she allowed it to fill her sight, her mind, her consciousness.

"Now," said Kandra in a voice like an incantation, "Close your eyes and think only of Vran, fill your mind, fill your heart. Dwell on your well-wishes. Picture him whole and well, see his smile that blessed so many of us. See his stalwart glance that lent us fortitude. Care for him. Care deeply. Hold him as a child. A child of your love. He is in need. Give him your love."

As they sat, several quiet sobs became audible in the room. Poppy concentrated on her sincere desire for Vran's recovery, picturing him as she had first seen him two years ago, smiling and friendly. Yes, Vran was a good man; he deserved good health, particularly when his had been taken from him so reprehensibly. Her thoughts swerved to Pule and Mari, and Serica. Criminals, all of them. They should be lying here dying instead of Vran. But these were not the kind of thoughts she was supposed to be thinking! Negative thoughts were not what was needed here, not what was intended. She remembered telling Kandra last night that if she stunk at this kind of thing, she'd leave immediately.

Her eyes popped wide open and she looked around for the least disturbing path to the door. But as her vision skimmed over Vran, lying so pale and helpless, she suddenly saw Mollie. Why, she had almost forgotten about the children in the hospital back home, and how she'd had to struggle to keep her empathy from spoiling her clown act. Those emotions came flooding back, a sudden quiver in her throat, a swelling in her chest. She remembered what Kandra had told her of the experience of birth—birth not only of a child but also a compassion like no other. Well, maybe it hadn't been as profound an experience as birthing your own child, but the compassion she had felt for those sick, lonely kids had certainly found a new, deep dimension inside her. With concentration, she replaced Mollie with Vran. It wasn't difficult; Vran lying there like a sick, helpless child. There was no real difference. The thought remained, the feeling grew. She cared. She cared deeply. She would not have to leave the room.

All had been silent for some time except for the few sobs that escaped several throats. Soft music now rose, a tinkling and a melodic whine, and they sat for some time with no other sound.

Finally Kandra's voice came again. "Now we will view the Uniplax again. Open your eyes slowly."

Poppy opened her eyes and stared at the drawing. "Begin at the outside," Kandra instructed in a low voice. Ask for guidance before following the pattern within, and continue to think of Vran."

Poppy stared at the outer lines. Before many moments passed, her eyes were drawn as if involuntarily along the lines, into the inner swirls of the pattern which now seemed to be moving like an actual swirling liquid. With no effort at all, Vran stayed in her mind, even as her eyes followed the movement. Then, quite suddenly, the swirling ceased and writing began to appear between the lines. She shook her head, and looked again. It was still there, but it was in foreign characters that she could not read. It was like the writing in the books upstairs, she realized, but how could this be? How could her mind have taken in and now be creating letters she had not yet learned. So far as she knew, she had never enjoyed a photographic memory.

"Ask for interpretation of anything you see, if it is not understood," Kandra murmured.

Poppy asked, and soon the writing faded and was replaced by pictures, vaguely drawn. Fascinated, she stared as they became clearer. She saw Vran in his finery, descending the steps of a dais, smiling his half-comical smile, with Avive by his side, beautiful as she had been two years ago. Well, this could be the recreation of a memory, exactly as they had appeared when she'd first met them. Then it all faded, and the lines took on the simple pattern they had formed before she had stared at them.

"Blest be Vran," a voice sang now. Poppy guessed it was the voice of the elderly man. The others joined in, making it a chant. After some time, the music faded and the chant died down. Eyes began to open.

Kandra stood in the center of the circle, wiping tears from her face. "Has any particular insight been given?" she asked.

Poppy startled herself by shooting up her hand. Kandra nodded to her.

"I saw Vran and Avive, all dressed up and looking healthy and happy," she said. "Coming down the steps of a dais."

A collective sigh issued from all present. "Let it be," Kandra said.

"Let it be!" Avive cried tearfully.

The words were repeated by all present.

After a silence, Kandra said, "I feel we have experienced a most beneficial palplath. I myself sensed the energy of healing pass through this room. I saw it pause and swirl over Vran's heart. Blest be Vran."

They all repeated her last words.

"Now, after a quiet time in which we will come back into our own concerns, we will depart, all blest."

"All blest," they repeated.

When they left, Poppy felt refreshed, and she was amazed at the expression of renewed hope on the queen's face, though the king lay as still and pale as ever. She was sure Avive had not remembered her, her attention so focused on her husband.

She spent the afternoon with Cherry and the children, learning to read, and ate supper with them in the storm room. Though she had not exerted herself physically, she fell asleep almost as soon as her head touched the pillow in Kandra's spare bed.

The women were so busy in the morning, Kandra guiding the help, along with her constant vigilance over Vran, and Cherry with her own baby and the queen's children, Poppy, following her resolve of two nights ago, was able to dig her laundress dress out of the rag closet and slip away, hoping the coins in the dress pocket that she had forgotten to return to Kandra would be enough for two more cart rides. Before leaving the house, feeling the frustration of not being able to leave a note for Cherry, she found Malina and instructed her that, if she should not be back by tonight, to tell Cherry that she had gone to visit Hesh, but to say nothing before supper. She would leave it to Cherry to tell Lorimar.

Malina's eyes skimmed Poppy's tattered clothing and perceptibly burned with curiosity. "And Cherry will know of this 'Hesh,' lady?"

Poppy nodded, and replied simply, "Yes, she will know."

Malina did not pursue the subject, but said with a slight bow, "I will do as you ask."

As usual, when she was shabbily clothed, the cart driver paid her little attention, and gave no reaction when she handed him half of the coins.

In the laundry, she had barely managed to stuff her cape beneath a pile of dirty laundry where it could easily be retrieved, rather than leaving it hanging on one of the pegs inside the door, before Etral's voice came at her from behind. "And where have *you* been for *two days*, my *lady!*"

Poppy started. Had they found out who she was? But turning to face the plump woman with hands on hips and red face nearly touching hers, she realized the overseer was simply making fun of her low station by calling her 'lady,' as had the men in the cart on the night of her arrival.

"I … was s … sick." She stuttered purposely, trying to sound intimidated.

"Well, I hope you are feeling strong now," the overseer said. "You have twice as much work to get done, unless you can persuade *that* Serica to do her share for a change. I would send the both of you on your way if it were not for the work being so far behind."

Poppy thought she saw a way to calm her boss. "I'll do my best, Etral. Serica was friendly to me the other day. Maybe I can talk to her."

The other woman turned away with a "Humph! That girl's *friendliness* will be her undoing."

If it's toward Pule, your gift of prophesy is right on the money, Poppy agreed silently. She found a pole and began stirring the nearest untended vat of clothes, watching Etral until she had disappeared into the steam on the other side of the room. Then glancing around and seeing no one close by, she quickly retrieved her cloak and balling it up to look like an armful of laundry, headed for the stairs, hoping the palace was built along the lines of a high school where the stairwells going down were usually directly under the ones going up.

She reached the stairway Mari and Pule had used and flattened herself against the wall under it, pulling on her cloak to make herself as invisible as possible. There was no stairway going down. Well, no use hanging around. She moved slowly along the wall away from the stairs, looking for a doorway. She found one and slipped through it. It was a relief site. Back outside, she continued along the stone wall until she found another opening. Through it, this time she found herself in one of those dark corridors with the only light a torch on the wall every several yards.

There was nothing to do but keep moving. After a few turns she realized the floor was slanting downward before her. *This must be the handicapped passageway.* Smiling at her own attempt at humor to keep up her courage, she continued until an opening appeared that led to a descending stairway. Embarking on a serious leg of her downward journey, she realized that, with all her plans of last night on how to get out of the house, then out of the laundry and into the depths of the palace, she hadn't given much thought to an explanation of who she was and where she was going, should she meet someone who wanted to know. And before she had a chance to come up with something convincing, a figure loomed at the bottom of the stairway.

Almost crouching under her hood, she racked her memory for the greetings Cherry had taught her the day she'd landed in Halderwold, but they all seemed to be remarks on the weather. Even the ones for a dark day: 'Water is needed,' or 'May the land never turn to swamp,' didn't seem to hold much probability of occurrence down here. Anxiety rising, she kept her head down and attempted to pass. The daunting figure blocked her way.

Peering from under her hood, she said shakily, "Fair weather ... outside."

"May it so remain," a deep voice growled.

"And ... may ... the land never turn to swamp."

A large hand came up to rest on the hilt of a sword. "Who are you, woman?"

She drew herself up to her full height which was about two-thirds of his. "I am Lady Poppy of the Wise House. I seek to confer with Hesh, keeper of the ... detained. Can you direct me to his apartment, sir?"

A low rumble rose from the man that she realized was a laugh, then he threw back his head and emitted a sound that made her wonder why he wasn't in prison himself. Maybe that was why he liked working down here away from everyone. "You seek Hesh, the watcher?" he demanded.

Poppy swallowed. "Yes. The watcher." She had even forgotten his proper title.

"You are on the far side of the palace from Hesh's domain." He sounded so amused he nearly ceased to be frightening.

Poppy licked her lips. "Can I get over to his side without going all the way back up?"

The large hand remained on the sword. "What business have you with Hesh?"

"I ... have been sent by Lorimar, the nashu, to tell Hesh that several new ... *(inmates? prisoners?)* ... several new *charges* are being sent to him on the morrow."

"Girls or boys?"

"Three girls and one boy."

"All under sixteen?"

"Yes. All of them."

To her great surprise, he turned abruptly, his short cloak swinging against her. "Come. I will take you to Hesh."

Dumbfounded, she followed him along corridors and down stairways for nearly an hour. Sometimes she had herself convinced it was a trick, they would end up someplace where she would immediately find herself under lock and key, or worse; and the people at Lorimer's house would never know what had happened to her. But true to his word, when the huge man finally stopped and knocked on a door, it opened and her old friend stood looking at them.

Hesh's mouth fell open as his eyes took in the tall guard, then darted to Poppy. Without acknowledging her, he looked back and addressed the guard, "What news, Guinar?"

"Do you know this woman, Hesh?" Guinar asked in a surprisingly mild tone.

Poppy shook her hood down. With a bow, and a widening of his mild, pale eyes, Hesh replied, "Of course. Lady Poppy has been my honored guest in the past and is most welcome."

Guinar studied them, first Hesh and then Poppy, his heavy eyelids drooping with what Poppy feared was suspicion. Hesh moved back, making a gesture of invitation to enter, and she moved forward, hoping Guinar would not stop her. He didn't, but her stomach tightened when Hesh added, "Please come in, Guinar. I have just yesterday received a gift fresh from the best vineyard."

"*Belda's* vineyard?"

Hesh smiled. "The very same. And I would be honored to learn your opinion of it."

Guinar stepped inside, nearing knocking Poppy out of the way, and stood looking around as if the wine bottle should be the most prominent item in the room.

"Please sit, both of you," Hesh said pleasantly, going to the cupboard.

They both sat. Guinar claiming the space of two people on a sofa and Poppy huddled in a chair near the fireplace, recalling the comfort this same chair had given her the last time she had been here.

Hesh brought a large jug to the table, then went back for cups. Guinar was now leaning forward, his elbows resting on his knees. *Why doesn't he just let his tongue hang out?* Poppy thought. He straightened up to receive a large cup of the dark wine. Poppy didn't care for red wine, but took her cup and pretended to sip from it, trying not to grimace at the loud slurping noises of the guard's hearty imbibing.

Poppy could sense Hesh's impatience to speak with her as he asked again, "Well Guinar, surely you have some news for me. I wait here in my unfrequented habitat for word from the world above. What of the king's illness?"

Guinar swallowed loudly. "The king and his family have left the palace," he said before filling his mouth again.

Looking alarmed, Hesh waited again for him to swallow. "Where have they gone? And why?"

"To the house of Lorimar, I am told," he replied, shooting Poppy another suspicious glance. "Of further happenings, I know nothing. I am but a humble guard." He finished his cup of wine in one long draft and held it out to Hesh, who got up and filled it again.

Hesh kept his eyes on Guinar as if he didn't want to force Poppy into the conversation, but she realized she must say something.

"I have been at Lorimar's house," she said quietly. "The king and queen and their children have been brought there so the king may benefit from Kandra's healing ministrations. So far, though, Vran remains the same—unconscious."

Hesh nodded, leaving his head hanging in a dispirited slump. Silence reigned in the room for a few minutes, until Guinar finished his second cup of wine, and Hesh said carefully, "Guinar, my good man, I wish I could enjoy your company even longer, but I worry that I may be found at fault for hindering your duties with my libations."

Guinar shook his head as if he had just emerged from a refreshing swim. "Yes, I am on duty," he said as if he had completely forgotten. "Shall I leave Lady Poppy with you or guide her back to her own world?" Poppy felt a shock until she realized he was speaking of ground level.

"Oh, please let me keep her a while," Hesh said pleasantly. "I have not enjoyed her company for some months now, and I have already reminded you of my customary isolation."

"Yes." The tipsy guard nodded his head. "I myself sometimes feel alone as I make my rounds through the passageways." He rose unsteadily and bowed to the old man.

Hesh stood and returned the bow.

"Good morrow to you, honorable Hesh," the guard said. "I will come by tomorrow to see if the lady needs further guidance."

"Thank you, Guinar," Poppy managed, standing to see him off. "And for your help today."

Guinar bowed again and left. Hesh closed and bolted the door, then came and sat facing Poppy who had collapsed back into her chair.

"Well, it has been some time, my lady."

Poppy sighed. "Yes, and I don't know where to start."

"Start with the king," was the simple suggestion, then noticing that Poppy had drunk almost none of her wine, he asked, "Would you like some tea?"

She perked up. "I'd love some tea."

Tea was soon provided from a kettle hanging over the fire, strange-tasting but calming to her fluttering nerves. Her host sat down again. "Lorimar has told me who you are," he said. "You may speak freely with me."

Poppy sighed. "I don't think I know who I am myself, when I'm here in this land. Have you seen Lorimar since … since I've been back?"

Hesh shook his head. "He finds his way to my rooms every few days. I saw him four … no five days ago."

"Then I'll start with my career as a laundress."

"You have become a *laundress?*" Hesh looked astonished.

"Not really." She felt a twinge of guilt at her predilection to relax in this cozy room, knowing what surrounded it. But the old man's reassuring manner gave her a feeling of security. She told him of the last several days and their discovery of fogbane in the king's bed clothes. "The women at Lorimar's house are washing him constantly with herbal baths, but no one, not even Kandra, knows whether he will recover or not."

The old man's eyes had opened widely at her mention of the poison herb. "Astounding!" he said. "No one has journeyed to the misty shores of the River Dystopia in decades, and that is the only known place where fogbane grows, to say nothing of the ban on it."

"Well, someone's been there and back," Poppy said. "Or else they're growing it in their backyard."

Hesh sat shaking his head for a while, then started as if he had forgotten something important. "But you must be weary, lady. And hungered. I will make us a meal."

"Oh, don't go to any trouble …" she began, but a wave of his hand silenced her. He bustled back and forth between the cupboards and the fireplace for half an hour. When he finally brought two steaming bowls of soup, her aching legs had to be forced to carry her the few steps to the table.

After their meal, Hesh invited her to rest while he finished his work day, and she was happy to comply, lounging in her chair, looking forward to his return. But an evening of talk brought them no nearer to a solution to the problem of Pule's impending grasp of power. Hesh sat swirling his third cup of wine, shaking his head. "We can do nothing until Vran either recovers or …"

"But even if he doesn't recover," Poppy said. "Wouldn't exposing Pule's part in the poisoning—and I'm sure he has one—give the wise ones and Avive grounds for sending him packing?"

The old man raised his bushy eyebrows at her figure of speech, but understood. "Pule already has more power than we like to contemplate. The miscreant already has a number of the king's people willing to back up his cause. If, in the king's absence, he manages to seize complete control, there will be no opposing him."

"I knew there had to more in that jerk's fan club than Mari and Serica," Poppy grumbled. "And whoever braved the jaunt to the River Dystopia. And that, once he took the wheel, he'd just blow off anyone who even hinted at becoming a bug in the system."

"Well said, lady," Hesh replied politely, though he had listened with a furrow of perplexity in his brow. "Clearly our best hope is for Vran to revive, then the case can be laid before him to pursue the villain through traditional means. The information gleaned from your labor in the laundry will then prove invaluable." He yawned widely.

"I sure hope so," Poppy said. Then glad to introduce the subject, added, "You're tired. Maybe we should call it a night."

The old man gave her a look of appreciation. "My visitors do not usually wish to leave in the dark, so my guest room is always prepared. And I have made a fire for you. But ..."

"But?" She looked at him in the flickering light.

"It should come from Lorimar, but yet ..."

"But what?" Poppy sat up straight, her tone was almost demanding.

"Has Lorimar, or anyone," he continued hesitantly, "ever spoken to you of ... the prophecy?"

CHAPTER 21

She had a strong feeling she'd be sorry she asked. "What prophecy?"

"There is a Halderwoldian prophecy of olden times," he continued slowly, stroking his abundant white beard. "It is said sorrowful times will come upon us, but a liberator will come to us one day. A female fair to look upon, who will bring us …" He paused.

Cold prickles made her draw her arms around herself. "What will she bring you, Hesh?"

"Fire."

Poppy slumped back in her chair and heaved a loud sighed. "Well, *I* didn't bring anything like *that.*"

"Indeed you did," he said with an apologetic smile. "Have you not noticed, lady, that no one in Halderwold, and I can assure you no one in Laria either, has hair the color of yours?"

She stared at him almost stupidly for a moment. "Oh, God, no." She covered her face with her hands and groaned. Looking up at him almost in desperation, she said, "Don't tell me you people are going to expect me to solve all the wild stuff going on here just because I have … *red hair!* I mean, there are thousands of people with red hair in …"

His smile reassured her even before he replied. "I have spoken at length with Lorimar about you and your possible origin. Where you are from, I do not know, and neither does Lorimar, but he believes the prophecy is to be fulfilled in you—at least he did before you disappeared. Now that you are back … he probably does not know what to think. Or perhaps his hope is renewed."

She sat there for a minute, not knowing what to say. Finally she said, "I wonder why Lorimar didn't tell me about this prophecy. I mean when he was preparing me for the Wise House and everything."

"The prophecy is not general knowledge. It belongs to the esoteric teachings of the wise ones and the ruling class. My father was a wise one and I myself spent several years in wise training, but I thought it more useful to assume charge of the young people in preliminary incarceration. Your instruction was soon to come, I believe. Particularly since you …"

"Since I might be the one," she finished for him weakly.

"As I remember," Hesh continued. "Lorimar desired you to first learn to read our script, then he intended to guide you to read the prophecy for yourself, so there would be no unanswered questions in your mind."

"I'd never have suspected him of *duping* me," she said thoughtfully. "But that does sound like Lorimar—always cautious. And I do remember his eagerness for me to learn to read, though I was just as eager. I felt shut out of all the knowledge—like a little kid."

Hesh nodded. "I believed his intention would have been the wisest course."

Poppy looked at the old man helplessly. "I don't know what to say, Hesh. I have no idea when I'll just disappear again and find myself back home. Then again, what if I don't? What if I stay here for the rest of my life? It can be absolutely *crazy-making* if I let myself think about it."

"I understand," he said kindly. "Best not to dwell on things we have no power over. The Unbounded One must be relied upon in such matters. Now, as I have said, your room is prepared."

"Oh, just like last time." In spite of her agitation, she suppressed a yawn. "I don't suppose …" she began, wondering how to say it. "Well, I surely don't need any help. I can put myself to bed, and get up in the morning." She had been afraid to ask about Nona, since he hadn't mentioned her. Maybe she'd had a nervous breakdown or something worse—committed suicide. That must happen now and then down here, especially with all those sharp tool the kids are allowed to work with.

His tone revealed his awareness of her concern. "Nona is strong and I believe she will weather the remaining years of her sentence in good courage. You may see her tomorrow."

She woke in the morning with Nona once again preparing her breach of fast over the bedroom fire. The face that peered at hers appeared considerably older, but joyful at seeing her again. "Lady," the girl greeted her, choking a little.

Poppy threw back the covers, held out her hands in greeting, but instead of performing the same gesture, the girl grasped them as if reaching for a life line. Pulling her onto the bed, Poppy received a shy embrace with a sniff of retracted tears.

"I feared never to see you again," Nona told her.

"Well, I'm here, but only for a short visit." Poppy forced herself to sound upbeat. It was obvious that very little encouragement would have the poor girl surrendering to her misery.

"Are you well, lady?"

"Very well, dear. And I see you've been holding it together too."

"Holding ...?"

"I mean you look as if you're handling your ... life here."

"Well, I'm alive," the girl said none too cheerfully. "And not mad, Uniplax be thanked. And ... just four more years."

Poppy nodded and gave her a little back rub. "You'll make it." In the moment of silence that followed, she realized the girl was waiting for news of her family but afraid to ask.

"Your mother is still alive," Poppy said quickly. "But not well. Deema has remained unmarried, waiting for you. She and Sil take care of the family, the four little boys."

"*Four* of them now?" Nona's eyes widened, enormous in her thin face. "Poor mother ..."

"You mother is well taken care of too," Poppy assured her. "You won't believe what a grown up woman Deema is now. And Sil does her share."

"Little Sil." The wan face took on a faraway look.

"Not so little, Deema tells me." Poppy sat up and swung her legs over the side of the bed. "Honey, they *loved* the gift you sent, and they're just waiting for you to come home and let them take care of you too."

"Oh, never." Nona gasped. "On the contrary, I will spend the rest of my life making up for the terrible mistake that took me away from them when I was so badly needed. Both Deema and Sil will marry, but I shall not. I shall do nothing but care for my parents and my brothers for the rest of my life."

"I'm sure they won't let you do anything of the kind," Poppy said. "Is that cof ... vivor?"

The girl jumped up off the bed. "Oh, I am sorry, lady!" She dipped out a scalding cup of brown fluid from the kettle hanging on a hook over the fire and, after wiping the outside with a towel, brought it to her. "I have the flatloaf all mixed. It will be fried very soon."

"Take your time. Take your time. And don't forget—you eat with me, just like last time."

Nona was now visibly cheered, and quickly finished the breakfast preparation. Then, with no further self-effacement, served up two helpings of flatloaf heaped with stewed berries, and pulled a stool up to the table to sit on.

After their meal, the girl registered astonishment at Poppy's clothing. "Are you not still dwelling at the house of Lorimar?" she exclaimed, holding up the ragged dress.

"I've been working in the laundry in the palace," Poppy explained, grinning at the girls's look of consternation. She leaned closer and whispered, "I've been *spying.*"

Nona was even more shocked. "On the *king?*"

Poppy thrust her arms into her clothing. "The king is very sick. The menders are doing some things necessary to help him."

"What ails him?"

"I can't talk about it right now. But as soon as it is all settled," Poppy assured her. "I'll come back, or send you word. We expect things to be better in Halderwold in the future." Where was all this optimism coming from? It seemed Nona's situation of despair had spurred Poppy in the opposite direction, into a more upbeat frame of mind. The girls embraced and Nona went off to her work.

There was not much left to discuss with Hesh, and he had work to do. He gave her a strong fatherly hug, along with some directions on getting home, but they sounded too complicated to bother trying to memorize. Poppy decided if she just kept taking the up staircases, she'd end up on ground level sooner or later. After Guinar, she no longer feared the palace guards. Apparently there was still enough respect for the wise ones to see her through. Still, she was just as happy to be starting off by herself, before her huge friend came by to offer his escort service.

Her hair hidden by her kerchief, her cloak and hood around her again, she set off down a dank corridor. It must have taken at least an hour to get here from the place where she'd met Guinar, and that was mostly downward, so she decided to allow herself as much time as she needed to make the trip back up. She set off at a comfortable pace so as not to tire herself on the many stairs before she reached the safety and comfort of 'home.'

Walking along, she realized she had given almost no thought this time to the worry her parents and Aunt Holly must be suffering, having her lapsed into another coma, or whatever they called it. She had taken her tumble by a well-traveled road, so by now they most certainly had her tucked up safely in the hospital, realizing she would probably come out of it again. Hopefully. But she hadn't time for their world right now, not with the problems to be dealt with here.

After some time, her ruminations her only company as she trudged along a dark and lonely corridor now far above the domain of Hesh, she became gradually aware of voices drifting from a side hallway as she passed. Pausing to wonder what this floor might be used for, she strained to hear the words rumbling along the stone passageway, but they were too faint to make out. Her curiosity mounting, she pulled her wrap close and, moving close to the wall, began a slow, careful advance in the direction of the voices.

As she crept nearer, she was intrigued to hear laughter included in the conversation—ribald laughter of several male voices, she realized as she drew closer. And she recognized one of those voices. It belonged to none other than Duke Pule. Holding her breath, she couldn't resist creeping closer. Good heavens, they were telling *jokes!* Huddled outside the door, she was struck by the simplicity of the humor these men were absolutely choking over.

"I took my wife on half a journey," one voice declared.

"How so?" another asked.

"I led her half way to the swamp and bid her go on without me."

Poppy shook her head in disbelief as whoops of laughter reached a crescendo.

"How far do you think she could walk into the swamp?" someone asked.

"Knowing Wera's stubbornness, she would probably attain some distance."

"More than half way?"

"Oh, I believe she would persevere much further than half way."

"Then she would not be going into the swamp."

"And why would she not?"

"Because after she got half way in, she would be going *out*. Ha, ha, ha."

Loud guffaws erupted. *Good grief, it sounds as if they're just repeating things they say all the time—like a ritual. I bet I could have them all rolling on the floor in five minutes!* Poppy pressed her hand over her mouth and nose for fear of snorting. Then another, much larger hand covered hers and a strong arm encircled her waist with crushing pressure.

"We meet again, Lady Poppy," said Guinar.

Unable to turn or even move, Poppy felt heavy legs behind her own forcing her to walk into the room, where the look of mirth dropped from a number of upturned faces. One face rose and rode a swaggering body toward her. As Guinar removed his hand from her mouth, another pulled her chin up with a wrenching jerk..

"I have been pondering this familiar face," said Pule. "I never expected to find it in the palace laundry or I would have recognized it at once."

"Hello … Pule." Poppy tried to speak, casting her mind about for something to say to the lowering expression hovering before her. *It's nice to see you again? No, not even close.*

He let go of her chin. "To what do my companions and I owe the honor of this visitation?"

"I am simply returning from a visit with Hesh." Guinar knew it anyway.

"Old Hesh is a friend of yours?" Pule sneered.

"Yes, he sheltered me from a storm … some time back," she replied, gasping for breath.

Pule looked down at Guinar's arm still around her and shot him a ferocious glance. "Such restraint is not necessary on a *lady*, Guinar!"

The goliath relaxed his hold and Pule assumed a sleazily polite tone. With a bow, he said, "Come and sit, lady."

Poppy had no choice. Guinar followed her to a bench and took a seat beside her, draping his arm loosely around her back.

Pule sat facing her. "A small amount of levity eases the social pressure of these uncertain times," he began slowly. "With the king ill and no one knowing where to turn."

"I can totally understand that, Pule," Poppy said, meaning it. "Where I came from, we have no restrictions on humor. We consider it necessary for good health."

A collective gasp filled the dank room. Pule turned to the others. "In Laria there are no laws against laughing, no restrictions on visual representation, or speaking with levity."

Several more gasps were heard as the men sat open-mouthed. Poppy was amazed. When Kandra had explained the history of the ban on humor, she had supposed it to be common knowledge. Now she realized it was probably because she was an outsider and a potential wise one that she had been given such historical information.

Not sure whether she was in danger or not, she felt she must take this rare opportunity to speak to these citizens of Halderwold. "It is true," she said with a sweeping glance over the men lined up on the benches, forgotten cups in their hands. "Only in Halderwold, several generations ago, did the king decide to ban humor." She paused, not knowing how far she should go. *Oh, what the heck. May as well get it out while I have the chance.*

"At one time the king—King Tullus—was a little … ahh, well, not handsome. Maybe even considered funny looking by some—even though he was a good king. Well, he couldn't handle the drawings—the *likenesses*—that made him look even funnier than he was, and caused his own subjects to disrespect him. Now, that had to be a tough thing for a king—a good king—to put up with. So you can hardly blame him for passing laws to prohibit his people from making fun of him."

The men were nodding and glancing at each other for re-enforcement of their agreement. Even Guinar dipped then lifted his huge head.

Pule sat for a moment as if he didn't know how to continue. "So our little secret is safe with you, Lady Poppy?" he asked with a sheepish look.

"Perfectly," Poppy declared. "In fact, I think a little party like this now and then is something Halderwoldians badly need."

The pressure seemed to ease. The nodding and smiling got to her, and her clown mentality began to kick in. "And I think I have a little question to ask you guys." She couldn't resist such a ripe audience. "Why does a chicken cross the road?"

Blank stares from all the men.

"What is a … *chicken*, lady?" Pule asked.

She was sure she had eaten chicken more than once in her stay here. She slipped from Guinar's relaxed embrace and tucked her hands under her arms. "It goes like this." She got up and hopped a few steps, proceeding to flap and cluck. "And it lay eggs." She mimed picking an egg up from between her feet and feeling its shape, then she pretended to drop and break it. "And it tastes good—you can eat a drum … a leg like this." She mimed eating a drumstick.

All the men were nodding again, crying out, "Pluken bird."

"Yes. A *bird!*" Poppy was on a roll. "Okay. So why does a *pluken bird* cross the road?"

Heads swivelled until all eyes were upon her in blank wonder. No one had an answer.

"Well of course … to get to the *other side!*" Poppy nearly shouted.

Pandemonium broke loose. The men dipped their heads, slapped their knees and stomped their feet, laughing uproariously.

"Okay, okay. Enough now," Poppy coached, becoming concerned, but no one paid any attention. Many were beginning to wheeze and choke. A fat man had slid onto the floor and was making helpless grabs at the end of his bench. Finally Pule rose from his seat and made some hand gestures at the men, who gradually settled down. The man on the floor was lifted back onto his seat by Guinar, who was still chuckling merrily to himself.

Poppy was sidling toward the doorway, hoping to slip away unnoticed but the dark, piercing eyes of the Duke were upon her as she glanced back, and he was coming toward her.

"I will of course escort you back to the common level, lady," he said in a tone that forbade her refusal.

"Oh, I'm sure Guinar will guide me," she began, looking around for her Hercules, but Pule had slid his arm through hers.

"We have much to discuss," he said, grasping her arm and steering her none too gently out the door and down the passageway. "Tell me first, lady," he said sarcastically, when they were out of the hearing of the other men. "What is the purpose of this laundress undertaking? Surely the Wise Lorimar is willing to provide more generously than that for his once intended."

"I ... like to earn my ..." she began, but he interrupted her with, "And where have you been these two years past? Did the nashu frighten you into hiding as he has recently done to the king and his family?"

Poppy bit her lip. On impulse she had nearly begun to defend Lorimar, but realized the conversation would amount to nothing more than Pule's baiting her for more information. "I have been ill," she told him. "Under the care of Kandra, the mender. But I am well now, and am able to support myself. First I worked in one of the vineyards, then I came to work in the laundry."

"You are a *Larian*. You were in wise training. Why would you now become a lowly worker?"

"I count it a matter of honor to earn my keep." Poppy flinched from his tightening hand. *I have to come up with something better than this!*

A guttural chuckle issued from his throat as his grip became painful on her arm. "I will not be toyed with, woman," he muttered through his teeth. "You will tell me what I wish to know before your blue eyes again rest upon the light of day."

Neither of them spoke as he steered her roughly down a side corridor and into a small room, bare except for a stone bench that encircled three walls, and one torch burning on the wall. He shoved her down onto the bench and went back to close the heavy, wooden door with a plank bar which he pulled down and shoved forcefully into a metal clamp. Then he came back and sat beside her. "Look at me!" he commanded.

Poppy forced herself to look into his lowering eyes, a coldness creeping around her heart. *If he kills me, surely I'll just wake up back home. Won't I?*

"We can do this one of two ways," the Duke was saying. "Either you answer my questions honestly, of your own volition, or your answers come by my methods. Which will you choose, Lady Poppy?"

She tightened everything within her chest in an effort to keep her voice steady. Why should he enjoy the satisfaction of sensing her fear? "I guess I may as well just answer them then."

"Good. You are a wise one indeed. My first question is, where have you been for the past two years?"

He didn't believe her story of being ill, that was plain. She grasped for something else—something he wouldn't be able to check out. "In the swamp."

He dropped his head and uttered a snort of disgust. "And what, pray, was your office there?"

"I was … gathering herbs for Kandra. The ones that do not grow here anymore."

"Such as?"

"Such as … cheroak moss." She probably shouldn't had said that, but it was the only name she could think of.

He looked startled. "Why would you be gathering that?"

"Just in case it should ever be needed. It was formerly a standard remedy in the medicine collection of a mender such as Kandra."

"And did you find any?"

She shook her head. "There's none there anymore either. The cheroak trees all grew so tall they blew down in the storms, and the moss won't grow on anything else."

He looked as if he half believed her. "Why would Lorimar allow you to travel to the swamp?"

"He thought I might be safer there than here, after what happened at our joining. That fairblow with rocks in it knocked me out, you know. And I was an invalid for several months. Then I was afraid to show myself, so he agreed to allow me to go to the swamp to look for cheroak moss, and some other herbs the women here were getting low on."

His eyes nearly burned a hole through hers as he appeared to be trying to judge her story, but she held her gaze steady. "And how did you find your way to the swamp?" He demanded. "Who went with you to guide you?"

"Two young men."

"By the names of?"

"… Zeno and … Alfred."

"I know of no one by those names."

"They were … very young. Fifteen, I think. And they both choose to stay there. They decided to build a 'wayfarer's shelter' like the ones that used to be there."

"And how did you get back to Halderwold by yourself?"

"They brought me a large part of the way. I had no trouble at all finding my way back. You just keep walking in the same direction."

"How long did the journey take you?"

"Several days. But I got a sore foot and couldn't walk very fast. I … stepped on a sharp stone and turned my ankle right after they turned back."

He sat studying her with a look of smoldering resentment of her cleverness. "And after you made this perilous journey that no one has taken in a generation for the purpose of gathering healing herbs for Kandra, Lorimar now requires you to earn your bread working in vineyards and laundries?"

Ouch! That's a tough one. She tried to sound out of patience. "Lorimar requires no such thing! I believe I already told you, I consider it a matter of honor to earn my own keep."

"And why has Lorimar not joined with you? It seemed he could hardly wait for your joining two years ago."

"He would have … but I refused him. One man has already tried to kill me rather than see 'an outlander' joined to the nashu of the wise ones. I will not put him nor his family in jeopardy by becoming one of them."

Pule sat silent, scratched under his nasty little pointed beard, and asked finally, "You have made the acquaintance of Serica?"

"Yes, we spoke a little in spite of our busyness. She seems like a nice young woman."

He cast a smirking glance at her. "She is a harlot. But that is of no importance to our purpose here."

She was gaining courage by his obvious bafflement. "And what *is* our purpose here, Duke Pule?"

Suddenly, he grasped her by both arms and pulled her to her feet, his face sickeningly close to hers. "To find out who you *are! What* you are! Why I was not *good enough* for you! I journeyed to Laria at the age of twelve and I saw no women there with fire in their hair." He gave her a bone-jolting shake that brought a cry from her lips. Then, as if realizing what he had done, he eased up on his grasp. "Sit down," he said in a strangled voice, as if struggling for control over himself.

She obeyed, and sat trembling as he took his place once more beside her. "What do you know of the king's illness?" He then demanded.

Shaking her head, she replied. "Nothing, except that he seems near death and has not opened his eyes or moved since being brought to Lormiar's house. But I'm not one of his caretakers—nor a mender. I saw him only once, as they brought him in."

"He has shown no change?"

"None before I left yesterday."

Looking up at the stone ceiling and rubbing his hands over his face as if to change his manner, he turned to her again. "Lady," he addressed her in a dramatically moderated tone. "I will ask you one more question. Your fate will depend upon your reply."

Unable to speak, she waited.

"Will you join with me and help me, as nashu of the wise ones, rule Halderwold, should the king die?"

The shock caused her whole body to lurch. Playing for time to think of an answer that wouldn't bring his violence upon her again, she asked, "What if the king recovers?"

"Join with me anyway, and we will await our chance. If not now, then soon."

"And what would become of Lorimar if I were to be made nashu?"

"Leave that to me."

"I'd … hate to think of anything bad happening to him, after all the kindness he and his family have shown me."

"*Kindness?*" He spit the word out. "A woman with your beauty and the talents of a wise one working as a *laundress?* That is his *kindness* to you?"

"I told you that is my own choice!"

He took her trembling hand in his cold one. "Make another choice now, lady. Do not be a *fool*. Make a choice that will in time put you over every laundress and vineyard worker, and indeed all other women in the realm."

They sat in bristling silence for a moment, until she looked up at him meekly.

"Well, Pule, what else can I say but … *yes.*"

He led her the rest of the way to his apartment in the palace, bidding her wait outside the door with two loitering guards who had snapped to attention when they appeared, while he went inside. She could hear nothing through the heavy door, but after a few minutes it was flung open and Mari appeared from inside with her tan face flushed maroon and shot Poppy a fiercely malicious look before flouncing away. The guards exchanged a lewd smirk, then quickly stood tall and sober again as Pule came to the door.

"Please, lady," he motioned Poppy inside with a sweeping gesture. Glancing around to calculate her chances of running, she decided there were none, and entered his domain. In a large and sumptuous sitting room, he motioned her toward a sofa. When she remained standing, he said, "Have no fear for your honor, lady, for you will be as unspoiled at our joining as you are at this moment."

Well at least *that* was ruled out—for the moment. Poppy sat on the sofa and Pule sat beside her, at a small distance. "I have sent for maids to help you bathe and keep you company through the night," he told her. "In the morning, they will dress you for our joining."

"In the … *tomorrow* morning?"

His smile spread like slime over his face. "Indeed. In this very room we will exchange our vows. My favorite manicule will be notified at once. Surely you did not think I would give you time to change your mind?"

She just shook her head and bit her lip. *With any luck, I'll crack my head on something tonight and go home.*

CHAPTER 22

But morning light pouring through the tapestry bordered windows found her still in the sumptuous bed he had given her. After a light meal, of which she ate nothing, she was bathed and perfumed with unfamiliar flower scents by the two large women he had sent last night to help—and guard—her. Dressed, for the second time, in a sky-blue wedding gown that smelled as if made of rose petals, her hair arranged in some kind of stacked-up perfumed complication, she was led into the over-furnished room where she had sat last night with her *intended*. And he stood there, looking, except for his change of clothing, as if he had never left. *Looking like the cat that swallowed the canary, Aunt Holly would say.*

"Good day, lady," he said with slick satisfaction. "I trust you are well rested and prepared for our day of days."

Poppy nodded. "There's only one thing."

"And what is that, my heart?"

"I would like to hold a cluster of my favorite flowers."

"And what are those, my love?" his voice belied a tinge of irritation.

"Bluets. I love bluets. It won't seem quite right without them."

He sucked in a breath. "Well, I suppose we could send someone out for *bluets*." He turned to the women and asked testily, "Have we any bluets growing in the royal gardens?"

Both women shook their heads. "Bluets grow wild, sire," the stoutest of them answered.

He gave a huff of annoyance.

"But I think I know where they can be found," the smaller one said.

"Then go get some." He waved her away with a gesture of great impatience.

Poppy sat on the sofa while Pule paced the room. After some time, a guard entered and motioned to Pule, who went to him and stepped outside, closing the door. Poppy and the remaining full-figured maid, whose name she hadn't even asked, sat silently glancing now and then at one another until the woman's attention flew to a stirring in the room opposite the door through which Pule had disappeared. Her companion jumped up and ran to open the door.

Two men in masks burst into the room and grabbed Poppy. Though startled, she put up no fight nor tried to cry out as they stuffed something into her mouth and wrapped her up, including her head, in a huge dark cloth, and carried her for some distance until she could hear their feet on stone instead of the luxurious carpets of the palace or the wooden floors of the terraces. Rather than panicking, she felt liberated. No matter who these captors turned out to be, she would thank them. Anything would be better than marrying Pule. She allowed herself to be carried along without a struggle.

After what seemed at least half an hour, Poppy was deposited on the floor against a wall like a sack of grain, where she lay listening to the voices above her.

"I want her *out* of Halderwold!" a woman's voice cried in a near hysterical tone.

"But where shall we take her?" A man's voice, sounding young, asked.

"Where? I do not care where, so long as she is out of the kingdom!"

"But there is no other habitation save Laria, and we cannot go there," another male voice, still quite young, pleaded.

"No other *habitation?*" the woman cried. "Is there no forest? No river? No *swamp?*"

She heard two simultaneous gasps. "*Mari!* Surely you do not …"

"Do not speak my name, fool!" Mari hissed. "Oh, well, no matter. She will never come back here again to accuse me."

There was a short silence, before Mari spoke again. "Yes, the swamp. Take her to the swamp."

"We will not go to the swamp," one man said. "Not even for you."

"Then take her as close as you dare go! Take her so far she cannot come back. Give her no water or food so she will have no choice but to continue on into the swamp, or die."

"It is so far," the other man whined. "If only we could take horses."

"*Horses?*" Mari cried. "Any fool knows there are no streams in the great grasslands. Can you carry enough water for yourselves and horses too? And am I to answer for horses missing from palace stable?"

The men muttered and a pacing of feet began around Poppy, which continued until Mari threatened, "Would you have me go to the Wise House with the tales I could tell about you two? Your journey to the River Dystopia and …"

"Woman, forebear!" the younger male voice pleaded. "We are *kin*."

"And how would *you* fair, *lady*," the other man asked. "We were ignorant of the intended use of fogbane when we were sent to gather it, but should *your* part in the king's illness be made known to the nashu …"

"*Enough!*" cried Mari, and Poppy felt a sharp prod in her side that had to be her foot. "When this baggage is gone from the city, Pule will be mine once more! And when he comes into power, I will share it with him, and you two *gallants* will be glad of my favor then. What will it gain us to stand here accusing one another? When it is dark, do what must be done. Just take her away!" Her orders were followed by the sound of fading footsteps on the stone floor.

Poppy was hoisted momentarily, deposited into what felt like a box, then the men left. Fighting panic at the feeling of being enclosed, she calmed herself by the thought that she at least knew of her immediate fate. There had been no mention of harming her directly, and they could certainly do worse than dump her somewhere. Maybe she could follow them back to Halderwold without being seen—or maybe she'd think of *something* by the time they'd left her there. No one had ever mentioned to her how long it took to get to the swamp, and she had never thought it necessary to ask. She'd come up with that 'sore foot' excuse yesterday to avoid answering that question for Pule.

Many painful hours later the two men returned and opened what she saw was some kind of chest after they removed her sacking and let her sit up. The cloth that had bound her head was taken away, leaving the scarf or whatever it was in her mouth. She looked at the two face masks, longing to be able to plead for water.

The men spoke to her with civility, even remorse.

"The first lap of our journey will be short," one of them explained. "We will take you in this chest to another house, then you will ride in a lighter carrier, a basket in which you will be able to breath freely, for we must carry you a great distance."

She sat calmly, knowing from the conversation she had overheard that there was no hope of them setting her free.

"However," the man continued, "You must keep the cloth in your mouth until we are well away from the city."

She nodded and offered no resistence as he pushed her back into the chest and closed it. She felt herself hoisted and carried.

When, after about another hour, the chest was set down and she was allowed to sit up again, two young men without masks squatted beside her. One removed the gag and gave her a drink of water.

"I regret that we cannot feed you," he said. "But you must be weak when we leave you in the grassland, so you cannot follow us back. Also, we cannot give you any fluid after tonight."

"How … how long will the journey be?" Poppy was afraid to ask.

The men were silent, exchanging glances as if each wanted the other to answer her question. The one who appeared younger looked away and said nothing. The one who had been speaking to her took a deep breath before replying. "No one is certain any more. Four or five days perhaps; more if we have to carry you."

"I can walk," she told him quickly.

He nodded. "Your cooperation will shorten the travail for all of us, but we still cannot give you food or water. After we leave you, you must have no choice but to continue on toward the swamp, or…." He pressed his knuckles against his mouth.

"I wouldn't want to come back here anyway," she lied, trying to sound convincing.

"We cannot depend upon that, lady," the man said with a little shake of his head. "Indeed the choice is not ours. Now let us begin the journey."

He got to his feet and tried the hinges of a wicker chest the younger man had dragged over beside them. He pulled a mound of material from the basket that turned out to be a cape and, turning to Poppy, said, "Stand up."

She stood with difficulty, her legs cramped and wobbling. He wrapped her in the cape. "It gets cold out there at night."

You are too kind, sir.

Her mouth was again stuffed with the now wet and disgusting gag. She was glad there was no food in her stomach or she felt sure she would wretch.

"We must carry you until we are without the city," he said, and she was stuffed, wrapped in the cape, into the wicker carrier, which was then hoisted and carried off. Nothing was said for a couple of hours. At least not to Poppy. The men muttered to each other now and then. She strained, when they spoke, to catch their names, but they used none.

They sat her down once in the dark and removed the gag by moonlight, then continued on their trek for a short distance. Finally, they let her out to sleep. A cord was tied around her wrists and another around her neck, the other end of which was around the older man's wrist. Then they wrapped her, and themselves, in capes, and slept.

It was well past dawn when they untied her. "Can you walk?" the older man asked.

"Just give me a few minutes." She stretched every muscle she was aware of having, walked a few steps, and finally told him she was ready to go. *The sooner we get there, the sooner I get rid of these goons and look for some berries. Dew-soaked blueberries would do just fine.*

"Good," the man continued. "It will be faster."

"I'll walk as far and as fast as I can," Poppy told him. "But I need some water and food."

Both men looked at her with what appeared to be genuine regret. "We cannot give you water or food, lady, as I have told you," the older one replied. "Because you must not have the strength to follow us back to Halderwold."

Poppy stamped her foot. "And I told *you* I have *no* intention of following you back! Pule would only have me thrown into one of your dungeons if I did. Or Mari would have me murdered. I just need *something* to navigate on. Think about it. You want to get rid of me as soon as possible and get back home. I want to get whatever I'm in for over with. So if you give me enough water and food to get where you're taking me, it will all be over sooner for all of us."

The men looked at each other as if confronted with a difficult puzzle, and Poppy realized that neither of them were what some would call 'the sharpest tools in the box.' No wonder they had been duped into criminal activity by a chamber maid.

"Well, what do you say, guys? Food once a day and water twice a day until we get wherever it is we're going, and then you go back without me. Is it a deal?"

"What is a *deal*?" the younger one asked stupidly.

"A deal is something people agree on."

"Oh, a bargain."

"Yes, exactly. A bargain."

The men looked at each other again, the older one spoke. "We will give you food and water once today and once tomorrow. The third day and after that, we will give you nothing. We can take no chances."

Poppy was ready to take what she could get. "Okay. How about my food and water for today?"

He opened the food basket slowly and took out a small piece of bread, an even smaller piece of meat, and a water bottle. He handed her the food which she wolfed down, then each of the men drank from the bottle before handing it to her. She drank deeply, knowing she would be panting before the next installment, but before she was ready to relinquish the bottle, he pulled it away from her. "Sorry," he said. "We must reserve what is left."

She let it go without complaint. She had already attained a higher level of sustenance than Mari had instructed. Soon they were on their way again, trudging through unending high grass with a few scrubby trees, scattered and small. They plodded on hour after hour with no conversation, not even between the men, who took turns carrying the wicker container with the capes inside, while the other carried the food and water.

When darkness finally brought them to a halt, they sat down, handed Poppy the cape to wrap herself in, and proceeded to wrap themselves in similar ones. Poppy noticed that they lay down with the water bottle and the food hamper between them, but she said nothing. They had made a bargain. Completely exhausted from walking all day, she fell asleep in spite of her thirst and hunger.

As soon as Poppy opened her eyes in the morning and realized the circumstances she was in, a painful hopelessness filled her.

"Time to get up!" came the command from the older man. Poppy had tried to get names from them yesterday, but they told her to call them 'One' and 'Two.' Showing a little smarts for a change, she thought. Well, they had spilled the beans on Mari, and if she ever got back to Halderwold ... She unrolled from the cape and struggled to sit up. "Breach of fast?" she asked.

"One drink of water," One said.

"And one piece of bread and meat," she reminded him. "Our bargain."

The men exchanged their usual glance. It was obvious they weren't really bad; they'd fallen in with the wrong crowd.

"Very well." One handed her a bottle from which she drank until he took it from her. "That will be all," he said. "Do not ask for more." He gave her a small piece or bread.

She ate her scanty meal, finally realizing why these guys seemed familiar. They looked just like those two orderlies who had dragged her back to bed in the hospital 'back home.'

Her one piece of bread, with no meat, wolfed down, they started walking. The whole vista now, other than the mountains in the distance, was grass up to the armpits, adding to the effort of moving forward. She was aware of the men pulling snacks from their pockets and eating them 'secretly' as they made their way, and their furtive exchange of drinks from the water bottle, but she knew asking again would do no good—and she wasn't going to beg. Before long, the sun became hot and the capes came off to be rolled up and carried underarm. Poppy became woozy and stumbled a few times, but the men appeared not to notice. They just kept walking.

It seemed impossible that late afternoon and the setting sun actually came, but she was still stepping along on automatic, a pain worsening in her lower back that competed with the hunger pang in her stomach. But worst of all was the thirst that parched her mouth and throat and brought torment to her whole body and mind. Her tongue kept sticking to the roof of her mouth, and when she tried to swallow, it hurt. A lot.

Finally, as darkness fell, they stopped again and prepared to sleep. Poppy literally fell onto her cape and was so clumsy in her attempts to pull it around her, Two came over the tugged it into place. "Thanks," she mumbled.

"No trouble," he replied in a low voice, and went back to his own spot. The movements she heard had to be their supper, but she remained unmoving and fell asleep.

Another morning dawned, to her utter misery. *Why or why can't I wake up back home?* She had concentrated hard every night, half-asleep, on waking up in her own apartment, or the hospital. Even down by the pond, alone with broken bones. But she still woke up here.

The only thing that got her into a sitting position was the hope of begging a morning drink of water. One looked thoughtful, but then relented and gave her the bottle, pulling it away, as usual, before she'd had enough. "No food." He answered her pleading look before she could even mouth the words.

"I ... don't think ... I can get up." She sank back into her wrapping. "Just go back and leave me. This must be far enough anyway."

"I am afraid we cannot do that, lady," One replied. "You know our instructions as well as we."

"But I can't. I just *can't!*"

They pulled her up, one on each side holding her arms at the elbow and under the shoulder. Once on her feet, she began to slide from their hold but they tightened it and made her move her legs. Knowing she must, she called on all her will power and found herself walking along like some creature from a movie about the living dead. And she almost wished she were—or maybe she was. "How much worse can it get?"

She hadn't realized she'd whispered it loud enough to be heard until Two said almost gently, "This is the last day, lady. Because you are able to walk, we will be able to leave you before nightfall."

"Leave me?" She had almost forgotten their mission, and her pleading this morning for them to do just that. Now it seemed terrifying. "You're just going to leave me out here—alone?"

"We must, lady," One replied. "If we do not, we, ourselves, would not dare to return. Forgive us."

In her surreal state of mind, she had come to depend upon these two men completely and could not imagine being abandoned by them in this endless grassland. She stumbled along, trying to reabsorb a situation that her mind had rejected in order for her body to continue on. "But ... we ... we three. We're in this ... together," she mumbled, then stumbled and fell flat, unable to make any effort to get up.

Almost as in a dream, she experienced the men, without a word, opening the wicker carrier, picking her up and putting her into it, and continuing on their journey, ignoring her occasional questions—so delusional she couldn't remember what they were herself. At the approach of another sundown, she was vaguely aware of them wrapping her again in her cape and placing her in the grass.

Before they stole away.

Poppy had no idea how long she had drifted in and out of consciousness, nor could she grasp which of her experiences were real or which were dreams: looking up at Aunt Holly or one of her parents—once Lorimar leaned over her, or was it Tremain?—even a couple of faces she didn't recognize, and glimpses of an empty blue sky rimmed with waving grasses.

She realized the men had left her and that her torturous thirst, when she was conscious, was no dream, and that she would soon die if she did nothing about it. Still she could not gather the strength to even begin to pull herself up and go looking for water. During the dark hours she felt cold and thought she had fallen into a lake, but when she tried to drink of it, her mouth ended up full of the dry edge of her cape. Finally, she gave up and accepted whatever came, no longer even trying to discriminate between dreams and reality. The dreams were better anyway.

She thought the voices were One and Two come back for her, and, unable to open her eyes, waited for them to pull her to her feet. They would soon realize it was impossible for her to walk any further. Then she felt her mouth becoming wet and supple as a male voice said gently, "You must take fluid, lady. Try and swallow just a little."

She tried to obey, but her throat would not work. She choked, and was pulled up and supported in a half-sitting position until a little more water dribbled into her mouth, finally softening her throat, and at last she swallowed.

"No more for now," she heard the voice say, as her body was lowered again. "It must be given gradually. Pick her up."

She slept, with an occasional half-awake impression of being joggled now and then, but with no idea how much time had passed before finally opening her eyes to find herself encircled in greenery. Not the pale, bland shade of the hospital walls, but a deep, bright bluish green like the trees in Halderwold.

"Water." She heard her own voice, a strange croak; and immediately felt wetness in her mouth. When she was revived enough to open her eyes, she saw a young woman bending over her, holding a cup, but pulled it away after she had obtained the smallest sip. "Another drink, please," she pleaded.

More wetness was applied to her lips. "You must drink very slowly, lady," a soft voice cautioned. "It will make you ill to drink too fast."

Next she was aware of her body being gently massaged with a warm, wet cloth, and she looked up into the kind, grey eyes of an older woman who smiled at her. "Rest now," was the gentle command. "Your fluid must be restored before you can put forth any exertion."

Poppy obeyed. Still too weak to do anything other than rest, she knew she was now in kind hands and no longer experiencing that agonizing thirst. With a new sense of peace, she slept again. When next she opened her eyes, she felt much more consciously present. She was hiked up onto a pillow and given a few sips of herbal tea, then a small cup of soup, by the young woman. She reached for the cup that was being held for her and found she could manage it.

"Do you have vigorwart?" was her first question after finishing the soup.

"Yes, we have vigorwart," came the gentle reply. "But Thalka must give me permission to make it for you."

"The … other woman?" Poppy asked weakly, noticing her own hand trembling like an old lady's.

The girl nodded and took the cup. "And I am Dendri. We welcome you among us, lady."

For the first time, Poppy took in her surroundings. The room, sort of an octagon or something, was walled by bare, rough-hewn boards with a vast and paneless window opening filled with the greenery she had been noticing: vines and branches with open spaces showing the same cerulean blue as the Halderwold sky. And some of the other walls seemed to have *pictures* on them, though all she could distinguish from the bed was some mixture of colors. But it was all so beautiful. "Where am I?"

"I believe the Larians call it 'The Borderland,'" the pretty girl pushed back her dark hair and replied. "And the Halderwoldians call it 'The Flatland Swamp.' But to those of us who dwell here, it is merely *home*, though we have named it 'Freeland.'"

Poppy had almost bolted upright but her body fell back from the first effort. "I'm ... actually *in the swamp?*"

"Indeed, lady." The girl shrugged as if to say, "*Where else?*"

"And you people *live* here? And you're ... *nice?*"

Dendri laughed merrily. "We are as nice as our circumstances afford. You may depend upon every kindness within our means until you are completely well."

"And what then?"

"Why then, it will be your choice how to occupy your time," the girl replied with a look of extreme amusement.

"I meant, will I be returned to Halderwold?"

"Would you wish *that*?" The question was posed with an air of incredulity, dark blue eyes flashing with astonishment.

"I don't know," Poppy replied slowly. "What would I do here?"

"Do?" Again, Dendri looked as if she found the question incomprehensible. "I imagine you would do as we all do. Live your life and enjoy it. What else is there to do?"

This girl was almost as carefree as Cherry had been when she'd first met her, though obviously several years older—probably seventeen or eighteen.

"Are you married, Dendri?" She hadn't really meant to ask the question aloud.

Dendri laughed again, a tinkling yet robust giggle that Poppy thought must easily be heard from outside. "No, but I have expectations. Do you find me so aged that I should be eager, lady?"

"Oh, no! Nothing like that," Poppy replied quickly, feeling her face tingle with embarrassment. "You're very pretty ... and ... *nice*," she added.

Dendri got up from her perch on the side of Poppy's bed, and said lightly, "I will tell Thalka that you are becoming amusingly insulting, which means you must be mending, and that you crave vigorwart."

Poppy lay back on her pillow with a smile that hurt her cracked lips. "Then I have expectations, too, Dendri."

Thalka allowed the vigorwart and brought it herself—a small wooden cup the size of a shot glass. Poppy took a long, slow sip, then lay back on her pillow. "I can get up soon, can't I?" she asked.

"Perhaps on the morrow," was the answer. Thalka sat wordlessly looking at her until she finished the drink and handed back the cup.

"Thanks, Thalka. Vigorwort was the first thing Kandra gave me when I arrived in Halderwold."

Thalka gazed thoughtfully at the ceiling. "Kandra. The renowned mender? Of the House of Lorimar?"

"Yes, she's a mender," Poppy replied, a little surprised. "And if she isn't *renowned*, she certainly should be."

"She had a beautiful daughter," the older women mused. "But a child when I beheld her. Ilan … Isan …"

"Isanda." Poppy said.

"Yes." Thalka nodded, still with a faraway look. "Black hair that shone like a rook's wing, and amber eyes …"

"I'm afraid Isanda died quite young," Poppy told her. "But she has a daughter who looks just like that. Lorimar's daughter. Her name is Cherry and she has been through her passage."

Thelka looked as if she had bitten down on a sour grape. "Ooh, yes. The *passage* … Such barbaric customs. My mother brought me here before I neared that age to spare me the anguish of self-repression … and child-marriage."

"Cherry is fifteen now," Poppy said. "She's married and has a year-old son, but she says she's happy. I met her husband once and he seemed like a very nice young man."

"And how comes it that you have met her husband only once if she has been married long enough to have a child?"

Uh-oh. Mouth in gear before brain, as usual. "I have been … away."

"And where could you have been, lady? You have never come here before." Thalka's thick, dark eyebrows formed perfect arches as she waited a reply.

Poppy thought fast. "I … was to be trained as a wise one. And it was decided that I should spend the past two years … learning the penal system, so I have been underground with Hesh, the watcher of the young people detained for 'undue jocularity.' I had just come above ground when I got *kidnapped* and left to die—and brought here."

Thalka's hands had gone up at the mention of the prison. "Uniplax preserve us! I had almost forgotten about all *that*. I left so young."

"And you have done well to miss it, I think," Poppy replied, thinking to turn the conversation back onto the other woman's concerns. "Is your life here … *happy*, Thalka?"

"Oh, indeed!" A beatific expression spread over the woman's plain features. "I thank the Unbounded One every morning when I open my eyes and see the tossing branches outside the windows, and again at night when I take one last look at the moonlight painting them with silver blue, that I am here … and not there."

"That was so *poetic*, Thalka," Poppy exclaimed.

"Well, I am a poet of sorts," Thalka admitted, flushing. She tossed a grey-streaked braid behind her shoulder and continued, "Though I was never taught to write. Still, words sometimes cavort through my mind, and Dendri has written some of them down for me."

"Dendri is a lovely girl," Poppy said. "Is she your daughter?"

"I have never married, but have given my time to learning of the plants and animations of the greenwold," Thalka replied. "But had I a blood daughter, I would wish her to be Dendri." She smiled brightly and another flash of something close to beauty suffused her tanned face.

"Is she a relative, then?"

"We are all relatives here," was the woman's reply. "Joined by our fugitive lives."

"From Halderwold?"

"From Halderwold, from Laria. Some of our inhabitants who appear to be Larian were actually born in Halderwold of Larian lineage; but, by their nature, found the repression in that fair realm a thing to flee from."

Poppy thought of the imprisoned young people. *Tell me about it!*

"Then," the woman continued, "after getting this far and learning from the Larians here that the journey to their own country is even more toilsome and imperiled than the one from Halderwold, they made friends—*families*, and remained here." Then she added with a smile, "And you will notice, lady, as you become acquainted with the people here, that the few who ever express a longing to return to Halderwold are those who grieve for their loved ones still living there."

CHAPTER 23

Poppy's curiosity about families being formed in this 'catchall' of people was piqued, though the thought passed though her mind how readily Lorimar's family had taken her in, and would have made her the lady of the house. Maybe the people of this world were just naturally gregarious. "So how did you and Dendri come to live together, Thalka?" She hoped it wasn't a rude question, after it was out of her mouth.

But her hostess responded pleasantly, "Dendri is a descendent of one of the first men from Halderwold to make his home here. He was a young man, one of the keepers of the 'wayfarer stations' of the old days …"

"Oh, I've heard of those!" Poppy interrupted, then, "Sorry, please tell me the story."

Thalka picked up her train of thought, seeming not to mind. "Well, word of course got back to Laria that the laws of Halderwold had become overly restrictive, and so fewer and fewer Larians came anyway …"

"Lorimar and his mother were the very last ones to make it through. Oops." Poppy put her hand to her mouth and saw the older woman favor her with a smile that seemed made for an antsy child. *Gosh, Kandra could be cool like this if she weren't a nervous wreck from looking over both shoulders all the time.*

"Yes, we know that, and the house of Lorimar is held in high regard here. So of those Larians who did come, most returned to their own land, but a few chose to stay here and create a community with the Halderwoldians who continue to drift in, bound for Laria. Many of them stayed also, when they found a colony here.

The last wayfarer keeper was called Alric. He was a strong and good man, a help to many who came here before our community was established as it is now. He had come here as a young man and lived almost as a hermit for many years; but eventually, after many more men and a few women had come, he married a Larian woman, young and beautiful they say. I cannot remember her name, but she had a daughter named Dendra, who was my Dendri's grandmother. Dendra's daughter, Shafrin, who was Dendri's mother, was nearly an elder and had become widowed shortly before Dendri was born. She was a Halderwoldian and my kinswoman, though not close—but that does not matter here—as I said, we are all kin in this settlement. Shafrin was poorly in health. I cared for her and the child until she passed on to the Unbounded One when Dendri was but two years old, so she knows no other mother but myself. Though, of course, any woman here would be mother to her if needed. So Dendri has been blessed with the beauty of both Larian and Halderwoldian women, the cheerful nature of one growing up among the joyful of heart, and wisdom beyond her years in the mender's arts—all I could teach her."

If only Cherry had enjoyed a carefree upbringing added to her mixed heritage and mender's training.

Thalka slapped her hands lightly on her thighs. "And so, that is the way many families have been created here. My parents fled from Halderwold when my father feared he had brought upon himself the displeasure of Vran's father, King Yador. My mother could have stayed, but she insisted on making the journey, both to stay with my father and to take me away from the life there. My parents thought they would have to journey all the way to Laria, not knowing of the small community established here. But when they arrived, they were warmly greeted, and weary, so they traveled no further. Now, there are many who have been born here and who are themselves parents, and so have created natural lineages, but more come steadily from Halderwold—the 'convicts,' as I believe they are termed there, but they are nearly all young men."

She stopped and actually giggled. "So you can imagine the wide range of choices my beautiful Dendri has for a husband! My only comfort is that she will have nowhere else to go after she has married. I shall still have her as my daughter and pupil."

"And you're a lucky woman, Thalka," said Poppy. "And so is your daughter."

Thalka sighed. "Yes, though our living must be carefully extracted from our surroundings, we live in plenty and in accord. We are indeed 'lucky.' I, in particular, since I long for no one who does not live here, and am joyfully devoted to my mender's arts."

"Well, I'm glad you know about vigorwart," Poppy said. "I've never experienced anything quite like it."

"That I learned of from my mother; who learned from my grandmother. I spring from a long line of menders, yet I think these living environs, the '*swamp*,' as I believe you call it, has drawn me into a tutelage that would have been impossible were I in a busier domestic role."

"Kandra has many worries, in addition to her mending," Poppy remarked. "No wonder she's nervous; not serene like you, Thalka."

"May the Uniplax make her way easier," Thalka said. Then she raised her hands and looked startled. "But enough of dallying over my silly pastimes. The council wishes to convene around you, lady, and I believe you are nearly well enough for it. They have sent word asking me to prepare you to meet with them."

"The ... *who?*"

"The council. Oh, I beg your pardon, lady. You come from a *kingdom*. Well, we have none of that here." She jumped up from her chair. "But I weary you with my prattle! You must rest and I will come back later."

"No," cried Poppy, raising herself up on her elbows. "You've got to tell me about this *council!* What ... who is it?"

Thalka paused. "I see you must know. Please lie back. I will bring tea, then we will continue."

Poppy agreed, resting again on the pillow. Thalka took a long time making the tea. *Probably hoping I'll fall asleep*, Poppy mused. After about twenty minutes, the tea came, along with some greenish cookies that tasted pretty good, like avocado.

"Now, about the council," Poppy said.

Thalka had settled herself on the bedside chair again. "Well, instead of royalty here," she began. "We have an appointed council. A group of twelve who agree on all that is undertaken. After they have taken a consensus of the general opinion, of course."

"And who are the members of this council?" Poppy was intrigued. "Are they Larians?"

"Some of them are. Others Halderwoldians. Some of mixed heritage. We take no notice of their origins. It is their wisdom that is valued."

"Oh, they are wise ones then?"

Thalka shrugged. "I believe a few of the Halderwoldians enjoyed that distinction before coming here, but now they are chosen on the basis of the people's confidence in them rather than any past honors."

"And how are they chosen, Thalka?"

"Every twelvemonth, each inhabitant of Freeland places a slip of paper into a cauldron. If unable to write, another will help. Then those who can read will count them. The twelve whose names appear on the papers most often form the council."

Poppy's mouth fell open, nearly losing a piece of half-chewed cookie. "Holy crow! You people *vote* here? You have a *democracy?*"

Thalka replied with a chuckle. "If that is how you term it, lady. I have heard neither of those words before."

Poppy stared at her, dumbfounded for a moment, then said, "I would very much like to meet with this council. As soon as possible."

The older woman rose with the energy of a child. "I will send a messenger immediately to find the council members and let them know you are well enough. But you still may not go out until the morrow."

"All right," Poppy said. "But one more question. Where do you get paper?"

"Paper? Oh, our paper is made from the fanna leaf. A plant whose leaves grow under water and last very well after they have been stretched and dried. But we are unable to make much paper. The few books we have are from Halderwold or Laria."

"And are those paintings on the walls?" Poppy asked. "I can't see them very well from here, but …"

"Oh, we paint on thin prackwood. After a coating of dried blainpitch, the colors last a lifetime."

"And what do you make the paint out of, Thalka?"

"A combination of many substances. You may learn all in time if it is your interest. Rest now. You must be alert to meet with the council on the morrow."

After another night of restful sleep, she enjoyed a heartier breakfast of what came very close to an omelet and some kind of seedcakes—not as delicious as the flatloaves of Halderwold, but not bad, with a beverage more like tea that the delicious *vivor*. The women then brought her a dress much like those worn in Halderwold, only several inches shorter, with matching trousers that reached below the knee. The knitted material was rougher than that of Halderwold; probably all done by hand here. But they did have woven material too. Apparently, looms were more in favor here than in Halderwold. Accustomed now to getting into strange getups, Poppy was soon comfortably clothed, and wrapped in a shawl with strings that tied at the throat.

"I don't need those tied," she told Dendri, as her nimble fingers entwined themselves in the strings.

"Oh, they must be tied," the girl answered, continuing with her task. "You could lose it climbing."

"*Climbing what?*"

Her companions ignored the question, finished dressing her and combing her hair, then began leading her through the house. Passing through the rooms, she could now see the wall decorations that she had wondered about when she had been in bed, with the daylight, or the evening lamp and the moon the only illumination. Now she looked on ornate tapestries depicting scenes of nature, people, animals and just about every subject imaginable. And the paintings that she had glimpsed from the bed: flowers, trees, people, both indoor and outdoor depictions of everyday life. How Kandra would rejoice to see these, she thought with a stab of chagrin, recalling her friend's tale of her grandmother being forced to burn their beautiful creations. She paused before two or three of the pictures only to be gently pulled along from the bedroom through a kitchen-sitting room with promises that she could take as much time as she desired to look at them later.

On the outer doorsill, after a glance outside, she shrank back.

We're ... up in the *trees?*"

Dendri giggled. "Would you dwell below, among the footslog of wet moss and slippery vines?"

"There is no danger," Thalka assured her soothingly, but with as much obvious amusement as the younger woman. "Just hold the handrail." When Poppy resisted her tug, she added with a hint of impatience, "Lady, that ladder is strong enough for a *dozen* like you!"

The climb down was a merry one. Dendri went ahead, inviting Poppy to lean on her shoulder with one hand and hang onto the rail with the other, and Thalka behind with a hand firmly under her arm.

"You are still weak, lady," she told Poppy soothingly, as if to make excuses for her timidity and apologize for their mocking.

But why am I so timid all of a sudden? Poppy wondered. Was she just weakened from the trauma of nearly dying of thirst, or had she completely lost her nerve? Only time would tell.

Once on the ground, she looked up at the house. It looked like the third story of a house missing the first two. Taking a panoramic glimpse, she saw to her amazement that she was in the middle of a leafy village of similar tree houses. A large village, as far as her vision went. She stood there fascinated. "I thought swamp trees grew low," she remarked, "with shallow roots."

"They did at one time," Thalka said. "until the people here learned to dwell in unison with them."

Poppy was unsure of her meaning. "You mean you've persuaded the trees to cooperate with the people's needs?"

The older woman shrugged and offered an enigmatic smile. "We have learned," she said. "We have all learned."

Poppy then glanced down to see that they were standing on a rough board-walk perhaps three or four feet off the ground. "You never walk on the ground here?"

Another shrug. "When there is occasion."

You could see a little between the boards, and Poppy gave a start as she saw something of a slightly different shade of green slip through the vegetation underneath. "What was *that?*" She shrieked.

The women's hands slipped around her arms, and, one on each side, they drew her forward. "Come, you will learn all in good time," Thalka told her.

Poppy silently allowed them to lead her, feeling sure that, in spite of their generous caretaking, she was to some degree the object of some kind of joke, particularly when she felt Dendri's arm tremble with what she suspected was suppressed mirth, and noticed that the girl was walking with her face turned away from her companions.

After about ten minutes, they arrived at an octagonal building in the center of the village, set about one story high with steps leading up to a railed board-walk around it, and a roof that came to a peak in the middle around a wide chimney. They stood on a lower, wider boardwalk surrounded by gardens and centered with wood sculptures of people, animals and abstracts, or at least what looked abstract to her.

Poppy peered under the building, which was well-lighted by beams of sun-light streaming between the space between the upper walkway and the build-ing itself, amazed at the spontaneous feeling of joy excited by the art. She must have been so preoccupied with the problems and possible solutions of the peo-ple of Halderwold, she hadn't realized how much she'd missed it. Ever a lover of museums and art stores, this place reminded her of a pleasant 'retreat' cen-ter where she had once spent a month in her summer teacher training courses. Dendri had told her they did nothing more important here than enjoy their lives, and she noticed her companions gazing at the gardens and the sculptures almost as if they had never seen them before either.

Then Thalka seemed to come abruptly back to business. "Come, lady. All are eager to meet you."

Poppy was every bit as eager to meet them. In spite of her physical weakness, she stepped lightly along the boardwalk and nearly bounded toward the nearest set of steps leading to the higher level.

"Not so swiftly," scolded Thalka. "You are still weak."

"I like this place!" Poppy cried, grabbing the smooth railing. "No one in Halderwold even *dreams* the swamp is like this. They think it's either a deserted wasteland or inhabited by criminals they've banished, living like animals."

"And so may their thinking remain," replied Thalka dryly. "We do not want them coming here with their laws and rules. Of course we do have many of their so-called 'criminals.' The merriest souls in our little community."

"What are your laws and rules here, Thalka?" Poppy asked.

The older woman tugged gently on Poppy's arm. "The council awaits you, lady. They will be your teachers. I am but your mender."

"*But?*" Poppy shot her a look of mock scorn. "But for you and your mending, I might not be walking around."

"True," Thalka agreed with a self-satisfied smile. "Now up the steps."

An arm held by each of her companions, Poppy climbed the set of board steps that brought them to the higher level.

"This way," Dendri said. "The main council room."

Soon they stepped through a large open doorway to meet the upturned faces of seven men and five women, all seated around a table.

"A *round table!*" Poppy exclaimed.

"It was wrought to accommodate the room, lady," said a smiling man with flowing white hair who had risen when the women came through the doorway, and now approached her with hands held out in the form of greeting she had received in Halderwold. Poppy performed the same gesture and wondered what to say; but before she could decide, he continued, "And also it was decided among us that, since we have no desire to be ruled by one, the table should allow all the council members to sit in equal fellowship.

"*King Arthur!*" was Poppy's bemused reply.

"No, we have no king," the man said quickly, looking at her with good-natured grey eyes. "I am Hap, the present chief council speaker. Please take a seat among us." He said this with a sweep of the hand toward an empty chair beside the one from which he had risen. Approaching the designated chair, she glanced around to find that Thalka and Dendri had disappeared, leaving her with a pang of insecurity. Obediently, she sat.

At first they all just sat there smiling at her. Were they waiting for her to begin the dialogue? Baffled, she looked from one face to another, until Hap said, "You are lately come from Halderwold, lady. Have you any new tidings to share with us?"

"Well," Poppy began slowly. "Nothing good. When I left, the king—Vran—was maybe dying. It looks as if someone's made the trip to the River Dystopia—which is forbidden as you probably know—and brought back the poison herb ... *fogbane*, they call it ..."

Gasps issued from the circle and all the heads nodded in silent understanding.

She went on, "Kandra, the mender, was taking care of the him—in Lorimar's house. He's the nashu of the wise ones and he's Kandra's son-in-law. Some people in the royal laundry had put the poison in the king's bedclothes. They'd been doing it for some time, so when I left, Kandra and some other women were washing him day and night, trying to get it out of his skin, but they really need the moss of ... a tree you have here ..."

"The cheroak," someone said.

"Have they no cheroak trees in Halderwold?" Hap asked.

"It seems they've all been destroyed by the storms," Poppy replied, then gaining enthusiasm, "If you have the tree right around here somewhere, maybe I could get some moss from it and take it back ..."

They were all looking at her with aghast expressions. "Surely, since you have been sent away," Hap said, "you may not go back. You would be imprisoned!"

"Well, I wasn't exactly sent here," she explained. "Not by the king or anyone in authority. I was dragged partway here by a couple of nitwits—the same two guys who went and got the fogbane. I think I must have been nearly dead when someone found me and brought me here because I didn't know a thing until I woke up in Thalka's house." She glanced around. "And I hope I meet those men so I can thank them."

No one indicated that they had any knowledge of these men, so she continued, "And I wasn't thinking of making the trip back all by myself. Couldn't some of you come with me, and we could just *sneak* back." She cast a look around at a circle of uncommitted faces. "Once we got to Lorimar's house, we'd be safe," she continued. "I can guarantee you that. And if Vran is still alive, then maybe ..."

They all sat in silence, until Hap said, "The king lives, lady. He has been revived from his deathlike state, though he is still unable to rise from bed."

Now Poppy was the one to stare. "You people know what's going on in Halderwold?"

Heads nodded as Hap replied, "Somewhat, but we are eager to hear anything you may have to tell us."

"Then you think Vran will recover completely without the moss?"

"Perhaps," Hap replied. "But he shall have it anyway, and soon. Runners have already left with some of the moss to be delivered to the House of Lorimar after nightfall today. Once the cheroak moss is in the competent hands of Kandra, if Vran is meant to recover, he shall."

"You guys know Kandra ... and Lorimar, and Vran? Then you must have known everything I just told you."

"Not all of it. But we knew about you, Lady Poppy, though we heard near two years ago that you had left the realm, or gone into hiding ..."

"I ... wasn't around for a while. But I'd rather not go into that right now."

"If that is what you wish."

"Then you have ... *spies* who go to Halderwold?" Poppy asked gingerly, wondering if it was perhaps none of her business.

A laugh seemed to make it's way around the circle.

"*Spies?*" repeated Hap with a smile. "We have *emissaries*."

"So, some of the people I met in Halderwold may have been from here?"

"Some were," was the reply. "Particularly the two in the back of the cart that carried you to Lorimar's house some days ago."

"Those men who made fun of me?"

The council members were all chuckling now; and one man held up his hands. "Forgive our rudeness of that evening, lady, but we needed to determine that it was really the Lady Poppy returned to the city."

"You were ... yes, you were one of them," Poppy cried. "I think I remember you."

"This is Mandar," Hap told her smiling. "He was indeed one of your ... escorts in the cart that evening."

"Well, I'll be a monkey's ... playmate!" Poppy cried.

A response of great mirth met her from the whole table.

"What is a *monkey?*" Hap asked.

I thought this was a political *meeting!* "It's just a ... funny animal. Looks something like a person."

They all roared with laughter.

"Then it must be a *very* funny animal, indeed," Hap said, followed by more laughter. "But, back to the matter at hand. I believe we should wait for those who left with the moss to return and bring us tidings before we carry out further plans."

"What … kind of plans are you making?" Poppy was intrigued.

"We try to think of some way to aid our relations in Halderwold," Hap replied. "Though all our contrivances are as yet unworkable. The vigilance of the officials of that city is not easily circumvented." Then he added with a smile and a glance around the table, "Though the ingenuity of some of our emissaries keep us in constant amazement."

Everyone nodded, many chuckled.

"Why do you go to so much trouble," Poppy asked. "When you all seem so happy living here?"

"Should that kingdom ever alter it's laws concerning the freedom of humor," the chief speaker replied. "Some living here would wish to return, mainly because of lost family members, though I think many of us would choose to remain. Also we have never forgotten the burdens under which our relations live. If we do not help them, who will?"

"Well, even if Vran recovers," Poppy told them. "I'm afraid none of those laws are likely to change any time soon. Vran had to take an oath to uphold the present laws, and that's very serious. There's nothing he can do about it. This was all explained to me."

"We have no wish that Vran should die or leave the throne," Hap said. "As you may know, the Duke Pule is next in line."

"Yeah, I know more than I care to about *Pule*." Poppy nearly spit as she spoke. "It was because of him that I was taken out into those grasslands and left to die of thirst."

Hap raised his eyebrows. "He ordered this?"

"No. *Worse*. He was going to force me to *marry* him! I happened on him and some of his cronies laughing and joking it up down in an underground room—underneath the palace. He kidnapped me under threat of injury. I think he would have actually *murdered* me."

Every face was turned toward her, transfixed. Several gasps came from the women.

"Well, he took me up to his apartment, had me guarded all night by two women, and in the morning, they got me all ready to *marry* him."

"I mean no offence, lady," Hap said gently. "But Pule has avoided joining—marriage as you say—these many years. He is actually old enough to be Vran's father. Why did he wish to force a woman who had no affection for him?"

"No offence taken." Poppy took in a breath and tried to calm down. Just reiterating the business with Pule had her so agitated she was hyperventilating.

"It wasn't my charms that captivated that creep. I was in wise training two years ago, and he'd already been vying for my attention—and I'd been avoiding him. I didn't really know what that was all about until he told me he'd make me the nashu, and he and I would rule Halderwold *together* when he became king. Naturally, his scheme was to get the Wise House completely under his command, instead of putting up with them as advisors. Then the rat would be an absolute monarch."

"Ahhs and Ohhs," came from all around the table.

"So the morning we were supposed to … get married, he left the room and two guys came in another door and kidnapped me. For the second time in two days."

"And who were these men?" Hap asked.

"Well, Mari, the queen's maid, who has serious designs on the duke, and the throne, had been in his apartment when he brought me home. He sent her packing, and she didn't look a bit pleased about leaving. So, it turned out, she was jealous enough to have me dragged away. And that's how I landed out in the grassland. Who those two thugs were, I have no idea."

"The queen's *maid* is allowed such authority?" one of the women asked.

"No, she isn't allowed it," Poppy explained. "She's got the idea into her head that Pule is going to marry *her* and make her queen."

"What a foolish girl," someone remarked.

"She's worse than foolish," Poppy told them. "She's an absolute *felon*. And I have it on good authority that there are more of the king's people ready to follow Duke Pule in some kind of revolt. But now that Vran may recover … well, that's wonderful, but there's no telling what they'll be plotting next. And no matter what it is, I'm afraid there still won't be much hope of changing the … humor laws, or the laws against art and publishing newspapers."

"Oh." Hap stroked his beard with a movement that reminded her of Hesh. "Then there is much we did *not* know, and we must think upon these things before another meeting. It is good that you came, lady."

"And it's great to be here," Poppy replied politely. "Well, it's okay now, but dying of thirst out there in that dry grass was no fun at all!"

Some of them actually began to chuckle, until Hap cast them a serious look.

Suddenly, something flew in through the long window on the other side of the room and whizzed past Poppy's head so close she felt her hair move, before exiting through the window on the other side of the room.

"What was *that!*" she shrieked, jumping from her chair. "It looked like a … a *flying snake! A snake with some kind of* side flaps!"

The others were all laughing so hard no one was able to answer. Alarmed, she looked at Hap who recovered enough to say, "It was merely a beguiler, lady. No cause for alarm."

"A *beguiler*?" she cried. "Like the serpent in the Bible? Then it *was* a snake. My God, they *fly* around here?"

"They are perfectly harmless, lady," a woman near her said soothingly, sounding as if she were stifling a giggle. "Please excuse our lack of concern for your alarm."

"We know nothing of this '*bible*,'" another woman told her kindly, "But I will escort you back to Thalka's house."

The first woman joined them as they left, each taking one of Poppy's arms. The two council women introduced themselves as Bya and Dursel. They both appeared to be in their thirties with smooth brown hair braided and wound around their heads, and both wore the same kind of simple dress Poppy had been given. Neither woman was beautiful, but their pleasant and relaxed manner exuded a freshness that, along with the beautiful surroundings, eased Poppy into a more relaxed mood. She asked where each of them lived and how they managed to raise families so far off the ground.

Laughing as they answered her questions, they explained that the children were trained from a very young age to cling to the vine and reed ropes along the steps and that, once down on the boardwalk in the morning, they usually played together all day in the common area, watched over by the elders who sat there talking. And those old enough attended school in the council house or learned the many skills needed to survive here.

"Like making paper," Poppy said.

Dursel nodded. "Making paper, making rope, poles, boards, soap, wine, walks, digging drainage ditches and wells for clear water, growing food, taking care of livestock. And, of course, building houses. There are many skills needed. Many are occupied with growing vegetables." She waved a hand toward the rough plank wall that bordered the walk.

Making her way to the council house between Thalka and Dendri, Poppy had noticed the low wooden walls on either side of the boardwalk, and the green leaves spilling over them, but had absent-mindedly taken it for decorative landscaping. Now she stopped to take a closer look and found a narrow vegetable garden running along the walkway. It looked like squash right here; farther back she thought she saw pea flowers, and toward Thalka's house were vines with red showing through. A few steps that way revealed tomatoes. The ground on the other side of the narrow garden was low and marshy looking, shaded by overhanging, mossy trees.

"Wow! You people use this narrow space to grow all these vegetables!" she cried, impressed. "Now that's really making use of every inch."

"We do that, lady," Bya replied, as the three continued on their walk. "But to us—I was born here, you see, and have looked upon no other landscape—it is but the natural way."

"Isn't there any dry ground around here at all?" Poppy wanted to know. "How did people pass through here to get between Halderwold and Laria?"

"There are a few natural causeways that pass through," Dursel explained. "And a number of higher, dry areas. The council house is on one of them."

"Oh. I guess I was so fascinated by the art gardens," Poppy said. "I didn't even stop to think it had to be on solid ground."

"And there are others," Dursel continued, "But none are very large, and so are used for crops such as grains and root vegetables, and for keeping sheep and goats, and plucken birds. That is why we choose to build our own houses in the trees."

"I've never seen anything like it." Poppy looked around and shook her head, realizing now that Halderwold actually seemed quite normal to her—at least it was sort of medieval earth. That had given it some familiarity. "In fact, I've never even imagined this could be done. Though I know some people live on boats ... and even in houses made of ice." Again, she realized she had been 'thinking out loud' and had said too much.

The two women stood staring at her.

"Tell us of these people," Bya implored. "Here, we listen to the same stories over and over all our lives. What is ice? And in what part of Halderwold do these people dwell?"

Oh, brother! "First," said Poppy, thinking fast. "I want to hear more about how you live here."

Luckily, Dursel seemed eager to take up her account again. "Well, we also make fabric. Though," she added with a sly smile, "Some of our clothing is brought here from Halderwold."

Poppy grinned. "I guessed as much. But what about all this wonderful art I see everywhere. When do you people find time to create it, living ... from scratch like you do?"

After both the women giggled, probably at the idea of their 'living from scratch," Dursel continued, "Those who wish to follow the arts rather than the more practical skills, if they show promise, are trained in sculpture, carving and painting; and many who work in the practical occupations enjoy creating art in their spare time. Young people from Halderwold are particularly enthusiastic in regard to these areas."

"Well, there's no mystery there," Poppy said.

"Indeed not, lady," Dursel replied. "I myself came from Halderwold as a young girl, and well remember the fears of my parents when, as a child, I showed a penchant for drawing in sandy areas."

The walk back was quite pleasant, informative and uneventful until Poppy felt a sudden sharp sting on her neck that brought a *"Yiiee!"* from her, as she swatted at a fly that quickly buzzed out of reach.

The two women giggled.

"I don't see anything so terribly funny about a person getting stung by a nasty fly!" Poppy couldn't help exclaiming.

"But does it sting now, lady?" Dursel asked.

Poppy felt the spot. "No. No, it doesn't seem to. But I still don't think it's very funny."

"It stings only for a moment," Bya said. "And do you realize what you said when it bit you?"

"I don't know. I yelled. What's the difference?"

"You said, '*Yiiee.*'"

Poppy let out a huff of impatience. "Well, what do the people here say when they get stung?"

"The same thing," Bya told her with a wide grin.

"And the fly is called the 'yi fly,'" Dursel explained.

Both women tittered merrily, but it cost Poppy more than a little effort to even smile. They took her arms again and jovially walked with her to Thalka's house, practically carrying her up the steps. After Thalka had put her back to bed, she heard them all laughing it up in the main room.

I'll bet they're laughing at me, she sulked.

What she seriously wondered, after having time to give it some thought, was why she wasn't happier here with these jolly people than she had been among the somber and fear-ridden inhabitants of Halderwold. She must have grown accustomed to the others, she decided. Or maybe she thrived on having a mission—the hope of helping them change things for the better. And the Halderwold houses were sturdy and secure, not a mile off the ground with snaky things flying through the windows almost into a person's hair. Though she had to admit the stone houses of Halderwold, stolid as they were, afforded no security from the real dangers, like their wacko laws, and Pule.

She lay mulling over her new, crotchety attitude. Of course, it was reasonably possible that this testiness was just the normal after-effects of two serious spills, nearly getting married—twice (neither of her own volition), kidnapped twice and murdered once, all in a matter of a few weeks, by her own time. Then add changing worlds way too suddenly and often.

After the women left, Thalka came into her room. "We have not come together here of an evening since you have been with us," she told Poppy. "I believe you are strong enough to enjoy a gathering tonight, but you must rest a while now."

"What kind of gathering are you having tonight, Thalka?" Poppy asked suspiciously.

"Just a gathering as we are wont to have of an evening. Supper and talk. Which oftentimes becomes a jestfest."

"A *jestfest?*" That definitely sounded like more than she was ready for; an involuntary moan was barely suppressed as she resisted the impulse to bury her head underneath the covers.

"Certainly, lady," her hostess replied cooly. "What else do people do after supper? Oh, excuse me," she added hastily. "You are just come from Halderwold. What do the people there do in the evenings?"

"Oh, we take nice long baths before supper, then we eat rather late so there isn't much evening left. Then we talk, go to bed and keep talking. Some people knit or sew. Lorimar always went to his study to look through his telescopes, I guess. Or read. He has a lot of books."

"What are these books about?" Thalka looked intrigued.

"I never found out," Poppy told her. "I would have learned to read in my wise training, but then I ..." *Rats! I've done it again. How do I account for those two years?*

But the other woman was gazing into space. "I never learned to read, as I have told you, but sometimes I wonder—as I did when I was a child and went to school in the Wise House for a short time—I did wonder what all those books could possibly have to say."

"Well, I'm not the one to tell you," Poppy said. "But Lorimar seems to look at the stars a lot, so I think they may have something to do with the heavens."

"Not unlikely," Thalka replied, then started as if coming back abruptly from a fantasy. "I must cook, and you must rest. Go to sleep."

CHAPTER 24

The sounds of people in the house met Poppy's ears when she woke, surprised that she had actually drifted off at Thalka's command. At first she thought she was home, hearing laughter mingling naturally with conversation, but the glowing lavender sky of near nightfall showing through the undulating branches greeted her eyes as she glanced out the long window. Still weak, and dreading to put forth the effort she knew it would take to face another unfamiliar assembly in another unfamiliar culture, she lay listening to the carefree prattle of neighbors. Soon, however, Dendri and two other young women appeared, and, seeing her awake, proceeded to pull her up and dress her as if she were their favorite doll.

"You will enjoy the gathering, lady," Dendri assured her when Poppy begged for a few more minutes by herself. "We will wait on you. You will do nothing but sit in your chair and allow the camaraderie to refresh your spirit."

Without strength to argue, she went out to the main room to be greeted like a resident celebrity by a couple of dozen people, causing her to worry that the whole house might collapse under their weight. But, though it seemed to rock a little now and then like a gigantic hammock, and no one else took any notice, she decided to try and relax. And much to her relief, these people didn't seem to be here to question her on her past life or her missing two years. They simple tucked her into a cushioned chair, wrapped her in a soft shawl, and brought her food and wine.

A good-looking young man lingered near her, but said nothing until Dendri hurried over and, taking him by the arm, led him close to Poppy's chair.

"This is Trael," she said. It was he and Weller ..." she glanced around and motioned another shy-looking young man to join them. After waiting for him to come near, she continued, "It was these two who found you in the grassland and brought you to us."

Poppy sat up straight and held out her hand toward Trael. "How wonderful to meet you," she said. "I owe you my life!"

The man glanced down at her hand and held his out in the greeting gesture. Annoyed at herself for forgetting, she immediately made the same gesture, then, with her hands in the same position, turned to Weller. "I can never thank you enough for saving my life. All I can do is … well, say it."

Both men smiled charmingly. "And only that is required, lady," Trael replied. Weller, who appeared a few years younger—just a boy, really, and very shy, merely nodded in agreement.

"I assume you were coming back from Halderwold when you found me," Poppy said.

"In fact, we were on our way there. About two days into our journey."

"And you had to turn around and come back with me?"

They both nodded.

"Well, I've caused you even more trouble than I'd realized," Poppy said.

Neither answered, both looking shy and uncomfortable, and she added quickly, "I was just wondering if you'd happened to see a couple of men about your age on their way back to Halderwold. They would be the scoundrels who took me out there to die."

Both shook their heads. "We did not, lady," Trael replied. "They brought you little further than half-way, unless you continued by yourself."

"That I did not," Poppy answered. "I could hardly walk the last couple of days. They wouldn't give me any water or food."

A look of ire crossed both their faces. "What a brutal thing to do," said Trael.

"Well, they were following the orders of a brutal woman," Poppy told them. "Actually, those men didn't really want to do it, but they wouldn't have dared go home without carrying out their mission. But I guess you wouldn't have seen them, anyway."

"No Halderwoldian has come out this way in many years," said Trael. "Except for the banished. Those we bring home, of course, as we did you. Though most of them carry abundant supplies, thinking they might get to Laria."

She nodded. "Of course. You, know, you guys travel back and forth so carefully, no one in Halderwold thinks anyone even lives here."

They both grinned widely, and Waller said shyly, "I fear the servants in that city must get blamed for many missing items."

Poppy laughed. "That's possible. But I don't think they treat the servants too badly over there. The people who work in Lorimar's house are treated with respect. Even in the royal laundry, some get away with goofing off."

The men gave her a perplexed look, nodded, and went to find places on the floor to sit.

They had a good supper, washed down with some pretty good wine. To their inquiries as to how she liked the meat, she replied, "It tastes just like pluken bird."

For some reason her remark brought chuckles all around, but then, they chuckled at just about everything. And it reminded her to ask them why the pluken bird crossed the road, which soon had them all nearly roaring with mirth.

By the end of the light-hearted evening, Poppy realized these people's humorous remarks were no more sophisticated than that underground gang that Pule partied with. She would have imagined this constant practice would produce a higher level of discernment between the types and innuendoes of humor, but their anecdotes were of people falling off the boardwalk and scurrying up covered with muck and moss, or of others who had been frightened by noises in the dark only to discover a nightbird trying to nest in their cupboards. They nearly rolled off their chairs recalling stories they seemed to already know, of the narrow escapes of those who made regular secret treks back to Halderwold to swipe rope and nails and tools, and dozens of other things to make their life here more comfortable.

Poppy didn't hold this kind of thievery against them in the least. After all, many of these people were here as a result of unfair banishment for perceived misdeeds that the upper echelon of Halderwoldians enjoyed regularly, as she had discovered by happening across Pule's little underground party. But as to the comic caliber of tonight's entertainment, it was hardly above the clowning act she'd performed for the children of Halderwold. In this world, among young and old alike, slapstick was definitely in.

In addition to the merry-making, another one of those horrible flying snakes—beguilers—had come soaring through the long window in one side of the room and out the other. Poppy cringed and let out a yelp that she had tried strenuously but unsuccessfully to stifle, to the rollicking amusement of the others. As it passed near her face, she'd noticed that the creature had a sort of ruffle along each side. That must be what enabled them to glide through the air. Try as she might to learn to take these reptiles in stride as the others did, she could only pretend not to be appalled by their short but sudden visits. And she thanked her good fortune that Thalka had put her into a bedroom with a window on one side only. That might be the only thing that discouraged those creatures from flying into bed with her.

Near the end of the rollicking evening, Hap drew her into a corner of the small main room. "I wish to speak with you tomorrow, lady. Perhaps just the two of us?"

She told him that would be fine with her, and he promised to come in the morning and take her for a walk. She went to bed looking forward to their conversation. She was worried about Halderwold and Vran—that was probably one reason why she couldn't seem to relax and get into the lighthearted mode of life that was prevalent here. Even if the king recovered, she thought, something had to be done about Pule and Mari, and soon, before the duke had time to hatch some new plot. This place had Halderwold beat hands down for a feeling of fellowship and safety from any harm from one's fellow inhabitants, but she couldn't help wondering how they got decisions made and things done in this atmosphere of 'fun first.' It must be natural, she decided, coming from a repressed culture, to go a little overboard the other way.

It was pitch dark when she woke in alarm, her bed swaying drunkenly, with the whine of a furious wind rampaging through the room. Her attempts to get out of bed found her thrown violently back, her calls to Thalka and Dendri ringing back into in her own ears by the wicked force that had possessed the house. Terrified, she waited, clinging to the reed ropes of the hammock type bed, until a voice near her ear—that of Thalka—cautioned her to remain in the bed and not panic.

"What's happening?" she cried. "It's a *storm*, isn't it? And us all up in *trees!*"

"No ... to worry ... over soon."

The few words she grasped seemed meaningless. She had already found out about the severity of these storms—the terror of Halderwold. How did her hostess hope to calm her with words she could hardly even hear, let alone trust? The motion only increased until the very room whipped from side to side like an amusement park ride.

Thalka slipped into the bed and, with one arm around Poppy's shoulders, she also clung to a rope that held the hammock into place. "Think of peace," she yelled into Poppy's ear.

Yeah, right.

But it was over as suddenly as it had begun. Thalka was up immediately, brought a lamp from somewhere and set it on a table. Both women looked around the room. To Poppy's amazement, nothing was damaged, or, except for the clothes she had carelessly draped over a chair, even tossed out of place. The wicker chests and light furniture hardly out of order. Now Poppy saw reason for the ropes that tied every piece of furniture to the floor poles. Thalka had the room in order in no time.

"H ... how could a storm like that do so little damage?" Poppy stuttered, surprised by the hoarseness of her own voice.

With one of her mysterious glances, Thalka said, "I already told you, lady. We have united with the natural forces. The trees have thrust their roots deeper than in former times and have learned to bend with the wind to help preserve us and our homes."

Poppy sat up and stared at her in the dim lamplight. "How can that be, Thalka? In Halderwold the storms wreak havoc with everything. They split the trees and knock them down. Even though the buildings are made of stone, the people—from the king down to the peasants—are terrified."

"This is not Halderwold," the older woman replied quietly. "My mother spoke to me often of the people there. Perhaps they dare not look into their own fears, nor ask the trees for help, nor the winds for mercy. Besides, their repression intensifies the energy of the strong emotions that are denied and causes them to be sloughed off into the atmosphere, making the storms much more fierce than those of old, or the ones we experience here."

"Are you *serious*?" Poppy immediately regretted her words. The people here definitely had *something* going for themselves.

As if reading her thoughts, Thalka said, "We have learned the art and spirit of communion." Then in a more casual tone, "It is close to daybreak. Would you like some tea?"

Poppy could only nod before flopping back down on her pillow. As she lay waiting for her tea, she recalled Kandra's telling her that the storms had become gradually worse in her lifetime. Were these people onto something or was it just their way of coping with life in a swamp? She had been underground with Hesh during the storm in Halderwold, so she had no personal point of comparison, yet she did remembered the fallen trees and scattered branches of the next day. And hadn't they wrecked all the cheroaks? They still had cheroaks here.

It was Dendri who brought her tea and food.

"I could get up. I'm not an invalid," Poppy began to protest, swinging her feet over the side of the bed.

A playful shove sent her flat on her back again, then Dendri said, "You may sit up, lady, but you will take your breach of fast in bed." A cup of tea was offered with a sly smile.

"What's so funny," Poppy asked, putting a small seedcake into her mouth. The Halderwoldians had made fun of her enough, especially when she'd first arrived, but here it was worse somehow. The people in Halderwold were nervous wrecks, stifling their amusement as they cast habitual furtive glances and worried about being overheard by the 'wrong ears.'

But these people seemed so cock-sure of themselves it was a little annoying. Did they really believe they could tell the trees and wind how to behave? Settling back and swallowing a large gulp of tea that tasted not unpleasantly like some kind of bark—at least what she thought bark might taste like (she still missed vivor)—she reminded herself again that neither of these places were real. Maybe anything could happen here, like in a dream. How had she become so caught up in the whole scene that she had forgotten that? Still, that storm had sure seemed real. Just like visiting those prisons and the asylum of Halderwold, and particularly that dying of thirst thing out in the grass. That had been about as real as anything she ever wanted to go through, in any world.

"It will all be explained," Dendri was saying. "Eat. You need to regain your strength." She sat down on the chair by the bed and crossed her legs, leaning her forearms on her knee.

Poppy ate another one of the seedcakes and looked at the other cake on her plate that looked like fish but tasted 'just like chicken.' She'd eaten a couple of them last night.

"What is this meat, Dendri? Is it pluken bird?"

"We have few pluken birds here," came the evasive answer. "And those we have give us eggs, so we cherish them."

"Then what is it?"

"All in time, lady." The girl's amused smile was gone; she seemed preoccupied.

Poppy put the plate aside and drank her tea.

Dendri leaned toward her, resting her chin on a fist. "What did you think of Trael?"

"That nice young man who saved me from certain death? Why, I adore him, and the other one too. Who wouldn't?"

"Who wouldn't, indeed?" the girl murmured.

"Oooh." It was Poppy's turn to smirk, and smirk she did. "And just yesterday Thalka was boasting to me of all the choices you have among prospective husbands. I'm thinking a choice has already been made."

She watched Dendri's tan face bloom like a lovely carnation. "I think Thalka is hoping that I will take more time, but ..."

"But you're probably not going to." Poppy reached out to pat her arm. "Listen, don't worry. Thalka loves you as much as any mother could, but she knows you'll get married—I'm surprised you're not already with the ratio of men to women here—and she's okay with it. She knows you won't go far away. She'll still have you near and she'll still be able to teach you the mender's trade, and ..."

"And communion with the spirits of the greenwold," the girl finished glumly. Then she looked at Poppy with a troubled expression. "I do want to learn these arts, lady. But Trael and I have spoken of going to Laria. I have kin there I should like to meet, and I have never looked upon any other place but this. He has been to Halderwold several times and claims it would also be a good place to live, if the laws were to change. He speaks of living in a house of solid stone, tending his own sheep ..." She broke off blushing even deeper, with a look of shame, as if confessing to a crime of concupiscence. "And I cannot stop imagining the beautiful cloaks and tapestries I could make from my own wool."

Poppy took a deep breath. The people here lived in merriment and sharing; but, after all was said and done, community property never had been known to satisfy everyone, permanently. There was still something to be said about owning your own home and—sheep, whatever. How could she advise this girl?

"Dendri," she began. "In the first place, I want you to know for sure that the people here are the best you'll ever meet ... *anywhere.* And secondly, it's perfectly natural for you to want to see other places, especially to find your relatives, but ... just don't be hasty about it. From what I hear, it's a really long trip to Laria, and who knows what's going on there now? So if you ever do go, you should know there's such a thing as ... well, wars and strife ... disagreements turned violent. I doubt if you've ever seen or thought much about things like that."

"Indeed, I have heard much from those come from Halderwold, of the terrible places some are required to live in, if they have been accused of ..."

"Jocularity," Poppy finished for her. "And they're not exaggerating. So I hope that rules out Halderwold, unless, of course, their laws do change. You wouldn't like it there, believe me." She put her cup down on the tray. "But I don't think you or Trael should make the long trip to Laria either, unless some-one comes from there to let you know how things are going."

"Have you been to Laria?" Dendri asked.

"No, I've never been there. I'm just saying you never know what changes might have occurred in a city over a long period of time. Better to wait until you get some word. You know, if Halderwold should change, and word gets around, the Larians will be coming through here again, and so will the people from Halderwold. At one time many people traveled back and forth. So I think you should wait until the coast is clear."

"Until the ..." the girl looked puzzled.

"The coast ... oh, that just means until everything is peaceful. Like it is here." *She doesn't even know what a* coast *is. If I could only get through to her how lucky she is; but still ... there's also something to be said about visiting exotic places, and I guess I ought to know.*

"Just think about any big step, Dendri. Really think, before you set off on any long, doubtful journey. It's a nice place to live here."

Dendri nodded, faraway thoughts still clouding her eyes. "I will."

Not knowing what else to say, Poppy finished her tea in one draft. "I'm sup-posed to meet with Hap this morning. I should get ready."

"Of course," said Dendri, getting up quickly. "I will help you. And I myself will be busy today. It is my turn to go to the dry pinnacle where the sheep are kept and help card wool."

So this girl who had seemed the very embodiment of a free spirit had her problems too. And no wonder her mind was on sheep's wool today.

Hap was waiting on a low step leading from the sidewalk level porch when Poppy came down. As she reached the bottom of the steps and took the arm he offered in a gentlemanly manner, she felt a sense of comfort in his genial com-panionship.

"We will stroll around the council house," he said. "The boards there are new and unwarped."

The day was lovely and, except for a few boughs that had already been peeled and piled off to the side, no doubt to become someone's porch rails or furniture, the bark someone's cup of tea, no trace of a storm was evident. After again noticing the greyish green motion under the boards, she made an effort to keep her eyes on the vista ahead: the various trees, supporting houses that swayed slightly in the breeze on their ropy stays, sporting 'hanging gardens' of flowers and herbs that blended with strands of hanging moss. From the vegetable beds along the walkway, abundant green foliage spiked upward and spilled over the sides of the rough-hewn edging that held the soil in place as if there had been no disturbance at all.

"It must be difficult to grow enough grains," Poppy remarked. Except for the seedcakes, she had noticed the shortage of baked goods, and remembered the vast planted fields and the delicious variety of the muffins and pancakes in Halderwold.

With a chuckle, Hap explained that "a bag or two of grain is lifted the odd time from that fair city. So, along with the grains and tubers we manage to obtain, we feast mostly on swamp nuts and green things. I hope you have not found our meals distasteful."

"Oh, not at all," she hastened to reply. "I love salads. Well, I love muffins and breads too, but I know fresh produce is very good for you."

"We believe it is." His look of concern vanished and his pleasant countenance returned. "And after a time, one grows to love whatever is available."

"How long have you been here, Hap?" Poppy wanted to know. "And you must be from Laria, right?" She had noticed his bluish grey eyes and fair skin.

"No, I was born in Halderwold," was the reply. "Though obviously I have Larian blood. But I have been here nearly all my life. Did you by any chance meet Hesh, the watcher of the young charges beneath the palace?"

"Yes, I visited him twice. Once when we were at the palace for a passage celebration, a storm came up. Lorimar took me down there for safety and, I think to meet Hesh and learn more about their ways of punishing the younger *criminals*." She held her fingers up in a quotation marks gesture, which only brought a look of good-natured puzzlement to the old man's face. "Then I visited him again just before I came here. That was when Pule got me—when I was coming back up to ground level."

"That reprehensible *varlet!*" Hap's good-humored crinkles contorted into angry frown lines.

"Hesh called him a 'scoundrel,'" Poppy observed.

Hap gave her a quick look, but said nothing.

"What?" she said in a mildly demanding tone..

After a short silence, he replied, "Hesh is my brother. We were separated when I was ten and he was eight."

"Oh, so that's why I'm so comfortable with you," Poppy exclaimed. "Just the way I felt with Hesh. That's why I went to see him this last time; to find out what he thought of all that was going on. Everyone in the city seemed so unsure, even Lorimar." She chose not to mention that part of her reason for sneaking off to visit Hesh was the discomfort of being around a man she had nearly married, in addition to her fear of being recognized and questioned about where she'd been keeping herself for two years.

Hap's crinkly smile returned. "So my brother is serving the people as well as he can, under the circumstances; and you and he are friends." He covered the hand that had slipped back onto his arm with his other one and looked up toward the sun-drenched bluish leaves.

"You know, lady, even in forlorn times—indeed, *especially* in forlorn times—kindred souls will find one another."

"I agree." Poppy sniffed back a tear and returned his hand clasp. "Can I ask why you and your brother were separated, Hap? Don't answer if you don't feel like talking about it."

But Hap had recovered his balanced humor. "We were of mixed Halderwoldian and Larian blood. Our father was a wise one, well recognized for his farsightedness. He advised King Yador—Vran's father—to abandon his oath, but the king became angry, advised of course by others of a different ilk, and my father thought it best to leave the realm. He brought me with him, but my mother, having been born in Halderwold, was terrified of the very idea of passing through the swamp. She kept the younger child with her, expecting us to return in time, but it was not possible. I have heard that Yador never held his disagreement with father against my mother, nor my brother, for which I am greatly relieved."

"Why did you stay here?" Poppy asked. "Why didn't you and your father go on to Laria?"

"My father had also been born and bred in Halderwold, though he was of Larian descent, and always hoped that some day things would change, then he would gladly have gone back to Halderwold. After all, his wife and younger son were still there."

"So he stayed here?" she asked. "Until he ..."

"Yes, until he died. And I have had no contact since childhood with my brother, though I have heard of his office in the youthful offender's prison." Again, he gazed into the foliage. "I remember how dear he was to me as a lad. I was but two years older, but there was much I could teach him. Reading, playing the iolta, tending our colt, learning to laugh only in the ..." His face took on an expression of distaste.

"The laughing room," Poppy said.

"Do they now call it that openly?" he asked.

"No, not openly," she told him. "It is still the storm room, but the children call it the laughing room."

Hap let out a long sigh. "To think that, after all these years of freedom and companionable ease here in Freeland, the children in Halderwold must still grow up under such restrictive conditions."

Poppy could think of nothing reassuring to say on the subject. "If I ever get back to Halderwold," she promised rashly. "I'll go visit Hesh again and tell him all about you. And that you still miss him."

The old man smiled sadly, his eyes watering. "That I would appreciate, lady. But you will not return to Halderwold while there is any danger to you there. I … we will not allow it."

"Everyone's always taking care of me," Poppy said peevishly, kicking a twig out of her way. "I don't see why I rate any more concern than the next person."

Hap looked at her in mild amazement, stopping in the middle of the walk. "You truly do not know?"

She thought a minute. "Well, there was this cock and bull story Hesh told me about a prophecy …"

"No idle tale! Whatever cocks and bulls may be. You would be wise to heed, lady. Have you yourself no sense of your mission?"

Poppy sighed deeply. "What I want to know is how in the name of conscience am I supposed to *save the realm?*" Exasperated, she stopped to face him. "I get banished and almost killed just for walking back from visiting an old friend! Apparently, I'm not all that valued by some of the citizens back there. And yet, I'm *too* valued by others who want to marry me—not for love but—on general principals, or evil schemes, or whatever! No, I absolutely do not get this whole prophecy thing. I'm supposed to change the crazy laws of Halderwald with my *hair color?* It's *insane!*"

"It may sound so," Hap patted her hand and drew her back into their stroll. "Many times the soul with a mission is unaware of it. But a prophecy must be taken seriously. Also, the people, especially the wise ones, who have kept the prophecy in mind, need something to give them hope."

"But hope for what?" Poppy almost wailed. "I just don't see what I can possibly do for them."

"You must not think yourself alone, lady," the old man said calmly. "Prophecy proceeds from The Unbounded Mind. Why do you think you did not perish in the grasslands? Believe me, the emissaries who discovered you came by quite by chance on their way to Halderwold, or so it would seem to those unschooled in the ways of the Uniplax."

"Okay, I've had pretty good luck ever since I came here, and I've never stopped thanking … the Uniplax that I was found in that field by Cherry, Lorimar's daughter, in the first place. But …"

He held up a finger. "Continue being thankful. And continue in your desire to help. There is a plan in the making, and you shall hear of it immediately."

"A plan? What's the plan?"

"We approach the council hall," he replied quietly, stopping again. "Where the others await us. However, before we join the others, I have a question. You may answer it or not, as you choose."

Poppy shrugged. "Let's have it."

"Well, it is simply: where are you from?"

She glanced around, sucked in a deep breath and let it out slowly. "I was afraid that would be it."

"And have you no answer for me, lady? I will accept your silence if that is what you wish to give, but I know you are no Halderwoldian, and you did not come from Laria …"

Well, Hesh was in on the secret that she was an alien, so why not Hap? "I'm from … somewhere else," she said slowly. "I don't know how I got here. I fell, twice, back home. The first time I landed in a field in Halderwold, and Cherry was out there picking blueberries. So she took me home to Lorimar's house. They thought I was from Laria and they really wanted to know how I got there. You know no one from Laria has been there in … a long time …"

"We know that, lady," Hap said, nodding. "They would have had to pass through here."

"Well, Cherry believed me, at first, which was lucky for me since she might not have taken me home with her and I don't know where I would have gone … But I guess Lorimar knew right away that I was … something else. Still, he treated me great and even took me into wise training. I realized later that it was because of … that prophecy. Hesh knows about it too, you know. He talks to Lorimar a lot."

"And I heard it from my father," Hap said. "Who was, as I have told you, a wise one."

"It was my way of talking that gave me away to Cherry. I guess I use a lot of expressions that are a little weird to you people."

The old man chuckled. "Cocks and bulls and monkeys and … well, your way of speaking, lady. We have Larians and Halderwoldians here, and those born of both …"

"And no one talks as wacky as I do," Poppy finished for him with a grin.

"I enjoy your accent, and your company," he told her. "And I will ask no more difficult questions. You have been as honest in your answers as I could have hoped."

With a gentle hand on her back, he urged her toward the council house.

Poppy mounted the steps feeling somewhat piqued at being led into another council meeting without warning, but Hap had probably only been sparing her apprehension. Before she had time to think about it, she was again surrounded by faces, beaming as friendly upon her as before, but much more serious.

"Well, Hap tells me you people have come up with a plan to save Halderwold," she said, after greetings were exchanged. "And I can't wait to hear it."

They told her of their plan.

For a few minutes, Poppy was shocked into silence. "If someone who has chosen exile over prison were to come back to Halderwod," she finally asked them. "Do they get another choice between prison and the swamp?"

Several heads were shaking as Hap replied somberly, "No, lady. Once one has chosen exile, he is not expected to ever come back. I believe the people of that city doubt that any who have left have even survived."

"They do doubt it," Poppy told the council. "It fact, they're pretty convinced of it. You have no idea how many people are languishing in those horrible dungeons because they were afraid to brave the outlands all by themselves. But I think it's mostly because no one has come from Laria in so many years. That makes them think no one from Halderwold has made it to Laria either. And they think those 'wayfarer stations' have long been abandoned."

"Well, they are correct in that assumption," a pale, elderly man of the council said. "Since they are no longer needed, with our settlement here. Still, the Larians have ceased coming, so many of us are still pining for our Larian relations as well. If the ways of Halderwold were to change, there would again be an interchange between the two lands, and I would die happy to think I helped bring it about."

Poppy glanced over the twelve. "Some of you are from Laria?"

Several heads bobbed. "Then you probably have no idea how awful the punishments—the prisons in Halderwold are. I was shown something of them in my wise training."

"We have heard, lady," Bya spoke up. "But we believe your coming is a sign that the time to help the people of Halderwold is come."

Poppy nearly groaned aloud. "Do you people *realize* how dangerous your plan is?" she practically yelled at them.

"We do not intend to take you with us, lady," Hap assured her. "We wish only instruction from you."

"*Instruction!*" Poppy almost spit out the words. "You think I'd let you guys go off to that place and put *that plan* into action with only my *instructions*? I tell you, I have *seen* some of these prisons, and not even the *worst* one. Even in wise training, I was not taken down into *that* dungeon! You people can't be *serious!*"

"But we are indeed," Hap replied calmly.

"Well, I won't do it," she declared. "If we do this at all, we do it together."

Some were nodding in agreement; others were shaking their heads. "You have suffered enough, lady," Dursel told her. "We had every intention that you should remain here when we formulated our plan. But *we* must do this for the sake of our people still living under those awful laws."

"For the good of both our lands," said another.

"For our future and the future of our children," said a youngish man.

Poppy was almost in pain. Their plan including not only these wonderful people, but her friends in Halderwold as well. If it failed, many of them could be killed; some would almost certainly be imprisoned. Her mind cast about for some other way. Any other way. She reached, she grasped.

"I know this is probably going to be an unpopular idea," she began, "But would it be the end of the world if Pule *did* end up ruling Halderwold? I mean he really *likes* 'jocularity.' I know that for a fact. So maybe he would change the laws …"

Every head around the table was shaking vigorously.

"Impossible!" Hap cried. "A villain who gains power becomes even more of a villain. It is most likely that he would preserve the present laws in order to hold an advantage over any who might betray or displease him. There are many here now who thought it wise to flee from his mistrust before any actual trouble came to them. Once he doubts one whom he has considered a fellow contriver, that person knows he must immediately leave Halderwold or suffer. How, then, could the duke be expected to cast away laws that would serve to keep his power absolute? Especially, since he himself regularly enjoys all the pleasures of law-breaking, as you have witnessed."

Poppy rubbed her forehead as if to erase the very image of Pule from her mind. *Once again, I got nothin.* "I guess you're right," she admitted. "I was just … reaching. Trying to think of some other way—some *safer* way, but maybe your plan is the only possibility. I can't come up with anything better." She cast a determined look around the table. "But I go with you. That's settled."

"Nooo," several voices rose together.

Some of the council members rose to their feet.

"Forget it." Poppy raised her hands. "Now, let talk about details."

They sat down again and, after a long discussion, the council was adjourned, and Mandar appeared at Poppy's side. He had been at Thalka's house last night, but had been one of the quieter guests, just sitting on a cushion on the floor smiling.

"May I walk you to Thalka's house?" he asked.

Poppy looked around for Bya and Dursel, but they were nowhere to be seen. Neither was Hap. With a definite feeling this was a setup, she agreed..

The walk was pleasant enough, given the newly-formed plan lingering in both their minds. Mainly to get her mind off it, she asked Mandor a question she had been planning to put to someone. "Can you tell me ... what is that ripple of greyish green I see under these boards sometimes?" She pointed toward the walkway.

He laughed a little. "That is merely the galters. Nothing to worry about, lady."

"And what are 'galters' exactly?" she asked without amusement.

"Well, they are ... there are none in Halderwold, I believe, so you would not have seen them before."

"No, I haven't. What are they?"

"Well, sort of a cross between ... ah, beguilers and ... well, you probably have not seen wunkers, either. They live in the deeper water."

Poppy shivered visibly, even though the air was warm. "Do they bite or anything?"

"Not if we bite them first." He began to laugh, then, glancing at her, pulled his face into a sober expression.

She was staring at him, the corners of her mouth pulled down.

"They are very tasty, lady," he said. "Nearly as tasty as beguilers."

"*What!*"

His forehead wrinkled apologetically. "This is a *swamp*, lady. We live as we can. We have found many ways ..."

Her hands went up, motioning back and forth.

"That's enough. Thanks just the same. I'm sorry I asked."

"But you did ask," he said in a humble tone.

"Yes, I did. And now I know."

After a brief silence of little comfort, Thalka's house came into view. Mandar stopped, putting out his hand as an entreaty for her to stop also. Much as she wanted to get up the ladder and into the house as soon as possible, she stopped and looked at him as politely as she could manage.

"I have somewhat to say to you, lady," he began in a rather formal tone. "As you may have noticed, we men outnumber the women here considerably."

Poppy nodded.

"Well, I would like to say, before we embark on out adventure to Halderwold, that should we be successful—or even if not—should the two of us return … or even if we should remain in Halderwold. Both unmaimed, of course. Well, I would ask for a joining with you, lady. As soon as possible."

When she didn't answer, he added, "I am soon to be twenty-five, and though aging, I would be a good husband. I have traveled to Halderwold many times and would bring you back any gift you desire … or we could live there, if you prefer."

She interrupted him. "Mandar, I don't think this is a good time to get into this. I mean, we've got this huge … *adventure* ahead of us, and details to plan and everything. And I'm very … nervous. I really can't think of anything else right now."

She began walking. He fell in with her quick stride.

"I apologize, lady. I ask only one thing. If we both find ourselves unscathed after the fulfillment of our plan, will you consider?"

"I … don't know."

"Will you give me an answer?"

"After it's all over? Yes, sure."

"Then I will wait. I suppose … our viewing of one another's bodies can take place then."

"Yes," she agreed quickly. "That can definitely wait."

Some day someone is going to ask me to marry him simply because he loves me.

They arrived at Thalka's porch, and she was up on the porch looking down on them. "Will you help the lady up the steps?" she asked Mandar.

As he reached for her, Poppy suddenly found new energy. "I can manage by myself." She grabbed the rope railing and practically flung herself up two or three steps. The last thing she wanted was for him to follow her into the house. If she knew Thalka at all, she'd insist he come in.

But her hostess seemed to intuit her mood. "I will aid her from here," she told Mandar, coming down down a few steps. Then she ignored him as she took Poppy's hand and climbed up to the house. When they looked around, he was gone.

"Mandar is a fine young man," the older woman remarked as she motioned Poppy toward the most comfortable chair in her main room.

"Thalka, I've got a lot on my mind right now," Poppy said, flopping into the chair. "We've got a plan. A plan to try and save Halderwold."

"Oh," Thalka said. "And may we not of the council hear of this plan?"

"I don't see why not. In fact, I'd like your wise evaluation of it."

Her hostess stood a moment with hands clasped in front of her apron. "Vigorwart?"

"*Yes!*"

CHAPTER 25

Arriving well after dark, Poppy was greeted by Lorimar himself, who had been waiting for her all evening in the vestibule. Ushering her quickly inside, he took her directly to the storm room where Kandra and Cherry rose from their chairs near lighted lamps to embrace her. They stared when she pushed back her hood to allow dark brown tresses to ripple over her shoulders.

"Is Vran up from bed?" was her first question.

"He is sleeping at this time," Kandra replied. "But he is able to get up when awake."

"Can he walk?"

"A few steps."

"Is he gaining strength?"

"Indeed. He is doing well."

"Good. That's all we need."

They all stared at her.

"What are you going to do to him?" Cherry asked.

"I'm not going to do anything to him." Poppy laughed a little and the others began to relax. "It's just that he needs to be able to at least walk a little for his … big party."

"His what?" All three of them stood looking at her as if she were the alien she actually was.

"Can we sit?" She moved toward a sofa. "And I could sure use some tea if it's not too much trouble."

"Say no more until I return." Cherry hurried out of the room.

The others all sat, Poppy a bit surprised—even amused—at Lorimar's silence; he who had always been so quick to take charge of every discussion.

"While we're waiting for Cherry, I'll tell you what has happened to me since I was here last," Poppy began. "I can fill her in later. We need to be all together to hear the plan."

Kandra drew the corners of her shawl together and her mouth moved as if in prayer. Poppy began her tale with her visit with Hesh. They nodded, having been told where she had gone by Malina, according to her own instructions. She then went into an account of her abduction by Pule, then her forced journey ("I guess it was a *double abduction*," she told them with a nervous laugh) to the grasslands where she had been left to die, but rescued by inhabitants—yes, there were inhabitants in the swamp—and they were super nice people.

Cherry was back with the tea and a plate with two blueberry muffins that made Poppy lose her train of thought until she had taken a large bite—almost half of the muffin—from one of them. "They don't have much flour in the swamp," she said.

Lorimar and Kandra had sat open mouthed and silent for a few minutes, now Lorimar was growing impatient. "Poppy, please continue your report of the people of the flatland swamp."

Cherry stared. "The people of ..."

"Shhhh," said Kandra.

She told them of life in the swamp, and the reason for her stealthy return of tonight. "But what is important," she said, after pausing to finish the second muffin and drain the teacup. "Is the plan that must be put into action as soon as possible."

They were aghast when she told them the swamp people were coming to Halderwold—that many had already arrived, and what they intended to do here.

"If they carry through with this madness, you shall remain hidden in this house until it is all over," Lorimar declared.

"No. I have to be there; I'm part of it," Poppy told him firmly. "But you three must do your part too." She looked from one to the other. "Unless you can think of a better plan."

"I believe I would rather things continue as they are," Kandra said shakily. "At lease we are accustomed to life as it has been."

"I have no fear for myself," Lorimar said thoughtfully. "If I thought it would work ..."

"I will do it!" Cherry cried. "But first you must have my son taken out of Halderwold to be cared for by these people who dwell so happily in the swamp. He must live if I do not!"

"I think I can arrange that," Poppy told her.

Cherry nodded and folded her arms in a determined manner.

Lorimar turned to his mother-in-law. "I would have you both remain at home. There is no need of your presence in such a dangerous situation. I alone will attend."

"I am going," Cherry declared firmly. "I shall not have my children grow up knowing I was too timid to be part of the event that gave them a new life."

Kandra drew in a deep breath. "Then I shall go as well. Neither my age nor my knowledge of the past shall render me a coward."

The next morning, Poppy invited Malina into the storm room.

"I and the inhabitants of Freeland thank you for you help," Poppy told her. "I wanted to say it now in case ... well, who knows for sure how things will turn out."

"I have been a go-between for those good people since my brother went to dwell with them five years ago," Malina said. "And I am proud to help, lady. I only pray the Unbounded One will favor the plan." She lifted her apron and dabbed at a tear that streaked down her face. "To think I may soon see my betrothed again ..."

Poppy mustered her most upbeat tone. "Sure you will, Malina. Keep praying. But we must live quietly and carefully until the day arrives."

On the appointed day, banners celebrating the king's good health flew everywhere. Garlands of flowers and herbs adorned every door, the palace apartments overflowed with baskets of flowers and fruits, jars of preserves, bottles of wine, and letters from well-wishing subjects. The city, for the first time in five generations, was readied for a public celebration unconnected with a passage of thirteen-year-olds, or a royal joining.

A vast semi-circle of benches for the elderly subjects had been constructed on the palace grounds, leaving a space in the front for children. Around the bench area, acres of palace lawns lay available for all to occupy, and adults and children of all ages placed their blankets and cushions on the grass. Many in the crowd had claimed their chosen places before dawn.

A dais carried from the palace ballroom and placed next to the buildings, looped with garlands of gigantic proportion, awaited the royal family, their guards and attendants. Already, Duke Pule and his sycophants had installed themselves in the rear seats near the tables loaded with wines and pastries.

All capable of standing rose to their feet as the first of several bands struck up a favorite anthem. The people stood now waving and shouting good wishes and thanks to the Unbounded One for the king's recovery.

Still visibly frail, the king, helped by aids and followed closely by Avive and the children, exited the palace amid deafening cheers, and mounted the steps to take their places at the front of the dais. Vran stood with his family and the merry makers behind them for several moments, waving to the people as more bands joined in and the music soared, carrying the spirits of the people with it.

After the royal family was seated and all had calmed enough for a single voice to be heard, Lorimar stood at a podium on a lower platform, close beside the royal dais, and welcomed the people to the celebration of the king's return to health.

Poppy sat in the field among the cushion crowd, not on the podium with Lorimar and the constituents of the Wise House. Very few knew of her presence.

More music rose toward the clear, lazuline skies that blessed the day, alternated with speeches by various magistrates, manicules and high-level wise ones, praising their king for his wisdom and kindly reign. Lorimar, having opened the ceremonies, retired to a spot near the outer edge of the podium.

After some time had passed, and during a particularly dull speech with many heads beginning to nod in the warm sunshine, and one child after another dipping a hand into a bag of treats, suddenly a man seated near the front jerked to his feet with a shrill *Yiiee!*"

Adult mouths were hurriedly covered, children turned abruptly, with wide grins, toward the conspicuous man who then settled sheepishly back onto his seat. Adult faces were quickly rearranged into solemn expressions, though hundreds of mouths were pressed unusually tight. Warning glances were shot at offspring.

No sooner had the children lowered their heads again, than a fat woman jumped to her feet with the same cry on a much higher octave. Suppressed smiles and smothered giggles made their rounds, hoods were pulled up, head scarves tugged forward, handkerchiefs raised to faces. The fat woman sank heavily back into her place with an intake of breath that ended in a sob. A little girl, who showed signs of becoming hysterical, was picked up by her father, pressed against his tunic and wrapped in his cloak. The dull speaker rambled on.

More '*Yiiees*' issued from various sections of the benches without anyone rising, as the stung victims learned to anticipate an attack and resisted jumping to their feet. Soon even the cries were stifled, although much swatting continued to go on. Almost no faces could be seen. Adults had pulled their headgear close, and children sat with heads lowered onto their knees, wrapped around by their arms. It seemed the confusion would pass.

Then a huge, bearded man jumped from his seat and shrieked in falsetto, "They're attacking me. These wicked pests—these *yi flies* are ruining my womanhood!" The man wore a flimsy woman's dress.

Oh my God, thought Poppy. *It's Guinar! He's one of us!*

The children lost all control. Even though many heads were still down, the volume of giggles that issued forth grew higher and higher. Several more large men jumped up, casting off their cloaks to reveal scanty women's garb, and pranced around, screaming that the flies were stinging them in their '*private parts.*' Even on the dais, no face lacked cover of cloak, hood, handkerchief or hand.

Then a dark-haired woman doffed her scarf to reveal comically garish make-up, jumped up from her cushion, threw off her cloak to reveal an outfit of too-large men's clothing, flourished a tri-corn hat before placing it on her head, and stomped around among the children.

"I'm a big, strong, married man," Poppy cried. "And I can handle any little fly that comes my way. Yiiee! Oh my! One just got me!" She reached around and grabbed her buttocks. Several other women in men's clothing had bounded to their feet and were now moving among the children, singing and yelling, getting stung by yi flies, or pretending they were, and assuming comical postures.

The cork was out of the bottle. The children were either jumping up or collapsing in hysterics. Parents pressed toward their children, but began losing all control and joining in their unbridled laughter as the clowning women performed zany dances in their midst. The men dressed as women came from every direction to join in the dancing with even more ridiculous antics.

The royal children had become as hysterical as the others. After realizing she could do nothing to stop them, Avive was first among the adults to join in. Seeing her children completely overwhelmed by the spirit of hilarity that had enchanted the others, she began to laugh, openly, throwing back her head and holding up her hands in a gesture of helplessness. Parents everywhere joined her, laughing along with their children as if to lend them the support of a collective. At last Vran joined his family and his subjects in public laughter, abandoning his oath of loyalty to his predecessor's edict.

Only Pule and his little gang resisted the spirit of mirth that swept through the whole gathering. He rose and stepped determinedly forward. Standing in front of the royal family, he attempted to address the crowd.

"Men and women of Halderwold!" he shouted. No one paid him any attention, but he continued to stand, repeating his address until some of the people in the front rows began to quiet down and look at him.

"Men and women of Halderwold!" he screamed again. "What is happening here today is a *travesty!* A *mockery* of all the values our realm has stood for these past several generations! A mockery upon the royal house of Yador, my uncle! What a blessing his royal majesty is not here today to countenance this unspeakable *debauchery!*"

The people in the front settled down a little more, as he continued, "These many years we have stood for the true values of seriousness and sobriety. Honor and honesty. Industry and usefulness. The beauty of … Yiiee!" He slapped at his neck, along with a little footwork that looked like bad dancing.

There was hardly a man, woman or child in the whole gathering who failed to laugh even harder than before. Hands went up over mouths as some in his own group tittered at the spectacle of their ring leader doing the dance of the yi fly at the very front of the dais with the royals in stitches behind him.

The Duke recovered quickly from the fly sting, but the sting of humiliation sent him wordlessly back to his chair. His cohorts tried to stifle their laughter when he sat down among them but, looking at each other again, most of them abandoned all attempts and buckled over in merriment. All except for Mari.

Poppy, now standing just below the front of the dais, saw Mari, with smoldering eyes and an angry countenance, drape an arm over Pule's shoulders and speak into his ear as he sat glaring at the floor. The only two people in the whole gathering who were not even smiling.

Vran was now struggling to his feet, and a hush gradually spread over the multitude. Every adult face was raised to him; every child unable to stop laughing was bundled into a parent's cloak.

"People of Halderwold," the king began shakily. "My beloved subjects. For many years I have longed for some way to lighten your burdens, to withdraw the oppressive laws than bind you, to allow the light of joy and humor to bless your spirits again in our realm as the sun shines upon us and blesses us with the good will of the Unbounded One. Yes, I have longed to bless you as it does. I have longed to make my reign one that you will remember as a good season, a time worthy in which to have lived." He lifted a handkerchief to his mouth and held it there for a long moment. Removing it, he cried, "But I have failed!"

A long "Noooo …" rose from the people, followed by many separate voices shouting, "We love you, Vran! Long live the king!"

An aid had approached Vran and slid a steadying arm around him. Accepting the help, the king held up his hand and all became quiet once more. "I have failed," he repeated in a trembling voice. "I have not been endowed with the courage …" A loud sob caused him to break off, but he recovered and continued. "I have not possessed the power of self-subjugation, nor the courage that would allow me to bring misgiving, maybe even shame, upon the house of my father, Yador, and to go down in the annals of the Wise House as the king who abandoned his oath."

The people remained unnaturally quiet.

"But today I do abandon it!" he shouted, seemingly strengthened by his own declaration. "For the health and happiness of my people, I now declare Halderwold henceforth a free realm where the people may laugh and draw and publish their thoughts and likeness throughout the realm! I, Vran, the King of Halderwold, I have declared it!"

Most of the people had risen to their feet already, now they were shouting, clapping, bowing, crying, tossing hats into the air. The noise was overwhelming. Poppy noticed that some of the people had remained seated, most of them elderly, others perhaps unable to imagine living in a free society. The king made motions for quiet and eventually the brouhaha quieted, some taking their seats again.

Vran spoke again. "Our laws shall be rewritten as they were in the days before King Tullus, and I charge Lorimar, Nashu of the Wise House, to oversee this process, and to publish a document weekly that will bring tidings to all the realm of the new laws, until all be revised. No one shall be ignorant of their freedoms or of their obligations."

He paused and looked toward the sky as if evoking the appropriate words, and the strength to bring them forth. "All in our prisons for the crime of *undue jocularity* shall be freed forthwith!" Plainly exhausted, the king sank onto his chair as the people's voices blended in one mighty roar. Poppy thought the joyful cry of mothers could be heard above all the others.

Then a new voice joined the fray as a dark-faced figure approached the front of the dais again.

"Rue the day!" Pule roared, "Rue the day that the ruler of Halderwold should turn lightly from that which he had sworn to uphold! That our king, because of the impotence of children and the intrusion of *deranged interlopers* into our realm, should abandon the solemn oath he took as the latest in a line of kings who took the same oath, and kept that oath—faithful unto their deaths! Is this weakened turncoat the leader you want? Is this spineless changeling the manner of man would have rule you?"

Many were the shouts of "Yes," and a chant of "Vran rules!" rose from the crowd.

But Pule was not to be discouraged. "I am a man who has upheld the laws of the land!" he screamed, waving both arms in the air. "I am a man who has honored our Halderwoldian way of life! I am the man next in line to rule this realm! The king is ill and weak, and has taken leave of his senses! We know he is even now barely drawn back from the hand of death. He is no longer fit to rule. Stand and give your loyalty to me and I will lead you back to the traditions and ways of the unmatched land of Halderwold! And I swear before you that no one assembled here today will be held responsible for breaking the laws of jocularity. All will be forgiven, and, as a people of one purpose, we will begin anew!"

To Poppy's astonishment, a small number of people stood and set up a chant: "Duke Pule, Duke Pule, Duke Pule shall rule!" Pule grinned and pumped his arms up and down while Vran and Avive looked on in amazement.

Doffing her tricorn hat, Poppy nearly bounded up the steps of the dais and stood beside the king. The crowd quieted. Pule was so surprised, he turned and stared at her in silence.

"I am Poppy of the Wise House," she shouted. "And I will state before any magistrate in the land that *that man* (she pointed her whole arm at Pule), the Duke Pule, has taken part in secret laughing parties in rooms beneath the palace, that he has commanded a following based on his favors, allowing his friends to break many of the laws of Halderwold. Not only the laws of jocularity, but those of kidnaping and attempted murder! That he captured me, and caused me to be carried to the grasslands near the swamp and left to die of thirst, and that he ..."

She paused to make sure she had the attention of everyone. She did. Even Pule. "That he was the direct cause of the king's illness. Duke Pule sent his people to the River Dystopia to bring back *fogbane*, a forbidden and deadly poison, and persuaded women in the palace—servants of the king and queen, and I can name them—to poison the king. That poison was the cause of Vran's illness and near death. But for the care of Kandra, the mender, of the House of Wise Lorimar, the king would now be dead!" She stepped to the very front of the dais. "Is this (waving her large hat at Pule) the manner of ruler you would have over your beautiful land of Halderwold?"

"No, no." A chant rose louder and louder: "King Vran! King Vran!"

Suddenly two young men materialized from the crowd and came forward, stopping at the bottom of the steps to the dais. With a shock, she recognized her old friends, One and Two. One went onto the lowest step and held up a hand. As soon as the chant subsided, he cried out, "I am Halam and my companion is Varge. We also will state that Pule ..." He paused to look behind him at those on the dais. "And Mari of the queen's service, sent us to the River Dystopia to bring back the fogbane that was meant to kill the king ..."

A loud stirring passed over the people. He waited until it died down once more, then continued, "We did this deed not knowing what the poison was intended for but we seek no impunity for our ignorance. It was a wicked deed. And we also ..." Again he waited for the crowd to quiet. "We also, upon the instruction of Mari, the queen's chamber maid and fellow plotter with Pule, took the Lady Poppy of the Wise House far out into the grasslands, leaving her there to die!"

The people roused again, fists were waving, and several men rushed forward to seize or injure Halam and Varge, but the guards stopped them, took Halam and Varge into custody themselves, and rushed them away.

Pule was on his feet and appeared to be shouting something, but was unable to be heard. He jumped off the edge of the dais and, after nearly falling on the ground, righted himself and ran toward the corner of the palace. Several guards stood looking at the king for instructions. Vran nodded, and they turned to pursue Pule, but he was already out of sight.

Lorimar appeared beside Poppy, slipping an arm protectively around her. "We are taking Vran and his family inside," he yelled into her ear. Then his arm slipped away as several others in the grey robes and silver clasps of the wise ones surrounded the royal family, picking up the children and helping the king and queen down the steps. Guards surrounded them all, facing the people, but no danger seemed probable from the king's subjects. Most of the people appeared to be in shock.

Because of the press of bodies on the dais, Poppy had gravitated toward the side, completely forgetting the small gang of Pule's people at the back, who had become completely silent. As she attempted to make her way to the front steps, someone bumped her hard from the side. Just managing to catch her balance, she looked up into the venomous face of Mari. Turning from the angry woman, she moved again to follow the people shepherding the king's family down the steps. But a hard punch in the shoulder sent her flying over the edge of the dais.

CHAPTER 26

Poppy languished in a semi-conscious state for some time. She made several attempts to sit up, but found herself unable. She needed a good rest anyway, she decided, giving in to her enervation. She was aware, at different times, of Cherry or Kandra bending over her. Sometimes there were two other people looking down on her. A young man with long, dark hair; he must be Armel. And a blond girl; someone she knew from the swamp? Even these mental challenges exhausted her. She allowed herself to slip back into sleep. Finally, she opened her eyes and Cherry was clearly there, sewing beside her.

"Cherry …" she managed.

The girl dropped her needlework and jumped from her chair to lean over her. "Poppy! Can you hear me?"

"Sure I can hear you," Poppy managed weakly. "You don't have to shout."

"I wasn't shouting … Oh, Uniplax be thanked. You are still here with us."

"I … seem to be," Poppy replied. "Have I been … out of commission long?"

"A few days, but way too long. So much has happened. There is too much to tell you."

"Could I have some tea first?"

Cherry laughed with delight. "Of course, dearest. Please do not go back to sleep while I am in the kitchen."

Poppy drew in a deep breath and raised her head a little before letting it fall back onto the pillow. "I won't. I need that tea."

Looking around, she saw she was in Kandra's bedroom and the windows glowed with lavender twilight. Cherry came back with the tea and some flat-loaf and jam. She propped Poppy up on pillows and helped her manage the cup. "Kandra has promised vigorwart, but must finish with a birth she is tending in the storm room."

"Oh, well for heavens sake," Poppy said. "A birth should come first. And I can do this myself." She indicated the plate Cherry had put down beside her on the bed. "Tell me all that's happened. Everything."

"I want to. As soon as possible," Cherry said. "But my father desires to speak with you, and I will allow him in now. If that is all right."

"Of course." Poppy crammed a large bite into her mouth and chewed hard. She felt very hungry but eating while Lorimar spoke to her still seemed a bit juvenile. But his seriousness and dignity usually had that effect on her anyway. Before she was able to swallow, Cherry had slipped out and her father entered the room.

Poppy nearly gulped down her large mouthful whole when she looked at the man walking toward her. Gone were the furrows of worry that had creased his forehead, the tightness that had claimed his mouth. His hair flowed over his shoulders again, appearing newly-washed and shining as silvery as the Uniplax clasp that held his tossed-back cloak. And his tunic, instead of the usual grey, was a bright teal. Most noticeable were his movements. Rather than the gait of a preoccupied old man which he had acquired in the two years she'd been away, he strode across the carpet like a twenty-year old. He even reached out for her hand as if spontaneously, which she gave, dropping the piece of bread.

"How do you feel?" he asked in a tone both concerned and lighthearted.

"I seem to be fine," she replied. "How is … everything?"

"Better than we could ever have hoped, but for your deliverance."

Poppy's other hand shot up to splay itself over her forehead. "Oh, come *on!* Don't tell me you're going to lay all that's happened here at *my* doorstep!"

"You are our deliverer, lady," he replied, lowering himself onto the chair Cherry had abandoned, without letting go of her hand. "To you we owe the riddance of six generations of repression."

She pulled her hand away as she sat up straight, shaking her head vigorously. "No. No, it's not going to be like that. I won't have it like that. With all you people have gone through, all the planning and bravery of the Freelanders, and you people here as well. You've freed yourselves. I've done almost nothing since I've been here but get myself into one pickle after another. I went along with the plan, yes. But I sure didn't create it. I didn't even think it would work."

He sat there smiling at her—beaming on her. A smile she'd never seen before. He was a beautiful man, though he seemed a stranger now. Of course, they never had gotten intimately acquainted in spite of nearly getting married. The pallor of worry that had glazed his eyes was replaced with a sparkle that reminded her of the blue diamonds these people had once decked her out in. *God, he looks like Tremain.*

For the first time since her return to this land, homesickness hit her with a wallop, swelled up through her like a weepy cloud. She'd been so preoccupied with the desperate problems of others, and her own hair-raising adventures, the longing for home that had persisted on her first visit had hardly had time to show up. Except of course when she was dying out there in the grass. She had sure prayed to go home then.

"There is someone outside. He is waiting," Lorimar was saying. "So I will not claim any more of your time at present."

"Who is it?" Poppy couldn't think of any 'he' in Halderwold who would be waiting to see her. She had been here such a short time before being dragged off to Freeland.

"He gives his name as Mandar."

"I … don't really want to see him."

She thought she saw a look of relief pass over his face. "I think you should. He has waited hours on each of the three days you have been … asleep."

Poppy sighed. "Oh, all right."

Lorimar left the room and soon the doorway was filled with the smiling countenance of Mandar. He approached, bowing.

"Well, we have both come through the great renewing of Halderwold unmaimed, lady," he said as he approached. Then, glancing at the chair Lorimar had recently vacated, "May I sit?"

"Sure."

He sat, then squirmed into a comfortable position, tugging at his robes. An outfit much finer than the homespuns he had worn back in the swamp.

"I have been waiting three days for your promised answer, lady."

Give the guy a medal someone. "Well, I've just come back to … consciousness. Less than an hour ago." *And I haven't given you a single thought.*

"And are you … well now?"

"I don't know yet. But I think not."

"What is your injury?"

"Well, I … can't remember who you are for one thing, or what question I'm supposed to answer. I can't remember much of anything. Maybe it will come back to me. I'm so sorry."

Mandar studied the rug for a long moment. "Then, perhaps we should … No, I will repeat my question. The question I asked in Freeland before we set out for Halderwold. I would wish to join with you, lady. We could live here if you prefer. My good friends and yours, Trael and Dendri are to join very soon, and they have leased a cottage in the sheep farming domain beyond the city. There is another cottage very close by theirs, so we could …"

Poppy could listen no longer. She held up a hand. "What did you say your name was, sir?"

He appeared crestfallen as he replied, "Mandar, lady. We knew each other in Freeland."

She allowed a minute to pass. "Well, you seem like a very nice young man, Mandar, but I don't remember you, and I don't recall ever learning a *thing* about sheep farming. Your offer sounds like a good life but I just don't think I'd be the best wife for you."

He stood, as if in a hurry now. "Then I will abide by your wisdom, lady. Thank you for allowing me this visit."

"Anytime, … Manzor, was it?"

"Mandar." He bowed and was gone.

As soon as he was out the door, Cherry came back in. "Who was that man? He has been sitting outside much of the time you were … asleep."

"Just a nice young man from Freeland—the swamp—who wanted to ask about my health."

"They all seem like such nice people," Cherry said.

"They are. Have you met a girl named Dendri?"

"Oh, yes, she was here yesterday. She and a nice man … Treil."

"Trael. They have been good friends to me. More than friends. Trael was one of the men who saved me from dying in the grasslands."

"Well, they should be back soon," Cherry said. "They both seemed very concerned about you. Particularly the girl."

"They are the best of people," Poppy said. "The man who was just here told me they are to stay in Halderwold, and keep sheep. Dendri loves to make tapestries and things."

Cherry's face took on a glow of excitement. "Oh, and I am eager to learn that very craft! Perhaps she will teach me."

"I'm sure she will. In fact, she would probably be willing to teach a whole class. You should see the beautiful wall hangings in her house in Freeland."

"It is truly a new day in Halderwold!" Cherry cried. "And much do we thank you for your part in it, Poppy. I am prouder than ever to call you my friend."

"Now, let's not go overboard with this, Cherry. I was only one cog in the wheel. In fact, when I first heard the plan they were hatching in Freeland, I told them it was insane. That they could all be killed trying a stunt like that. If it had been up to me, it wouldn't even have happened at all."

But her friend was shaking her head. "No one will believe that. You are being called our *deliverer*, and festivities in your honor are being planned."

"Oh, *no.*"

"Yes, indeed."

Poppy slid down under the covers, fighting the urge to pull them over her head. "Wasn't there supposed to be some vigorwart coming?"

"Kandra wanted to bring it herself. She will be up soon."

Good, she'll be more mature about this whole thing.

Kandra came in, a tray in her hands and a rare smile on her face. Poppy sat up again, surprised at the large cup being offered to her. "Isn't this … too much, Kandra?"

"You are to drink it slowly, dear. Do not gulp it down in your usual manner—as if it were the last drop of vigorwart on lara." She sat the tray down on the bedside table with a twinkle in her eyes.

"Whatever you say, mender lady," Poppy accepted the cup with a grin. After a long, slow sip, she replaced the cup on the tray. "What I need most is to hear what's been going on these three days. What happened to Vran and Avive? Are they still here? And what happened to Pule and Mari and all their cohorts? Are they in jail?"

Cherry, who had pulled up a lighter chair so her grandmother could take the large one by the bed, began eagerly, "Vran and Avive are back in the palace, and several of those offenders are being held somewhere in the prison, but Pule has not been caught."

"No!" Poppy cried.

Kandra took up the tale. "Indeed, where that man can be is a conundrum. They say all the passageways and rooms under the palace have been scoured for him, but still he evades capture."

"Well, if he gets to Freeland," Poppy mused. "He won't be welcomed there. Those people know all about Duke Pule. How did he get away anyway? I saw some guards go after him when he ran toward the palace."

"Some of them were on his side," Cherry put in.

"All has not yet been sorted out," Kandra said. "But with Vran in good health, and the former authority of the Wise House restored, Halderwold will soon be a homeland to be envied."

"What about Mari? And Serica? And those people who were yelling for Pule to be king?"

"Mari is in custody, and so is Serica. They will each be given a fair trial."

"I think they should go easy on Serica," Poppy said. "She had a very disappointing life. Her husband went to prison for jocularity, you know, and she lost her home."

Kandra nodded. "All that will be taken into consideration. She may well be forgiven. But Mari ..."

"That Mari is another kettle of fish," Poppy said. "But I wouldn't want her put in some dungeon because of what she did to me. Maybe she was really in love with Pule. Or something."

"Humph," said Cherry. "That is no excuse."

"She will be dealt with fairly," Kandra said. "Now you must rest, Poppy. There are many who have been waiting to speak with you, to say nothing of the celebration being planned."

"Ughh," Poppy said, settling down again, but her mind was still whirling. "What about all those kids in the dungeons for jocularity? Have they been freed?"

Cherry came over and tucked in the covers. "So many changes are being made, Poppy. Halderwold is a new land; a land such as I have never seen. You will be visited by your friend, Nona, very soon," she added happily. "And the guards have been put on a workday like the other workers. Vade now comes home every night."

"Wonderful, Cherry," Poppy replied. "You should go to bed too."

"Straightaway," her friend agreed. She rose and turned to leave, then turned back. "Oh, and Poppy—imagine! Alvar is to have a baby lipkin! Father says it is all right now."

"Way to go, Alvar," Poppy said, laughing weakly.

Cherry left the room and Kandra got up to do the same. "Yes it is a new day in Halderwold," she sighed. "A day such as I never thought to see."

"And I'm so glad, Kandra. But there is one person I worry about. Someone who will not be so happy about the changes."

"Surely not one of Pule's people," Kandra said.

"No. Of course not. The woman I stayed with in Freeland. Her name is Thalka and she's a mender, like you. I told her about you and she would like to meet you some day."

"Well, perhaps it shall be," said Kandra. "And I would like to meet her. What is there to cause you worry?"

"Well, she never married. She gave her life to learning her art—and bringing up a lovely girl whom she loves as a daughter. And I've just heard that the girl, Dendri, is here and going to get mar … joined and stay here, keeping sheep."

"Dendri has been here every day, asking about you. I have spoken with her, and she did tell me of her mother, Thalka the mender. It is sad that they are to live so far from each other. I never think about it, but if Cherry were to go live in another land, it would indeed break my heart. Perhaps we should invite Thalka to come live in Halderwold."

"That would be a lovely thing to do, Kandra," Poppy said. "But I don't think she would. I mean, she has this thing about communicating with the spirits of the trees in Freeland. She says the storms have been lessened because of it."

Kandra stared across the room. "That I would like to learn. I must send her a letter. If she does not want to come here, perhaps I could visit her some day. Is it so far?"

"It is quite a distance to walk," Poppy told her. "But probably not that bad if you have food and water. You know those rats who took me out there gave me almost nothing to eat or drink. I was dying of thirst when two Freelanders found me. Oh, yes, and Trael, Dendri's husband to be, was one of them."

"Then they shall be honored in this house. And I shall beg Dendri to persuade her mother to come to us."

Poppy yawned. "I'll go to sleep happy, Kandra."

"And so shall I."

Kandra gave her a motherly pat on the head and picked up the lamp.

"One more question," Poppy yawned.

"One more," her hostess said firmly.

"That young wise one who was here before I left. Armel. Has he been visiting me? I mean since I've been … out."

"No. Armel went back to the Wise House when the king and queen left. Why do you think he visited you?"

"I dunno. It seemed a young man with long black hair's been leaning over me now and then. And a girl with light hair."

Kandra shook her head. "There have been no visitors to your chamber these three days but Cherry and myself. We have all been afraid that …"

Poppy opened her eyes. "Afraid of what, Kandra? Have I been in worse shape than I thought?"

"No. Just that … well, the last time, when we brought you home in that cart, and then you were gone …"

"Oh. I forgot about that. Of course I wasn't here so … So no one has been looking at me? Besides you and Cherry?"

"Not even Lorimar has come in to you. Let alone any other men or Larian women."

"Okay. I guess I just dreamed it."

"Sleep well, Poppy."

"You too, Kandra."

Poppy dozed off.

Waking, she vaguely recalled leaving the road, but decided that, after a rest, she'd be able to get up. There were people with her. Several times, she heard herself say, "Not the hospital." Surely there was no need for all that bother again.

"Where does she live?" a male voice asked.

"Wait, it's right here," a female voice replied. "I got her wallet. It was in her skirt pocket."

Yes, they had her address right, whoever they were. But their discussion continued, the snatches she caught of it.

"That car never stopped, no need for the cops."

"No way, we'll take her home. Fish's got a sidecar on his hog."

She dozed again.

She was comfortable now, looking up at a bedraggled couple bending over her.

"She's awake. We can't leave 'till she really awake, Neal."

"Hey, you awake, lady?"

She dozed off again, but the faces were still there when she opened her eyes again.

"You don't have to call me 'lady' here," she told them.

"Just bein' polite, miss. You okay? You goin' t' stay awake now?"

"Am I home?"

"Yep. Accordin' to the address in your wallet." The stringy-haired blonde hovered over her. "You got any pain?"

She looked up at the girl, then wiggled. "I … don't think so."

"Good," Neal said. "'Cause we gotta go. But we want you to be okay."

"We should call somebody," the girl said. "Is this 'Tremain' the right guy to call, Paige?"

"Who?"

"Tremain. And you're Paige, right?" The girl was holding her little address book.

Paige lifted her head and looked around at her apartment and then at the bikers. "You two brought me home?"

"Yeah, but we can't stay," the man with long black hair said. "And no cops needed. That car that cut you off never stopped."

Paige went over her body mentally, then sat up. The girl helped her. "Just hand me my phone," she said, pointing to it. "And you guys can go. And, thanks a lot for bringing me home."

"No problem," Neal said. "We're not the kind to leave you out there."

"My bicycle."

"It's still out there by the pond, lady. Sorry, but it's kind of bent up and we didn't have no way to bring it."

"That's okay. Look, I really appreciate this."

"Happy to do it, miss." Neal touched a finger to his red headcloth. "Now, you take care yerself. Okay?"

"Goodbye, Paige," the girl said.

"Goodbye …"

"Babe."

"Goodbye, Babe."

Paige took another nap with her phone resting on her stomach, then she was able to get up from the sofa. She put the phone in its cradle, then went to the computer and turned it on. The date was displayed as it booted up. It was still Saturday, but it would have to be, wouldn't it? Those bikers had just brought her home from her ride. And her spill. Her lovely ride by the beautiful pond.

It was getting dark. She went to bed.

And woke up to a sunny Sunday morning. Actually, it was almost noon, she realized when she looked at the clock. Good thing it was Sunday. She got up and made coffee and toast, and tried to feel at home. She had a strange sense of

... what could she call it? Psychic exhaustion? Well, she had an appointment with Dr. Blanchard on Wednesday, anyway. An after-check or something. That should be soon enough to address the bruises she'd become aware of, and the scraped shoulder.

Then Tremain called to tell her he was on his way.

"Where to?" she asked.

"A real clown, aren't you?"

"Sorry, I woke up late," she told him. "Guess I haven't got my brain in gear yet."

"Well, get the brain in gear, and the rear too. And wear a sweater, there's a fall chill in the air today. I'll be there in half an hour to pick you up."

"Okay. I'll be ready."

She went to her appointment book. The football game—and they were going to lunch first. Now it was all coming back. Well, she didn't need much time to get ready for a game. Just a quick shower and some casual clothes. She'd washed her hair Saturday morning. A long time ago, but it felt clean. And it was red again. She remembered the dye job Dendri had given her.

In the bathroom, she realized she had intended for the tenth time to buy a decent shower cap yesterday, but had forgotten again with Ethel Parker muttering about the price of asparagus and toilet tissue. She'd picked up a cheap one a couple of weeks ago at the corner store but it had ripped after the second wearing as she'd hastily pulled it off. Maybe there was an old one under the sink that she'd forgotten about. She got down on her knees to rummage among the shelves.

Pay dirt right away. Aunt Holly had left her shower cap, a true 'madcap' of bright plastic, sporting a ring of tacked-on multicolored flowers behind the double edge ruffles.

She had just stepped out of the shower and dried off when Tremain knocked. Throwing on a robe, she padded barefoot to the door.

He took one look at her and burst into a guffaw. "You wear *that* to shower in?"

Then she remembered what she had on her head. "You don't find it attractive?"

He laughed again. "It's ... definitely *you*."

She turned to the mirror on the wall beside the door and gazed at herself for a long moment, then turned back. "You know something?"

"Very little."

"Well," she said slowly, with proud satisfaction. "I do believe I have *found my hat!*"

The End

978-0-595-40785-
0-595-40785-4

Printed in the United States
69730LV00003B/176